P9-BYD-725

Killing Kelly

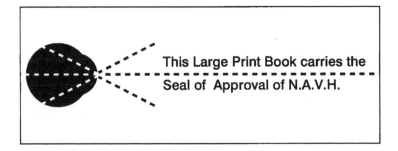

This Large Print Book carries the
Seal of Approval of N.A.V.H.

Heather Graham

Killing Kelly

Thorndike Press • Waterville, Maine

Published in 2005 by arrangement with Harlequin Books S.A.

Thorndike Press® Large Print Basic.

The tree indicium is a trademark of Thorndike Press.

The text of this Large Print edition is unabridged. Other aspects of the book may vary from the original edition.

Set in 16 pt. Plantin by Elena Picard.

Printed in the United States on permanent paper.

Library of Congress Cataloging-in-Publication Data

Graham, Heather.
    Killing Kelly / by Heather Graham.
      p. cm.
    "Thorndike Press large print basic" — T.p. verso.
    ISBN 0-7862-7563-4 (lg. print : hc : alk. paper)
    1. Actresses — Crimes against — Fiction. 2. Florida Keys (Fla.) — Fiction. 3. Ex-police officers — Fiction. 4. Dance teachers — Fiction. 5. Soap operas — Fiction. 6. Large type books. I. Title.
PS3557.R198K55 2005
  813′.54—dc22   2005002055

Dedicated to Teresa Davant,
with all the thanks and love in the world.
Okay, so none of us look alike.
But you'll still always be a "sister."

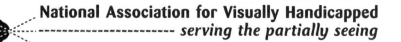
National Association for Visually Handicapped
------------------------ *serving the partially seeing*

As the Founder/CEO of NAVH, the only national health agency solely devoted to those who, although not totally blind, have an eye disease which could lead to serious visual impairment, I am pleased to recognize Thorndike Press* as one of the leading publishers in the large print field.

Founded in 1954 in San Francisco to prepare large print textbooks for partially seeing children, NAVH became the pioneer and standard setting agency in the preparation of large type.

Today, those publishers who meet our standards carry the prestigious "Seal of Approval" indicating high quality large print. We are delighted that Thorndike Press is one of the publishers whose titles meet these standards. We are also pleased to recognize the significant contribution Thorndike Press is making in this important and growing field.

Lorraine H. Marchi, L.H.D.
Founder/CEO
NAVH

* Thorndike Press encompasses the following imprints: Thorndike, Wheeler, Walker and Large Print Press.

Darkness and Shadows

Prologue

What was it about the night and the little places where secrets lurked that caused unease to stir in the human heart? It was the unknown, of course. Primeval fear. Something deep within human instinct that all of the civilization in the world could not change.

Dr. Dana Sumter knew all about the psyche and the innate responses to stimuli. Yet she didn't like it one bit that it was still dark when she returned, sliding her sleek Mercedes into the driveway. She started to hit the garage door opener, then remembered that she couldn't park in the garage; she was refurbishing the house and the garage was filled with old furniture that would be picked up by a charity organization.

With a sigh, she simply parked. The engine now off, she was suddenly aware of more than the darkness. She heard the sounds of the day dawning. From somewhere far away, the shrill whine of an emergency vehicle's siren mingled with the distant, deep bark of a large dog. There was a clattering and a screeching as alley cats fought somewhere. Then . . . just whispers in the shadows as the wind picked up slightly, then died down again. The sound was slightly ominous, like a deep, menacing breath . . . right down her spine.

Dana was irritated to be out at that time of the morning, irritated that she'd agreed to do the crack-of-dawn news show. Why had she? Oh, yes, her ratings had slipped because she'd come down rather hard against a womanizing drunkard. The switchboard at her daily syndicated show had gone off the light beam after that. But still, there had been complaints. A lot of people — men, mainly — calling in to say that she should be shot, or coming up with various other colorful phrases, all in the same vein.

She pulled down the visor mirror and studied her features. Good. Maybe her face was a little narrow, a little hard, but basically, for her age, she was sleek, professional, attractive. She lived carefully, didn't smoke, seldom drank and exercised regularly. She gave a little sniff. She'd gotten a lot of flak the time she'd given the overweight housewife the advice to do something about herself. She knew that people had expected her to say that the husband was simply a louse for ignoring his wife. But on that occasion, she'd gone the other way, telling the woman to buy the *South Beach Diet* book, or do Atkins, or get thee to a gym! The phones had rung off the hooks with people calling in, raging that women were worthy of love no matter what their size. She'd done one of her best shows ever after that, saying that being worthy of love didn't make it happen, that both men and women were responsible to keep themselves up.

However, despite the fact that she had definitely improved herself to an even greater degree, she'd still caught Harvey red-handed with a young thing half his age. But at least she'd had the self-respect to follow her own advice! Yes, she was swift and brutal. The best lawyers in town had helped her keep what was hers intact. He'd made his pixie mistress into a trophy wife — until the trophy wife had discovered that, without Dana, good old Harvey didn't have any money. And suddenly there was Harvey, out in the cold with his dick in his hand.

When asked about her divorce, Dana was cool and calculated, saying that in any marriage there could come a time when both parties simply fell out of love. She forced herself to talk about her ex-husband with affection, as if they were still friends. She had survived the dissolution of her own marriage before the public eye with great esteem, maintaining that, despite the fact that their children were long grown, it was important to be friends for their sakes.

Friends, my ass! She never should have married. Men were all disloyal egoists who used women. She had simply learned to use them back. Even the one fiasco she had endured years ago in weakness was something she had turned to her advantage. And over and over again, at that!

Done with the introspection, she opened her car door, ready to head into her house. Yet she was surprised to still feel a faint sense of unease as she sat in her car. She lived in a gorgeous house on a well-lit main street in a very fashionable district of Westchester, New York. Even when it was midnight, or in the wee hours of the morning, cars went by constantly. She'd never felt in the least bit of danger, no matter what time she returned to or left her house. But now . . .

She looked into the rearview window, but saw nothing. Still, she waited.

Finally, feeling silly, she got out of the car and walked to her front door. But she couldn't help looking over her shoulder. Then she chided herself. It was ridiculous for a grown woman to be afraid of shadows and the sound of leaves rustling in the summer breeze.

At the front door she paused and looked around again. This was odd, so odd. She felt the hairs at her nape standing on end. But there was nothing, no one.

Telling herself to stop being an idiot, she slipped her key into the lock and stepped in. Then she keyed in her number on the alarm pad as she started to close and lock the door. But the door wouldn't close. She frowned, pressing at it. And that was when it burst back in upon her.

For a moment, she just stared, stunned, trying to fathom just what . . . who . . . Then she opened her mouth to scream as she launched for the alarm pad.

But it was too late.

Several thoughts went through her mind. *It wasn't ridiculous to be wary of shadows, of darkness, of little whispers of danger. She shouldn't have been so mistrusting as to refuse to keep a live-in housekeeper. She should have been more careful about things she said . . . and did! She should have . . .*

From somewhere far away she could hear her dog, Muffy, barking. Then, with a sudden squeaking sound, the barking was cut off — just as every other noise and sensation faded away.

Chapter 1

"There's only darkness . . . shadows . . . Kelly, remember that you start off confident, then begin to feel the menace of the night, of something not quite right," Joe Penny directed.

"Four . . . three . . ." Grant Idle, the assistant director, mouthed the last two numbers in the countdown, his fingers raised. Kelly Trent could barely see him. Because it was supposed to be night, there were areas of pure darkness surrounding the intricately planned lighting. She knew, however, that beyond Grant, Joe and the camera, sound and lighting personnel, there was still something of a crowd. Matt Avery, one of her least favorite people in the world, was there with some of the other executives from Household Heaven, the giant mega-cleaning-product corporation that was the major sponsor behind the show. There were guests, friends of Joe

Penny, as well as a few people her agent had brought.

Videotaping a popular soap opera was surely one of the strangest ventures in a world that was already strange. Sometimes the sets were closed. Other times it seemed as if they were having a party and anyone could attend. Usually they filmed in the studio; it was cost-effective to do so. Tonight, however, they were out at Hibiscus Point, a man-made private development where they had been all day, filming every exterior shot they could in a matter of hours.

They weren't on anything that resembled a high-traffic public street, because the first houses hadn't even been sold. In fact, many of the high-priced lots remained empty. And the property they were using was high on a hill, rather remote. Still, it seemed as if they were at a busy crossroads, though many of the cars and people hovering behind the cameras had nothing to do with the actual production. Kelly didn't mind one way or the other. She'd been a part of this world for far too long to do anything other than go with the flow and, for the most part, enjoy herself. However, she did find it strange. The producers had put out a gag order regarding the

16

shoot, so presumably, no one but those involved should have known that they would be working outside the studio. But given the number of people around, they might as well have posted an announcement in *Billboard*.

On cue, she exited the driver's seat of the BMW parked in the driveway, decked to the nines as Marla Valentine. She allowed the car door to slam behind her. And though Marla was supposedly doing nothing more than returning to her home, she paused, adjusted her skirt and straightened her hair. After all, Marla was a Valentine. To the Valentines, appearance meant the world. She was one of the three redheaded sisters who ruled the valley, through scandal after scandal, affair after affair.

A few steps across dirt and she reached the tiled path to the door of the cliffside bungalow. For a moment — without batting an eye or displaying so much as a hint of a smile — she felt a certain amusement. Marla Valentine should have been fair play for criticism just for the shoes she chose to wear. The stiletto heels weren't so bad in the studio. But here, on location, they were murder themselves. She had to take great care with every step. First, because if she didn't, she'd sink right into the earth, and then because they'd be as loud as an exploding bomb on the tile. But whatever Marla Valentine's shoes, she reflected, she loved her job. Melodrama was simply fun, most of the time. Hard work, but fun. And when they finished here tonight, they were on a three-week hiatus. Which didn't actually mean she was off next week, though, for a number of the actors were going to be guests at a theme park for Soap Week.

She paused, just as she had been directed, and acted out a niggling feeling rising in Marla at the first hint of danger — the slightest tightening of her brow, the faintest frown indicating that she was perplexed.

She looked ahead at the door. The front light, which should have been on, was off. And despite the camera lights, it *seemed* dark. There was the softest whisper of a breeze that night, just enough to ruffle the trees and give a strange, barely audible whistle to the air.

She had to admit, she was having fun being Marla Valentine now. After many seasons in which Marla had been the nice sister, the shy sister, the used sister, she had developed a streak of nastiness that was pure entertainment. And now Marla was finally facing danger. She'd gotten very tough, so surely she would face it well and come back fighting.

Kelly took a step, then played up her character's sense of unease. She squared her shoulders, as if she had put down the demons of hesitance and fear. She started walking again, keys in her hands. She wasn't going to run away from her own front door.

But then she paused, as if uncertain once again. From the corner of her eyes, she could see one cameraman moving around to her left, the other to her right. The focus was on her, then on the door, the bushes, the shadows . . .

Lights stung Kelly's eyes for a moment, but Marla Valentine convinced herself that there was nothing there. Just as Kelly had been directed. Just as she had rehearsed.

She climbed the steps in her stiletto heels. Then, on cue, her attacker appeared from the shadow of the bushes to her right.

Hugh Thompson was the ultimate pro. Stuntman for dozens of shows and movies, he was a solid six foot four. Tonight, he was clad in black from head to toe, a ski mask covering everything but his eyes, a black coat concealing the rest of his frame. Standing perfectly still, he might have been taken for a shadow.

She screamed. It was a damned good scream, she reflected ruefully, but then, in truth, his appearance was rather frightening. He lunged for her and she spun around. Though they were often able to do their takes without so much as a run-through, they had rehearsed this scene several times. She didn't come straight down the steps, but headed for the mound of earth on the side.

Hugh should have caught her. And she should have been there to catch. Instead, the pile of earth gave way. To her astonishment, she had no footing whatsoever. In sneakers, she might have had a chance. But in the stiletto heels, she went down. And with nothing to stop her, she began to roll.

For a moment, pure panic seized Kelly. The house was on a cliff. If she kept rolling and rolling . . . She was vaguely aware of screams coming from the rest of the cast and crew. Hugh was shouting. They all seemed very far away. Dirt and grass were tearing at her. She felt a sharp pain as her elbow hit something, then her knee. She saw a branch and made a mad grasp for it. The rough limb burned her palms, but she held fast. Her impetus halted, she was able to inch along and catch hold of the tree with the low-hanging branch.

One of the stiletto heels was already gone. She kicked off the other and struggled to her feet. Turning around, she saw the edge of the cliff, not very far away at all, deceptive in the darkness. Her knees nearly gave on her again. Her fear was so deep that it truly seemed her heart leaped to her throat and a chill weakened the length of her body. Sheer physical reaction to the manner of her near-death raked her limbs.

Hugh Thompson reached her first.

"Kelly!" Despite the knit ski mask, his voice boomed with concern.

"I'm fine!" she called quickly, shaking like a leaf.

He caught up to her and pulled her back toward the house, half lifting her. "Kelly, jeez!" he breathed.

"Hugh, please, put me down. I'm fine, really. I just don't understand . . . that little mound by the porch was solid as rock before!"

"You can never trust the ground in California!" Hugh said, shaking his head. "Oh, man, Kelly, I about had a heart attack there, watching you go down!"

By then Joe Penny had reached them, his perfect silver hair nearly standing on end.

He looked as white as a ghost. "Kelly . . . Kelly!" He threw his arms around her, shaking. Camera and light crews followed him, along with people from costume and makeup, and the two extras with whom Marla Valentine had recently conversed.

"Joe, everyone, please, I'm fine. Of course, I must look like muddy hell, but hey, I can wash up!" Then she heard the sound of a siren and looked at Joe with concern. "Please tell me you didn't call an ambulance!"

"Kelly, you might have been killed!" Joe said, shaking his head, his face still ashen. "My God, I went over all this myself. What on earth . . . ?"

"Like Hugh says, it's California!" Kelly said cheerfully.

"You're bleeding," Hugh said.

She looked down at her knee. "It's just a scratch. Really, I'm fine."

"You could be clamoring for workmen's comp!" one of the extras called out, attempting a note of levity.

"A paid vacation in the Caribbean," Hugh agreed lightly.

"But I'm fine!" she protested again. "Please, guys. Thank you all so much for your concern, but I'm not hurt!"

"Oh, my God, Kelly!" That came from

Matt Avery, who had just made his way through the crowd surrounding her. She was glad that she wasn't gasping for air — she certainly wouldn't have gotten any! And then . . . Matt.

He reached for her, drawing her into the shadow of his arms. Matt Avery was tall and good-looking, with a smooth manner, a deep, rich voice and an easy charm that attracted women of all ages. Women just tended to gravitate to him. But as he tilted her chin upward, she fought very hard not to let him hear the grinding of her teeth.

"Kelly, good God! Are you all right?"

She tried to extricate herself politely. "Please, please, everyone. I swear to you, I'm fine."

"The ambulance is here," Joe said firmly.

"But I don't —"

"Kelly!" Her agent, Mel Alton, burst through the crowd then. She smiled because she knew that his concern was for her and not his ten percent.

"She's getting into that ambulance!" Joe insisted.

"I'll hop in with her," Mel said tersely.

"Look, we can finish the scene —" Kelly tried.

"Are you crazy?" Joe demanded. "Kelly, you're bleeding!" He hesitated. "Besides, the scene actually . . . well, what we've got on camera is amazing. But you! You're getting checked out, and then you're going home!"

"My knee is scratched!" she protested. "I don't need to be checked out."

"Kelly, we may not know what else is wrong right now. A doctor must see you," Matt Avery said firmly.

"She could probably sue," someone from the crowd muttered, and an uneasy silence followed.

Joe quickly managed a dry laugh. "Kelly, you'll need to get checked out . . . for insurance purposes, all that." He suddenly looked stricken. "I hope you're all right! You're due in Florida, at the theme park, on Tuesday!"

"I'll be there," Kelly said.

"Not if it jeopardizes your health!" Joe said.

She was fairly certain that he was sincere. Joe was a character. So were most of the people with whom she worked. Still, they'd been together a long time, and she believed that he did care about her.

Once again, Kelly tried to reassure everyone. "I'm fine." But it didn't seem to matter. The police had arrived along with the ambulance.

"Kelly, this is the way it has to go," Joe said.

She knew that he was right. The show couldn't afford a lawsuit, so the least minor accident required an investigation.

A gentle officer with graying hair and a kindly manner quizzed Kelly as she was seated in the ambulance. Mel hopped in with her. Like Joe, he was more than a co-worker. He was a friend, almost a father figure to her. He grinned, but looked a little worried.

"On the bright side, it will be in all the magazines," he told her.

"The rags," she said dryly.

"There is no such thing as —"

"Bad publicity, I know."

"Miss, please lie down and relax," the emergency medic said gently.

"But I'm fine. And whatever you do, please don't put the siren on —"

But it blared, despite her protests.

Despite the obvious legal repercussions, Joe Penny wasn't worried about the future of his show. After all, accidents happened. This one, however, was baffling. They'd chosen the place specifically for the cliff-top scenes. He'd been delighted to get the property for the price they'd paid for the

25

day. He hadn't been forced to pay travel bills to create the look of an island. Yes, they'd had to shuffle things around from the set — the cameras, the lights, costumes, trailers — but it had been a song compared to what they would have paid to find the right look on a Caribbean island. Everything had gone smoothly . . . until now.

The crowd had been dispersed. The officer in charge of the investigation, Ben Garrison, was a fellow with an easy manner that kept everyone calm. He and his men had asked dozens of questions of everyone involved, from the set director to the lighting personnel and camera crew. Even a few of the bystanders had been asked about what they'd seen.

Waiting to speak with the officer himself, Joe suddenly groaned inwardly. He loved his show. It was a good show. It held its own in an ever-changing world — and an ever-changing market.

He'd been through serious problems on the set before — murder could definitely be considered a serious problem — but the show had prevailed. And that was all in the past now.

He could feel himself sweating though the air was cool. As he waited, he stared at the house on the cliff, suddenly hating the edifice as if it had human qualities. Matt Avery walked up behind him.

"I don't produce or direct," Matt said quietly, "but we are vested in this show just as deeply as anyone else. And I have a suggestion, because this was one of the scariest 'accidents' I've ever had to witness."

Joe turned to look at the man and forced a smile. The show *had* prevailed through its problems because of Household Heaven — and the company's advertising dollars. Matt Avery was the man with the power to say how Household Heaven would continue to spend those advertising dollars. And Matt was a businessman first and foremost — and a very rich and powerful one at that.

"Your suggestion?" Joe asked, knowing what Avery was going to say. And understanding his concern.

"If it had been any other cast member, I might be inclined to think it was an accident," Matt said. "But it was Kelly who fell. She could have gone over that cliff. The very landscape that meant so much to us as a location could have killed her."

"The police are investigating."

"But you rehearsed that scene. Over and over."

"Maybe that's what dislodged the earth," Joe mused.

"Maybe one of those hundreds — or thousands — of people sending in hate mail meant for Marla Valentine to die."

"Matt! We kept this shoot hush-hush."

"There was a crowd here tonight."

Joe waved a hand in the air, looking around. Matt Avery and some of his crew had been invited. There was the fellow he'd met through another executive on the show who was looking to do a rock video. The guy in the shades *was* the rock star. And one of the cameramen had asked if his visiting sister could be there. As to the others . . . he didn't know. No one had pushed forward out of the crowd. The curious and the fans that had gathered around had politely kept their places out on the street.

"Matt, Kelly is an actress," he said.

"Yes, and one we care a lot about. Come on, Joe, you don't want another scandal with this show."

"Actually," Joe said uneasily, "scandal can be good. The audience thrives on who is doing what — and who," he added dryly.

"We're not talking about the sex lives of the stars, here," Matt said. "We're talking lethal scandal, and I don't believe you want

28

any kind of that ugliness tingeing the show again. I know that I sure as hell don't."

"What are you saying?" Joe demanded.

"We've got to take care of Kelly."

"And how do you propose we do that?" Joe demanded.

"Well, Mel will have to be in on this, and Kelly's manager also. But this is very serious. We have to work this out, for the sake of the show. And for Kelly, of course."

"Of course," Joe agreed, but he wondered why he was already feeling so ill. *Valentine Valley* was his show. He'd conceived it, worked it, tended to it like a lover. And he liked to believe he called the shots. But he also knew that, even as he professed his deep concern, Matt Avery had it in for Kelly.

Lance Morton remained outside the hospital emergency doors, having followed the emergency vehicle that had brought Kelly. There was not another soul outside the hospital doors. No one. It had apparently been a slow night in the City of Angels, a place so named despite the fact that every sin in the world was committed there.

It still awed him. Lance was a hometown boy. From the Midwest. Corn-fed, as he liked to say. In fact, people not from there liked to make fun of Ohio. But it had been a good enough place to grow up, and definitely a good enough place to study music. It had been a great place to get a garage band together, that was for sure. And now . . .

He still stood on the walk just beyond the emergency doors, even though she had already left with her agent. The outside had been thronged. How people had heard so quickly, he didn't know. But there had been a crowd, mostly waving and wishing her well, a few calling out that Marla Valentine was getting what she deserved.

He probably could have gotten in. *She* didn't know him. But Mel did. Besides, *she* would know him very soon!

Yes, he could have tried to get close . . . but he hadn't done so. Instead he had stayed outside, like a scorned lover, or a would-be idolizer, just watching from afar. He adored her. And just knowing how close he was — not just touching her from the fringes, but being close, *really* close — gave him a feeling of rapture.

He felt a trembling all over. Soon they would dance. She, the object of his absolute affection, would be with him. Him, a nobody from the Midwest. Little Lance

Morton, a nerd to some in high school. But the world was about to change. He was going to work with Kelly Trent.

With Kelly, he was going to tango right into terror!

Chapter 2

"Okay, you two. Why, exactly, am I here?" Kelly demanded.

A week after the incident, Kelly was just as frustrated, if not more so, than she had been the evening she had fallen. In the fleeting space of those few seconds, it seemed now everything had changed.

At the hospital, she had been given the exact diagnosis she had realized herself — she had a few scratches and bruises. She had been stunned by the concern that had arisen, even from her friends. Yes, she had been terrified at the time of the accident. But it had been an accident, and it was over. In *her* mind at least.

But no amount of protesting on her part would keep others from being concerned. She had been forced to forgo Soap Week at the theme park, yet found herself in Florida at Mel's insistence, anyway. Something to do with the people who had been at the shoot and a music video. She hadn't been in the least interested when he had first mentioned it. Yet he had kept nudging, telling her that since Joe Penny had been adamant about her not attending Soap Week, she could at least take the time to meet some of the people involved.

Ally Bassett was so concerned that she was in Florida as well. That Mel could sound cheerful about Ally's presence meant they'd finally found something to agree on. Mel thought that, as her manager, Ally should be watching Kelly's earnings and expenditures with a far more jaundiced eye. Ally was of the belief that you had to spend money to make money.

But since even her closest friends seemed really concerned about the accident, she had agreed to take the trip south that they had urged. It was to be a "vacation" combined with a fact-finding mission about the offer she'd had to do a music video. And though the very thought made her wince, Mel had been insistent on her finding out more about it, at the very least.

So now she sat on the balcony of her South Beach hotel suite staring at the two of them, and wondering why they were looking at her so seriously. And, for that matter, not only being polite to each other, but seeming to be allies, completely of one mind.

"How's the coffee?" Mel asked.

"It's fine, thanks. It's coffee," she said.

"Do you want anything else?" Ally asked.

They'd ordered up room service, and it, too, was just fine. Everything was fine.

Kelly sighed. "Just talk, you two. I swear I'm fine. Happy as a lark, though I can't believe that you two are ganging up on me."

Ally looked at Mel. "We're not ganging up on you!" she protested.

"Never," Mel assured her somberly. "We're both here in your best interest, Kelly."

"I know. And thank you. So . . ."

"So!" Mel looked at Ally, took a deep breath, then looked at Kelly very seriously. "Kelly, you should take the video."

"Guys, I really don't know. I find the idea very risky, career-wise. And I don't really know that much about it."

"That's why we're here," Mel said. "You can meet the people involved, get a firm grasp of everything that will happen."

"You might as well take the gig," Ally said flatly. "Your character's been attacked and is in a coma. Quite frankly, I'm afraid that Marla is going to die."

"What?" Kelly said, so startled she nearly spilled her coffee.

Mel shot Ally a look, obviously annoyed. Then he inhaled on a deep breath. "Kelly, it's gone too far. They're very afraid for you right now." He hesitated. "And Ally's not wrong. There *has* been talk about having to kill you off."

"Oh, come on! You have to be exaggerating. They can't kill me!" Kelly said, somehow managing to keep her composure despite the words being stated. She wanted to sound as if it absolutely couldn't be true, but even as the protest left her lips, she wondered, *could it be true?* Is that why Mel had gotten together with Ally to break this news to her?

"This will blow over. And with Marla in a coma, I'll get a few weeks' vacation out of it. But I don't understand why they would kill me off."

"Kelly, you became a ball-buster," Mel said. He lit a cigarette, puffed twice and tamped it out. Mel was always trying to quit smoking. He sighed. "I'm not explaining this well."

"No, you're not," Ally agreed.

He shot her another severe stare. "You're not helping much!" He turned to Kelly. "We're speaking about your character on the show, of course. But many people think that you *are* Marla Valentine. And people really hate you."

Despite her resolve, her voice was thick as she added, "A ball-buster, yes, but . . . I've never gotten more fan mail. I've never felt . . . well, more important to the show!"

"Well, there is that. And Kelly, everyone with the show knows that you're one of the nicest, most dedicated actresses in the business. The thing is, everyone *does* care about you. So they're worried. And because of that, they've decided that you will be written out for *at least* the next four months."

She gasped with surprise and dismay. "Four months! People will forget me."

"Hopefully not. You'll be the subject of a lot of conversations as they try to solve the dilemma regarding what happened to you," Ally put in.

"Four months . . ." Kelly murmured. "I just can't believe it!"

"But you have to believe it," Mel told her, shaking his head. "Kelly, do you ever read your mail? It's deadly serious! The powers that be have no choice but to take it all to heart."

She could do nothing but stare at him for a moment, shocked. Yes, her character was hated, hated in absolutely the best way a soap actress can be hated. Once sweet, Marla Valentine had become the evil vixen on the show, and in the show within the show. Marla had become an advice diva. Not that she had any credentials, but in Valentine Valley, no credentials were necessary. Kelly sometimes wondered just who in the writing department had such a deep, almost manic loathing for men. But there had to be someone in there with a very real and seething emotion, because her character now spent a certain amount of each half hour spewing venomous advice regarding cheating husbands, alcoholic husbands, nonworking husbands and, in fact, any poor fellow who just wasn't nice. She'd been a little wary of the turn in the scripts at first, but then she'd had to admit herself, she'd never received more mail.

Apparently, there were a lot of women who did feel burned — and enjoyed the chew-'em-up, spit-'em-out suggestions given by her character. And though Kelly knew that many women were taken in by the wrong man and emotionally injured, her own opinion was that the bad out there worked both ways. Men and women could be incredibly cruel to one another, and, unfortunately, in most relationships, someone got hurt.

But Marla Valentine was a character, nothing more. And since they were talking daytime soap, she was really more of a caricature, whose opinions were as far from Kelly's own personal philosophies as it was possible to get.

"It won't happen," Kelly said firmly. "Being evil has brought more attention than anything else the character has ever done before. She's flying like an eagle right now. People love to hate a villainess."

"And they love to see a villainess get her just rewards," Mel said.

She shook her head again, dismayed that a rupture in a hill of earth could have done this to her. "Okay, I'm in a coma now. But things have never been so hot for Marla! We both know that what really matters is money, and I'm making them a lot of money right now. Trust me. The few months will go by, and I will get out of the coma."

"No," Mel murmured, looking away. "I really don't think so."

"Then, if they kill me off, I'll come back as a ghost?" Kelly said lightly. "Or as my innocent twin sister from Peoria, whom I knew nothing about because we were separated at birth?"

Mel breathed a deep sigh. "Kelly, please listen. I'm trying to explain everything. There was trouble on your set before. Real trouble. So people are a little gun-shy these days. And they're afraid. Some of these letters your character has received are extremely threatening. The show can't afford any more trouble like this. And since they've made Marla so despicable, some people feel that it's time to put an end to her."

"Dead and gone, we're afraid," Ally said. "Joe said as much when we met with him the other day."

"Great. Why wasn't I at this meeting?" she demanded.

"Joe said you weren't to come," Mel said flatly.

"Joe's a coward!" Kelly muttered. She stared at Mel. He was her friend, as well as her adviser. A man in his late fifties now, he was fierce when he needed to be, dignified in any situation and as kind as Santa when his clients were distressed. She believed with her whole heart that he never meant anything but the absolute best for her. And that he fought for her like a tiger, as well.

She looked at Ally Bassett. Though she wasn't as close with Ally, she had liked her from the moment they met. Ally, too, was fierce. She meant to do the best for her clients, because she meant to further her own career.

"Okay, so I may actually be fired," Kelly said. "What do we do now?"

"Just consider the music video," Ally said.

"Consider it very, very seriously!" Mel said.

"Okay," Kelly said, resigning herself to the idea. "When do I meet these people?"

"There's going to be a party on a yacht," Ally told her. "It will be fun."

"Fun, right!" Mel agreed, though he gave a little shudder as he said the words.

"You'll get to meet the people involved. Kelly, they want you so badly! They'll pay extremely well. Just remember, Courteney Cox got her start dancing with Bruce Springsteen!" Ally added.

Kelly looked at her. "She was very young at the time. I'm afraid I'm not that young! And I've been working on the soap forever!"

"This is a new venue that can keep you from winding up being typecast," Mel said flatly. "It's time to stretch your wings a bit."

"I could do a play," Kelly said.

"You could. But this will be big money, and it will keep you in the public eye. The commitment isn't forever. After, you'll be a more wanted and valuable commodity. Trust me. Then, if you want, you can do your pick of plays."

"You're both going with me, right?" Kelly said.

Mel shot Ally a stare and said, "I'll be there."

"I have a few things to take care of here today, then I have to get back to California tonight," Ally said. "Actually, I would love to go. It's Marc Logan's yacht. No expense spared. I'm truly sorry not to be there!"

"But I'll be there," Mel said. "Wouldn't miss it for the world."

"Hi!"

Doug O'Casey eased his sunglasses back and looked up. He had been lying on the beach, something he seldom had occasion to do. Born and bred in South Florida, he was accustomed to sea, sun and surf. His recent musings, however, had been on the fact that, because of that, rather than in spite of it, he never just lay out in the sun on the sand. It wasn't that he didn't appreciate the water, he just preferred to be out on it or taking part in sports involving it.

And besides, it provided him with too much time to do nothing but think — and the thoughts racing through his head didn't particularly make him happy.

He'd come out here with Jane Ulrich, to keep her company. They were out on the private beach area of the Montage, an old deco hotel known for its old-world service. He'd never seen the place before today; it wasn't one of the big, showy places that had become renowned. Last night, they'd put on a private performance for an embassy party. A weekend stay at the hotel had come with the gig. Therefore, an occasion to stop, to keep Jane company, to lie in the sand. Except when he twisted, he saw that Jane was no longer lying on the sand. He hadn't heard her leave, and that disturbed him.

"Hello!" the stranger said again, waving a hand, determined to draw his attention.

The woman looking down at him reminded him of a stereotypical valley girl grown up. She was petite, compact, blond beyond blond, blue-eyed and . . . perky. On the beach, she was dressed in a short skirt and high heels that she was obviously having trouble standing in. Her smile was irritatingly cheerful.

"Hi," he responded, waiting.

"You're Doug O'Casey? Shannon said that I could find you here," she said.

He didn't want to admit to his identity — not right away. He arched a brow slowly and carefully. The woman didn't look like a friend of Shannon's, or even an associate. She was too . . . Was there really such an adjective as *Hollywood?* She was simply *plastic,* from features that seemed stretched to the breaking point to breasts that seemed anatomically impossible.

"I have an offer for you," she told him. "A business proposition."

Offer, he thought, wondering why his heart had quickened for a minute. *Not case, problem, dilemma . . .*

"My name is Ally Bassett, and I'm the head of Bassett Management." When he didn't respond she continued. "I represent one of the most popular actresses on the daytime circuit. She's about to become involved in a special project, and I'd like to hire you to accompany her. I think we need a man with your special . . . qualifications, shall we say."

"My special qualifications?" he asked, slightly amused. "What's your offer?"

She sighed, shifting her weight in the sand, and he realized with an odd pleasure he shouldn't have been feeling that she was entirely annoyed by the fact that her designer sandals were covered in sand.

"Perhaps you'd be willing to meet with me in the café . . . say, in thirty minutes?"

"What's your offer?" he demanded again.

This time her sigh was pained and impatient. "A very lucrative one, Mr. O'Casey. It has to do with a music video."

He arched a brow, unable to suppress the grin that came to his lips. "A music video? Who's the group?" he asked, now completely intrigued.

"Kill Me Quick."

It was a bizarre name, but he'd actually heard of the group. He'd heard quite a lot about them, in fact. Though hitting the rock scene with numbers that veered toward heavy metal, they were still incredibly geared toward the beat of their work, making it perfect for dance. Their timing was impeccable.

"I'm sorry, I'm just not getting this. Do you want to hire me on as a teacher or as a dancer?" he asked, frowning. Of all the things he had expected as he pondered his next career move, this had not been among them.

"Well, officially we want to hire you to teach my client how to dance. Unofficially, we want you there to keep an eye on her."

His brows shot up. "Sorry. I'm really confused now. You want a dancer or a bodyguard?"

"Both, actually," Ally said. "You've been highly recommended for your dance skills. And we know that you had a very different career before you went into dance. The skills you have from that job may come in very handy."

He rose, dusting sand from the back of his legs. Though he wasn't interested in spending his time with some spoiled star, he had to admit that the "bodyguard" aspect of the job had him intrigued.

"I'll meet you in the café. Give me twenty minutes," he told her. He was smiling slightly, shaking his head as he turned toward the hotel. She was swearing as she made her way through the sand in his wake.

Strange, he'd been lying there thinking he was ready to take his life in a different direction. And now . . . What the hell. It just might be interesting. He liked the music. And, yes, he did want to know what celebrity was being wooed for the project.

Chapter 3

Kelly wished she were just about anywhere else in the world.

The party on the yacht was pretty much what she had expected — full of strangers. These were people she was supposed to work with, but so far, they seemed to be a group of suntanned beach bums and bunnies, heedless of anything beyond the pursuit of another drink. As she leaned against the railing, sipping a cosmopolitan with Mel by her side, a bone-thin, huge-breasted woman walked by, offering a smile that was surely half collagen. "Drinks, anyone?"

Kelly smiled back. "Still have this one, thanks."

"Fine, thanks," Mel said. When she had moved on, he asked, "Having fun yet?"

"Um — sure," she lied.

"We don't have to stay that long. You should just meet a few more people."

Beyond Mel, she saw a tall blond man. He was broad-shouldered, deeply bronzed and decked out in a handsome suit that gave credence to the width of those shoulders and the tapered line of his hip. She was certain that the guy was artificial, like the woman — pumped up on steroids, the kind of man who spent his every waking hour in a gym, or in the sun, or shaving or waxing his chest, or God knew what else.

He turned, as if aware that he was being watched. He didn't smile, just assessed her gravely in return. His face was both classic and rugged, with clean strong lines and eyes an almost shockingly deep blue. Contacts, probably. And his posture was so perfect, it made him seem even taller than the six two or three that he must be. He wore the handsome suit with a casual ease that made her think of a latter-day Cary Grant or Errol Flynn.

Gay? she wondered.

He belonged on a remake of *Baywatch*, she decided. And she felt a moment's discomfort, aware that they were both staring at each other, and that he was surely doing the same sort of mental deduction regarding her. She didn't know why, but she was afraid that his assessment of her wasn't a very good one. Maybe he was deciding that she'd had a nose job, and that her lips were mainly collagen. That she was anorexic, maybe a cocaine freak.

She flushed suddenly as the man inclined his head slightly, then turned away. She had no right to be judging him. She knew how unfair stereotypes could be. Those who worked in soap operas far too often endured the snobbery of critics and their peers.

The "producer" was a rich, middle-aged, super-tanned, silver-haired, would-be Casanova named Marc Logan. She'd seen him before. He'd been in the crowd her last night of work on the soap. No surprise. The video offer had been on the table then; she should have met him that night.

She'd forced a smile and slipped from beneath his arm about forty times already tonight. She flushed, lowering her head slightly, thinking again that she had no right to judge these people. She was just feeling so . . . well, lost. And betrayed. And paying for something that hadn't been her fault!

When she looked up, she realized that Marc Logan was watching her. He was against the opposite railing, across the deck from her now. When he lifted his glass to her, she forced a smile and lifted her own. Okay, so he had been a little too touchy. But his admiration for her seemed genuine. He had been there the night of her accident, and he seemed to admire her all the more for her "get back up and go!" attitude. And, she had to admit, he didn't seem the least concerned about hiring her. For that alone, she knew she should be thankful.

"You sure do look beautiful on this old scow!" he called to her.

Right, the yacht was an old scow. He was waiting for her to reply, to say that it was a magnificent vessel. Then he could walk over and start talking.

She called out a simple thanks, and he started walking toward them, anyway.

Luckily one of the bikini-clad waitresses snagged his attention. He slipped his arm around the girl, and his hand fell — *slimed* — down her back. She didn't seem to mind.

Kelly turned away, wincing. Okay, so he was admiring and flattering. He still made her uneasy. Was she really going to take a job working for *him?* She shook her head, amazed to feel the prick of tears behind her eyes. "I can't believe Joe Penny would fire me — and that I'll be reduced to this!" she whispered.

"You're not being fired. You're being a savvy businesswoman by keeping your name out there!" Mel assured her.

She gave his arm a little hug. "If I'm not being fired, why are you so worried about me? Worried and determined that I take this video job. Mel . . . these people are scary!"

He laughed and seemed more at ease. "Kelly, you just don't know them. Hey, you've survived Hollywood a long time. You can deal with anyone."

"You really want me to work for him?" she asked Mel, indicating the producer.

"He's just footing the bill. Trust me," Mel continued, "Logan won't be around much at all, he's just getting things going. And he's spent hours bitching about every cent of the budget *except* for the off-the-chart money he's willing to spend to have you."

Money. She suddenly knew why she'd felt such fierce betrayal and fear. She had actually been so complacent about her work, without ever really looking to the future and change. *Valentine Valley* was easy and comfortable. Her job paid the bills and paid them well. She loved her house off Sunset Boulevard, and loved having the wherewithal to take her nieces and nephews on trips to theme parks around the States, to help out when her sister and brother wound up in any kind of trouble. She'd bought the house in Palm Springs for her folks, and when her mother had been ill, and then her father, she'd been lucky enough to pay for the best private care available until she had lost both. And she'd been given time then, twice. Everyone had been so understanding.

As if reading her thoughts, Mel spoke softly again. "Kelly, I can see your mind working. And I know what you don't want other people to know."

"Oh?"

"Your role was a sure thing. You're scared for your future. But it's good for you to take a few chances." He took a deep breath. "Okay, Logan is a sleazebag, yes. But he's a rich sleazebag. You probably won't even have to see him again. Jerry Tritan is the director you'll be working with, and I swear, he is 'A' list. He's the new 'it' man for this kind of work." Mel began to tick off a number of recent videos the man had done. She'd seen a few and they were good — almost like miniature movies rather than bursts of op-art images. "He's the guy in the nice suit, with the very serious dark eyes and shaggy haircut."

She felt somewhat mollified. Jerry Tritan was known to be exacting but ethical. Shy, not much of a player. He was in the midst of a serious discussion with the tall blond man, and both seemed to be listening intently to each other. They both looked up, as if a sixth sense warned them they were being watched. The blond man stared at her. Jerry Tritan lowered his head in a polite acknowledgment and she returned the gesture.

"See?" Mel said softly. "It will be all right."

"Sure, if you say so!"

If her spine were any stiffer, it would probably crack. She forced herself to look out over the water. The scenery was actually very beautiful. The downtown lights from Miami and Miami Beach reflected on the bay and the sky was touched with a few puffs of clouds just visible in the night.

It was beautiful here. If she just gave it a chance . . .

"And here comes another principal in our new venture," Mel murmured.

"There she is!" came a cry.

One of the beautiful people on board, a young man with a thick head of blond hair that curled at his nape, was coming toward them. He was slender, dark-eyed, with a lean, almost classic face. She had seen him before as well, she was suddenly certain. He'd been with Logan, hanging around behind Mel on the night she had fallen.

"Kelly! Kelly Trent." Arriving directly in front of her, he took both her hands, smiling at her. His look was thoroughly adoring, and she should have appreciated it more. However, what with recent revelations . . .

"Kelly, this is Lance Morton, lead singer with the group Kill Me Quick."

Kill Me Quick. Great name.

"Lance, how do you do? A pleasure," she murmured, wishing she could extricate her hands from his. She didn't mean to be impolite; she was just feeling ill.

"Great. Thrilled. I wanted you, you know. Right from the very beginning. As soon as we heard we were getting the contract and the video," he told her. He looked at her sheepishly. "I was there in L.A., dying to meet you, but after the accident we all kept our distance. But . . . wow. I feel like a little kid getting to meet my idol!"

"Well, thank you very much," she said. "That's very kind of you."

"No, thank you. It's just way beyond rad that we're going to be working together. Way beyond."

"Well . . . cool," she said, finally drawing her hands from his grip. "But the deal hasn't been finalized," she murmured, glancing at Mel. "It isn't exactly written in cement yet."

"Oh, but it will be!" he told her, giving her a thumbs-up sign and offering Mel a broad grin. "We start in two weeks, and it will be the time of my dreams!" He was being summoned, she realized, by one of the cocktail waitresses, a dark-haired beauty in a bikini and sailor's cap. But before leaving, he kissed her cheek, managing to slobber enough that her face smelled like sour bourbon and old smoke.

"Mel!" she said, when he had walked on. "This is no done deal."

"Kelly, they're offering big bucks for you. Really big bucks. And you need it, Kelly. You need to sock it away in case . . . well, you just need to sock it away. What's to say no to?"

"Hmm, let me think. Some videos come out like pure crap, and the exposure could turn on me. I'm sorry, Mel, but it is true!"

"Kelly, Lance Morton may be a bit . . . rad, but the money people behind this are the best. Hey, you guys could take Best Video at one of those music-award things — and you could wind up hosting a show. Trust me, the good outweighs the bad. And once again, you need it."

She flushed. She was bad with money. Horrible, as a matter of fact. She should have accrued a savings account that would have seen her through such an unforeseen circumstance, but . . .

She cleared her throat. "Okay, Mel. You and Ally got me here, so let's get to it. What am I supposed to do? Just stand around looking ethereal? Jump off a cliff . . . what?"

"You'll be dancing, doing some backup singing. . . . It will be great," Mel said.

"What?"

"Dancing, doing some backup singing, that's all. It will be easy. A piece of cake for you. This will pay more than some feature work might. Seriously, wait until you see this contract. It will be an easy slide into the future."

She groaned. "No, it won't."

"Ah, come on. You can carry a tune. The boys have heard you — remember Marla Valentine's stint as a nightclub entertainer? And you've always wanted to do musical theater."

"Yes, I can carry a tune."

"Then?"

"I can't dance."

"Don't be ridiculous. Everyone can dance."

"Well, I can't. Honestly, Mel. I can't dance."

"You majored in theater arts —"

"And the dance majors laughed at me when I took the compulsory courses. I have two left feet."

"We'll deal with that," he assured her confidently. "They've already been advised that you need a coach."

"All right. Tell me about the video."

"The song is called 'Tango to Terror.'"

" 'Tango to Terror' — by Kill Me Quick. You've gotta love it," she murmured, shaking her head.

He smiled. "It will be fine. You just have to tango."

"Oh, Mel. Please listen to me. I cannot dance."

"They've got that covered. You'll have a coach."

"What I'll need is a stand-in."

"Kelly! You sound like a defeatist. You've got a crackerjack dance coach," he said.

"She'll quit in three days," Kelly assured him.

"He."

"Great. *He'll* quit in *two* days."

"Ah, come on, Kelly. You sound scared, but don't be. They love you, they want you."

"Yeah, well, at *Valentine Valley* they have affection and respect for me, and that's why we're in this situation. You want to explain that?"

He hesitated, then said, "Kelly, Dr. Dana Sumter was murdered three weeks ago."

She frowned, not understanding what that fact had to do with her. "Yes, I know about that. It's been on television and in the papers. But I understand that they arrested her ex-husband a few days ago."

"Yes, they did," Mel said, making a clucking sound. "And motive? Hell, the guy had plenty. She completely emasculated the poor fellow. But he's crying innocent."

"Most criminals do claim to be innocent," Kelly reminded him.

"All right! I doubt you've heard about this one because, in comparison, it was small time."

"This one what?"

"Sandusky, Ohio. Sally Bower, a local personality with an advice show who was found drowned in her bathtub last week."

Kelly looked at him. "Murdered?"

Mel shrugged. "Apparently the autopsy was inconclusive. She'd had a tremendous amount to drink and had taken some Valium. She was known to abuse prescription drugs."

"Mel, that's tragic. And I'm very sorry to hear about it. But I'm not an advice therapist. I'm just a soap actress."

"Yes, I agree. But that's the point. There's been enough trouble over the years involving *Valentine Valley*. The producers aren't taking any chances with your life. And that's that." Mel pushed away from the railing, looking out over the crowd on the yacht.

"But I'm not afraid!" Kelly told him.

"Kelly," he said with a soft sigh. "I'm sorry. The sponsors have spoken."

"The sponsors!" Kelly exclaimed, feeling another surge of anger, certain she knew the real "truth" behind her situation.

But she didn't have a chance to try to explain what had happened to Mel, for he was looking past her, whispering quickly, "Hey! There he is! Coming over to meet you now."

Kelly turned. It was the blond man with the perfect posture whom she had observed earlier. His expression was impassive as he approached.

"Doug, good to see you again. Meet Miss Kelly Trent. Kelly, Doug O'Casey. Your coach."

Great. Just great. She took the man's hand and forced a smile. She didn't mean to be rude; she was just so miserable. "How do you do?" she murmured.

"Miss Trent," he replied. His voice was distant. A little static seemed to snap between them, and she felt a new rise of bitterness, hostility and, admittedly, sorrow. Why hadn't she seen this coming? She had stared at him in judgment, and he was doing it now, as well, no matter how polite his words. There was a certain amount of disdain about him as he stared down into her eyes.

Great, a no-talent personality, high-maintenance, hard work, his look seemed to say. *Dental floss between the ears.*

"You two will get on famously together, I'm certain!" Mel said cheerfully.

Her face was about to crack. She withdrew her hand, thinking it would burst into flame then and there. His eyes were intense. That deep, deep blue.

"What's your dance experience, Miss Trent?" he asked politely.

"None. Absolutely none," she assured him sweetly.

Mel landed a hard hand clap on her back. She nearly staggered forward. He didn't even notice. "Kelly won't have a problem in the least, Doug, not with you. I've been told you're the best. And I've been told that with a male dancer such as yourself leading, any woman can be made to look good."

Doug O'Casey gazed at Kelly again. She could almost hear his thought process. *Any woman? Well, maybe, except for this one. . . .*

"Well, I just wanted to introduce myself and say hello, Miss Trent. I hear we're to start working together very soon, so . . . I'll be seeing you then."

"It isn't a done deal," Kelly insisted.

"We just have to sign the papers!" Mel said cheerfully. She couldn't believe it. He actually stepped on her toe to shut her up.

"Good evening, then."

Doug O'Casey turned and walked away. He'd been perfectly polite. There was no reason for her to be feeling so hostile. But he had brought out a certain . . . wariness in her, at the very least.

One of the bikini-clad cocktail waitresses sidled up to him. Kelly heard laughter from them both and wondered why she felt so annoyed.

Mel was grinning at her exuberantly. "See, Kelly, it will be great."

"Oh, yeah, just great," she murmured. Her head was suddenly pounding. "Mel, please, can we go now?"

"We haven't mingled enough."

Music was playing on the deck below them. There were shouts, laughter, a rise of drink orders, and then people were pressing together, gyrating, dancing. . . .

"Kelly, another drink," Mel suggested.

"No, please, I really need a little time alone. You go ahead, Mel. I can see myself back to the hotel."

"Kelly —"

"I'll sign the contract, Mel, because I trust you. If you're convinced it will be good — and a good move to stay in the public eye — I'll do it. But let me out of here tonight, please? You just shot down my entire world, you know," she reminded him reproachfully.

Seeing his expression, she softened her tone. "Please forgive me. I've really got to go."

"It's all right. I'll see you home."

"No, Mel, if you're having fun —"

He glared at her. He hadn't really wanted to come himself in the first place. "I want to see you safely back at the hotel.

You know, I'm not much, but I'll do my level best to protect you from any bogeyman!"

"I'm not afraid of bogeymen," she told him.

He shrugged. "Well, maybe I am. You can protect me."

She was finally able to say thank-you and goodbye with a real smile — be it one of relief — and depart the yacht. Somehow, though, it seemed that eyes watched every second of her departure. Having descended to the dock, she looked back. No one was even looking their way.

"What's the matter?" Mel asked.

"Nothing. Nothing at all." But she shivered. "I was looking back. For the bogeyman."

"Did you see him?" Mel teased.

"No, I guess he's hiding," she said. "But that's all right." She linked her arm with his. "I have you to protect me."

"Right, my girl. Onward!" He led her to the limo that had brought them and would now return them to their hotel.

He seemed grave, however, as he looked back at the ship.

"What's the matter, Mel?"

He gave a little shiver. "I don't know. I think I just realized that I'm worried about you myself!"

"Don't be."

He nodded. "The video is being shot on a private island. I'll be relieved once you're there."

"Mel! There is no bogeyman!" she assured him. Yet, even as she said the words, she felt a strange chill. And she wondered, would those words come back to haunt her?

Sitting in his chair, Marc Logan watched *Valentine Valley*, which he had watched for as long as he could remember. Not at the regular time, of course. He was a busy man, so he taped the program. But he loved *Valentine Valley*. It was his guilty pleasure — and a secret he kept to himself.

The show came on at two in the afternoon. He liked to watch the episodes the same night when he could. But sometimes, when he was especially busy, he taped the week's worth and watched them all in one orgy.

It was late. The party was over, and everyone was gone. He was thrilled. Tonight had been special. He had met her before, of course, but tonight . . . *she* had been on his yacht. And she had agreed to do his video. Of course, the world would see it as a video done for Kill Me Quick, but that didn't matter. It was *his* video.

The show had touched various emotions in him at times. It had made him cry. It had made him laugh, it had made him feel glad to be alive. It had made him feel justified at times, sympathetic, in tune, and then, at other times, angry.

The thing was, it was so real. He just loved it. She managed to have such a voice of truth, and also be a caricature. She epitomized every self-righteous egotist giving others advice. Asses who knew nothing about real situations and probably wouldn't even begin to realize just how richly they were being lampooned.

He started to watch the newest episode, then realized that she wasn't in it and flicked back. End of last week. He had been there when the episode had been filmed. When she'd fallen. Lord, she could have died, but it made for amazing footage. He imagined that it would be one of the most watched episodes ever in daytime TV. And he imagined the folks running the show must be tearing their hair out. Kelly was hot.

He rewound again, listening to the whir of his tape. They were back to her being the advice diva! What an actress! She played Marla Valentine superbly. She was smug. So good. The damned poster child for all those idiots who seemed to believe they had the voice of God whispering in their ears, dishing out advice.

"Let's see . . . oh!" Marla sat in the chair and glanced at the oh-so-professional clipboard in her hands, her red hair falling forward. "I have an answer for Sarah, in Ohio. This one did not take a rocket scientist to figure out. Sarah, I sure hope you're out there today, because you need to listen to me. Leave him. Did you hear me, honey? Do it. Leave the no-good, dirty piece of slime. You've seen his past behavior. What do you think will happen? Please, get serious. Remember, one definition of insanity refers to doing the same thing over and over, expecting a different result. And, honey, when you walk out that door, you make sure you've already got yourself a good lawyer. Take that filthy varmint for everything that the law will provide. In short, scalp him! Go straight for the . . . well, you know what to go straight for, Sarah, don't you? And don't hesitate. He deserves it!"

Logan laughed out loud. "Oh, baby, skewer 'em all!"

He shook his head, smiling. Okay, so he

was a rich old geezer, reaching desperately for his youth by way of a plastic surgeon. The operating word there was *rich*. He had been able to afford the price to open his own studios and music label, and could afford even the outrageous price tag that went with making a quality music video. So he liked to gripe about the budget. That was expected, but it didn't matter. This was a dream. He was going to be the power behind a rock video that starred Kelly Trent.

Rising, he mused that he was getting everything he wanted, basically, because he had just always loved music. And there was nothing like a good tango.

Chapter 4

"So, how was the party?" Quinn asked.

Doug shrugged, then offered his brother and Jake Dilessio a dry grin. "Kind of what you'd expect. Actually, *everything* that you'd expect. A total stereotype."

"A total stereotype," Jake said, imitating Doug's shrug as he turned to Quinn. "Expensive booze, beautiful babes, a millionaire's yacht . . . ho, hum. Poor boy."

"The booze was probably good — I don't know, I wasn't drinking," Doug said, sitting back with a broader grin. "The babes were okay, but a little hard-core. The yacht was great. The millionaire is a creep."

"Well, there you have it in a nutshell," Quinn said. "I spent last night in a car watching a front door that never opened. How was your evening, Jake?"

"Very sad," Jake told them. "Down in the projects, picking up a kid whose girlfriend thought he wouldn't cheat anymore if she removed his penis. She took a swipe at him, missed and hit his femoral artery. He's dead and she's in jail awaiting arraignment."

"Well, you definitely win for worst evening," Doug murmured, looking out toward the water. They were lunching at Nick's, a rustic place on the water frequented by both those who did and those who did not have boats. Jake Dilessio, married to Nick's niece, still maintained a permanent berth at the dockside marina. Both Jake and his wife, Ashley, were with the metro police force, she in forensics, he in homicide. Doug's brother, Quinn, actually kept his permanent residence in the Keys, where he worked as a private investigator, but since the Keys could be deadly quiet at times, and many cases brought to him in the Keys area tended to have ties up in the far more crowded Miami-Dade County area, he kept a berth for his boat here as well. Quinn had been through the FBI academy and worked with the bureau for several years before returning home and going into business with another friend in the private sector. The youngest of the three, Doug had worked hard to earn the respect of his older brother, Jake and others of their ilk. They all still thought that he was crazy, having suddenly given up his education and career to enter the realm of professional dancing. He had taken his first lessons at the studio first managed and now owned by Shannon, née Mackay and now O'Casey. The studio was where he now taught, where he practiced with Jane, and the institution he represented when he competed.

Quinn was watching him now, deep blue eyes sparkling. "You mentioned the yacht, the millionaire, the booze and the women. What about your little soap star?"

"She's not exactly little. More than five seven, I'd say," Doug told him.

"Thin, though, huh? The anorexic type?" Quinn asked.

"Thin . . . but, no. She's got a shape to her," Doug said.

"Is she nice or a bitch?" Jake asked.

"I don't know. We didn't talk that long," Doug told him.

"How about the hair?" Quinn asked. "Is that red real?"

Doug smiled slowly. "It looks real."

"You ever watch that show, Quinn?" Jake asked.

"If I did, I wouldn't admit it," Quinn said.

"Me, neither," Jake responded. "Yet everyone at the station seemed to know who she is when we received those warnings about her."

"Warnings?" Doug asked.

Jake shrugged. "Kelly Trent's manager, a woman named Ally Bassett, got in touch with the local police for some advice. She wants protection around her star, especially after the accident on set."

Doug leaned forward. "What kind of an accident?"

"The kind that really appeared to be an accident," Quinn said.

Jake groaned. "Don't you ever read the papers?"

"Sure, I read the papers," Doug said impatiently. But he hiked a brow toward Jake. "Okay, what papers?"

Jake grinned. "Well, mainly the rags. But all the show business and *People*-type weeklies had information on it, too. They were on location, some new development in the L.A. area. A mound of earth became nothing but a puff of sand and she nearly rolled off a cliff. The cops were called in to investigate, but there was nothing to indicate any tampering. People had been around the site all day. Seems there's been trouble on the soap before, and, because of it, not to mention the death threats, the people surrounding Kelly Trent are on the nervous side."

"Death threats? Against a soap star?" Doug said. He was angry. Ally Bassett had told him about the accident, and that she and Kelly's people were worried about their star. But she hadn't mentioned death threats.

Quinn looked at Jake and shrugged. "He really doesn't watch daytime TV, huh?"

Doug glared at Jake. "Right. Like you sit home on a daily basis and watch television. Why would anyone want to kill a soap star?" he asked.

"Why does anyone ever want to kill anyone?" Jake muttered.

"All right, guys, come on," Doug said. "People kill for greed, passion, fear. Motive is one of those things they usually ask you to prove in court, unless you're dealing with a psychopath. Even then there's still a motive. Sexual gratification through abusive power, something!"

"Hate," Quinn said softly.

"A soap star can be that hated?" Doug asked.

"Apparently, in this case, yes," Jake said. "The FBI has just started taking an interest in a couple of murders across the country."

"Soap stars?"

"Advice columnists, talk-show hosts, that kind of thing."

"And that has what to do with a soap star?" Doug demanded.

Quinn groaned, shaking his head. "You should watch the show — at least once."

"Hey," Doug protested. "I was offered the teaching job. Quinn, your wife suggested me for it, and the pay was awfully damned good. And yes, it intrigued me that I needed to be looking out for her as well. That doesn't mean I have to watch the show!"

"Seriously, Doug," Jake said, "the soaps apparently receive more mail than can be handled on a regular basis. Half of it is nasty, some of it threatening, and an awful lot of it is from people who take the characters far too seriously. Anyway, they've gotten all kinds of mail lately on your new protégé because the character she plays on her soap is an advice diva. From what I've heard, a vicious advice diva."

"What's the department doing?" Doug asked.

"Trying to offer a little protection, but nothing specific. Miss Trent has never come to us herself seeking assistance. But because of what has happened, the powers that be are not entirely ignoring the situation, either. She's staying on the beach. The place has in-house security. The beach cops have cruised her hotel, and the chief of guards down there has been instructed to check on her now and then. There's no solid danger that I know about, but you should be aware of what's going on."

"I intend to be aware. More so now that you've given me more information than Kelly Trent's manager did!"

"Miss Trent should be in good hands, then. They miss you at the station, you know," Jake said lightly.

"There's always an opening with me," Quinn said.

"I like what I do," Doug told them. And it was true. Still . . .

"Well, son of a bitch!" Jake muttered suddenly, staring past Doug to the docks.

"What?" Doug started to turn.

"That's Kevin Lane."

"Yeah, it is," Quinn muttered.

Quinn and Jake had both gone still. "All right, I've been out of the loop too long," Doug said. "Who the hell is Kevin Lane?"

"A major player who winds up coming off as clean as a whistle most of the time. He's wanted for questioning in the Leon

Thibault murder," Jake said.

Doug almost made a sudden swing, but caught himself in time, turning gradually. Leon Thibault had been a pure scumbag — suspected of being the money behind a dozen or more major South American drug buys. Some of the cops felt he was personally keeping half the Colombian cocaine dealers in business.

He'd been found dead, shot in the back of the head, in his custom Jag three weeks ago, just prior to the influx of a new drug on the streets of Miami known as sweet coke, a substance slipped into drinks that rendered the imbiber all but incoherent and yet as malleable and cooperative as a newborn pup.

"They got anything on Lane?" Doug asked quietly.

"An eyewitness ID for being at the scene," Jake murmured.

"You have legal grounds to arrest him?" Doug asked.

"Yeah."

"Let's flank him, then," Quinn said.

"I'll go left," Jake said.

"Right," Quinn agreed.

"I'll do the head-on," Doug said.

"You're not in on this kind of stuff anymore," Jake reminded him.

"Quinn's no cop. He's a P.I.," Doug said flatly.

"Yeah, a P.I. who was once —"

"Yeah, yeah, you want this guy, Jake? Then I'll take the head-on. You never heard of a citizen's arrest?"

"I'm willing to bet that he's armed," Jake warned.

"And I'm willing to bet that both of you are, too," Doug said.

His brother shrugged. "Let's go."

They left their table, Quinn and Jake fanning out to flank either side of their objective, Doug heading straight to the docks. There was a young, pretty blonde headed for one of the boats, and Lane was apparently following her.

"Hey, Lane!" Doug called out, determined to stop the guy before the blonde wound up caught in their pincher movement as well.

Lane stopped and looked at him.

"Who the hell are you?"

He was somewhere between thirty and forty, wearing designer leisure clothes. An oxymoron if Doug had ever heard one. His shorts were ragged, and his shirt, with palm-tree images, looked as if it had been bought at one of the pricey shops in Bar Harbor. His dark hair was slicked back, and he was tanned to a deep brown.

Doug didn't reply but kept coming forward, smiling as if he were anxious for a friendly meeting. Perhaps a business meeting.

"What do you want?" Lane called to him.

He still didn't reply.

"Look, buddy, who the hell are you?" He made a slight movement with his hand, as if he had a small sidearm tucked into the waistband of his cutoffs.

Doug didn't have to reply. Quinn was coming around by then.

"He's my brother."

Lane snapped around, his eyes narrowing as he saw Quinn. "O'Casey," Lane breathed. "Well, what the fuck. You ain't got nothing on me, you asshole. You're not a cop, so why don't you clear away from me. And get your brother out of here, unless you want him hurt. Or, what is he? CIA, FBI?"

"Naw, he's a dance teacher," Quinn said.

"But I'm a cop," Jake said, coming in from the other side. "And you're coming down to the station with me. You're under arrest —"

Lane flung around in a sudden movement, the small revolver drawn and aimed.

"Don't want to shoot a cop, now, do I?" Lane asked softly.

Doug weighed his distance from Lane, then was spurred into action. Lane was forced to turn, but he couldn't get the gun around fast enough or even squeeze off a round. Doug butted him dead center in the midriff and the two of them went flying off the dock, weightless for a minute, then into the drink together.

He might have been a big man with a gun, but he didn't put much into physical fitness. A straightforward jab in the jaw rendered the man senseless. Doug caught him around the neck in a life-saving hold, kicked hard and brought them both to the surface. Jake caught hold of Lane, dragging him out. Quinn offered his brother a hand.

"That was asinine," he said softly.

"It worked," Doug said.

"I get you hurt — or killed — and Mom will flay me alive."

"Hey, I passed that twenty-one mark some years ago, you know," Doug told him. "He could have shot Jake. In my position, you would have done the same thing."

Quinn couldn't argue that. They both stood on the dock, Doug dripping, as Jake bent over Lane and showed a small, gathering crowd of onlookers his badge. "Clear out. Nothing happening here. This gentleman is just taking a little trip down to headquarters, that's all, folks."

Lane had opened his eyes and was blinking. He met Doug's eyes, his own narrowed and venomous. "Dance teacher, my ass!" he hissed.

"I *am* a dance teacher," Doug said.

"Wow, I forgot to tell you that he was a cop before that," Quinn told Lane. "Sorry, slipped my mind. Top of his class in the academy."

"Get up," Jake ordered.

"Police brutality," Lane muttered. "You'll be in court for this."

"Police brutality from a dance teacher?" Jake queried. Then his features grew taut. He read Lane his rights and the handcuffs came out.

"Look, I swear to you, it's going to be fine. Perfectly fine," Mel said.

They were at breakfast on South Beach. It was May, a good time to be here, Mel had assured her, since they were still in the season before the area was swept beneath the true dead heat of summer. She had to admit that it was beautiful. There wasn't a cloud in the sky. The blue above them was extraordinary. And the people around them were . . . eclectic.

The small but prestigious deco hotel Mel had booked them into offered a little breakfast patio right on the street. So far, she'd seen half a dozen skaters go by, some on wheels, some on single blades, a few of the girls a bit strange looking in their bikinis, socks and heavy shoes. Some elderly women in huge flowered hats had passed by, a couple with little teacup dogs they seemed to dote upon. But the really nice thing about the place was that no one seemed to care much about anyone else's business or appearance. People smiled, waved, bid good morning to total strangers. He-man construction workers waved their hands at young gay men without seeming to have any taints of homophobia. One of the elderly ladies was delighted when a dark-haired Latin beauty a fourth of her age — and nearly naked — paused to ooh and aah over her little Yorkie. Spanish and English mixed in the same sentences along with a little Portuguese, compliments of a growing Brazilian population, according to Mel.

Actually, Kelly decided, she didn't mind being here at all. If she were here just on vacation, she would really be enjoying herself. But there was that whole thing about being put on hold for *four* months to make her tense and worried. And then there was the video . . .

Mel's hand came gently over hers. "Kelly, it will be fine."

She sighed softly, feeling a sudden surge of both amusement and affection. "Hey, did I ever tell you that you're really a top-notch agent? Lots of guys would have made a phone call — worried that they were representing a sinking ship — and told me, hey, there's a job, take it or leave it."

"I've made some money off of you in the past years, you know, young lady," he reminded her.

But Mel really was something special, she thought.

"Okay, so it's going to be fine. Where do we go from here?"

"You sign the contract." He leaned forward. "We can head back to L.A. for you to get a few things together, and then we head back here."

She looked around, enjoying the scene. Then she sighed. It was time for her "denial" phase regarding the fact that she could be fired to be over. "All right," she said.

"While all this is happening, we'll be looking ahead. You'll be all right financially, Kelly. Honestly, I'd never have you make this move just for the money. I think it's the right thing to do."

"I sure hope so."

He looked uncomfortable. "Well, frankly, I didn't believe it myself when they made the decision to keep you off the show. I can only believe that the people in charge actually must care for you a great deal."

She stared at him, adjusting her sunglasses to look him fully in the eyes. "Either they're worried about my life, or I never should have dated Matt Avery from Household Heaven."

"Well, that, too," Mel said uncomfortably. He cleared his throat. "He is the CEO, a huge wheeler-dealer — despite the fact that he's really nothing more than a snot-nosed, obnoxious, immature brat."

"Well disguised," Kelly agreed with a murmur. She'd come to that conclusion herself, after their first date. When she'd first met him at a party, he'd seemed too good to be real. Tall, fit, with beautiful gray eyes and dark hair. He'd been polite, courteous and charming. Then their first date had been in his penthouse and it quickly became obvious that he wasn't interested in getting to know her. He'd brought her there, bought the right champagne and brought in a high-priced celebrity chef. That, apparently, meant that she was supposed to sleep with him on the dinner table when the meal was done. He'd gotten as nasty as a two-year-old with a toy taken away when it hadn't worked out. If she hadn't taken a lot of yoga and some basic judo, it might have turned into date rape. He'd gained her sympathy at first by telling her about his ex-wife and how she'd managed to take him to the cleaners. By the end of the evening, she'd been certain that no matter what the ex had gotten, it hadn't been enough.

Thinking that it might have been Matt to make the final call on her being basically sent to the cellar actually made her feel better. Well, it made her angry, and that was better than feeling lost and hurt.

"Where's the contract?" she asked him.

"In my room."

"I take it you've had it awhile."

He arched his bushy salt-and-pepper brows, then nodded. "Yes. And I honestly believe this is a good thing. But if you had been dead set against it, I'd have certainly bowed to your decision. Naturally I've had the contract for several days now. I read it the minute it was offered. I tinkered with it, making some additional demands. Every one was met. You read it. You don't think I'd ever have you sign a contract without making a few adjustments, do you?"

She smiled. "No." She took the last sip of her coffee. "Well, let's go up and I'll sign the damned thing. Then what?"

"We'll make a stop by the ballroom in one of the big old hotels to the north."

"Is that where we're going to be filming?"

"No, that's where they're having the dance auditions."

She groaned. "I told you last night, I can't dance —"

"You're not auditioning, Kelly," he said with a patient sigh. "They're finishing up choosing the backup dancers. Filming takes place on Dead Man's Key."

Kelly groaned. "Tell me that you're joking now?"

He grinned. "No."

She stared at him, shaking her head. "This is really too much. I'm doing a video for a song titled 'Tango to Terror' by a group called Kill Me Quick and we're doing it on Dead Man's Key?"

He listened, nodding. "Well, yes, that's the gist of it."

"Great. Just great. Let me sign the contract before I start thinking the whole project is jinxed or something!"

"Tomorrow we'll head home so that you can gather up what you'll want for a longer stay. You're going to love being in the Keys, and the work will be easy."

"Really? I'm just going to come back and learn how to dance in one day?"

"Oh, no. We've got the dance coach coming out to L.A. You can work with him there, and by the time you come back, you'll be moving as if you've done it all your life!"

She arched a brow. That was certainly doubtful!

Chapter 5

They were down to the last ten dancers and the competition was stiff. Only four would be hired — two men and two women.

Seeing the talent involved, Doug was somewhat amazed himself that he'd been hired for the project. Not that he was knocking his own ability, but the world was filled with talent. After the words he'd heard from Ally Bassett, and now that he knew more about the situation from his brother and Jake, he understood why he was here. Frankly, he might well be a sacrificial goat. If there were any real danger to Kelly Trent, he'd be around her to absorb it. And he did have what was considered the proper aesthetic for a dance with Kelly — a good frame. He was tall and broad-shouldered, and if he hadn't already been in fairly decent shape, his stint in the police academy would have put him there. The sergeant in charge of his class had become a cop fresh from the army, and he had been merciless.

Size mattered — though he'd seen plenty of powerful smaller guys — when doing the lifts that were such a part of professional dance, and especially, so it seemed, in this video.

The remaining hopefuls on the floor followed each command of the dance director with such precision it was staggering. Their bodies were taut, toned and perfect. They had muscles most people were unaware even existed. Doug was glad that he wasn't making the final decisions. They were fluid, incredible, unbelievable.

Still, he found his mind wandering back to the morning. He missed being a cop. It had been an itch ever since he'd left the force. Though Quinn had given him a hard time that morning, his brother had suggested that he get his private investigator's license and do some work for him on occasion. And he had done so. He was still trying to figure out if it would be possible to live in both worlds. There was, after all, a tremendous sense of satisfaction in nabbing a guy like Lane.

Then again, there was the tango and a soap diva who looked as if she'd rather eat glass than be involved in the undertaking.

Well, he'd agreed to the project and he intended to see it through. And now, admittedly, he was more intrigued than ever.

"She's here," Jane Ulrich, his one-time instructor and frequent partner, said, poking Doug in the ribs. "Wow. She's prettier in person. And that is some head of hair. But then — and I suppose you don't know this — the red hair was part of the family thing on the soap."

"Frankly, no, I never watched the soap," Doug answered softly, his gaze directed toward the ballroom doors. Indeed, she had arrived. And everything had stopped. The music was still playing, but not a dancer was moving. And Herb Essen, the dance coordinator for the project, hadn't even noticed because he was staring at the doorway as well.

"Kelly! Kelly Trent!" someone called out.

"Marla! It's Marla Valentine!" someone else said.

To her credit, Doug thought a bit begrudgingly, the woman flushed and looked a little taken aback by the attention. She was escorted by her agent, Mel Alton, who seemed to be a decent enough sort. More like an older scholar than a Hollywood mover and shaker. For a moment, Kelly

Trent looked as if she wanted to run behind him and escape the entire scene.

But she gave everyone a wave and offered Herb an apologetic smile. "I'm so sorry. I didn't mean to interrupt!"

"That's fine," Herb called back, obviously smitten. He left his position by the CD player, hurrying toward the entry. That seemed to give everyone the freedom to leave the dance floor. Heading toward the woman, Herb, usually somewhat fierce and completely dignified, now looked like a puppy dog eager for attention. Herb was gay — and still idolizing the woman.

Doug wasn't sure why, but he found the scenario irritating. These people were vying for important jobs, and they were flocking to Kelly Trent, either just to touch her, bask in her celebrity or ask for autographs.

"Did you meet her yet?" Jane asked.

"Last night."

"That's right. *You* were invited to the party."

"I asked you if you wanted to go with me," he reminded her.

"I couldn't!" she reminded him. Jane had recently started dating a local hockey player who'd had a charity event the night before.

"Lots of people like sports stars better than TV actors," he reminded her. "And your Mike Murphy is one hell of a hockey player. I'd have been at your event if I could have been."

She flashed him a narrow-eyed grimace, flipping back a length of her dark hair. "Mike is all right," she said softly. "Of course I was happy to be there."

"There you go. And you're right. Mike is more than all right."

She arched a brow. "Are you happy to be passing me off? Afraid I might have been getting too into you?"

He grinned, shaking his head. He liked Jane. Really liked her. They were very good friends. But he'd had a brush with a dancer once and she'd wound up dead. Having gone into the competition ring, he'd made a personal decision that his love interests in the future would not come from the same arena.

"Jane —"

She kissed his cheek. "Sorry. I like being best friends. I'm getting really into Mike, and I was very proud to be there for him last night, but . . . Kelly Trent plays on *my* soap," Jane reminded him.

He had to laugh. Jane looked so indignant. Like thousands of people — perhaps tens or hundreds of thousands — she taped daytime television to watch later.

"Don't you dare laugh at me!" Jane told him.

"Sorry, wouldn't dream of it."

"Well, are you going to introduce me?" Jane demanded.

"She looks a little busy now, don't you think? Why don't we let the crowd die down, then we'll zero in?"

"You're still laughing at me!" Jane protested.

"I'm not," Doug assured her.

"I don't know why they insisted on a male coach for her. I could have taught her the tango."

Doug hesitated. "I'm dancing with her in the video," he said. "Of course, you could have danced with her, but I think that would have changed the tone of the video."

Jane stared at him, her eyes huge. "You're dancing with her — actually dancing *with her* — in the video?"

"Yeah. It was an offer I couldn't refuse. There's some big money behind this."

"Why didn't I get that kind of an offer?" Jane muttered.

"You did. You're coaching the group chosen today," he reminded her. "You're the total authority."

"Beneath Herb Essen. And I'm not actually in it!" she said.

He arched a brow, smiling. "Like I said, it would change the dynamics of the piece if you were dancing with her."

She sighed. "I'd still like to be in the video."

"Tell someone," he suggested.

She shook her head. "There you go — that's life for you! You were my student. Now you get to be a star and I get to be a coach!"

"I'm willing to bet that if you want to be in it yourself, all you have to do is say so," Doug suggested.

"How embarrassing that would be. Like begging for a position. I'm a professional!" Jane protested. "That would be obnoxiously aggressive. They could say no and then I'd want to hide under a rock."

He laughed. "Jane, that could be seen as assertive rather than aggressive. And they will most likely say yes."

"It's all scripted. And they are the backup dancers," she said, pointing to the crowd now hovering around Kelly Trent, who was dutifully signing cocktail napkins and whatever else people could get their hands on.

"Scripts have been known to be rewritten," he said. Jane was staring at him with her huge, dark eyes. "Okay, how about I suggest you want to dance in the thing?"

She rewarded him with a bountiful smile. "That works for me." She grabbed his hand. "Now, introduce me to Kelly Trent."

They walked over. Kelly was signing someone's address book, using the fellow's back as a desk. She glanced up, realizing that someone else had arrived. She managed a smile, but he thought that it was a very wary one.

"Good morning, Miss Trent," he said politely.

"Hi," she said, then, finishing with her task, returned the address book to the tall, tightly muscled and striking black man for whom she'd been signing.

"Thanks! My girlfriend is going to be so jealous!"

"Want something for her, too?" Kelly suggested.

"Wow, would you? Cocktail napkin, I guess."

She smiled, asked the girlfriend's name, signed and gave him the cocktail napkin.

"All right, people!" Herb called out then, apparently remembering what they were there to do. "Back on the floor!"

The others moved back to their positions as Herb called out the order of the routine that had been given to the group before their impromptu break. The music started.

"Tango to Terror." Looking a little pale, Kelly Trent watched the action as she stood by Mel's side. Alton reached over and shook Doug's hand, wishing him a good morning.

"Miss Trent, Mr. Alton, I'd like to introduce an associate, Jane Ulrich. Jane, Kelly Trent, Mel Alton."

Mel instantly smiled, not a lascivious smile, just an appreciative one. Jane was very attractive.

"How do you do, Miss Ulrich?" Mel said.

"Hi, nice to meet you," Kelly said, offering Jane a smile and sincere interest.

"Thank you. I can't tell you how excited I am. You're on my favorite soap," Jane told her.

Kelly glanced at Mel, her beautiful eyes — a strange, hypnotic blend of blue and green with something like a touch of gold right around the pupils — somewhat questioning, but she went ahead and said, "Well, thank you. I'm going to be off it for quite a while," she told Jane.

"No!" Jane gasped, horrified.

"I'm afraid they've got me in a coma. Apparently, Marla's venom has been a bit too scary lately," Kelly explained.

"No!" Jane gasped again.

Kelly smiled deeply at that, a full, rueful grin. "I'm afraid so."

"No!" came from Jane's horrified lips one more time.

"Yes, but hush on that, please," Mel said, putting a finger to his lips. "They want to keep the audience guessing just when she's going to come back."

"Ah, so you're moving on to bigger and better things while you take your break," Jane said.

As Kelly Trent looked at the dancers, Doug could tell that she wasn't at all sure she *was* moving on to bigger and better things, but she wasn't about to say so.

She turned to Jane. "Quite frankly, I'm watching these people and feeling a surge of pure panic. I can't do that — any of that."

"Oh!" Jane waved a dismissive hand in the air. "Don't worry, he's just making them show their stuff right now. The song is, amazingly, an excellent tango. That's what you'll be doing. And you'll learn it in no time! Doug will make you look good. Honestly."

Kelly's kaleidoscope eyes fixed on him and she didn't appear in the least certain. "Well, we can hope," she murmured, smiling at Jane again.

"I promise you, Doug is great," Jane said.

"Unfortunately, I somehow missed ballroom dancing entirely while growing up," Kelly said. She seemed to honestly like Jane because, once again, her smile appeared deep and sincere. "I had so many friends who at least went to cotillion . . . but not me."

"I'm willing to bet you'll be amazed at how quickly you learn," Jane assured her.

A security guard entered the ballroom right behind them, looking around. He approached their group a little hesitantly. "There's a phone call, a gentleman calling about something important having to do with the video. Could one of you take the call?" he asked apologetically.

"I'll take the call and see if I'm able to help," Doug offered.

"Thanks," the man said, looking relieved. "There's a house phone on the wall over there."

Doug excused himself and the man walked with him, indicating the phone. "Sorry, I couldn't quite figure out what he was saying. Sounds as if he's on a cell phone or something. He might have been asking for Kelly Trent, but since I've no idea who this guy is, I thought I should get someone involved with the project on the phone."

"It's fine, don't worry about it," Doug said. "If it's a kook, I'll hang up. If it's important, I'll either get Miss Trent or make sure the right people get the message."

"Thanks!" the fellow said, and, turning, left Doug at the phone.

He picked up the receiver. "Hello, can I help you?"

There was a strange sound in the background, like a whooshing noise. Then a voice came on. "I need to speak with Kelly Trent."

"I'm sorry. I'll see if she's available. Who is this, please?"

"She's going to be doing the video, right? We'll be able to see her? Can she speak now? That entire *Valentine Valley* thing is . . . well, her character could be dead!"

Doug took a breath. "Excuse me, who are you and just what do you want?"

"Kelly Trent!" Suddenly the caller wheezed with laughter. "Kelly is going to be dead, Kelly is going to be dead!"

"Hey —"

There was a sudden click. The line went dead.

Chapter 6

When Doug O'Casey returned from having taken the phone call, he had a strange look about him.

"Who was it? Is there a problem?" Mel asked.

O'Casey shook his head. "Whoever it was . . . asked for you, but then hung up," he said, looking at Kelly. He added, "Sorry."

A bit puzzled, Kelly shrugged. "I doubt it could have been anything important. I'm certainly not managing any part of this. Actually, Mel and I just stopped by, so no one even knows that I'm here. If friends are trying to reach me, they have my cell phone number."

"Sure," O'Casey said, but his eyes still seemed intense. He was staring at her as if trying to fathom some mystery, and she found it unsettling. She didn't think she'd ever seen eyes of such a dark intense blue.

And the way that he watched her made her feel a bizarre combination of heat and unease. There was a wired energy about him, as well as a taut composure, as if he were watching, waiting, all the time. Like a snake, he seemed coiled, ready to strike.

At the same time, there was something about him that offered a sense of security. He was definitely toned, almost to a fault. Agile, muscled, with tiger-quick reflexes. And she realized — with more than a bit of dismay — that he awakened a sexual core within her. That was, in itself, frightening. She was actually afraid of the man, she thought. No, not of him, exactly, but . . . She was afraid to be around him. Afraid of herself, maybe.

Mel cleared his throat and Kelly realized uneasily that she and Doug had been staring at each other too long. Not a great deal of time, surely, but too long. Enough for Mel to notice that there was a touch of friction in the air. She pulled her gaze from the man and looked at Mel.

"Is this group the rest of the cast, then?" he asked.

The auditioning dancers had been called back to the floor. They were working their hearts out.

"A few of them, at least," Doug said.

"This isn't going to work," Kelly heard herself murmur uneasily. She winced. She'd been honest about her lack of experience, but she hated that she sounded so pathetically uncertain.

"Oh, don't worry. You're not going to have to do those kicks and contortions," O'Casey said.

Great. She'd be okay because they weren't really expecting anything out of her.

"Actually," she said, feeling her lips twitch, "I can kick."

"Good for you," Doug said. "That's right. You're from California. Pilates, yoga, Taebo, the exercise of the week, huh?"

"Doug," Jane murmured, an almost imperceptible note of reproach in her voice. Maybe he wasn't aware of the way he had sounded.

Why the hell was he giving her such a hard time? The guy was a dancer himself. A performer. A man with no right to make it sound as if she were living in an entirely plastic, *worthless* world.

"You've never seen the inside of a gym, have you, Mr. O'Casey?" she inquired, letting the sarcasm drip just slightly.

"Touché," Jane offered, so softly that Kelly wasn't quite certain she had heard the note of support.

"Hmm. You've a point there, I imagine," O'Casey murmured.

"Hey, Doug . . . Jane!" the dance coach called from the floor.

"Excuse us, will you?" Jane said sweetly. Doug had his hand on her arm, ready to draw her away. "Miss Trent, I really am your biggest fan. It's such a pleasure to meet you, though I suspect you must hear that all the time. I sound like an idiot —"

"You sound just fine, and I'm terribly flattered. The pleasure is mine," Kelly told her.

Doug O'Casey nodded to her — a little curtly, she thought — then went on toward the floor with Jane. Kelly found herself wondering about the relationship between them. They seemed to know each other backward and forward, and yet . . .

"Can we go now?" she asked Mel softly.

"Sure, except . . . don't you want to see a little more?" he asked.

"Why? I'm already daunted, and my cowardice is growing," Kelly told him dryly. "You're a good agent, you know. You've taught me that I'm never supposed to voice my pathetic uncertainties to anyone, right? And I think I've already given away my cowardice enough."

Mel laughed. "Kelly, you haven't. I swear.

I know this has really shaken you, but when one door closes, a new door opens. And this is a great door we're entering."

"I haven't actually left anything yet," she reminded him.

"Quite right. That's why this is going to be so good. Think of it as an adventure."

"Right! It's going to be great, Mel! I'm grateful for the support. You sound like a scruffy-jawed Mary Poppins! But you know what? I am going to be good. It's going to take some hard work, but I know how to work hard. It's going to be an education." She squared her shoulders suddenly and looked at him. Screw the dance instructor. She hadn't asked to do the video; she'd been aggressively pursued.

"They're dancing something of what you're going to be doing now," Mel told her. "Let's just hang in a few minutes more, okay?"

The music was playing again. Doug O'Casey and Jane Ulrich were on the floor alone. They might have been one entity, they were so close. The woman's position was perfect. They were smooth as silk — and sharp as tacks, head movements exact, on the split second, arms, bodies, every piece of musculature attuned. Inwardly, Kelly groaned.

"Never!" she whispered to Mel.

"Oh, don't be ridiculous."

"Mel, those two have obviously danced together forever. They're like Fred Astaire and Ginger Rogers. You think I can look like that in a matter of weeks?"

"It will be video. Mistakes are edited. There will be close-ups, backup dancers, and the band themselves. This isn't half of the choreography."

"That's reassuring!" she murmured.

"It will be fine."

"Right. I can tell. Maybe I can play pro football in a movie after this!"

"Kelly, Kelly, Kelly!"

"Mel, Mel, Mel!"

"You got a better idea for the immediate future?" he inquired.

She looked at him. "No," she admitted.

He grinned deeply. "Okay, kid, enough torture for today. Think of it this way — after the video, you'll just have another talent to add to your résumé. How's that?"

"Lovely," she assured him.

Mel glanced at his watch. "I'll leave you to pack up. I have a few things to do, a few bases to touch, and then we need to head for the airport."

"Home!" she said with an appreciative sigh.

"Sanctuary?" he teased lightly.

She laughed. "Yeah, maybe."

Mel gave a wave toward the group on the dance floor. Barely noticed, they slipped out.

Chapter 7

"Hey, kid. What's happening?"

Doug grinned, shaking his head. Quinn couldn't see him, since they were talking over the phone. But to Quinn, Doug knew he'd always be "kid," even if they both made it past ninety.

"I'm heading out. The 6:00 p.m. flight to L.A."

"Cool. When are you coming back?"

"In a week."

"Where are they putting you up?"

"Someplace on Sunset."

"Sounds like a good gig to me." Quinn could almost see his younger brother shaking his head. "I'll bet it's a decent place."

"You used to travel a lot more than me."

"Yeah, on taxpayer dollars. We didn't get much in the way of hotels."

"I guess there is big money behind this," Doug agreed.

"You almost sound as if you're feeling guilty."

"No," Doug said. "Just a little disturbed."

"How come? What's up?"

"Well, it was probably some kind of a crank call, but at the dance auditions, I took the phone when the person on the other end asked to speak with Kelly Trent. The man — or woman — definitely sounded deranged. At first, he just wanted to talk to her, but then he wanted to know if she was really in the video. The call ended with 'She's going to be dead, Kelly Trent is going to be dead,' or words to that effect."

"Did you tell Kelly that she got a threatening call?"

"I just said that someone had asked to speak with her, but then had hung up. I called Jake, asked him if he could trace the call. But it will be nearly impossible, because it came in on a switchboard, with hundreds of other calls. So, what do you make of it?"

Quinn was silent for a minute. "What did you make of it?"

"I just asked you that question! You're the damned P.I."

"Well, yes, but you were a cop."

"Right. It probably meant nothing. When

I talked with Ally Bassett, she admitted that soap stars get crank and threatening calls all the time."

"But this one bothered you."

"Yes."

"Okay, so think like a cop. Jake will do what he can, but it's like looking for a needle in a haystack. For you, it's a gut-level thing. So keep it on the front burner."

"If I hadn't been with you guys and heard all this stuff about advice divas dying, I would have believed it was just a crank. Hell, she's an actress, not a therapist. But we both know there are enough whacked-out psychos out there who may not make such a distinction. I don't want to be an alarmist, but it's something to definitely keep on the front burner."

"You're still a cop at heart, you know," Quinn said.

"Whatever, big bro," Doug said, then hesitated. "Listen, you know Jake is great, but he's a cop, bound to certain ethics and rules. Everyone knows it can be a different thing for a P.I."

"Good God, you're not suggesting that I'm unethical?"

Doug laughed. "You're just in a better position than Jake or I am right now to do some digging."

There was silence at the other end, then Quinn said, "I'll do some checking around, see if I can get someone to find out where the call originated."

"I'd appreciate it."

"I'm willing to bet it came from a pay phone."

"Me, too. But I wouldn't mind knowing."

"All right. Have a good flight, then. Keep in touch."

Doug hung up, then picked up his jacket and headed out to the living room, where Jane was waiting. She'd offered to take him to the airport.

"All set," he told her.

She'd been holding his ticket.

"First class, huh?" she said, looking up at him.

"Yep."

"Why did I go into dance instead of music?"

"Because you move like a symphony, how's that?" he responded.

"This whole thing is wild, isn't it?" she asked.

"Different, anyway. By the way, I mentioned that you'd like to be in the video," he said.

"And?"

"Well, some other poor female is going to be out of a job."

"Really? I'm in?" She threw her arms around him, giving him a big hug.

"Jane, you're championship material. This isn't that big a deal!"

She shook her head. "Are you kidding? Championships are hours and hours of hard work. And no matter how hard you work, you can reach a competition and be knocked out by someone else. But a video, a sure-shot at my fifteen minutes of fame? This works for me."

"Well, then. Good."

Jane studied him. "It really doesn't matter that much to you, does it?"

He shrugged. "I don't know. I honestly don't know. Anyway, let's head out." He grinned. "I wouldn't want to miss out on first class by being late."

"Aha!" she said. "So first class is cool!"

"A big seat and a free beer? You bet!"

Matt Avery sat in his richly upholstered desk chair and stared out at the superb skyline view of Hollywood offered by his floor-to-ceiling glass windows. Life was good. Well, today it was good.

By now, she knew . . . He hadn't demanded that she be fired. That would have been insane. Because, as wicked as she was, she was a big name out there now, and that meant money. No, it was far better to be a man who was more concerned with human life than advertising dollars. Putting her on a paid leave was . . . brilliant. And with any luck, as time rolled by . . . she would receive a good substitute for the ax he had intended. The thought made him smile.

But his smile faded as he remembered his evening with Kelly. He'd offered her everything. The very best. Himself. And she'd kicked him in the balls.

She'd had so much dignity, so much pride — rejecting him. Well, he didn't like rejection. She should have known that. And now . . . it was all set into motion. Good old Mel had delivered the news and the lovely little redhead would be cut down to size. *Rejected.*

Matt looked around his office. Again he felt a deep sense of pleasure. He had a good head for business. And in a town that was filled with the renowned and the beautiful, he really had it all going. Celebrities could be like the flavor of the week. Pretty boys could fall prey to gossip and innuendo. Beautiful women arrived daily in truckloads. Here, in Hollywood, there was

only one thing that really mattered —
money.

Money was power. Starlets learned
quickly that it was more important to get
to know the big boys than the pretty boys.
He knew how to play and he played well.
He'd never lost, never even dreamed of
facing humiliation until . . . Kelly. But no
more!

A buzz sounded on his desk. He pressed
the intercom to speak with his secretary.

"What?"

"Your ex-wife is on line one, sir."

Grimly he punched another button and
leaned back in his chair.

"Matt?"

"What do you want now, Veronica?" he
asked. He leaned back, lifting a hand,
forming a trigger with his forefinger and
thumb. "Bang!" he said softly.

"Matt, damn it, are you there?" she
asked, her voice as irritating through the
blank air as it was in person. Well, nearly.

"Oh, yeah, I'm here. *Bang, bang, bang!*"
he repeated under his breath.

"What is that noise, Matt?"

"Nothing. Talk, Veronica, what do you
want now?" He closed his eyes, gritting his
teeth. Who did he hate more? This woman
who had used him, then tried to use him

up? Or . . . Kelly, the one who had rejected him? Who had looked through him? Found him . . . lacking?

Veronica's voice droned on. And as the words meshed and blended, it was as if he couldn't even really hear her. But then, he had left Veronica, bored with her, sick of the sound of her voice. While Kelly Trent . . .

Bang. Bang. Bang. You're hurt. You're bleeding. You're dead.

Sleeping on a flight was the only way to go, as far as Kelly was concerned. She boarded, plumped up her pillow and closed her eyes. She was vaguely aware of Mel playing with the headphones and magazines in the seat pocket in front of him, but she paid little attention to him. By now she was becoming annoyed with herself. Her pride was wounded. She should have quit the damned soap. Quit it a long time ago and taken a few chances.

She vaguely heard the preparations for takeoff, the words of the flight attendants. Then, just as they started to taxi down the runway, she opened her eyes — and realized that Doug O'Casey was in the seat across the aisle from her. Her eyes widened with surprise. He was leaning back in his seat, eyes closed as well. Then he turned, as if aware that she was staring at him.

"Hey."

"You're on this plane?" she asked.

He arched a brow and looked around with a small, rueful smile. "Apparently."

She didn't know why she felt so off guard. "You're coming to L.A. already?"

"There's not a lot of time," he reminded her.

Her initial hostility suddenly faded to a flash of humor. "You could have all the time in the world and it still wouldn't work the way it does with your girlfriend."

"Jane?" he said.

"Yes. Miss Ulrich."

He shrugged. "Jane is a true pro. But like you said, you can kick." She felt the sweep of his indigo gaze. "You're in excellent shape, and you don't even need to be to learn steps." He snapped his fingers. "You'll have the basic tango down in an hour."

She looked forward for a minute, then shrugged. "I'd like to think I'm capable of learning the basic steps. But the way your heads snapped and the speed with which she made a lot of those turns . . . I don't know. That could be tricky."

He smiled. "That's why we're going to

work. Starting tomorrow."

"Tomorrow?"

"That would be why I'm on the plane."

She flushed with annoyance and glanced at Mel, wondering why she was the last to know everything. Mel, however, had ceased to play with his magazines and earphones. He was snoring softly at her side.

"It does take work," Doug told her quietly.

"I'm not afraid of work."

"Then why are you afraid?"

"I'm not afraid."

"Then what's the problem?"

She stared at him. There were dozens of problems, especially with the very core of her life, but she certainly didn't want to get into a deep conversation on the rights and wrongs of the world, particularly not across the aisle on an airplane, and definitely not with this man.

The flight attendant, a cheerful, bald fellow with huge dark brows, stopped to ask them what they'd like to drink. Doug ordered a beer. Kelly hadn't wanted anything before but suddenly, now she did. "Jack and Coke," she murmured.

The flight attendant walked on by. Kelly leaned toward Doug's chair. "There isn't a problem. I'm just being as honest as I can about the fact that I haven't the least idea of how to do the tango."

O'Casey shrugged, staring back at her intently. "So? They're sparing nothing to teach you."

"Of course. They've acquired nothing but the best to teach me, right?"

He grinned slowly at her tone. "I do know what I'm doing."

"Then it's all just lovely, isn't it?"

"How come you're so hostile?" he asked.

"How come *you're* so hostile?" she flung back.

His smile deepened. "It's interesting. I've never worked with such a 'star' before. And . . ."

"And what?"

"Well, it's rather what I expected."

"And that would be?"

"You," he said.

"Jack and Coke!" the flight attendant said, setting a drink down before Kelly, along with a cup of warm mixed nuts. "Let's see. The beer here, right?"

"Thank you," O'Casey said.

She looked around the flight attendant. "Me. And just what exactly does that mean?"

"Nothing."

"Oh, bullshit!"

"All right. You're a prima donna."

"What!"

" 'Oh, I can't dance!' You sound like a petulant child."

"You're an ass!" she told him.

He arched a brow, looking around. She had spoken too loudly. People in the seats ahead were turning around uneasily. Inwardly, Kelly winced.

She lowered her voice. "I'm not being petulant, I'm being honest. I'm trying to give them an option out of using me if they don't want to!"

"They want you. They've made that obvious."

"And I'm going to do it. So what's your problem?" she demanded.

Again, he hiked up a brow. Then, after a moment, he shrugged. "I don't know," he told her. "I honestly don't know."

Something about his answer touched Kelly strangely. For a moment — a brief moment — she thought that he might be feeling something of the strange loss and confusion with life that she was feeling herself. But then the moment was gone. He stared at her with those ever-probing, ridiculously dark blue eyes and said, "If you're unhappy with having an ass for an instructor, you can have me replaced. You

115

are the star, after all."

"I'll bear that in mind," she assured him.

"Chicken kiev, salmon or steak?" the flight attendant asked.

"Salmon," Kelly ordered.

"Steak," O'Casey said.

"Would you like to order for your companion?" the flight attendant asked Kelly.

"Oh, no, let him sleep," Kelly said sweetly. She suddenly wanted to strangle Mel as well.

"Sure thing. He can really have dinner anytime," the man said.

"Thanks," Kelly told him.

"Sure thing!"

She was starting to dislike the flight attendant; he was far too cheerful. She picked up her in-flight magazine, determined to show that she had no desire to continue their conversation. Doug O'Casey ignored her, leaning back.

Two seconds later, Kelly stared at him again. He was frowning, playing with the arm of the chair. She sighed, undid her seat belt, leaned across the aisle and hit the right button to make the seat go back. He went with a jerk.

She was pretty sure he was gritting his teeth, but he smiled over the fact. "Thanks."

"No problem."

But before she could straighten and return to her own chair, the plane suddenly hit an air pocket and she wound up strewn over his lap and halfway in the empty seat beside him. She was certainly closer than she had ever intended, and trembling from the fear that had clutched her heart.

"The captain has turned on the seat-belt sign!" a flight attendant announced, her tone stressed. "If you're out of your seat, please return to it immediately and fasten your seat belt."

Kelly tried to straighten just as there was another serious bump. Cups and glasses went flying. She might have hit the roof on that one, except for the fact that he caught her, sliding her fully into the empty window seat at his side.

"I'd fasten that seat belt right now, if I were you," he said.

"Now *you're* going to tell *me* how to fly?" she demanded awkwardly.

"No, I'm suggesting you try a seat belt."

She was aware then of the male flight attendant rushing by, holding on to seats, hurrying into the main body of the cabin. There were cries of fear coming from the rear of the plane. The bumps were continuing.

The pilot came on. "I'm going to ask the

flight attendants to please take their seats as well. Seems we've encountered something of a lightning storm, folks, and we'll do our best to get out of it as quickly as possible."

Kelly glanced over at Mel. To her absolute disbelief, he was still snoring. Another bump rocked the plane and the woman in front of Kelly started to scream. "We're all going to die!"

"Oh, Jesus!" someone swore furiously from a seat behind.

O'Casey leaned forward, looking at the hysterical woman. "Hey! It's all right. Messed up a few good drinks, but it's all right. Honestly. Just as if we were hitting some rough spots on pavement."

"No, no, I've flown before! This has never happened —"

"I've flown a lot and been in the same situation at least a dozen times. Honestly, trust me," O'Casey said. He had a way of talking that was actually lulling. Kelly had flown dozens and dozens of flights herself; this had definitely given her a few twinges. She found that she was listening to him herself and feeling lulled.

"Want me to come up there?" O'Casey asked the woman.

"No, no, I wouldn't want to take you

away from your wife," the woman said, her voice stressed.

"I'm not his wife!" Kelly announced.

"Oh, honey, everyone sleeps together these days without being married. Don't worry about it. I certainly wouldn't judge anyone. Especially not . . . not when we might die any minute!"

"We're not going to die!" Kelly snapped. "And I'm not —"

"It's just turbulence, that's all," O'Casey said, his tone assuring again.

The violent rise and fall of the plane stopped as quickly as it had begun. The flight attendants were up in a few minutes, running along the aisle and picking up the cups, glasses, bottles and everything else that had flown. The seat-belt sign remained on.

The woman in the front seat turned around. "I'm so sorry. I'm afraid I'm not much of a flier."

"It's perfectly all right, and perfectly natural," O'Casey assured her.

Kelly got her first sight of the woman's face as she peered at the two of them through the crack in the seats. She was beautiful. Slim, classical, features perfectly formed.

"I'm such a . . . coward," the woman said.

"It's all right!" Kelly told her.

The woman's eyes widened suddenly. "Marla! Marla Valentine!"

Inwardly, Kelly groaned, but she forced a weary smile. "My name is Kelly."

"Simone Montaige. What a pleasure." The woman focused her huge topaz eyes on O'Casey.

"Douglas O'Casey," he said.

The woman nodded and stared at Kelly again. "I didn't know you were married." She flushed. "I read the soap opera trades," she admitted. "Oh, that's right, sorry. You said that you weren't his wife."

"We're friends," Doug explained briefly.

"I see," the woman said, flashing another perfect smile.

"Acquaintances," Kelly said, wondering why she was feeling so irritated.

"Oh." She gave Doug another assessing gaze.

"His girlfriend is back in Miami," Kelly offered.

"Oh." There was a definite insinuation in the single syllable.

"Actually, I have lots of friends in Miami," O'Casey said pleasantly. "Miss Trent and I just met."

"We're . . . working together," Kelly said.

"Oh, yes, right. Of course," Simone said.

"How nice. How . . . *very* nice."

Kelly could have groaned. No matter what she said now, it wouldn't come out right. Fine, let the woman think whatever she wanted.

"So, you're from Miami," Simone said to Doug. "Great place. I love South Beach. I work out there now and then."

"I can imagine," Kelly murmured.

"Pardon?" Simone said.

"I'm sorry. You're very attractive," Kelly said. "Are you a model? If so, I imagine you work out there frequently — doing print ads," Kelly said, feeling her jaw lock.

"Oh, yes. On the beach. Bathing suits."

"Bathing suits. Imagine that," Kelly said politely.

"Where is home? L.A.?" O'Casey said, actually elbowing Kelly with a little jab.

"Yes. L.A. It's been home forever."

"You look familiar," O'Casey said.

Again Simone offered a perfect smile. "Miss Trent hit it right on. I'm a model. I've done some cosmetic ads. And I've worked for a number of magazines." She flushed modestly. "Some high-impact magazines. Actually, I'm Miss February."

Kelly turned to O'Casey, a brow slightly arched, a pleasant grin in place. "There you go. This lovely lady is Miss February."

121

She couldn't help allowing a small purr into her voice. "Of course you recognize her."

He was nonplussed. "Miss February. Sure." He returned Kelly's gaze. "You're so right. Miss February."

"As I said, I do many print ads," Simone said with a shrug, and offered the name of the very well-known lingerie company for which she also worked. Thankfully, the angle at which she had twisted to speak with them seemed to be getting to her at last. She offered O'Casey one last brilliant pout of her lips and told him, "I'll write down my numbers. You were so kind to me. Call me if you need anything — anything at all — while you're in L.A."

"Great. Thanks," O'Casey told her.

The young woman stared at Kelly again, offering her a rueful smile. "You two are really . . . just working together?"

"Really. We're working together," Kelly said.

"I didn't mean to be forward. Or hone in on anything."

"Trust me, you certainly didn't," Kelly assured her.

Miss February passed back a slip of paper. O'Casey thanked her, then he looked at Kelly.

"What about Jane?" she asked him softly.

"Well, you won't tell her, will you?" he asked.

"I barely know her," Kelly said. "However, it seems my sympathy should be with her."

"I'm willing to bet Jane can handle it."

She went to undo her seat belt, ready to cross over and return to her own chair. A glance across the aisle showed her that, despite the violent turbulence that had rocked the plane, Mel was still snoring.

"Does he take something to fly?" O'Casey murmured.

"He must have. Now, if you'll excuse me —" she said, starting to rise. But as she did so, the dinner cart came to a halt by O'Casey's side, blocking her exit.

"You've moved over here, Miss Trent!" the too-cheerful flight attendant said. "Salmon for you . . . and what was the dressing you wanted on your salad?"

She eased back in the chair, gritting her teeth, aware that O'Casey was staring at her and that he was amused. Yes, she could just say that she was moving back to her own chair. But strangers sat next to each other on airplanes all the time. It would look rather silly if she were to insist she had to be back in her own seat at this point.

Worse, it might just look as if she were a little afraid of remaining too close to him. Or as if she were a *prima donna*. Or *petulant!*

"Peppercorn," she said, offering O'Casey the sweetest, most disdainful smile she had ever acted out on any stage. He lowered his head as if just ever so slightly amused.

Dinner was served. Then wine came around. The flight attendant was great at keeping glasses full. He was determined to get his passengers soused and out for the majority of the trip, perhaps. And still Mel didn't move, though every once in a while he let out a snore.

O'Casey leaned near her. "Still want to move back?"

"I've slept to the hum of Mel's snores many a time," she assured him. But the trays remained down, making the move not an easy accomplishment, so she stayed. And some time before the trays were picked up, she leaned back and dozed herself.

The next thing Kelly knew, they were landing. As she lifted her head, she realized that she'd been sleeping on the man's shoulder. She refused to look at him, and refused to acknowledge her own accidental act. They were here. At last, the interminable flight was over! L.A. She was home, except . . . home, like everything else in her world, would never really be the same again. As she contemplated the tarmac, she felt the absurd desire to cry once again. She had been all but fired, for God's sake! And home wasn't at all what it had once been. Get over it! she warned herself sternly.

She turned, startled to discover that O'Casey was studying her. "Sometimes," he told her, "a whole new world can be a damned good one, you know."

She unclipped her belt. "I'm really not sure what you're talking about," she murmured, glancing over at Mel. He was just awakening. She found herself irritated that he had managed to sleep through the entire flight, bumps and smooth sailing, eschewing drinks and dinner.

Rising, she whispered to O'Casey, "Don't forget Miss February's phone numbers. I think you left them in the seat pocket." She crawled over him, awkward in her haste, aware of his stature and the scent of his cologne, still somewhat teasing and alluring after all the hours in the air. She was more anxious to deplane than she had ever been, at any time, in her entire flying history.

O'Casey let her crawl, making no effort to either stop her or assist her. Of course not. Miss February had risen as well. His attention was diverted. Once again, the delicate, frightened flier was telling O'Casey to call her, that she would love to show him L.A. In fact, she was just dying to do so.

Chapter 8

"It's shocking, absolutely shocking," Serena said. "That they would kill you like that! So brutally, so coldly!"

"No, no, no — they don't see it as cold or shocking. She's on a long paid vacation. They can imagine themselves as saints! And if, in reality, it is brutal and cold, it's not truly shocking at all," Jennifer argued. "This is Hollywood." She snapped her fingers. "Face it, we're in a cutthroat business."

They were sitting at their favorite haunt, a little Italian restaurant on Sunset. It was a beautiful spring day, the temperature in the low eighties, and Kelly was seated with her two soap "sisters" — the other "Valentine" daughters — outside beneath one of the brightly striped umbrellas.

"Money is always going to be the bottom line," Serena said.

"Actually —" Kelly began.

127

"But Kelly's character has surely made them a fortune lately!" Jennifer argued indignantly.

"Maybe the whole soap is going down," Serena suggested.

"It's really —" Kelly tried again.

"Impossible! The ratings are up like they haven't been in years," Jen scoffed. "There's something malicious in all this and I'm certain it has something to do with you accepting that dinner invitation with Matt Avery."

"It doesn't —" Kelly began.

"The lech!" Serena said, shuddering with distaste.

"How dare he," Jennifer said, all but snarling.

"Jen, honestly —"

"You don't think there could be any truth to the idea that the powers that be are actually worried that Kelly is in danger because of her role, do you?" Serena said.

"Listen, Serena —" Kelly tried.

"Oh, come on!" Jennifer said. "Serena, do you believe that? They know the ex-husband killed the one woman. And the other . . . she was doling out advice while being hyped up on drugs herself. She drowned in her bathtub. Besides, Kelly is an actress."

Kelly stared at her. "Everyone seems to know so much about all this!" she marveled.

Jen shrugged. "The newspapers, CNN, MSNBC, local stations *and* the Internet have carried all kinds of stuff on it. We're living in the information age, you know. It's hard to imagine Serena missing much, since she's married to a P.I. And what intrigues Serena, I get to hear all about. It makes sense, trust me."

"Great," Kelly murmured.

"It's going to be all right, you know," Serena told Kelly, her beautiful eyes wide and sympathetic.

Kelly exhaled a long sigh, shaking her head. "Hey, both of you, it's fine. Honestly. Things really haven't been the same since . . . in a long time." And they hadn't been. Too much friction — lethal friction — had occurred at the set and around the folks involved with the show over the last years. And both Jennifer and Serena had married, Jennifer to another actor and Serena to a private investigator. Jennifer had a three-year-old daughter and infant twins, while Serena now had a bouncing baby boy, just one year old. Both had gotten involved with their husbands and families, the future and other projects. As a result, their time on the show had just

about gotten down to guest appearances —
which is why Kelly had taken over the
reigning position.

"A video!" Jennifer said, her eyes sparkling with envy.

"That's really too cool," Serena agreed.
"Think of the exposure."

"Think of the fun," Jennifer said.

"Well, that, naturally. I'm sure it's going
to be hard work, as well," Serena said,
frowning. "I think that Matt Avery is behind you being on 'paid leave,' I really do.
And though I honestly can't believe that
you could be in danger for a role you're
portraying — or even that the deaths of
two people in different states can be related — there is no sense in taking chances
with your life! So what's happened is actually good."

"Exactly. That's the way I see it," Kelly
said. Was she telling the truth, or lying?

"Oh, Lord!" Jennifer exclaimed suddenly.

"What?" Serena demanded.

"Don't look now, but someone just went
inside to the to-go counter," Jennifer said.

Both Serena and Kelly immediately
looked.

"I said not to do that!" Jennifer told
them.

There were a number of people heading in to the restaurant's take-out bar area where one could get cappuccinos or gourmet drinks to go, as well as meals. At first, Kelly had no idea to whom Jennifer had been referring.

"Speak of the devil incarnate," Serena murmured.

"Who . . . ?" Kelly began, but then she saw.

Matt Avery was there, along with Joe Penny. Kelly stiffened instantly. Matt was simply an ass, slick and plastic. She had once been fooled, but never again. However, seeing Joe Penny with him was like a kick deep in the gut. Joe had been the man to hire her at the show's inception. He had been a friend for many years and she had stuck with him through the many trials and tribulations that had rocked the soap.

"They haven't seen us yet," Jennifer murmured. "Kel, if you want to move somewhere, we can."

Kelly smiled grimly. "Oh, no. I'm pleased to see them both."

As she spoke, Joe turned. The deep crimson flush that lit his cheeks as he saw her displayed his instant discomfort. She lifted a hand and waved, her gaze hard and unfaltering. If she hadn't been the one put out on a long "vacation" without so much as a discussion after all those years, she might have felt sorry for him. He actually looked a little sick.

She didn't think he spoke to Matt — he was just staring at her. But Matt must have sensed some change in his companion because he turned to look, too. As usual, the man was dressed in perfectly tailored designer clothing — polo shirt, jacket and dark, sharp-creased pants. For a brief moment, alarm seemed to touch his eyes. Then pleasure. She was certain he was enjoying the thrust of his knife.

The woman behind the counter drew the men's attention, handing them their designer coffees to go with their designer clothing and designer attitude. They turned, Matt in the lead, coming out the door.

"Girls! Good to see you three," Matt said, voice low, with a careful modulation intended to be sexy.

"Matt. Hi, Joe," Serena said, addressing the man behind him.

Joe nodded, took a gulp of his coffee and, to his horror, spilled it on his shirt. This allowed him to excuse himself quickly, saying he needed cold water.

"Kelly, I've just heard the news about

you leaving the show for an extended period," Matt said. "I'm so terribly sorry."

"Are you?" Kelly said, pleased that she sounded entirely surprised but not terribly concerned. "Actually, it worked out rather well," she said firmly.

"Could we speak privately for just a minute?" he asked her.

"Why?"

"Please, Kelly. Just for a moment. I really do feel terrible about all this."

She indicated the busy street, smiling. "Where?"

"Just . . . there," he said.

She rose, following him to a spot just beyond the tables. He leaned against the wall, smiling at her. "Things could get bad for you, Kelly," he said softly.

"I see how concerned you are."

"Honey, I could make everything work out for you."

"Please, don't worry or be concerned. Mel will make things work out for me."

"Still a total bitch, aren't you?" he queried, his tone so soft that, for a minute, she didn't quite catch the loathing in it.

"Matt, why are we talking?"

"You are a tease, baby, you know that? You came on to me like gangbusters, then turned into Marla Valentine. You know what they call women like you, Kelly?"

"Excuse me, Matt. Thanks again for your concern. I'd like to get back to lunch."

"Cunt, prick-tease. . . ."

He had somehow managed to slowly edge her back to the café wall, his own form in front of her, almost touching. His arm rested on the wall, blocking her in.

"Matt," she said sweetly. "I'll scream."

"Kelly!" Serena's voice suddenly rose loud and cheerful. "Hey, I think there's someone looking for you here!"

"Move!" Kelly said firmly to Matt.

He smiled. "Prick-teasers always get what's coming to them, Kelly," he said. "And I'm in a position to make sure it happens."

She pushed him backward, forcing her way around him. To her amazement, he followed her back to the table, smiling. She was certain Serena had called out just to rescue her, but her friend was pointing toward the podium seating station. There was O'Casey, looking toward their table. He gave her a little nod of acknowledgment, a wry, almost apologetic smile, then began talking to the hostess again. She knew that he had no intention of coming toward her table, interrupting her when it appeared that she was with friends. The soaps apparently meant nothing to him; celebrity meant nothing to him.

She didn't know where he had gone from the airport last night. She had given him a brief goodbye after she and Mel claimed their luggage; there hadn't been an opportunity to do more since Miss February had still been telling him about the delights of L.A. She just knew that she was supposed to be at a private studio at four to meet him, but that was still hours away. L.A. was a big place. It seemed a bit surprising to see him here. Then again, Mel had probably given him the names of some eateries, and this was one of Mel's favorite places.

She stood staring at him a minute, aware that Matt remained right behind her, pretending that nothing hostile had happened between them.

"Seriously, Kelly, if you need some help finding work in the interim, I can surely put in a word here or there," Matt said, the sympathy in his voice false and dripping.

She ignored him, telling Serena and Jennifer "That is a friend of mine" as she made her way through the outside tables to the podium. "Doug!"

He turned, frowning, apparently surprised that she was coming toward him. "Hello," he said, actually looking a little wary. "Sorry. I didn't follow you here. Mel said this was a good place for casual Italian."

"It is. Come over here, will you? I'd like you to meet a few friends."

"Look, I didn't come to hound you. It's all right. We'll meet at four."

"I have a table for you, sir, right over there," the hostess said, smiling brightly.

"I'll just take my seat —"

"I'd *really* like you to meet my friends," Kelly said. Good God! If he shook her off like a virus, she was going to appear a fool.

"You know, I might be meeting friends," he told her softly.

"Are you? Oh, God, yes. Miss February," she murmured.

"I said I *might* be meeting friends."

"So you're not?"

"Not now."

"Do you mind meeting a few people or not?" she demanded, her tone growing a bit irritated with her sense of unease.

He shrugged, the sweep of his eyes questioning. "Sure." He glanced at the hostess. "Sorry, I guess I won't be needing that table."

Kelly knew that she was being watched

as she slipped an arm through O'Casey's, drawing him along with her. What the hell was she doing? she wondered. She had never felt the need to play games before or that she needed to prove anything. Now she was calculating, surmising that, although O'Casey's clothing certainly hadn't come with the price tag that accompanied Matt Avery's, he wore them with a greater natural ease and disdain. The feel of the muscles in his arms was rock hard, vibrant and powerful. He was a very good-looking man, rugged as well as aesthetic.

"Why are you pretending to like me?" he asked, and the question worked well for her charade as he bent close, whispering in her ear.

"I never said that I didn't like you," she reminded him.

"Hmm. Well, there's been body language, you know."

"I like you just fine, O'Casey," she said tautly.

"Yes, at this particular moment. What's up? Seems like you're using me, doesn't it?"

"I'm just introducing you to a few people. Good God, this isn't Mystery Dinner Theater or anything."

"It's all right. You can use me," he murmured. "In fact, use away."

She flashed him a wary glance right before they reached the table. "Doug, these are a few very special friends of mine, Jennifer and Serena. And this is Matt Avery. Jen, Serena — Doug O'Casey."

"How do you do, Doug?" Serena asked, a light of mischief in her eyes as she extended a hand.

"A pleasure," Jennifer said.

"Sure." Matt Avery shook O'Casey's hand. Matt was shorter and his fingers appeared far too manicured against the other man's. Actually, he paled all around when compared to Doug O'Casey. The man might be a tango expert, but there was something far more down to earth, even *masculine,* about him. She hated the thought, but he was actually more *macho.* And she was glad that she had brought him over.

Okay, she was standing a little too close. Her hold on him was a little too proprietary. But she was trying to make it appear as if there was something between them. As if he were her . . . protector and her lover.

Though a little bit ashamed of herself, she was also extremely glad of his appearance. She would surely have to answer for this later, and she was definitely betraying a weakness, but she didn't seem quite able to help herself. And for the moment, it was good.

Matt Avery was sizing up the man. And he was irritated. "Mr. O'Casey is new to Hollywood? Actor . . . stunt man . . . director?" Matt asked.

"Dance instructor. And I'm not remaining in Hollywood. The opposite coast is my home," O'Casey said. He looked at Kelly, and she decided he could pull off any acting job, he was looking at her with such admiration. "I'm simply privileged to be working with Miss Trent on her latest venture."

"And that would be?" Matt said.

"A video."

"By Kill Me Quick!" Jennifer supplied.

"Kill Me Quick?" Matt said, his tone derisive.

"Matt! Where have you been?" Serena demanded, her tone wonderfully teasing and reproachful. "They came out like gangbusters and the experts predict that everything they do will go platinum."

"So you're teaching our Miss Trent to dance?" Matt said, staring at O'Casey.

O'Casey gave her another look that was startling in the extreme, his eyes as warm as indigo. She realized that she was still locked to his arm. "Teaching Kelly?" he repeated softly. His voice was great — rich, deep, husky. "Yes. And I have the pleasure of dancing with Miss Trent." He focused on Matt Avery. "The tango," he said. He made the single word sound as sensual as silk.

"Well, wonderful. Just wonderful," Matt said.

Joe Penny came out of the restaurant at last, looking as if he wanted to slink right by the table rather than face Kelly. Except that he, too, saw O'Casey there. He walked toward them, frowning, the look on his face indicating that he should know O'Casey, yet he couldn't quite place him.

"Joe Penny, a dear friend — and director for the show," Kelly said to O'Casey. "Joe, Doug O'Casey."

The how-do-you-dos went around again, but Joe didn't get to ask any questions, because Matt was irritated and ready to drag Joe away. To his credit, Joe held his ground solidly, long enough to get in a few words to Kelly. "Kelly . . . we are really going to miss you. You were the show. *Are* the show, beyond a doubt. This is really necessary, because if anything were to happen to you . . ."

He swallowed, his Adam's apple wiggling. She knew he was sincerely bereft.

"Joe, honestly, it's fine. I might not have been able to do this video — and I can't tell you how excited I am about what I'm doing — if it weren't for this vacation. Joe, don't look so sad! Time goes by. I'll be back at work before you know it. Until then, I'll still be around, all right?"

She felt O'Casey watching her as she spoke and hoped she wasn't turning a dozen shades of red as she lied through her teeth.

"Joe, we've got some work to discuss," Matt said irritably. "Ladies, have a great day." He physically grabbed Joe's elbow.

"Nice to meet you," O'Casey said pleasantly.

"Yeah, sure," Avery muttered as the two left.

"Thanks," Kelly murmured very softly.

"Think nothing of it," he murmured back.

"Wow!" Serena said, bursting into laughter when the two men were out of earshot. "You are something, Doug. Will you take a seat, join us?"

"Don't let her scare you," Jennifer said, smiling. "She's married. To a big he-man-type P.I."

"Oh, good Lord, I wasn't scaring the man," Serena said.

"You're salivating!" Jen warned.

"I am not!" Serena said indignantly. "I have a really wonderful husband, just as you said, Jen. But I also have good eyesight and instincts. And it's delightful to meet you, Doug. Especially here and now," she admitted.

"Thanks." He took a seat easily. Until he freed himself to do so, Kelly hadn't realized what a death grip she'd maintained on his arm.

"We were all sisters," Jennifer explained.

"I see," O'Casey said.

"On the soap," Serena said.

"He doesn't watch soaps," Kelly said.

He shrugged ruefully. "I don't really watch any daytime television," he assured them.

"If he did, he wouldn't watch soaps," Kelly said, and wondered why she was now feeling so awkward.

He turned to her, that deep, chilling sweep of his eyes raking over her once again.

"I think he likes cop shows," she heard herself say. What the hell was she doing? She actually owed him a thank-you.

"I'm into the old sitcom reruns, actually," O'Casey said to Serena and Jen.

"The older the better," Jen said, agreeing with him. "*I Love Lucy*, *The Honeymooners*, *My Favorite Blonde* —"

"To name a few," O'Casey said with a rueful half smile.

"While you're here, we'd love to have you for dinner. I mean," Serena said with a frown, "you are here for a while, right?"

"A week."

"It would be lovely," Serena said. "Jen and her husband could come . . . and your mom, Jen." Her eyes were light and wickedly teasing again. "You have heard of Abby Sawyer, haven't you?" she asked O'Casey.

"You bet. She's one of our finest living actresses," O'Casey said, gazing at Jennifer. "She's your mother?"

Jennifer grinned. "Yep, she's my mom. She's a delightful person, too. But if we all have dinner, be warned. Serena has a one-year-old boy who is just learning to walk. He's a terror."

"My child is not a terror!" Serena protested, but with laughter. "Here's one for you. Jen has a darling little girl and twins. The twins are infants, and they scream blue blazes."

"I'd love to come," O'Casey said.

Kelly frowned fiercely at Serena, but Serena just ignored her. "It's a date. Friday night. Jen, is that good for you?"

"You bet."

Frustrated, Kelly stared around the table. They hadn't even asked her. Assumptions were being made far too easily.

O'Casey was the one to look at Kelly. "Do you mind?"

"Don't be ridiculous," she lied quickly. "It's a . . . fine idea. Just fine."

"The food is actually very good here," Serena said. "Now that we've nabbed you away from your table, you should order."

"What do you suggest?" O'Casey asked.

"The penne with vodka cream sauce," Jennifer said, and when the waitress appeared, that's exactly what he ordered.

"Jerk!" Serena muttered.

"Pardon?" O'Casey said.

"Matt Avery. Since he shot up to CEO at Household Heaven, he's had a thing for Kelly, though Kelly didn't have a thing for him. He's a jerk. He caused this whole mess."

"Serena, really, we don't have to discuss this now," Kelly murmured.

"What do you think about Joe agreeing to all this?" Jennifer asked, as if she hadn't heard Kelly speak.

"Joe is a nice enough guy. He's capable of being a little jerky himself, but we all know he's really decent beneath. In his way," Kelly said. She lifted her hands. "Hey, with the trouble before, he had his hands full. And he has to bow to Avery."

"You think he sold out. I think he's really frightened for you," Serena said.

Kelly let out an exasperated sigh. "I don't think he sold out. And it's really no big deal."

"But that woman, Dr. Sumter, was killed," Serena said. "And Liam says that from what he's seen and heard, the ex-husband just might not be guilty."

"Who is Liam?" O'Casey asked.

"My husband," Serena explained. "He's a private investigator."

"Great. Will I get to meet him?"

"Of course," Serena said.

"Good."

O'Casey appeared to be more intrigued by the idea of meeting a P.I. than even meeting Jen's mother, even though he had said he admired her.

Serena looked at Kelly. "Liam is actually a little worried about you, you know."

Kelly moaned. "A woman, reputed to be one of the greatest bitches of all time, was murdered. I'm not saying that it should be . . . understandable that she was murdered. Not at all. What happened was terrible. But I'll say it again. I'm a soap actress. She was real. And of course the ex-husband is denying the charge. Everyone denies the charge!"

"There was that other advice therapist killed in Ohio," Jennifer reminded her.

"In Ohio. She drowned in a bathtub." Kelly tried not to show her irritation. She really wished they were not having this conversation with O'Casey at the table. True, she had dragged him over. And true, he had done a great job in front of Matt and Joe. But now . . . She sure as hell didn't want his sympathy or pity!

"Regardless of whatever crock Matt has been feeding Joe Penny and the other powers that be, it remains a crock. The point is, it doesn't matter. Admittedly I'm a little scared right now. But you two haven't been on the show regularly in the last years —" She paused, glancing at Doug. "Maternity leave sent Serena off to Egypt, and Jennifer has been doing a lot of theater work, so she's supposedly been off doing all kinds of international travel as well. Anyway, the show hasn't been the same in a long time. And I'll be damned if I'll ever suck up to Matt Avery. I'm not in any danger. I won't even say that I rejected the wrong person because he's a jerk and I'd do it again. But let's not turn it into anything else!"

They were all staring at her as she finished her tirade. No one responded.

She groaned, burying her face in her hands, then looked up again. "Please! I am not in any danger."

"Well, you were nearly killed on the set," Jennifer reminded her.

"This is California. An earthquake could swallow us all up at almost any time," she reminded them.

"But was it an accident?" Serena mused.

"Oh, please. You've been married to a P.I. too long," Kelly said, shaking her head. "You guys are supposed to be my friends!" she pleaded. "Do you want to turn me into a paranoid?"

"Of course not," Serena murmured.

"We want you to be careful," Jennifer said.

"I am careful. End of subject, please!" Kelly pleaded.

At last, Serena looked at O'Casey. "How's the penne?"

"Very good, thanks."

Jennifer looked at her watch. "Well, this has certainly been an interesting lunch.

And long. You two are due at the that dance studio in a little less than two hours."

Marc Logan's South Beach office was in the penthouse of one of the tallest buildings in the area. Though not nearly as tall as some of the skyscrapers now gracing downtown Miami itself, the building still gave Marc one hell of a view. From his height, he could see the Intercoastal waterway and the bay. Gorgeous. Plate-glass floor-to-ceiling windows, rich carpeting, solid dark oak furniture, a fantastic bar — his office had everything. He liked his yacht, but he liked his office even better.

In fact, he thought with a smile, he just liked being Marc and being exactly where he was. Because here, no matter how old a man might be, no matter what his looks, money could buy almost anything — sex, drugs, beauty, revenge . . . anything. As a young man — one with a big nose, a thin build and a lack of natural charisma — he'd put in some major elbow grease. He'd used his mind and he'd made a hell of a lot of money.

Now, of course, there were three exes in the picture, scattered about in various places collecting on his hard work. The first was living quietly in a fine community on the west coast of the state. She collected her alimony and kept her mouth shut. The second was a royal pain, always asking for more. With his third marriage, he had seen to it that he had a prenuptial agreement, so she didn't have much of a leg to stand on. She'd been a trophy wife, but not a terribly bright one, so despite her scheming, she wasn't much of a thorn in his side. After her, he'd decided that it was better not to marry. Yes, he paid a great deal for companionship at times. But wives were just the same, really, only more expensive in the long run. Then again . . .

He was smarter these days. Women were essential. They could be hell, but they were one of his weaknesses, he had to admit. But he had learned better how to deal with them. And after his last escapade, he had learned a whole lot better. These days he was just damned careful.

He ran his fingers through his rich silver hair. The color wasn't exactly natural, but then again, neither was the hair itself. Transplant. He touched the bridge of his nose. Now it was a damned good one. And as for his skinny build, it still required a fair amount of work to keep the paunch down and the muscles up, but he had never shirked hard work.

And there was still some hard work in his business, but he could delegate. He had bought the right stocks and his stocks made money. He had a nose for selling off when something was going to take a dive. He had a construction company and good people to manage it. So now he could take a few chances. Most times, even those were calculated. He could make money on things he enjoyed. He enjoyed music. Loved it. If he hadn't been a bone-skinny kid from the Bronx who had to make it somehow, he would have tried to be a drummer. He loved the drums and he'd always enjoyed the whole rock thing. The sounds, the action, the energy, the fans . . . screeching women throwing themselves at musicians.

But now he had discovered that most of the screeching women figured that the money behind the music was damned cool, too. So it all worked for him. Producing Kill Me Quick's album and video was pure enjoyment for him.

And then, like icing on the cake, there was Kelly Trent.

And because he was who he was, he could afford Kelly Trent. He was still basking in the pleasure that he'd accomplished that coup. She didn't know just how good she was going to look once the video was complete. He meant to be there for the filming, even though he'd hired a producer, a money cruncher. He still meant to be around. To watch.

With a smile, he left his window view and went to his desk. He pushed a button. "Betsy, get me Harry Sullivan on Dead Man's Key."

"It's after five, sir. We might not catch him."

"After five, yes, but I'm willing to bet he'll be available for me."

"Yes, sir. I'll put the call through immediately."

A second later, he heard his secretary's voice. "Harry Sullivan on line one, Mr. Logan."

"Thank you, Betsy."

In a number of instances, his hiring practices didn't have much to do with ability. But not in the case of his secretary. She was pure efficiency. Tall as a man, built like a Norwegian lumberjack, ugly as sin and as capable as they came. The trophy wives had never been able to complain about her.

"Mr. Logan, good evening. What can I do for you?"

"Harry, I'm just checking on my arrangements for the video."

There was a split second of silence. "Sir, Betsy assured me that —"

"Yes, yes, I'm sure Betsy has seen to the facilities. I just want to double-check on the arrangements. You've made sure that we'll have the island entirely to ourselves? No one there but absolutely essential personnel?"

"Two cooks, four maids, four housekeepers and me, Mr. Logan. Other than that, the island is yours, entirely yours. There won't be any spying eyes around, trying to catch the action before it's ready. I've made certain that you'll have everything you want. And, of course, I'll see to it that you get anything else you might require while you're there."

"Good. Privacy for an assurance of safety is what I want, Sullivan."

"Yessir! I understand that."

"You're a good man, Sullivan."

"May I say, Mr. Logan, that we're grateful for your business, and will happily do anything in our power to assure that you're pleased with every amenity."

"You may certainly say so. What I want, Sullivan, is your absolute assurance that my star is going to be safe on that island of yours."

"Safety. Of course! It is an island, sir. No bridges. Pleasure boats will be forbidden from docking. There will be people out on the waters, but —"

"Yes, yes," Marc said impatiently. "But no one gets on the island."

"Right. Absolutely right."

Marc had a few more questions for the man, and when they were answered satisfactorily, he hung up and smiled. Arrangements guaranteed. No idiot fantasy freaks were getting close to his Kelly!

Chapter 9

With lunch over and a little time to spare, Kelly had suggested they walk a bit on Sunset. They'd stopped at a music store and an antique store, and Doug had to admit that he'd been impressed with her friends. Both beautiful women, they were grounded and fun. He looked forward to the dinner.

Since she had her own car and he had a rental, they drove separately to the studio. It was a perfect space, nothing but an audio system and a vast hardwood floor. Mel was already there, delighted to give them the keys — it was theirs for the duration of the time in California.

Mel had ordered a variety of practice and performance shoes for Kelly, and she chose a pair with which to start work, oddly enough more than willing to listen to his advice regarding her footwear. Mel didn't stay after assuring himself that he had acquired the right supplies for his client. He gave them the keys and told them good luck.

"So. Tango," Kelly said a little awkwardly after he had departed and the door had closed.

"Basically very easy."

She laughed softly. "I'm going to look like Jane Ulrich?"

"Not by this afternoon, but we've got some time. So . . . we start with the basics."

And they did. Working separately in front of the mirrors, he showed her the very basics; then they worked together.

"I'm not looking a lot like Jane," Kelly commented ruefully.

"Learn the steps, then the close contact, then the sharpness and the shaping. A lot of what looks so great is the shaping, and that will come," he assured her.

She was smiling at last, he thought gladly, realizing that once she started something, she was determined. She was also agile, light, flexible and toned. And whether she was willing to admit it or not, she must have had some kind of dance experience in the past, because she was up on steps.

She was a pleasure to teach, quick to laugh at her own mistakes while ready to correct them. And she was a pleasure to touch, to hold. The scent of her hair teased his nose. The feel of her was warm and supple.

This was a job, he reminded himself. He taught lots of women to dance. Young, old, thick, thin . . . it was something he did. He hadn't gotten into it because he loved music, loved movement. He had an edge in him that liked to compete. He had discovered that he was a good teacher almost by accident. Simply by doing it. Since his affair with the brilliant champion who had wound up dead, he had forged a distance. And there had never been a chance of his becoming involved with either a fellow instructor or a student again. He hadn't even been sure that he liked this woman. But now . . .

The tango was close. Her essence was intoxicating, her laughter fluid and enticing. Once into this, despite her heavy denials, she was passionate. And time ticked away without either of them seeming to notice . . .

Finally, Kill Me Quick's electric rendition of Tango to Terror came to an end for the last time. They were locked together as the music ended. And for a fraction of time, they were left in silence, their eyes meeting. Then, as if on cue, they simultaneously moved apart.

He cleared his throat. "You'll be looking like Jane in no time," he said lightly.

"Do you really think that will be possible?" she asked.

"You moved mountains today," he told her.

"Well, great." And then she smiled again, a deep, happy smile for the work she knew had been well done. "Maybe!" she murmured. She backed away a step. "Same time tomorrow."

"Same time tomorrow," he agreed.

"Um . . . you're all right here, right? The hotel, rental car, all that kind of stuff?"

"Yes, I'm fine. Thanks."

"Have you called Miss February yet?" she asked him.

He lowered his head, smiled slightly, then looked at her again. "Not yet."

"Well, she was certainly . . . Miss February," Kelly said, suddenly in a hurry. "Well, tomorrow, then." She turned and departed quickly.

He watched her for a minute and a strange sense of unease filled him. She didn't seem concerned in the least, but he couldn't forget the threats that surrounded her. And he didn't like the way she had left.

Maybe he was making a mountain out of a molehill just because he had once been a cop. And admittedly, putting death threats made against a soap star together with the murder of an advice diva was reaching. But he had been hired by Ally Bassett specifically because he had been a cop. And he missed investigative work. So . . . there was no reason he shouldn't do some investigating. He just didn't need to follow the woman everywhere.

He shook his head and walked over to make sure the stereo equipment was turned off. And beside the shoe boxes he noticed a wallet on the floor. It must have fallen from her purse. Opening it, he looked quickly for her ID. Yes, it was her wallet.

He set the wallet down, changed his own shoes and turned out the lights, ready to lock up. He would give Mel a call, let him know that he had the wallet. And he would return it to Kelly tomorrow.

It was dark, very dark.

Kelly's house was situated off the road, up a small hill from the Strip and set back from the road. She had always loved the privacy of it. But that night there was no moon. And there were no stars. Not even the streetlights were able to penetrate the lush trees and foliage that grew so beautifully in the front.

When she pulled off the street and up the driveway, she winced, shaking her head with self-disgust. She'd forgotten to turn on the porch lights when she'd left that day. The front of the house was completely shrouded in shadow.

She kept the car lights on, staring at the house, wondering why she was suddenly so uneasy. She'd come home dozens of times in the dark. Besides, her dog, Sam — who had been staying with Serena during her absence — was back in the house, waiting for her. During the drive, she'd been almost euphoric. She could dance. All right, she wasn't great yet. She was far from looking anything like a professional. Yet . . . she had felt good. She had felt great! Moving, learning, putting everything he said into practice, doing it wrong, trying again, getting it right. She should now be in a state of cheerful bliss. But she wasn't. Kelly took a deep breath. All she had to do was get her key ready, head for the house and walk in.

Maybe her unease was simply due to the fact that she had seen Joe Penny with Matt Avery today. And Matt had been an ass,

159

actually threatening her in his slimy way.

So? Get out of the car. Go in. The front door isn't that far from the drive!

But she sat for a moment, suddenly really unnerved as she remembered that this was the scene she had played on her last day of work. The darkness.

Shadows . . . A woman alone. No one around. A prowler in the bushes. A murderer waiting to strike.

She let out a sound of pure exasperation. She'd lived here for several years. It was a great neighborhood. There was no reason for anyone to want to hurt her. She wasn't going to stay in her car all night, and she definitely wasn't going to give in to the fears that everyone else had for her!

Kelly exited the car, clutching her keys in her hand. Being paranoid was one thing. Being smart was another. And she should have been smarter, she thought, suddenly wishing she had a little container of mace or pepper spray on her key chain.

When she closed the car door, the loud bang echoed in the night. The shadows at the front of the house were deep. The trees bent and whispered in a soft groan. She couldn't really see, yet shadows seemed to dip and sway. She blinked, and they seemed to grow. And there was movement, as if, indeed, the shadow of a man began to emerge on the porch from the bushes that surrounded the tile of the steps.

She felt a sense of acute and growing danger, as if there were tiny pinpricks of alarm at the base of her spine. As if . . .

From within the house, Sam, her weimaraner, began to bark. The sound was aggressive, not like the excited woofs he let out when he knew that she was coming to the door. She looked back at the car just as the inside lights went out. Darkness seemed to loom and grow around it. She heard a sound, something that really caused an icy chill of panic to streak down her spine. A sound . . . like a footstep against the tile, a scraping sound so light she might have imagined it. Yet she had not.

Suddenly she was certain there was someone, something, on the far side of the porch, concealed by the bushes. And it was moving. Darkness against darkness, a shadow growing . . .

She turned, afraid that she wouldn't make it back to the car and, suddenly, absolutely certain she was in terrible danger. She raced for the street and heard a whooshing noise behind her, as if someone was indeed coming in pursuit. Her feet took flight.

Just as she reached the sidewalk and the quiet street, a car came around the corner. She was on the pavement. A horn began to blare. She looked back to the house, but it was silent. Dark. Except for the movement of shadow.

Movement!

A shadow. Coming toward her. And then . . . light. Blinding light.

Mel Alton seldom simply answered his cell phone. He had caller ID, and he was careful. But he was tired. He'd been putting in an awful lot of time with Kelly Trent. Granted, the video was netting him a tidy sum also. In fact, he was doing damned well by her, considering that she was on a paid vacation from the soap. She was worth his efforts, but she wasn't his only client.

His day had been busy, hectic. Many of the clients he had taken on were doing so well that they had become demanding. It was a "know when to hold, know when to fold" business. Ask for too much for the wrong person and that person would be replaced. But if he didn't ask for enough, he would lose the reputation he had garnered for being an ethical and tough — very tough — agent. Many of his clients needed their hands held a lot. And he had to explain over and over that this was a game in which a good actor could lose out just because a director had decided on a certain look. Some clients needed to be encouraged every day. Others were just idiots. A perfect audition would be set up and they'd fail to show. Then they'd whine. If they were big enough, another audition could be set up. When they weren't all that they thought themselves to be, they just got mad at Mel.

So it was with exhaustion that he entered his Beverly Hills condo and answered the phone without thinking.

"Mel?"

He winced instantly and thought about making a noise, pretending that he didn't have a good connection. But he had to talk to her eventually.

"What is it now, Marlene?" he asked.

"My check bounced."

"Impossible."

"Impossible? Well, it bounced!"

"All right, all right, I must not have transferred funds correctly or something. I'll have Sally at the office find out what happened in the morning."

He could just see his ex-wife. Once upon a time, she had been adorable. That had been back in their high school days. When they had married. When she had believed in him, putting him through college by working as a waitress during all odd hours to do it. Once, they had been good together.

So what the hell had happened? He couldn't blame it on a particular place. Marriages fell apart all across the country. He worked longer hours, she became involved with the kids. She began to complain about the time he put into his work, and he began to get angry at her nagging. She took up tennis. And then she took up with the tennis pro.

He didn't even notice at first, because there had been that one indiscretion with an eager young actress. The end had been rough, really rough. Maybe Marlene had a right to ask for the moon. She had been there from the beginning supporting him. Two of the children were grown, but they still had a fourteen-year-old daughter, Ariel. He adored her. Marlene had wanted more than custody of their girl. She'd taken the dog, the cat, the house, the Rolls . . . everything. Fine. He'd have felt really guilty about the young actress if it wasn't for the tennis pro. And then Marlene's plastic surgeon, who had fallen in love with his own work. That was a new one. Mel had just learned about that. He'd spent a fortune on her face and body just to have them enjoyed by the good doctor.

"I need more, Mel."

"Too bad, Marlene."

"I'll take you back to court."

"The kids are grown and gone, Marlene, except for Ariel. I already gave you everything. There's nothing else to take me for."

"Let me just say this, Mel. Everything you have, you have because of me. It's my turn. I gave my youth to you. I gave my looks to you."

"Thank goodness Dr. Shales got them back for you, right?" he asked lightly.

"There had better be a little apology amount in that new check you issue, Mel," Marlene said sweetly.

There was something in her voice that hit a field of irrational anger within him, something he didn't deal with all that often. Just now and then.

He smiled icily before he spoke. "Hey, did you hear? Another old bat died under anesthesia for liposuction."

"Cute, Mel. Old men can die getting tummy tucks, too, you know."

"There have been a few nasty bitches around the country having serious accidents lately, too. Have you noticed?"

"What the hell does that mean, Mel?"

"Nothing."

"Mel, was that a threat?"

"Ah, Marlene! A threat, from me to you?"

"I'll really sue your ass, Mel."

"Wouldn't dream of threatening you, my dear. Sorry about the check, Marlene. It will be reissued."

"I really do suggest that you pad the amount. I never did bring up that actress in court. How old was she, Mel?"

"Old enough. And I didn't mention the tennis pro."

"You weren't neglected."

"Are we going to go through all of this again? Christ, Marlene, it's been over for nearly three years."

"Fix my check, Mel," she said, and hung up.

He was tempted to fling the phone across the room, but he didn't. There was a way to deal with Marlene. There were always ways to deal with people. Reason was one. But when reason failed . . . there were other ways. That had become quite obvious to him.

Chapter 10

Lord! What was the woman doing, standing in the middle of the street?

Doug brought the car to a screeching halt just a few feet in front of Kelly Trent. Her eyes were wide, like those of a doe blinded in the headlights. He leaned out the window, perplexed, angry and frightened, he might have hit her.

"What the hell are you doing?" he demanded angrily.

"What?" she said, blinking, looking at the house, then back at him again.

"Kelly, what are you doing in the street?"

She shook her head. "Nothing. I heard . . ."

"You heard what?"

"Nothing," she said, then frowned, stepping toward the sidewalk. "What are you doing here? How did you know where I live?" she asked suspiciously.

He picked up her wallet from the passenger's seat of his rental car and tossed it to her. "You left your wallet at the studio. I guess it fell out of your purse. Your address is on your driver's license. I thought you might need it."

"I . . . yeah. Thanks."

"All right. Good night."

"Hey, wait! Since you're here, why don't you come in for a minute? You can meet my dog. I'll be taking him with me to Miami."

"You want me to meet your dog?" he asked.

"You don't like dogs?"

"Yeah, I like dogs."

She stooped down halfway up the long walk and he realized she was picking up her purse. He frowned, puzzled. Had she dropped it, lost it as easily as she had her wallet? Had she left it there on purpose? If so, *why?*

At the door, she inserted her key into the lock. He realized that she hadn't even been in yet. From inside, it sounded as if the dog was going crazy.

"It's me, Sam!" Kelly called out.

"Come on in," she said as the dog — a very large weimaraner — came bounding toward him. "Sam!"

168

Kelly caught the animal by the collar. The dog wiggled and wormed, but seemed fairly obedient. "Sam, this is Doug O'Casey. Doug, this is Sam. Sam, sit and be courteous. This is an introduction."

Sam sat and offered Doug a paw, which he dutifully shook. The dog whined and didn't seem in the least at ease, but he didn't bound at Doug again. Instead he went running up and down the entry, barking.

"Sam!" Kelly said. She shook her head, then looked at Doug. "Cat."

"What?"

"There must be a cat out there, prowling around in the bushes. He's a good dog, but cats drive him crazy. Sam thinks they're demons."

"I see," Doug murmured. "Sam, there are no cats out there."

The dog looked at him, almost as if he understood every word. Sam really was a beautiful animal, large, toned and sleekly muscled. His eyes were as silver as his coat. He wagged his tail, then whined again.

"Want me to go check for cats, make absolutely certain?" Doug said, hunkering down to pet the dog as Sam trotted back to him.

"Well, he does have to go for a walk," Kelly murmured.

"I'll take him."

"No, no, don't be silly. Make yourself comfortable. Have a seat. Get yourself a drink . . . kitchen is right down the hall to the left, through the archway."

"I'll tell you what. You can get me a drink, since you know where everything is, and I'll take the dog out. It's not a problem."

"Really . . . ?"

"Really. Sam and I will be fine."

She hesitated, still seeming uncertain in a way that she hadn't before. He was aware, even more than he had been that afternoon, that she was beautiful. Her hair was a really rich, deep red, and her eyes were an amazing shade between blue and green. She was slender, yet exceptionally well toned and muscled. Her stature was delicate and somehow strong, as well. He remembered the first night he had seen her. She had been just as attractive then, surely, but when he had looked at her, he had seen nothing but a spoiled star. Maybe that was what he had expected. But now . . .

She was no different; he was just seeing her as she was — far more down-to-earth than he had ever imagined. She didn't have a chauffeur, a ridiculously palatial estate or any pretensions. She worked hard. She could be hesitant or she could plow right in. She was a mass of contradictions, all of them alluring.

"Knock when you're back," she said at last, smiling slightly. "And thanks."

Doug opened the door, and they stepped out. He was taken by surprise when Sam let out a woof and dragged him toward the bushes. He nearly tripped off the tile steps of the porch. The dog was strong. And determined. As he continued to pull Doug with him into the foliage, he barked in a frenzy.

"Sam!"

The dog had been trained at some time, because at the sound of his name, he stopped, looked guiltily at Doug, thumped his tail and whined.

"We're going for a walk," Doug said. "Heel!"

The dog obediently did so. But as Doug started down the walk, Sam whined and then stared at him again. Doug stopped, looking curiously at the house. "All right, boy."

As they headed back, Doug thought he heard a rustling. He was tempted to let the dog go but held tight to the leash. He doubted a coyote had come down this far, but he didn't want to take a chance of having Kelly's pet tangle with another creature that might leave it injured in any way. Hell, maybe there was a skunk crawling around. Or the dog was simply after a cat.

Still, he let the animal go through the bushes. Sam sniffed, traced his ground, sniffed, barked and started around the side of the house, running with the free lead that Doug gave him all the way through the backyard, over a small hedge, through a neighbor's yard and then out to the opposite street. There, the dog sniffed, whined and walked back and forth on the pavement.

"Whatever it was, it's gone now, bud," Doug told the dog dryly.

Apparently the dog now agreed with him. And after marking a few trees, he seemed happy to head back to the house.

Kelly had locked the door, and when she answered his knock, he realized that she hadn't just hit one lock, she'd slid the top bolt as well.

"Thanks," she said as he brought Sam back in.

"Sure thing."

"I made rum and Cokes. I wasn't sure what you liked and I figured that was a fairly safe drink."

"That's fine."

She handed him a glass, and he realized that she had nearly consumed her own. "Well," she murmured, sweeping out an arm. "This is the entry."

"Lovely. Nice tile."

"Thanks. It was built in the late twenties."

"It seems a great place, the old tile, the archways — actually, it kind of reminds me of some of the old places around me, on the beach, in the Grove. Mediterranean or Old Spanish."

"Kind of," she agreed, leading him in. Sam whined, sliding beneath her hand as she walked. "Hey, you!" she said, patting the dog's head. She turned back to Doug. "This is the living room or parlor, or whatever you want to call it."

"Once again, very nice," he told her. And it was. The floors were hardwood, with handsome throw rugs. The sofa was soft, fine leather, and there were richly upholstered chairs facing a large stone hearth. The room was rustic and stylish. Neat, yet comfortable and inviting.

"I guess you have designers out here for

your um . . . decor."

She smiled. "You can. I haven't. The sofa was from a garage sale. You can get great stuff out here if you prowl around."

"You live here alone?" he asked.

She nodded. "It's my house. I love it."

"It's . . . great."

She smiled. "Want another drink?"

"No, thanks. I don't usually have so much as a drink and then drive."

"Well, you don't have to leave immediately, do you? Oh . . . sorry. I guess Miss February might have called by now. Pretty girl, but not as attractive as your Jane, though it's really none of my business."

He wondered if he should let her go on or tell her the truth. "Jane is my *dance* partner. We're not dating."

"Oh?"

He saw the question in her wide eyes and had to smile.

"She's dating a hockey player."

"And you . . ."

He laughed. "Are you trying to ask me about my sexual preference?"

She flushed. "I guess not. You were interested in Miss February, after all. Not that your sexual preference means anything in the least. I mean . . . oh, Lord, I mean as far as I'm concerned, people are

174

people, whatever their likes, dislikes, beliefs, color and so on. I certainly don't mean criminal types or . . . never mind. I'm rambling, I'm afraid."

"How many drinks did you have while I was walking Fido here?" he inquired.

"Sam."

"Sorry. Sam. And he is a great dog. How many drinks?"

"Two. I'm heading for my third."

"Strange, you didn't drink like a lush on the yacht."

She flushed. "I've decided I'm entitled to one night of total insobriety."

"Because of the whole job thing?" he asked.

She lifted her glass to him. "Right on. You see, I might have pretended to have a great deal more disdain for the whole thing, pretend that I don't care in the least since I have job offers coming out the kazoo — except that my friends were all so blunt today. They're wonderful girls, but they could have displayed a bit more decorum since you are, if you'll forgive me, a stranger. To them, at least. And to me, as well."

"Maybe they know a kindred soul when they see one," he said. "And honestly, I'm trying not to be too strange."

"I didn't say that you were strange. Just

a stranger," she said softly. "I'm having a third drink," she said, and swirled around, heading for her kitchen.

He followed her. The kitchen was nice, too. Warm. Done in shades of blue and white, with some dark wood trim. He leaned on the counter, watching her. "Do you usually drink a lot?" he inquired, oddly touched and amused by her behavior.

"No," she said simply.

He frowned. "Are you *that* disturbed by being put on an extended vacation? I just assumed there are a million roles you could have and that you might have actually enjoyed the time using it to do something else."

She stared at him as if he were utterly insane.

"Oh, come on! Sure, it's hard out here, but I take it you're supposed to be something of an accomplished performer."

"Thanks for that vote of confidence," she said dryly. "And in a way, you're right. I was just really stunned at the timing and the speed with which I was simply out for the count." She frowned as she reached for ice and cracked some out onto a kitchen towel on the counter. When she finished preparing her drink, she turned to him. "Honestly, I do have confidence in myself," she said thoughtfully, then sighed. "I think it's just that . . . I've thought about leaving the show before — but I didn't. Now I'm on 'vacation.' And I'm furious because I think that I know why I'm really on 'vacation,' and it hasn't a thing in the world to do with being in danger. And the point of my being on vacation so long is so that the character will lose her popularity. And if I'm no longer popular, I don't have the clout. And then it would make sense to fire me."

"You don't think there's any possibility that you *are* in danger?" he asked.

She hesitated — just a split second — then shook her head. "I play a bitch who manipulates human lives. It's a role. I'm not that woman." He wasn't sure what his eyes or expression said to her then, because she lifted her glass to him, saying, "Honestly! Oh, I know what you were thinking when you met me. Frankly, you've more or less told me what you think. I'm a petulant little television star, low on the rung, a soap personality! One who thinks she's too good for a video. Well, it isn't that at all."

"I know. You're afraid."

"Not *afraid*. Hesitant. Nervous. All right, a little afraid. But only because I've never done anything like this and because . . . well, like I said before, I can't dance."

"But you can dance," he told her. "Surely you proved that to yourself today."

She smiled ruefully. "I didn't entirely suck, did I?"

He laughed. "Do you put that on your résumé? *I didn't entirely suck.*"

Her smiled deepened. "No. I'm quite good, actually. You have to be, you know, in a soap. Most of the time, there's only one take. We learn our lines in a snap. If you can pull off a soap role without looking like a total lie, you've got to have some talent."

"But there is more out there."

"I know. And I will find it. Tonight, I'm going to feel a little sorry for myself. But the anger has already kicked in. As they say, success is the best revenge. So I'm going to be so good in this video that it's going to be incredible, and then —" She paused, grinning ruefully. "Then, dammit, if I choose, I'll move on!"

"Good for you!"

"Thanks," she said regally, inclining her head.

"Do you think you should have some food to go with that alcohol?" he suggested.

She thought about that for a minute. "Maybe. It doesn't matter much to me at the moment." She yawned suddenly. "Come to think of it, I don't really want to go out. And I'm not so sure I have the energy to cook. Actually, there must be something in the cupboard."

"Do you have any real food? You only picked at a very small plate during lunch."

She grinned. "Sure. I have lots of power bars, that kind of thing. There's a bowl of fruit on the counter. Help yourself."

"I would have cooked for you."

"Why? I intend to enjoy my misery tonight."

"And have a hangover when I have to work with you tomorrow?"

She stared at him indignantly. "I always work when I need to," she informed him.

"You'd work better without a headache."

"What makes you think I get hangovers?" she inquired.

"I'm going on the odds."

"If you insist on food for me, just order pizza." She waved a hand in the direction of the refrigerator. "There are some numbers beneath the magnet."

She left him standing in the kitchen. She intended to make a regal exit, walking around him to depart to somewhere beyond the kitchen, but her footsteps weren't that steady and she sidled next to him instead. She had the pure and total sensuality of a cat. He was forced to catch her. Rum and Coke teetered dangerously. He braced her with one hand on her waist, rescuing the drink with the other. "Three — and you're this smashed?" he asked.

She let out a sound of pure irritation. "They were strong. It's not actually a habit of mine . . ." She looked into his eyes and started laughing. "Unhand me, stranger. Order that pizza, if you want!"

"Sure you won't pass out before it comes?"

"I never pass out." Her face was close to his, her lips curled into a defiant smile. Her scent was . . . absolutely evocative.

"Pizza," he said, letting her go. He walked to the refrigerator, where, as she had said, there were several small brochures held by magnets. One number for pizza delivery was beneath a magnet that held a picture of children — a pack of little redheads. So the red hair was genetic and definitely natural.

He placed an order for a large cheese pie, but when he hung up, she was gone. Sam was in the kitchen, though, staring at him with those huge silver-gray eyes that seemed to speak volumes. The dog's tail thudded on the floor.

"Where is she, boy?" he asked.

As if Sam understood, he barked, thudded his tail again and started to the rear of the bungalow.

The back area was large and appeared to be something of a family room. She had a computer station set up and had rigged an old-fashioned secretary with a notebook. Nearby, on an old phone stand, was her printer and fax. A massive pool table took up the center of the room, and to the far rear was a sofa and chairs, and beyond them, a large-screen television. Bookcases offered numerous volumes, many of which looked like first printings, and a collection of CDs and DVDs.

Kelly was stretched out on the sofa, a trail of hair falling over the end, as if she were Rapunzel. He was definitely tempted to climb up that long hair.

He walked into the room, taking a seat in one of the chairs. She had flicked on the television to a news station. Her eyes, however, were closed.

Sam went to her side, placing his nose on the sofa by her hand. Absently, she gently laid her fingers on his head.

"Is the pizza coming?" she asked.

"It is."

"Maybe that's good."

"I think it is."

"I'm not . . . feeling so well. Maybe I should have eaten lunch."

"Great. I knew all you'd done was move green things around on your plate!"

"I ordered food." To his surprise her eyes flew open, falling upon him with accusation. "No, I am not anorexic! I don't starve myself. I was talking when the food came."

He shrugged. "Who are the kids on the fridge?"

She smiled. "Nieces and nephews. My brother has the two girls and my sister has the two boys. They're cute, huh?"

"Yep. Very cute. Do you have any little ones of your own stashed around anywhere?"

A frown passed over her forehead; she was annoyed with the question. "Of course not! When — if — I have children, they'll be with me." She swung around to face him. "What about you? Children stashed anywhere?"

He smiled, shaking his head.

"Ex-wives?" she asked.

Again, he shook his head.

She lay back on the couch and groaned softly. "I think I'm grateful you've ordered a pizza."

"You did kind of inhale that booze."

She lifted a hand, waved it in the air. "I'm . . . well, it hasn't been a good week."

Doug folded his hands, watching the way her hair draped over the couch. "Tell me about Matt Avery," he said evenly.

She made a face. "There's not a lot to tell. He's a total creep and I bruised his ego."

"You really think that this whole thing is his way of getting you fired?"

"Yes, I do."

"But apparently your accident was serious."

She sighed deeply. "A few scratches."

"But it could have been fatal?"

"Look, I'm not an idiot. Yes, I could have been killed. I wasn't. There were dozens of people on that location all day. No night stalker was running around the place."

Sam suddenly let out a woof. Doug was startled when Kelly nearly jumped a mile high.

"Pizza guy, probably," Doug said softly.

"Oh, yeah. Of course."

Doug went to the door, Sam at his heels.

"It's okay, boy, just pizza," he said. But he looked through the keyhole and assured himself that it was a kid with a box before opening the door. He paid, thanked the teenager, closed and locked the door, then headed back for the family room.

Kelly had risen and gone for paper plates, napkins and a big bottle of cola. She was setting up on the coffee table when he brought in the pizza. They politely went through the motions of selecting slices and dealing with the gooey cheese.

"Your turn," she said then.

"Pardon?"

"First, how did you get into ballroom dance? Your folks? Have you done it forever?"

He shook his head, smiling. "I got into it late. A few years ago. I went to take some lessons for a friend's wedding."

"You're kidding."

"No."

"You've only been dancing a few years?"

"Right."

She winced slightly. "I've only got a few days."

"You've got some background training," he told her.

"Tap lessons when I was five. Some dance in college."

"And all those Pilates courses," he teased.

She lifted her chin. "I like exercise. And you forgot the yoga."

"I'm not making fun of you, you know. Those practices are great for exercise. Body and mind, so they say."

She frowned. "I'm a little curious . . . "

"About what?"

"Never mind. It's none of my business."

"Shoot."

"Okay. Why aren't you dating your partner? She's stunning. And incredibly talented."

Doug lifted his pizza with a shrug. "I dated a dancer once. Actually, I don't think you could call it dating. We had an affair. I was in way over my head."

"So . . . ?"

"I was having an affair. She was having several of them."

"Ah."

"And then she was killed."

"Killed?"

"Murdered." He fought with a tangle of cheese. That was the past; he had learned from it.

Kelly frowned, obviously sympathetic. "I'm so sorry! Was it an act of terrible violence? What happened?"

He shook his head. "Far more subtle. A mix of drugs and alcohol. The guilty are dead, and it . . . well, it wasn't that long ago but long enough. Anyway, I haven't thought it a good idea to mix work with pleasure since."

She seemed fascinated. Since the pizza had arrived, they were sitting close on the couch. Not touching, but his senses were so attuned to her, he could almost feel her form. He was so tempted to slide next to her that he rose abruptly, pretending to wad up a napkin for the trash. She was different tonight, completely off guard. Eyes like a Caribbean sea, the very subtle scent of her cologne hovering in the air, like an aura of innocence and seduction surrounding her. Her hair was tousled, and she was quick to smile, quick to look at him with an open warmth he'd not even imagined she could offer. The alcohol?

Warning bells sounded in his mind. Either she was a shining star, feeling a bit tarnished, and still out of his range, or she was a victim, intended for a danger and demise she refused to acknowledge. He needed to keep his distance. Yet . . .

It had been forever since he'd felt such a compulsion to come closer. To touch. In a dream world, he would step forward, slip his fingers through that fascinating mane of burning hair, tilt her head and test the fullness of her lips, the endless magic in her eyes. Taste. A sensation of pure fire leaped into his lower extremities. He gritted his teeth, stepped back.

"More soda?"

"Pardon?"

"Can I pour you more soda?"

"No, I'm fine." She didn't actually move away or create more distance between them, but she straightened, as if she had decided she'd been too relaxed, too at ease. As if she, too, must remember to hold on to a certain wariness.

"I guess I should head on out for the night," he said.

She turned away. He wondered if she was disappointed. Or if she was just uneasy. Scared.

"Yes, well, you don't live in L.A. I'm sure there's a lot you'd like to do."

"Actually, I thought I'd get some sleep."

Her head remained down. He couldn't gauge her reaction. She looked up. "Your hotel is okay?"

"It's great. White, very white. Walls, floor, bedspread." He grimaced.

She laughed. "It's supposed to be chic."

"I'm sure it is. It's also — white. But very comfortable."

"I'm glad," she told him.

He hesitated. "Want me to take Sam for a last run?"

"No, no. That's all right. I'll take him. You're the dance teacher, not the dog walker."

"I told you, I like dogs."

She swept back a massive length of her hair. The red glinted in the light. Her eyes touched his. "You sure?"

"Lock me out. I'll knock when I'm back."

He took Sam out, but the dog remained interested in the bushes and the same path he had followed before. Had someone been there? Doug let the dog have his way. Sam sniffed, moved forward, and came to the street again, then seemed lost. A cat? A prowler? Or worse? Was he letting his imagination get away with him?

Once it had been the curiosity alone that had tugged at him. Curiosity and the wonder if he had taken a turn in life too rashly. But now it was Kelly herself.

He stiffened with resolve. No involvement. It was always a mistake. When he had viewed her as cold, untouchable and affected, he had still seen her as a seductive beauty. But now . . . hell, now she was the stuff of dreams. The kind that caused tossing and turning. And if something were to happen to her . . .

"Sam, time to head back," he told the dog, but he paused, taking another look around. He'd circled the house several times; if there had been anyone present who shouldn't have been there, he was long gone. So he walked back to the house, determined to leave, yet loathe to do so.

Kelly let him in. "Thanks. That was really nice of you."

"No problem."

They stood in the hallway. They weren't touching, but the air all around them seemed electric. He wondered what would happen if he stepped forward. Touched her. Spoke the truth. *You're the most sensual creature I think I've ever come across. I'm about dying, on fire, in agony, just being near you.*

"Are you going to be all right?"

"Of course. Why wouldn't I be?"

"You seemed . . . nervous."

She laughed. "All those caring people around me are doing a bit of a number on my mind. I've had this place for years. Besides," she said with a smile, "I have Sam. He'd alert the world if there were any

189

trouble, I assure you. I'm fine. Go on. I'll see you tomorrow."

He nodded and turned. "Lock up before I leave."

She started to turn back into the house, then paused. "I can meet you earlier, if you wish. I'm not doing anything, being here at home. And —" She shrugged ruefully. "I'm not used to not working."

"All right. We can start earlier."

"Okay."

They still just looked at each other.

"If you don't have other plans, we could meet for an early lunch . . . say, about a quarter of twelve."

"Sure. Where?"

"Mirabelle. It's about five or six blocks from your hotel. Walk out and take a left. It's a pleasant place with a nice menu."

He nodded. "Sounds great."

Her smile deepened, and at that moment he mocked himself that he was in love. Or definitely in lust.

"Good night," he said again. "Lock up."

She went in, and he listened for the bolt. Then he walked to his car and sat in it, staring at the house for long moments before heading back onto the street.

It hadn't been at all hard to get her address. Lance Morton sat in his car, staring at the house. He felt a thrill of elation rip through him. *Kelly! Kelly Trent.* The house was wonderful, just what he had hoped. It was just so . . . Kelly!

He hesitated behind the wheel, staring at the front porch. A bright light blazed from it, but the property was surrounded by trees and foliage. He was tempted to get out. No . . . not now. He could wait.

He sat in his car a long time. Staring. Thinking. And feeling the same thrill over and over again. *Kelly. Kelly Trent.*

Uneasily, he looked around the street. It was quiet, dead quiet. Lance rolled up his windows, turned on the CD, listened and imagined. He closed his eyes, letting his thoughts take him where they would. He gave in to the deepest desires of imagination, listening to the music, seeing in his mind's eye. Feeling. The music came to a crescendo. So did he.

He swallowed, looked around and remembered that, quiet as it might be, he was on a public street. He'd been an idiot. What if a cop had come by? But he lingered still, just another moment. *Kelly . . .* There would be time for them. Plenty of time. He just had to wait. The right moment would come.

Chapter 11

Kelly was pleased to discover Doug already at the restaurant when she arrived. He was wearing a polo shirt and casual jacket, and had a large knapsack at his side. He rose as she walked to the table, and waited for her to sit.

"Thanks," she murmured. She noticed his glass.

"Iced tea?"

"The drink of the South," he murmured.

"Sounds good."

She wondered why she felt a little awkward. It wasn't a date, for heaven's sake. But she still found herself looking at the menu with the determination that she wasn't going to order anything messy. It wasn't a date, but she was ordering date food — something that came in bite-size pieces, that didn't dribble down the chin. No pasta.

He didn't seem to have the same problem. He was having the shrimp linguini. She opted for the fruit plate.

"Did you sleep well?" she asked.

He nodded. "Surrounded by white. I dreamed I was in the clouds."

"Really?"

"No. I had a peaceful, dreamless sleep."

She smiled, toying with the condensation on her glass.

"How about you?" he asked.

"Well, I definitely went out like a light — with Sam sleeping at my feet. So, did you do anything this morning?"

He shrugged. "Walked. Went to the record store. Looked up whatever they might have on Kill Me Quick."

"And?"

"They've released one album. I bought it. They are good, more than a garage band. Lance Morton apparently went to Juilliard."

"How did you find that out?"

"Well, I can't swear it's true, but it's in his résumé."

"He's given you a résumé?"

"I looked him up on the Web."

"Oh." She shrugged. "He seems okay."

"Yeah. So far. He hasn't been arrested for anything, anyway."

"You looked that up, too? On the Web?"

He hesitated. "I did some research on him and the group."

"And what else did you learn?"

"They were all music majors at some kind of an accredited school. Hal Winter, the guitarist, was with a gospel group for a while."

"From gospel to Kill Me Quick, interesting," Kelly mused, smiling.

"Aaron Kiley has played backup for a number of important groups. He's keyboard."

"Aha!"

"And the drummer, Ron Peterson, was considered to be something of a genius. Graduated head of his class at seventeen, chose to take off and tour Europe, came back and worked with a stomp group, then met up with the rest of the fellows. They played coffeehouses, school gigs and weddings. Then they were picked up by a label for their first album. After that, apparently, they were seen by Marc Logan, who decided to make an investment in the guys."

"And what do you really think of them?" Kelly asked.

"I think they've definitely got talent. I like what I've heard."

She hesitated. "Do you honestly think this

is going to be a good career move for me?"

"Yes, I honestly do — if my opinion means anything."

"I asked you for it," she reminded him.

Their entrées arrived. She carefully skewered a strawberry. "Are you always so thorough?"

He had a talent for winding linguini. If she'd chosen the entrée, she'd be trailing long strands with every bite.

"So thorough?"

"Yes, you looked up the entire band."

"I like to know what I'm getting myself into."

She laughed. "Did you look up my résumé as well?"

She was startled when he appeared to flush slightly. "Actually, I looked you up last night. An Emmy, huh?"

"One."

"One is more than a lot of actresses ever acquire."

"True. I'm grateful." She played with her glass. "What would happen if I were to look you up?"

"I don't have a Web page."

"But you're a professional dancer."

"I don't have a Web page."

"Maybe mine has a lot of lies on it," she murmured.

"I don't know why, but I'm doubting that."

"A Web page can be all hype."

"Yours is too modest."

"Not enough hype?"

He didn't answer. He was looking past her shoulder, and she realized they were being approached by a man. For a moment she tensed. Then she saw who was coming and eased, smiling.

"A friend?" Doug queried lightly.

She nodded. By then, Liam Murphy had reached the table. He bent to kiss her cheek. "Hey, kid." He nodded to Doug. "Sorry, excuse me."

"Liam, sit, please!" Kelly said. "Doug, this is Liam Murphy. Serena's husband. Liam, this is Doug O'Casey, my dance instructor for the video."

The two men nodded to each other in acknowledgment.

"Didn't mean to interrupt. Just saw you here, kid," Liam said.

Kelly groaned softly. "I'm inching toward the thirty mark and you're still calling me kid."

"You're not interrupting. Can you join us?" O'Casey said.

"I'm meeting a friend in a few minutes, but sure, if you don't mind." Liam pulled up a chair while sizing up O'Casey. "I hear we're having a dinner party tomorrow night."

"Yes, thanks."

"Glad to have you," he said, then turned to Kelly. "I heard about the video."

"And the 'vacation' I've been put on?" Kelly said.

"I think it's a good idea," Liam told her.

"Liam is a private investigator," Kelly explained.

"Right, so I remember Serena saying," Doug said. His attention was on Liam. "So, you do think it's a good idea that Kelly is off the set."

Kelly groaned.

"Yes," Liam said. "Being safe is always better than being sorry."

"I take it you have a lot of friends on the police force?" O'Casey said to Liam.

"Yes."

"What was the final report after Kelly's accident?" O'Casey asked.

"Hey! I am here, you might have asked me," Kelly reminded him.

"I'd have gotten a different answer," O'Casey said.

Liam shrugged, grinning as he glanced at Kelly. "Accident — as far as the official report went. But I know some of the guys who were there. They were baffled, so, unofficially, there was no concrete decision. There was an investigation. No one saw anyone tampering with the mound. It was raw earth at a building site, supposedly in solid shape. The area hasn't really been opened yet — the houses up there that are completed are on the market." He lifted his hands. "There weren't any clues to follow. People had been over the place all day. No one saw anything. Everyone was stunned and appalled. So it appears that it was an accident."

"Because it *was* just an accident," Kelly said.

"Right," Liam agreed. "So she's better off away."

"I understand there was trouble on the show before," O'Casey said.

"Oh, please! None of this can be associated with that," Kelly protested.

"No one is suggesting that it is," O'Casey said. "But, Kelly, you've got to understand why people are feeling nervous for you." He turned back to Liam. "What do you know about the Dana Sumter case? According to the news, the ex-husband is under arrest but adamantly denying the charge."

Kelly let out an impatient sigh. "Did

anyone really think that he'd rush in with a confession?"

Neither of the men seemed to hear her. "I'd be interested in talking with the fellow," Liam said. "Sure, he could be acting. But I've seen him in front of some news cameras, and he is passionately denying any part in the murder."

"What about the Ohio case?" O'Casey asked.

"It was in *Ohio!*" Kelly snapped.

"Could be related, could be an accident," Liam said. He looked up, then excused himself, offering O'Casey a hand. "My friend just showed up. It's good to meet you. I look forward to seeing you at the house tomorrow night."

"Thanks for the invitation."

"I'm glad you're with Kelly."

"He's not actually with me," Kelly said, flushing with dismay. O'Casey was going to think she was a clinging vine if she wasn't careful.

"I agree, she probably shouldn't be alone," O'Casey said.

"Bye, kid," Liam said.

Kelly shook her head as he walked away. Wincing, she brought her gaze up to meet O'Casey's. "Please, I know I . . . um . . ."

"You used me yesterday?" he said lightly.

"Yes, I did. I'm sorry. But you don't have to feel responsible for me in any way."

He lifted his hands, staring back at her. "Hey, my only reason for being these days — and being here in L.A. — is to teach you the tango." He was looking past her head. "He's meeting a cop," he murmured.

"What?"

O'Casey took a sip of his tea. "Your friend, Liam. The fellow he's meeting is a cop."

Kelly twisted around. The man was in plainclothes, but she happened to know him. It was Detective Olsen, the officer they had worked with years ago on the set. He looked like a kindly St. Nick, but was as sharp as a tack when the need arose.

Frowning, she stared at O'Casey. "How did you know?"

"You know him, too?"

She nodded.

"And he is a cop, right?"

"Yes. How did you know?"

O'Casey shrugged. "He just has the look. Want coffee? Dessert?"

"No, no, thank you."

"I'll get the check, then?"

"I asked you here."

"I'll get the check."

"You got the pizza last night."

"And I'll get this now," he said firmly.

She frowned. "But —"

"Don't worry. I won't consider it a date," he said, and rose, signaling to the waitress before she could protest again. Having handed over his credit card, he turned back to her. "Want to walk a little, then head to the studio?"

"Um, sure."

As he walked to the hostess's station to sign his bill, Kelly sipped the last of her tea. When she looked up again, she noted O'Casey leaning against the podium. His dark blue eyes seemed fierce in study. She turned slightly. He was watching Liam and Detective Olsen.

She frowned. But when his gaze turned to her, his expression changed in the blink of an eye. He smiled, lifting a hand. She rose to join him and they exited the restaurant.

"Who's the guy with Kelly?" Olsen asked. He was a big man and suspicious by nature.

But then, Liam realized, he tended to be a suspicious fellow himself. He turned and looked toward the retreating couple. "Dance coach for the video thing she's doing. His name is O'Casey. Doug O'Casey."

"You know him?"

"Just met him today."

"Looks like a cop to me."

"I think he's legitimately a dance coach," Liam told him.

"What do you know about him?"

"Nothing. I never knew he existed until yesterday. Serena mentioned that she'd met him last night. I intend to check him out."

"I'll do it from the station," Olsen said.

"Good."

"Well, it's good to know the background of anyone she's got an association with now. Who are the people involved in this project?"

"No one involved with the soap," Liam assured him.

"Well, that's probably good."

"You were on site at the location where they were filming before it was cleared," Liam reminded him. "I can't figure out how someone could have tampered with a mound of earth without anyone seeing him. Or her."

"Hiding in plain sight," Olsen said.

"What?"

Olsen shrugged. "There are dozens of

people walking around on a set all day. Lighting, gofers, cameramen, makeup guys — who the hell knows exactly who else? If someone was walking around looking like a production assistant, prop boy, whatever — someone who acted like they had a right to be there — who would notice?"

"So you don't believe it was an accident?" Liam persisted.

"Hell, I don't know. But I do think that show is cursed. I'm glad that Kelly is off it. I think she should watch herself real good."

Liam shook his head. "Okay, what if there is a psycho out there? Someone out to rid the world of advice therapists. Would such a psycho be organized enough to manage an accident like the one that happened on the set?"

"You can profile people all you want," Olsen said. "Doesn't mean you'll always have the answers. Hell, we've still got lots of crime going on, right?"

"What about Dr. Sumter's husband?" Liam said. As Olsen mulled the matter, he added, "Any chance I can talk to the guy?"

"I'll see what I can do," Olsen told him.

The tango. Close, hot . . . friggin' downright sizzling, when you got to it.

Kelly was talented, far more talented than she wanted to believe. She had grasped the steps almost immediately. What she hadn't remembered exactly from the day before, she picked up as soon as he refreshed her on their work. Yesterday, they'd worked apart or in practice holds. But today she was ready for timing. And shaping. And close body contact.

The woman held herself slightly to her left. Hips met. Legs moved in tandem. He had never been so distracted. Not as a student when coached by a woman who was actually his lover, and never, certainly, as an instructor. But distracted he was. There was the scent of her hair and the color of it. He knew the full firmness and softness of her breasts against his chest. The taut touch of her pelvis, thighs, limbs. There was no way in hell that a healthy male with any kind of kicking libido could avoid the swell of internal excitement she elicited. He could only pray to control the external. And she was so damned deep in concentration!

A misstep. She looked up at him, frustrated. "God, I'm sorry, but when I watched you and Jane . . . your legs seemed to move at exactly the same time. Almost as one."

"You just have to let me lead. We're doing the same timing, yet you're a fraction of a second behind. Let me lead before you move."

"But I'll trip you."

"No, because you move as soon as I lead."

He realized that they were having the conversation while locked together. She didn't seem to notice. He was amazed that he could talk.

"I'm snapping my head at the wrong time, too."

"You'll get that. Right now, let's zero in on the footwork. Heel leads."

"Heel leads . . ." she murmured, looking down.

"Don't look at your feet."

"Right."

"Head up, back slightly curved. You don't stick your butt out, you tuck it in."

"I'm not sticking my butt out!"

"Beginners have a tendency to lean forward with their chests. The chest is back. It's the pelvis that remains forward."

Her brow remained knit in serious concentration. Her pelvis inclined against him. A tremor shot through him and he prayed she hadn't felt it. Sweat was breaking out on his forehead. He released her, stepping away.

"I'm sorry! What did I do?"

"Nothing. We'll just talk about . . . the head snap and the timing," he murmured. He directed her next to him, walking through the moves, showing her head position, foot position, contra body movement. She listened and imitated, an excellent pupil.

They worked apart until he was certain he had regained his composure.

"Ready?" he asked, putting on the track to "Tango to Terror."

She nodded, a bit grimly, and slid into his arms. He helped her adjust her position, wishing that they were doing a do-wop or swing. He moved with her, through all the basic steps. She erred, but for someone who had been working only two days, she was amazing. The softness of her hair tickled his nose. The scent she wore . . . it was all that he breathed. Her body . . . He made it through once, twice, then was relieved to note the time. Outside the studio, it had grown dark.

"That's it for today," he said, tossing her a towel. "There's some bottled water in the little refrigerator."

"Thanks," she said, but she didn't move. He'd sat in one of the few wood chairs surrounding the walls to change his shoes.

She was still standing in the center of the room, looking at him.

"Something wrong?" she asked.

He frowned, looking at her. "No. In fact, you're doing everything amazingly right. Why?"

She shook her head, looking a little lost. "Obviously I'm not going to dance like Jane. But it's as if . . . as if you can't wait to stop dancing with me."

He flung his towel around his neck. "You've worked hard. For hours. You've done excellently. They're not just going to get a soap star, they're going to get a dancer. There's nothing wrong with your work."

"Is it me?"

"Pardon?"

She lifted her shoulders, offering a little grimace. "Is my deodorant not working or something?"

He inhaled on a deep breath, staring at her.

"I mean," she continued a little nervously, "I've always thought that I was fairly attractive, and I know that I'm supposed to look somewhat sensual. . . ."

Doug stood and walked over to her. Close, he circled around her, then met her eyes again. "Miss Trent. You are achieving your goals. Trust me. Most men would crawl on their knees through broken glass to be near you. To touch you. In fact, if you were any hotter, they'd be sensing you through the walls. They'd be rushing the stairs to this place, ready, just like moths to the flame, to burn to cinders just for a chance to have sex with you."

His words had come out far too angry, he knew. But she just stared back at him, those aquamarine eyes a fathomless sea. He thought for a moment that she was going to lash out in anger, say that she was just trying to emulate Jane with some kind of accuracy. But she didn't. And after a moment, a very small smile curled her lips. "Most men?" she murmured softly.

"Um."

"What about you?"

"What about me?"

"Would you . . . want me?"

He stared back at her, body and brow whipcord-taut.

"You bet. I'd be crawling right through that broken glass, into the flames, for you. For one hot night. Day. Hour."

"The sex-drive thing, huh?" she whispered.

"You bet."

"But . . ."

"That, Miss Trent, is supposedly what separates us from the beasts. We have our wicked, carnal desires."

"We do."

"But we can control them."

He turned away, heading toward the door. "Come on. Let's lock up the studio."

Driving home, Kelly felt like a fool.

Well, so much for daring to give in to attraction. It wasn't that she had actually meant to ask him to have sex, but she had felt such a sense of elation, comfort . . . attraction. Excitement. Well, what exactly had she wanted? Whatever it was, she wasn't getting it.

A new flush rose to her cheeks, the heat of embarrassment sweeping over her again. They had been getting on amazingly well. He had seemed pleased with her as a pupil. He had seemed to like her. So she had . . . She groaned out loud, wondering what had possessed her to behave in a way that was completely contrary to her nature. She was going to have to face him every day!

She pulled into her driveway and, to her amazement, the discomfort and shame that had been riddling her disappeared as if in a puff of fog. But what settled over her then was worse. Fear. Two words haunted her thoughts. *Darkness. Shadows.*

There sat her house, totally benign. Inside, Sam, good old Sam, ever protective, awaited her. She had only to make the walk from her car to the house. She bit her lower lip. *She* was the one who kept insisting she wasn't in any danger. Yet, last night . . . Had there been someone sneaking around the house?

She let out a sigh, wincing. The world was filled with people who were . . . ill. Maybe Dana Sumter's husband hadn't killed her. Maybe there was a psychopath out there who hated anyone who wrote advice columns, talked on television or practiced any form of therapy, whether they were real or fictional.

"So, what's it to be?" she asked herself out loud. "Do I sit in my car all night, staring at my front door?" Why hadn't she gone out and bought mace that morning?

"I'm coming, Sam."

She hesitated another second, then opened the car door. The distance to her front porch was not great. Her porch light was on, but that only deepened the shadows surrounding the light. She quickened her step. And just as she did so, a shadow very definitely moved.

★ ★ ★

Leaving the studio, Doug had waged a silent war with himself. On the one hand, he was proud and feeling strong. No involvements where work is concerned. But on the other hand, he hated himself. He ached, yearned, and a number of his body parts totally despised him.

What the fuck is the matter with you? Not every sexual encounter is meant to turn into a relationship. He certainly didn't run around like a cad, but spending the night with a woman didn't necessarily mean that he'd see her again, either. Both sexes were sometimes just out for a little companionship, for some sheer physical, carnal pleasure. Besides, he had to face this woman on a daily basis.

Why Kelly? Chemistry, he thought irritably. She had a way of slipping beneath his skin. Holding back, rushing forward. Ice in the sun.

He was halfway to his hotel when he'd decided to follow her home, despite the fact that he had been right to step away from her — even if certain parts of him remained torn with agony and reproach. They were business associates. She wasn't just any woman. She wasn't a stranger he'd met in a bar, just out for the night, looking for what she could find. She was . . . Kelly.

Despite all that, he had an uneasy feeling. Liam had agreed that she might be in danger. And last night she had been scared. Really scared. So he'd just see to it that she'd gotten home okay. That Sam was walked, that she was locked in. That was all.

Was it? he mocked himself. Was he heading over there because he wanted her to say — do — something more? And what about him? When she answered the door did he tell her, "Oh, God, please. Yes, you are the most sensual, sexual experience I've ever had, and I haven't even seen you without clothes on. Please, let me in, give me another chance, let me just kiss the ground where you walk?"

Get a grip, he warned himself firmly. *Just see to it that she's safe!*

He pulled around her corner, and as he did so, he saw that her car was in her driveway. A breath of relief rushed through him. Then he saw the shadow move. And he heard Kelly scream.

Chapter 12

Screaming. It was an instinctive gut reaction to shock. Like a shadow moving. Becoming a man.

"Kelly! Hey, please, it's me, Lance Morton. Wow, I'm sorry, I didn't mean to scare the hell out of you!"

She blinked because he was out of the shadows. Lean body, aesthetic face, shaggy hair. He was decked out in a nicely fitting suit, and there was really nothing menacing about him at all. He might be in decent shape beneath the threads, but he was slender and not in the least intimidating. She would never have screamed at the sight of him if she hadn't seen him move like that out of the shadows.

"Lance —" she began.

But then another scream of shock tore from her throat. A figure tore by her with the speed of lightning. The whir of darkness catapulted against Lance. Lance screamed and went down with the figure on top of him.

"What the hell are you doing?" a voice growled.

She knew the voice. "O'Casey!"

He didn't hear her gasp. "What did you do to her!" he exploded again.

Lance Morton, surely about to become one of the hottest voices in rock, was flat on the ground. O'Casey had brought him down like a felled tree, and he was straddled over his prone victim now, hands grasped around the collar of the man's expensively tailored casual jacket.

"You!" Lance gasped.

"O'Casey, it's all right!" Kelly said, finding life again at last, racing forward and reaching for his shoulders, as if she could drag him off Lance.

Lance was swearing by then, and his words weren't going over well with O'Casey. "Shut the hell up!" he said, rising, dragging Lance to his feet. Lance staggered in his attempt to rise. He'd gone down hard.

"Let me go!" Lance demanded.

O'Casey shoved him free.

"Hey!"

"What the hell did you do to her?" O'Casey demanded in a barely leashed fury.

"I said hello!" Lance snapped. O'Casey, his blond hair disheveled, turned on Kelly. "He said hello?"

"Something like that," she murmured.

He lifted his hands, staring at her. "Why did you scream?"

"He startled me."

"Startled you?"

"He just startled me, that's all. I'm sorry, it was ridiculous. I didn't see him at first. He walked up and I . . . screamed," she finished lamely.

"I came by to say hello because I was in the city!" Lance said.

O'Casey spun back on him. "What were you doing, stalking her in her yard?"

Lance let out a wounded sigh. "I was just hanging around, hoping she'd come home so that I'd get a chance to say hello and introduce myself a little further. It is *my* video," he said indignantly. He glared at O'Casey. "You might have broken my neck! My back is killing me!"

"Has anyone ever suggested that you *not* hang around a woman's door in the dark?" O'Casey demanded.

"I don't know how I'm going to sing, to manage this video now myself!" Lance continued, deeply wounded. He pointed a finger at O'Casey. "You're a madman, an animal, rushing someone like that."

She could almost hear O'Casey's teeth grating.

"Yeah? Well, you don't seem too sane yourself. She screamed, you ass. Screamed. That usually means someone needs help."

By then, Kelly became aware of Sam, barking his head off inside the door. She winced, angry because she had let everyone spook her so badly that she had screamed blue blazes just because someone had walked toward her. *No!* She wasn't that much of an idiot! He had been in the shadows, and he had scared a year's worth of life out of her!

Yet, the way that O'Casey had slammed him might have broken every bone in Lance Morton's body. This could really be a disaster.

"Let's go in," she said.

Both men turned and stared at her.

"Look," she said, "there's been a mistake, a major misunderstanding here. Lance, you scared me. You shouldn't have been in the bushes. I should have recognized you, and I shouldn't have screamed like that. And Doug . . ."

"I should have let the guy strangle you if he had been a deranged killer?" he demanded, hands on hips.

"I'm not a deranged killer!" Lance announced indignantly. "Jesus Christ, who the hell do you think you are, the CIA?"

O'Casey cast him a look that was chilling.

"You know, your ass can be fired, just like that." Lance snapped his fingers.

"Fire me," O'Casey said.

"Now, stop it!" Kelly insisted.

"He's out," Lance said. "In fact, I think I'll call the police and file assault charges!"

"You file assault charges and I'll file for trespassing," Kelly said, stepping in far more smoothly than she might have imagined for the situation.

"What!" Lance said, blinking.

"You heard her."

"You're fired." ˙

"If he's out, I'm out," Kelly said softly.

"What?" Lance said again. "He's a two-bit teacher."

"I don't think you should insult him right now," Kelly murmured.

"He can't insult me. He doesn't know anything. From him, words are meaningless."

"Hey!"

Sam was going crazy inside. Kelly shook her head impatiently. "Okay, you two can just stay out here and hurl insults at each other. It was a bad situation. I'm sorry. But now I'm taking my dog for a walk." She started for the door. Both men were silent behind her as she slid her key in the door. Then, to her horror, Sam pushed past her and bounded, barking in a frenzy. She spun around, stunned. Sam was protective, yes, but he'd never been an attack dog. And he was making a beeline for Lance Morton.

"Sam!"

The dog ignored her. There really would be an assault charge if her dog bit the man! she thought with dismay.

"Sam!" O'Casey's voice rose high. He took a step forward, placing himself between the dog and Lance Morton. Sam slid to a stop, barking furiously.

"Sam! It's all right. Here, boy, here!" Kelly said desperately.

Sam remained where he was, whining then rather than barking. His silver-gray body trembled.

"Sam, it's okay." O'Casey stepped forward, a hand out, patting Sam's head. The dog's little stub of a silver tail wagged.

"I think I'm going to hurl!" Lance said.

"You're going to be all right. Come in," Kelly told him.

"I have a headache, big time," Lance said.

"I'll make you a drink. Or get you some aspirin."

"I'll take a drink," Lance said. He stepped by O'Casey, staring at him. Sam growled.

"Hey!" Lance said.

"He's quite a judge of character," O'Casey said blandly.

"Was that another dig?" Lance demanded. He walked toward the door, obviously still irate. "Next thing you know, he'll be saying the music sucks."

"The music is good," O'Casey muttered, implying that other things might not be.

But Lance didn't hear the intonation. He dropped his anger like a fallen coat. "Yeah?" he said to O'Casey. There was a lot of hope in his voice, a lot of uncertainty.

"Yes, the music is good," O'Casey repeated.

"Wow. Thanks."

"Both of you, please come in. Let's all chill out a bit, huh?" Kelly said.

They both stared at her. Lance shrugged. "Hey, you're the one who screamed."

She looked at him as if he had really gone mad for a minute, then she shook her head. "Yes, I screamed. I've apologized.

Shall we make it go all around?"

He stared back at her. "You wouldn't really leave the video, would you?"

"I wouldn't want to."

"I, uh —" He paused a second, looking at the dog warily and then at O'Casey with the same care. "I'm sorry I scared you."

O'Casey shrugged. "I'm sorry if I broke any of your bones."

Lance Morton smiled then. "Hey, cool. No, I don't think that any of my bones are broken. You really like my music?"

"Yes," O'Casey said. "I like it a lot. I don't think you guys are going to be a flash that comes and goes. You're real musicians, you've got talent and flair. And now you have money behind you."

"Cool. Way cool!" Lance said, walking up the steps. "You got any good whiskey?" he asked Kelly.

"I imagine I can find some," she said dryly. She looked at O'Casey. "I think that Sam . . ."

Her voice faded as Sam came to life, running, trotting over to one of the bushes that lined the front of the house, lifting his leg.

"Sam . . . ?" O'Casey said, arching a brow.

"Doesn't really need a walk anymore,"

she said. She walked into the house, followed by Lance, O'Casey and then Sam. The dog didn't seem to want to go for a long walk. He was far more interested in being in the house with her . . . guests.

She walked into the kitchen. Thankfully, she kept a decent whiskey in the house. She heard the men following her, and the tap of Sam's nails as he followed as well.

"Great place," Lance said.

"How did you know where it was?" O'Casey asked.

He caught Lance off guard. The singer wiggled his shoulders, as if he were in pain from the assault. "Man, that hurt!" he murmured.

"How did you know where Kelly lived?" O'Casey persisted.

"Easy," Lance said. "I got the address from Logan, who got it from Mel — your agent."

"Really?" Kelly said, taking down glasses. "Mel doesn't usually give out my address."

Lance shrugged. "Well, Logan had it somehow. Maybe for payments or something."

"I'm paid through Mel," she said.

"The IRS?" Lance suggested. "Hell, I don't know."

Kelly handed him the glass of whiskey.

"Thanks!" Lance said. He looked at a grass stain on his jacket. "Ruined, I think."

"I know a good cleaner," she told him. She glanced at O'Casey, indicating the glasses. He shook his head. She opted for a plain Coke herself.

"Man, but my back is killing me!" Lance said.

"I know a good masseuse, too," she told him.

He walked into her back room, looking around, then sinking into the couch. "You'd give me the name of your masseuse?" he said, grinning.

She shrugged. "Why not?"

"Radical," he said, pleased.

"I'm still a little confused," O'Casey said. "You just came by, and you were hanging out in Kelly's yard, waiting for her to come home? What the hell are you doing in California, anyway?"

"Recording."

"You couldn't record in Miami? I thought some of the best studios were there."

"Oh, sure, there are great studios in Miami. But we were scheduled to work out here. Hey, I don't know why. I'm not financing this thing. We're laying a few more tracks. They want them ready to go when we start the video."

"But hanging out in someone's yard, waiting?" O'Casey persisted.

"Hey! I didn't know that you two were an item," Lance said impatiently, shaking his head.

Kelly's protest froze on her lips. She waited for O'Casey to say something. He didn't. Lance was still looking around the room with interest. "Really cool place," he said.

"Glad you like it," Kelly murmured.

Lance nodded absently, then stared at her. "Hey, how come you didn't know I was here? They said you'd be doing some backup singing for the final track."

"Actually, yes, that was in the contract. But no one gave me a schedule for when to be in a studio," Kelly said.

Lance shrugged. "Well, maybe they're not ready for that, but I would think they'd have you doing some practices with us. Usually we wouldn't just let anyone come in that way, but . . . hey, Kelly. It's you."

"Thanks."

He'd finished his drink. He looked at the empty glass.

"Would you like another?" she offered.

"Sure."

She took his glass, ready to get him another drink. O'Casey was still watching him as if he were a bomb that might explode. "Where's your car?" he asked.

"Car?" Lance repeated.

"Your car. Auto. Vehicle. How did you get here?" O'Casey asked.

"Taxi, man. I took a taxi."

"You don't have a car here?"

"Sure, I've got a rental. I'm just not that good with the streets, the canyons, the up and down. Man, I couldn't live out here! I was in the back seat of a limo yesterday and I could have sworn I was going to vomit the whole ride. It's a great place, but not for me."

Kelly gave Lance another Scotch on the rocks.

"You took a taxi, got out at an empty house and just waited?" O'Casey said.

Lance glared at him, lifting his hands. The ice in his glass rattled. "I told you, I came to say hello."

"Finish your drink. I'll give you a ride home," O'Casey said.

Lance grinned suddenly. "You won't freak out in the driver's seat? Who'd have figured the dance teacher for a tackle in another life! Man, I am bruised top to bottom."

"Want me to make you a doctor's appointment?" Kelly asked.

"Hell, no. I don't go to the doctor for bruises," Lance said. His glass was empty again. He looked hopefully at Kelly.

"It's late. Kelly worked hard today. I'll take you home," O'Casey said.

Lance shrugged, then rose, wincing.

"Try a long hot bath," Kelly suggested.

He looked at her, grinning again. It was a look that made her uneasy. His words, as he stared at her, didn't help any. "A long hot bath, huh?"

"Come on, this taxi is heading out," O'Casey said. He looked at Kelly. "Lock up good when we're gone, right?"

She nodded. "I've got Sam, you know."

"Yeah. He should be with you at all times," O'Casey murmured. He set a hand on Lance's shoulder, directing him toward the front door. When he had the singer out on the porch, he turned back. "Are you all right?"

"Perfectly," she assured him, then added softly, "I really shouldn't have screamed. I was just so startled."

He didn't reply to that, and his gaze was fathomless. "I'll get him out of here," he said.

She nodded. "Tomorrow at . . . ?"

"How about I pick you up?" he suggested.

She shrugged. She'd been humiliated that day. She really wished she could tell him she'd just meet him at the studio at four, as had been planned for the week. But screw humiliation. She'd been terrified when the figure had emerged from the shadows. O'Casey was welcome to come and get her. That way, she wouldn't be coming back alone in the darkness again.

"What time?" she asked him.

"Noonish?"

"Fine."

"Hey, taxi man, are you coming?" Lance asked.

"Lock up," O'Casey told Kelly.

She heard the footsteps of the men as they receded down the walk. Sam whined and looked up at her hopefully. "I hope you did what you wanted when you were out there, young man, because there is no more walk tonight!" She scratched his ears, very glad that she had him.

She was feeling all right as she picked up Lance's glass and the remains of her own Coke. She was even okay as she brushed her teeth and washed her face. But when she went into her bedroom, she discovered that she couldn't stand the darkness. She lay down with the lights on and turned on the television, calling for Sam to hop up by her feet. Eventually, she fell asleep.

She woke to the cold dampness of Sam's nose pressing against her fingers. It was morning and he wanted out.

"Okay, Sam, I'm getting up," she murmured sleepily.

The television was droning away with the morning newscast. The day was going to be smoggy. Big surprise. The dry weather would continue. Another big surprise.

"And in the case of Dr. Dana Sumter, Gerry Proctor, attorney for the defense, has announced that he will prove beyond a doubt his client's innocence."

Kelly cracked open her eyes, then sat up. The defense attorney came on briefly, claiming that his client was being railroaded and maligned just for having been married to the woman. As she stared at the television, the husband himself came on. "She was the mother of my children, for God's sake!" the man protested. He was a decent-looking fellow, middle-aged, mildly receding hairline. "Dana and I had our differences, but I'd never . . . she was the mother of my children!" he repeated.

Kelly hit the power button. The screen

went blank. She rose and walked into the bathroom, eager for a quick shower before taking Sam out for his morning constitutional.

Doug had watched the news as well. He was reflecting on the impression Sumter gave in the interview when the phone rang.

"O'Casey?"

"Hey." It was Kelly.

"Did you have plans for this morning?"

"Not really. What's up?"

"I thought I'd come by for you."

"Yeah, that's fine. Didn't we agree on lunch yesterday, before practice?"

"Yes, right . . . but you were coming for me just before twelve. I thought that I'd come for you instead, since you don't know the city the way I do. I thought we'd have lunch maybe a little earlier, then practice. I'll bring clothing to change into, then we'll head back to your hotel and straight over to dinner. They're expecting us around eight. Of course, there's no pressure. If you'd rather just stick with the original plan . . ."

She added the last in a rush, as if afraid she'd been too forward. Times and mores might change, but people didn't. Even with something as simple as dinner or deciding who was driving meant putting oneself out on the line. No one liked rejection. It was a matter of pride.

"That would mean you'd be dropping me off, and I should be seeing you back to your house," Doug rationalized.

She hesitated just a fraction of a second. "It's all right, really. I intend to get one of those little cans of pepper spray for my key chain today."

"I'll pick you up," he said.

"But —"

"You can tell me where we're going. How's that? Look, it will just make me feel better to get you safely back to your place, Kelly. Let's pretend that none of this is happening. Pretend we just met in a bar."

"I really don't go to bars."

"Okay, we met at the bowling alley."

She laughed. "I don't bowl."

"Okay! We met in a Pilates class and I asked you out to dinner. I'd still feel better about picking you up and seeing you home safely. I'll be there in half an hour, all right? That way, I'll get to see Sam."

She laughed then. "All right."

He hung up, stared at the receiver and shook his head. "You're getting in too deep, kid," he said aloud. It's exactly what Quinn would have said to him. Hell, it was like being caught in a current. There was nothing to do but ride it out, and hope that you eventually made it to shore.

Chapter 13

Kelly climbed into close-fitting knit workout pants and a T-shirt for the day, then packed a shoulder bag with dress and sandals to change into for the evening. Sam watched her as she walked around the house, and she was careful to stop and give him a fair amount of attention as she got ready. As a puppy, he'd consumed a fantastic number of shoes, seasoned a few floors and gone through one couch, but now he was a perfect gentleman. They'd gone through training classes together and he'd gotten over his urge to consume leather. She didn't like the fact that she'd be leaving him alone for long hours that night, but he was a good boy and he'd deal with it.

"We'll go out again before I actually leave," she told him. He cocked his head and looked at her as if he knew exactly what she was saying and still didn't like it.

"Sam! I'm taking you to Florida, you

know. You'll love it. I think. I have to get you to like Lance Morton, but then again, I'm working on that myself."

The doorbell rang. O'Casey was there, his sunglasses giving him the look of a fictional spy, despite the fact that he, too, was in casual clothing — short-sleeved tailored shirt and Dockers.

Sam woofed excitedly.

"I take it he wants a walk?" O'Casey said.

"I promised him a good one," she said apologetically. "Come in. I'll take him, then we can go."

"I don't mind."

"I don't, either."

"We'll go together."

She got Sam's leash and started out. Doug was still on the porch when she was halfway down the walk.

"Kelly."

She paused, turning back. "Yeah?"

"What are you doing?"

She waited, wondering what on earth he could be talking about.

"I'm walking the dog."

"You've left the door open."

"I'm just walking the dog. I'll be right back."

He groaned. "Kelly. Once again, if there

were no hint of danger and we were living in Utopia, you'd still need to lock your door!"

"But we're just going around the block."

He groaned again. "It would take someone split seconds to slip in and wait. Damn, do you do this at night?"

"No." Well, she hadn't lately. She'd not even gone out at night since she'd returned from Florida. He'd taken the dog, and last night Sam just hadn't gone out again.

"Kelly." O'Casey said her name flatly.

"All right, all right." She hurried back, handed him the leash and went back in for her keys. As they left then, she locked the door. "Happy?"

"Only if you intend to keep it up. Don't you ever go to neighborhood crime-watch meetings or anything?"

"No, actually," she murmured.

"There's paranoid and there's common sense," he told her.

"Right. Except," she argued, "Sam would know if there was someone in his house."

"Probably. Would he know in time, though? This is a ridiculous argument. I'm right and you know it."

"I should have just let you walk the dog!" she murmured, hurrying on ahead.

She noted that he was studying the yards as they walked along. "What now?" she asked him.

"Lots and lots of foliage," he said. "And trees."

"They're big yards, irregular. Some of the newer places have been built around the trees," she said. "Why are you wondering about the foliage?"

"Lots of places for people to hide."

"Will you stop, please!"

"Just observing," he said. He gazed at her but she couldn't see his eyes. "Were there any repercussions over Mr. Morton's appearance last night?"

She shook her head, smiling. "He must have talked to someone, because I got a call from Mel this morning telling me to be in the studio Monday morning to do some vocals. He apologized. Apparently he knew, but he'd forgotten to tell me. A call from Lance had jogged his memory. Mel said that he's been so busy with me — which he has been — that he's gotten into some serious work regarding his other clients. I don't think Lance Morton even mentioned that there had been a run-in of any kind. I'm glad."

He shrugged.

"Okay, you were in the right again. But

don't you want to continue this rock video?"

"I'd never kowtow to Lance Morton."

She grinned. "He could be really famous one day."

He looked at her, but she couldn't read his expression. "You're really famous."

"No, I'm not. Soap stars aren't *really* famous. Now, a hot rock star — that's famous."

"No matter how famous he gets, he's still an idiot."

Kelly laughed. "Back to my original question," she said. "Don't you want to do this? You agreed to it, and I keep thinking that it isn't just the money."

"Sure. I'm having fun. And," he added a little gruffly, as if it took some effort, "it was really decent of you to stand up for me, even though I was right to tackle the guy."

"I seem to be learning the tango," she murmured, and gave her attention to the dog. "Sorry, Sam, it's time to go in."

O'Casey watched her every move as she locked up. Then they got into the car.

"Where to?" O'Casey asked her.

"Back to the Sunset area near the studio, I guess. Do you like sushi?"

"Why did I know that you would?"

"People usually love it or hate it. Well?"

"I eat just about anything."

She let out an impatient sigh. "But do you like it?"

"Yes."

"Back to Sunset, then."

As he drove, he asked her questions about Mel, the soap, her life. They seemed casual enough, so she answered them quite freely.

They parked in the studio lot and walked down the Strip. The weather was beautiful, so they opted to sit outside. Apparently he did like sushi. They got into a long discussion on whether to get a large boat or not, on which rolls were the best and just exactly what they should order.

"What about you?" Kelly asked.

"What about me?"

"No ex-wives, kids. Family?"

"My dad passed away. My mother lives in north Miami. I have a brother who's also in South Florida."

"No nieces or nephews?"

"I imagine I'll have one or the other or both soon enough. Quinn is married. To my boss, actually."

"To your boss?" Kelly wasn't sure why, but she found that amusing. "Competitive dancers have bosses?"

"Shannon owns the studio where I usually teach. She hasn't a mean or autocratic bone in her body. I'm here because your manager, Ally Bassett, approached me through Moonlight Sonata studios. According to Mel, you're the easiest person in the world to accommodate. No demanding posse to deal with."

She laughed. "No, I don't have a retinue. I'm not even picky about makeup or hair."

"Well, I guess you don't need to be, do you?" he asked.

Her Boston roll nearly stuck in her mouth. It was quite a compliment, coming from Doug.

"Thanks," she murmured.

"You're really not at all what I expected," he said. "Want to walk?"

"Sure. I'll get the check today."

"I'll get it."

"O'Casey, haven't you been living in the modern world?"

"Sure. I just turn the checks in for expenses, so it makes more sense that I get them, right? Saves face, too."

"There are lots of decent guys out there willing to lunch Dutch treat. Even to let the woman pick up the tab now and then."

"I'm sure there are," he said, but his credit card was out.

When the bill was paid, they wandered down Sunset. Kelly pointed out some of the strange new fashions in the windows. She had paused to study some knit workout clothing that looked as if it might suit the Florida weather when she realized that he hadn't caught up with her. He was about fifty feet back, paused just beyond the seating area of one of the restaurants on the Strip.

"O'Casey, do you mind if I run in here for just a moment?" she called.

He didn't turn to her; he might not have heard her. She walked back to him. He took her by the shoulders, leading her in front of him, then pointing into the restaurant.

At a table together were Matt Avery, Marc Logan and Joe Penny. As they watched, Joe looked at his watch and rose, excusing himself. The minute he was gone, Marc Logan and Matt Avery moved in over the table. It appeared their words were hushed and intense.

"What do you make of that?" O'Casey asked softly.

"Matt Avery is probably telling Marc Logan that he should be firing me for my own good," Kelly told him.

Joe Penny came walking out, then stopped short, seeing them. "Kelly! Mr. . . . uh, O'Casey."

"Hi, Joe."

"Hello," O'Casey said.

"I guess that you two are on your way to . . . dance, or whatever."

"Yes."

Joe stared at Kelly. He looked a little sick every time his eyes touched hers. "I miss you on the set, Kelly."

"Thanks."

"It won't be that long."

She laughed. "Joe! This is hardly a tragedy! I love what I'm learning. I'm really excited about the video. Who knows, I may not want to come back!"

He looked stricken.

She shook her head. "Oh, come on, Joe. Face it. Avery wants me to lose any popularity whatsoever while I'm gone. He wants me out."

"It's my show," Joe said indignantly.

"His money."

"Well, it's Household Heav—"

"His money," Kelly repeated pleasantly.

"How did Marc Logan wind up in that lunch group?" O'Casey asked.

Startled, Joe looked from Kelly to him.

"Oh, well, he comes around. He's got his boys here, recording now. I guess he had this dream about Kelly being in the video for some time. Seems a decent enough guy. Anyway, I've got to get back to work. Kelly . . ."

Impulsively she hugged him. "I love you, too, Joe. We'll just see how things go, huh?"

He nodded and they parted. "Nice to see you, Mr. O'Casey. Kelly, take care. And keep in touch."

Kelly nodded.

"Strange," O'Casey said.

"What? People having lunch?"

He shook his head. "Never mind."

"What?"

"Logan and Avery. That conversation."

Kelly shrugged. "Are we going to analyze every word someone utters? They're both slimy money men. Anyway, do you mind if I run into a store for a minute?"

"Not at all."

"Are you going to keep staring at the restaurant?"

"Yes."

"Suit yourself!" Kelly said impatiently.

Shaking her head, she went into the shop. She took longer than she'd expected. The salesgirl was a fan of her soap. They talked, Kelly explaining she'd be off the show for a while. She told the girl about the rock video, which made the young woman more excited. Kelly thanked her and left the store, her purchases in hand.

O'Casey was leaning against the wall. He looked at her, arching a brow. "Just a minute or two?" he said.

"Sorry. What, no one else to spy on in the restaurant?"

"They left a while ago."

"Did the three of you chat?"

"They didn't see me."

"You were right out here!"

He looked at her. "I didn't want to be seen."

"Why?"

"I don't particularly like either of them," he said.

"Well, that makes sense," she murmured. She lifted her bag. "Clothes. For the island, or whatever it is exactly that we're shooting on."

"Island."

She turned and started toward the crosswalk. She stepped onto the street.

"Hey! There are cars out there!" he warned.

She turned back to him. "Big-time law, big-time fines! Cars have to stop." As she said the words, she started into the street.

Suddenly she heard O'Casey shout. When she turned, there was a dark sedan shooting her way. She heard O'Casey shout again, then she was tackled. He hit her like a ton of bricks. His force propelled her far out of the way of the speeding car. They landed together, all but entwined, almost on the sidewalk on the other side of the street. Her butt hurt, her arms hurt, her shoulder hurt. She was dazed, still held down by the weight of the man.

She looked up into his eyes. It was then that she started shaking, realizing that, once again, she had very nearly been killed.

Chapter 14

"Oh, my God!" a woman shrieked from her table at a sidewalk café.

"Are you all right?" a man demanded, rushing forward.

Suddenly, there were people everywhere. "Can you imagine!" someone shouted. "Asshole!" someone else cried. By then, bystanders had helped them both up.

O'Casey had lost his sunglasses. The look he gave Kelly was of naked concern. She was startled to feel a sweet heat cascade into her even as she trembled in the aftermath of fear. But he quickly tore his eyes from her, looking at the crowd.

"Did anyone get a license plate number?"

There was silence. Then, "I think it might have been an out-of-state tag," a woman offered tentatively.

"No! It was a rental plate, I'm certain," a pretty young blonde said.

"Well, it was a black sedan, that's for certain," a bearded man with his paper coffee cup still in hand said with assurance.

"Black!" A clean but scruffy-looking teen protested. "It was dark green."

"Green! It was one of those really deep blues," an older man said, shaking his head.

"It was a Chevy," someone said.

"No, it was a Ford!"

"It was a foreign car!"

"We should call the police."

O'Casey had been staring at them all, and he shook his head incredulously. "No, thanks. It won't do any good."

"That was nearly a hit and run!" the blonde said indignantly.

"But we have nothing to tell the police," O'Casey said patiently. "They can't go stopping every green, black, blue, Ford, Chevy and foreign car with out-of-state, in-state and rental tags," he explained.

"Oh, my God!" the blonde said. "You're Marla Valentine!"

Kelly cringed. "I'm Kelly Trent, yes."

Her pants were ripped, she was totally disheveled and she was beginning to hurt in half a dozen places. She sure as hell didn't want a big deal made out of this.

The next thing she knew, she'd be off limits from every workplace in the world because of the insurance costs, since she'd appear to be a terrible liability.

"Thank you all so much for trying to help," she said, tugging at O'Casey's sleeve. "But it's true, there's nothing that can be done. Thank you. O'Casey!" She dropped her voice to a whisper. "I beg of you, let's get out of here! Please. I don't want to wind up on the five o'clock news."

"It didn't used to be like this!" the older man was complaining. "Californians! We know how to stop for crosswalks. It's all the foreigners we've got here now. All those folks from New York!"

"Idiot drivers are everywhere," someone else said.

"You're really all right?" the blonde asked.

"Yes, yes, fine . . . just shaken, scratched up a bit," Kelly said. "O'Casey!" she whispered more strongly.

"Excuse us," he said firmly to the gathering crowd. "Thanks so very much. We're going to go clean up now . . . and shake this experience off."

His arm around Kelly, he started moving her down the sidewalk toward the studio.

"Wait!" someone called.

Kelly stiffened. O'Casey turned back.

The blonde rushed forward, bringing Kelly's over-the-shoulder bag and the clothing she had just bought, which had wound up flung near the curb. They both had completely forgotten Kelly's belongings.

"Thank you!" Kelly said.

"My pleasure!"

Kelly smiled weakly again, really anxious to escape. The crowd had inched up to where the blonde was.

"Thank you again everyone!" she called.

O'Casey started walking. Quickly. She could hear the crowd continuing as they departed.

"Kelly Trent! Wow. Better in person."

"So natural!"

"Who's the guy?"

"Hot as hell!" someone said. Kelly couldn't see over her shoulder, but she was certain it was the blonde.

She glanced up at O'Casey. "I think the blonde likes you."

"Maybe that good-looking gay guy does, too," he said with a grin, but then the grin faded. "You could have been killed."

"Yes, but it was stupidity, not a conspiracy," she told him. "I was determined to prove to you that Californians could cross a highway when they wanted. I guess that guy — or whoever was driving — just didn't see me."

He was quiet, and she didn't like his silence. "What?" she demanded.

"Kelly, that car didn't just miss seeing you. It sped up."

"Well, of course it sped up. Since the guy nearly hit me, he sure as hell wasn't going to stay around."

"I don't like it," O'Casey said flatly, wondering why she was misunderstanding his words.

"Well, I didn't think it was a ton of fun, either!"

"No, I mean . . ."

She groaned. "O'Casey! No one was trying to kill me! Think about it. Who the hell would know just when and where I was going to cross a street!"

"How badly are you hurt?" he asked her.

"I'm not. A rip in my pants, a scratched knee and elbow."

"No aches and pains?"

"A few."

"Think you should see a doctor?" he asked.

"No!"

He was silent again. "You can't be up to dancing right now."

"Actually, I could be. Except that I really am filthy."

They had neared the studio. He didn't direct her up the stairs but around back to the parking lot. "Where are you taking me? I don't want to go home right now, O'Casey. There is nothing wrong with me!"

"I won't take you home."

"Where are you taking me, then?"

"My hotel is just down the street. Let's go there, clean up, regroup."

"All right."

He drove the short distance down the street. The valet took the car, and they headed quickly for the elevator. He opened his door.

Kelly stepped in, impressed.

"Nice."

"Yes, actually, it is. Pretty good lifestyle for a simple man like me," he commented, grinning. "I've got to admit, I did like the legroom on the plane. The meal wasn't great, but it beat the hell out of the bag of chips they throw at you now in coach. And as for the room, I could get used to living like this." He walked across the spacious room with its bedroom and sitting areas and opened a door. "I'll take off for a while and leave you with the bath."

Kelly arched a brow and followed him. The bathroom was great. The tub huge, with all kinds of whirl jets.

"Very nice," she agreed.

"So I'll get out of your way for a while, go for a walk. Take your time."

"You went down on the pavement, too, you know. And it *is* your room — maybe *you* need a hot bath."

"I landed on top of you," he reminded her ruefully. "I've got a little dust on me."

She nodded slowly. "All right. A good soak is in order." She hesitated, almost afraid to breathe, and spoke as casually as she could. "I don't want to throw you out."

"You're not."

"The bathroom *does* have a door, you don't need to leave," she reminded him.

"Yeah, I know." He walked across the room again, then hunkered down in front of the minibar. "Think they keep brandy in these?"

"Doubtful, but you never know."

He struggled with the catch for a minute, then got the door open. "Um . . ."

"I'll take the little bottle of Chablis."

He nodded and handed it to her. After a moment, he took a beer for himself. He popped it and took a long swallow.

"Wow," she murmured.

"Well, I was scared as hell for you, even if you weren't. Hey, want a glass for that?"

"No, thanks. I guess I can swig wine

out of the bottle, too."

He nodded. "Take it in with you. There's all kinds of bath salts in there. Hot water will help a lot with your muscles."

"My muscles are all right."

"They tensed, trust me."

"Did yours tense, too?"

"You bet."

He finished the beer and set the can down. "All right, I'm going. I'm serious. Hot, hot water. It will help a lot."

She frowned, putting her hands on her hips. "So where are you going?"

"For a walk."

"Why?"

"Okay, I didn't see the license tag at all, but I'm pretty sure the car was black, had four doors and was a foreign model. I'm just going to take a look around."

"O'Casey, that car is going to be long gone by now!"

"Probably. But I think I'll retrace our steps a bit, take a look around at the metered parking, in the lots."

She threw up her arms. "Okay, fine. Make yourself happy, knock yourself out." She headed toward the bathroom, then came back, taking her shopping and shoulder bags from him. "Thanks!" she said softly. At the bathroom door, she paused again. "Really, thank you for saving my life."

"It's all part of the dance, huh?" he replied, a slight smile teasing his lips.

"All in a day's work," she agreed. She stepped into the massive, beautifully marbled and decorated bath, and closed the door.

Quite frankly, she was right, Doug thought. It was absurd to attempt walking around the area looking for the car. But Kelly didn't want to go home, and he wasn't sure he should be around while she soaked. So he walked.

Pity that with all the witnesses, not one person had been able to catch sight of the license plate. But then again, who stared at license plates? It was a miracle most of the time when someone actually caught the numbers on a tag. But in a hit-and-run case, there was usually damage on the car. Thank God there wasn't going to be any damage on the car.

Here, as in his hometown, expensive cars were plentiful. Sleek black sedans were parked in many places, along with green ones and dark blue ones. There were small, ritzy sport cars as well, but the sedans were plentiful. He was looking for a needle in a haystack where the needle might not have even fallen. Or, if he were to find the needle, he wouldn't recognize it from the hay. Still, he took his time, walking several miles in the area, stopping off at a little place near the bookstore for an espresso.

Bad driver? Clever assailant? He didn't have the answer. He'd researched the people connected to Kelly's soap and the video, but he hadn't found anything too incriminating. Yet something nagged at him. The incident with the car just seemed to make it all the worse. At last, he turned back to the hotel. Tonight he could talk to Liam.

When he reached his room, he hesitated, then slipped the plastic key into the lock. "Kelly?" he called.

"I'm here."

He walked into the room, and there she was, scrubbed clean, hair damp, stretched out in the hotel-provided white terry robe on the elaborate white bed.

"Hey," he murmured, closing the door behind him.

It wasn't as if she was in some flimsy lace garment, something see-through, low-cut, offering an erotic display of cleavage. It was worse, for he knew she was naked beneath the terry robe. She wasn't wearing any kind of musk, no perfume sworn to be an aphrodisiac. She was just . . . bathed.

And there was a subtle scent to whatever soap, shampoo, bath salts or body wash she had used that was . . . compelling. No, alluring. In truth, on her it was the most exotic tease that had ever wafted toward his senses.

She was on an elbow, reading one of the in-room magazines. Though her hair remained damp, just brushed, she had probably made a halfhearted attempt to dry it because the wisps around her face were light and curling slightly, becoming a softer shade of red. There was nothing about the way she was stretched out that intended to taunt and seduce. The robe was respectably closed, the hem reaching below her knee, only her calves and feet visible. But then again, why was she in the robe?

He walked over to the side of the bed. She looked up at him, those eyes of hers as clear and beautiful as the glaze of a perfect day in the islands. "Did you find the car?"

"No."

"You weren't really expecting to, were you?"

"No," he told her.

"Are you afraid of me?" she asked him softly.

A smile teased his lips. "No. And yes."

"Why?" she asked.

"Because we shouldn't become involved," he told her.

She nodded, looking down for a moment. Then she looked back up at him. He noted that her lashes were very dark and sweeping, a perfect frame for those eyes.

"Ah," she murmured. Her gaze met his squarely. "Why not?"

He lifted his hands, surprised that words were failing him. But instinct wasn't. Natural inclination was all there. He could already feel the pounding of his heart and the pulse of his blood in his temple. Reaction to stimuli. Damn, she even had good feet. Her toenails were a delicate shade of pink. Feet connected to ankles. Ankles to calves. And above the hem, the edge of the terry robe. And beneath it, nothing.

He met her eyes again. "Because," he said gruffly, "you're Kelly Trent."

She offered him a small, wistful smile that did more than seize hold of his libido. It catapulted to his heart. "What if I weren't Kelly Trent? What if I were someone you just met at a bowling alley?"

"You don't bowl," he reminded her.

"Okay, what if I were just someone you met at a Pilates class?"

He shook his head. "I don't take Pilates."

"All right," she said softly. "I understand." She stood, shaking that mane of
long red hair. She started walking toward
the bathroom, then paused, turning back.
"No, I don't understand. Am I that . . .
*un*intriguing?"

He groaned out loud. He'd tried. God
knew, he'd tried. There was a point, however, at which every man had to cede a
losing battle. He walked over to her. Her
hands were on the belt of the terry robe;
she'd been getting ready to give it up for
her clothing. His fingers curled over hers.
He gave a tug to the belt and the terry
split. Her eyes were on his. He returned
her stare, cupped her chin, angled her
head. Her lips parted to his instantly. They
were great lips — flush, full, sensual, deep,
rich . . .

His fingers tangled into the red-fire
mane of her hair. The warmth of her
mouth seemed like a honeyed mire, dragging him more deeply into a realm where
he knew that, once entrapped, he would
remain forever. That didn't stop him. No
inner warning, no pretense of intelligence,
reason or self-control could have begun to
budge him. His tongue raked her mouth,
the need for greater depths gripping the
length of him. There, in the liquid inferno,

came the knowledge. The point of no return had been reached, ignored and bypassed.

At last his lips rose from hers. Her eyes were on him, her lips damp, more evocative. Her chest rose and fell. She didn't smile as she searched out his eyes. "No recriminations," she said softly. "No regrets, no commitment, no demands." He realized that she wasn't whispering her own independence; she was simply telling him that he'd owe her nothing.

"You really think that I'll forget this moment?" he asked her, smoothing a strand of red-gold silk from her forehead.

She studied him. "Nor will I. But you owe me nothing."

"I didn't suggest that I did. After all, you are seducing me."

"Yes." With that honest admission of the obvious, she turned away from him, letting the robe fall. It wasn't a calculated move. It didn't need to be.

If he hadn't already been fully convinced to give way to madness, he would have been at that moment. Her back was perfect, flawless, her shoulders tapering to her waist, dimples just inside her hips, hips slightly flared, buttocks, thighs, back to those calves. Perfect feet. Upward again . . .

The unruly red mane of hair.

She ripped the great expanse of white covering from the bed. He took the opportunity to kick off his shoes, shed his clothing. Thank God for knits. They shed fast. She slid onto the sheets and he had to stop himself from flying on top of her, forcing a slow path, crawling next to her, finding her eyes again, engaging her lips as he allowed his fingers to slide down the length of her arm, feel the softness of her flesh.

Fingers played downward next, over her hips, slightly down her thigh. He felt her knuckles as they curled against his chest, locked there by the force of his position. He caught her hands, kissing the knuckles, allowing them freedom. Felt them against his shoulders, a butterfly touch over his chest. Felt her move against him. Her lips, freed from his kiss, left a sultry tease of heat and dampness against his shoulder. He groaned deep in his throat, aware of the spasms shaking his length. God, he'd be like a kid in a minute, drowning in sensation, unable to . . .

He caught her wrists and flipped her down, staring into her eyes again for a minute. They were a sea, he warned himself, a sea he was going to drown in. Oh, well, no man lived forever.

Her breasts were firm, evocative to his hands, reacting to the slightest tease of his fingers. The nipples were rose, a perfect match for the redness of her hair. And a perfect fit for the light edge of his lips and teeth, eliciting a rise of movement from her, a gasping sound, a twist against him.

Her fingers in his hair, tugging slightly. He inched downward, burying his face against her ribs, abdomen. His hands slid down the outer length of her legs. The inner length. Teased. Explored. Probed.

She surged hard against him, almost struggling to touch him as he touched her. He didn't dare let her. He inched downward, fingers stroking, tongue doing likewise, following the same track in a swirling, slow, tantalizing action.

She was frantically whispering, twisting, arching, in one second trying to elude his touch, in another ever more eager for it. She cried out, fingers biting into his shoulders, body becoming as stiff as a jackknife, muscles taut, strained.

Easing suddenly, he inched swiftly upward, hips wedged between her legs, fingers capturing her chin and cheek again, mouth finding her lips, body thrusting into her with the same motion.

She was fire, lava, movement, friction, magic. He broke the connection of their lips, encapsulating her in his arms as he fit more tightly to her, body rocking, the force of desire racking through him with a fever. The room seemed to become nothing more than a haven of white, blinding white, like the clouds. He could almost imagine that such a vision was Heaven. Against the expanse of white, her hair seemed like tendrils of real flame, her flesh vibrant, their hands laced together.

Somewhere in it all, he lost sight of everything except for the blinding white, the scent of her, the agony that twitched throughout his length and the almost savage hunger with which he came to move. The feeling was . . . so good, so agonizing.

He climaxed with stunning force, his body shuddering. He didn't know if five minutes had passed or five seconds. He felt an echoing tremor and a new surge of heat as her body eased beneath his own, felt the slow shift downward from rapture and radiance.

He shifted his weight from her, coming to her side. She curled against him, eyes downcast.

"What are you thinking?" he probed.

Her eyes met his and a smile teased her

lips. "I'm thinking that at least now I'll be able to do the tango without . . . well, you know. Without wondering."

"Miss Trent, have you been out to seduce me all along?"

"Not all along, no. I really didn't like you at first."

He laughed and tilted her chin upward. "Did you raid the mini-bar for the rest of the booze after I left?"

"I consumed my one small bottle of wine. I am not in the least inebriated," she assured him. "Honestly."

"Um. Nice."

"You did inhale that beer," she informed him.

"I admit, I'm high as a kite."

She frowned. "You went somewhere and had something?"

"Espresso."

She smiled. "So you're high on me?"

"Absolutely."

"Then why were you resisting with such determination?"

"You're Kelly Trent."

"And what does that mean?" she asked a little desperately.

"It means we're working together."

"This could help the tango," she reminded him.

"I dance with lots of women."

"Ah." She frowned again. "What exactly does that mean?"

He laughed softly. "Exactly what I said. I dance." He shifted and noticed her wince. "Are you . . . did I hurt you?" he said puzzled.

"Kneecap."

"What?"

"It's nothing. I have a scraped kneecap."

He maneuvered around and tenderly touched the area where she did indeed have a good scratch. "Wow, sorry."

"I'm not in that much pain!"

"Still . . ." He touched his lips gently around the area.

"Left thigh," she said huskily.

He shifted around again. "There will be a bruise."

"Afraid so."

He brushed the area with his lips as well. She twisted beneath him, catching his face between her hands. "You didn't hurt anything, did you?"

"Shoulder is a little sore," he said.

Long, delicate fingers traced over it. "Where?"

"There."

She kissed the spot.

"I think I hit this rib."

"Um . . ." Again, that incredulous touch of delicacy and wicked flames. "Anywhere else?"

"There isn't a part on me that couldn't use a healing touch," he assured her solemnly.

"Then perhaps I'd best spread a little tenderness all around," she murmured. And she did. Here. There. With each brush of fingers and tongue, the world began to spin.

He let her have her way, until he could bear it no longer. Then his aggression surged forward. She was in his arms and they were locked to each other once again, her limbs climbing his hips, a surge of energy ripping through them both with force and fire. Her skin was damp, her hair a tangled red halo, her body a work of pure erotic rhythm. He was rocked that time into such a climax that he was blinded, half soaring in the sublime physical elation, half in an agony of easing tension. Elated, he drew her close just to feel the pounding of her heart, the rise and fall of her breath, the whisper of it against his cheek. He smoothed her hair, marveling at the feel of it.

She had been sidling into his heart and soul since he had first seen her and tried to deny that there was anything special about her. Now here she was, so trusting at his side. So trusting that she had dozed off, he realized after a moment. And that fact tore at him. She was sleeping because she probably hadn't slept much at all lately. Because she kept denying that she could be in danger. But she was afraid.

Chapter 15

Kelly woke with a start. The room was in shadows. She sat up, seized by an irrational panic at finding herself alone.

"Hey!"

He was there, standing at the foot of the bed and dressed nicely. Damn, he wore a suit well. Of course, now she knew why, how she knew every inch of him. She had gotten exactly what she'd wanted and more. And she was both elated and nervous.

"Hey," she managed.

"Nightmare?" he asked. "Scary thought, if it was."

"No . . . no. I just woke suddenly, that's all."

"You were really tired."

"I guess."

"Well, you said we were supposed to be at your friend's house at eight."

"Yes! Well, thereabouts. What time is it now?"

"About seven-forty-five."

"Oh!" She jumped out of bed, heading for the bath, yet she had to pause. She walked back to him, frowning. "I'm sorry. I know you really didn't want to get involved, but I rather pushed the issue."

"Kelly!" His hands fell on her shoulders. "I'm not sorry in the least. I couldn't be. My God, let's leave it at this — I couldn't be. In fact, if you don't get into the shower and get some clothes on, I can be even less sorry, and then we'll be really late."

She smiled, turned and raced into the bathroom. In fifteen minutes she had taken a quick shower, dressed and put on a bit of makeup. He seemed somewhat surprised that she was ready so fast. Though he'd been at his computer in the sitting area, he shut down the moment he saw her, whistling. "That's a casual go-to-a-friend's-house dress?"

She frowned. It was just a black knit.

"It's at least six years old. Wash and wear."

"Wash and wear well," he murmured.

He escorted her out. At the elevator, they ran into a crowd of teenage girls. "Did you see him?" one of them was demanding of the other. She was thin as a rail, in jeans and a cropped tank top, with short ebony hair. The majority of her stomach was showing.

"Are you sure that was him?" another asked. Blonde and cute, she had long hair, a stylish cap and a zodiac sign tattooed on her shoulder.

"Of course! All the rock stars come to this hotel!" a brunette in a miniskirt declared.

"It was him!" the dark-haired girl insisted. Then she fell silent, seeing Doug and Kelly. She smiled a little awkwardly. "Sorry, but do you know if Rick Garrison is at this hotel?"

"I'm sorry, I don't know who he is," Kelly said.

"Lead guitarist for the Cobras, fairly new group," O'Casey informed her.

"Is he here?" the dark-haired girl asked.

"Sorry, I don't know," O'Casey said.

"Your rock star may be here," Kelly offered. The girls seemed sweet. "It's true, a lot of rock musicians stay at this hotel."

They had just stepped out on the lobby level when one of the girls began shouting "Oh, oh! I know it's him this time. It's Lance Morton!" the girl cried, in ecstasy.

Kelly's head jerked up. O'Casey was already looking across the lobby. The man to whom they were referring was headed out to the pool and garden bar area.

"Oh! Lance Morton! Yes, yes!" The girls started to move.

Kelly and Doug looked at each other. "Lance, here?" Doug said.

"Let's not hang around, please, in case it was Lance and he comes back," Kelly said.

"I wonder what he's doing here. Actually, I wonder why he's not here."

"What are you talking about?" Kelly asked.

"He's not staying here. Remember? I dropped him at his hotel last night. He's staying in Beverly Hills."

"Maybe he wanted to stay in Beverly Hills," Kelly said.

O'Casey had turned around and was looking toward the bar. "He's here now."

"It's a popular bar and he wants a drink," Kelly said, sighing. "O'Casey, please, let's have a nice night. I beg you, don't make a mystery out of every move someone makes!"

His attention returned to her and those magnetic eyes softened.

"Miss Trent, you're right. I'll speak with the valet and we'll be on the road. We'll have a great time at your friend's place and then we can come back here and —"

"No."

"No? That was it?" he asked politely. "Curiosity sated, all done?"

She shook her head, smiling. "I have Sam, remember? We'll have a nice time at my friend's house and then go back to my house. If you don't mind."

One of the very slow, rueful smiles she found so appealing curled onto his lips. "I don't mind at all. Frankly, all that white was beginning to feel a little too heavenly. And God forbid, I wouldn't want you thinking you were too much of a goddess."

She arched a brow. "All right, Adonis, let's go, shall we?"

"Adonis?" he queried.

"Goddess?" she said skeptically.

"Well, it was one hell of an afternoon," he murmured politely.

"And it's going to be a good night. A normal night," she said firmly.

"Yes, of course." He offered her his arm and led her out the front door of the hotel, where he asked the valet for his car. Yet, Kelly noted, despite his words that they would enjoy the evening, he was staring back toward the bar. And there was something about his expression that elicited a core of fear in the bottom of her heart.

Just as they arrived, Kelly said, "Please

don't tell them about the incident with the car today. They'll make something out of it and just go nuts worrying."

"Maybe something should have been made out of it."

She shook her head, distressed. "You don't understand, O'Casey. If I become a liability, no one will ever hire me for anything!"

"If you're dead, you won't have to worry about it," he warned her. "And these are your friends."

She shook her head. "Please don't say anything tonight."

The scene at Serena's house was exactly as Kelly had warned — wild. And delightful. Doug didn't like to think of himself as the star-struck type, but meeting Abby Sawyer could only be described as awesome. Her beauty was ageless, and her manner as charming as her looks. She was a doting grandmother, and apparently more than fond of Jennifer's brood, as well. There was nothing "Hollywood" about the gathering. Serena was in an apron, dangling her infant on her hip, able to prepare drinks while she shouted out to the patio to tell her husband that it was time to get the fire geared up. Doug met each of the kids in turn, laughing when he discovered that it was true, watching a toddler tear about probably demanded more energy than dancing the hottest salsa.

Besides the kids, there were the animals — a huge wolfhound and some kind of a fluffy little thing in the backyard, a massive cat on the rear of the sofa and love birds in a gorgeous antique cage.

Doug recognized Conar, Jennifer's husband, almost immediately, though he said nothing when they were introduced, reading that the man didn't want anything said. The actor had been in a number of top-rated movies and lauded in the papers for his choice of roles. But he was home now, just a husband and dad. He, too, was at the mercy of the kids. There were no housekeepers, cooks or attendants of any kind at the gathering.

Conar and Liam Murphy had apparently been friends for some time; there was an ease about their relationship. And when the children had been collected and tucked away in various beds, Doug found himself out on the porch where the two men were working the barbecue. He was glad. They were scoping him out, that much was evident. And it was all right. He already knew that there was a steely quality about Liam Murphy he liked. And Conar seemed made of the same stuff, entirely down-to-earth, bright, into and aware of the real world. There was some general conversation between them at first — politics, weather, sports. Then, as he pushed foil-wrapped potatoes around on the barbecue, Liam said, "So, you went from being a cop to being a dance instructor slash competitor."

Taken off guard, Doug froze slightly, then shrugged. The guy was a P.I. And he and his wife had a deep friendship with Kelly. Naturally, he'd been checked out by this crew.

"That's right."

"Interesting change in careers."

"I know."

"You hated being a cop?"

"I loved being a cop."

Conar and Liam exchanged glances. Liam cleared his throat. "Are you, uh . . ."

"He wants to know if you're gay," Conar said. "Which would be fine, of course."

"He does have damned good clothes," Liam said ruefully.

"Heterosexual. It's not a requirement in dance to be gay, you know."

Both men reddened. "Lord, I didn't mean . . ." Conar muttered.

"It's all right," Doug said. "Some of the

most talented people in the business are gay. I just don't happen to be. Sorry, you caught me a little by surprise there, knowing about my previous employment."

"But you've got your private investigator's license now, too, right?" Liam asked.

Doug shrugged. "Sure. I've got the license. I have a brother who's a P.I. and, naturally, lots of friends still on the force."

Again Conar and Liam glanced at each other. Doug was glad to feel that he was passing muster. "Is there a problem?" he asked, because they seemed to be holding something back.

"Problem?" Conar said.

"Hell, no," Liam said.

"Frankly, we're relieved," Conar told him.

Doug's brows shot up.

"I think Kelly is blind to possible danger," Liam said.

"She is," Doug agreed.

"So we're glad she has an ex-cop dance teacher," Liam said with a shrug.

Doug was seated on a patio bench by the wall and he stretched against it. "If someone is after her — and managed to rig something on the location set when the soap was filming — wouldn't that someone have to be associated with the soap?"

"We had some serious incidents that involved the soap several years ago. Since then, everyone has been checked out big-time," Liam said.

"What about this Joe Penny?" Doug asked.

"Joe? He'd be the last person in the world to hurt Kelly. He was delighted with the response her character was drawing in. The soap was flying high. It must be killing him to have her off the set," Conar replied.

"I agree with that one," Liam said.

"The possibilities are endless. Kelly has gotten a lot of crackpot mail. Then the earth crumbles, and that's that. Accident. Coincidence. Maybe, no matter how good a front the guy is putting up, Dana Sumter *was* killed by her husband. And the woman in Ohio was simply an abuser of drugs and alcohol. Maybe we're all a bunch of alarmists," Conar said with a shrug.

"Actually, I'm glad she's going to be working in Miami," Liam said. "At least she'll be out of here for a while."

"Away from accidents," Conar said.

Despite Kelly's words, Doug was tempted to tell them about the car that had nearly run Kelly over. For the moment, he decided to remain silent. Liam had said something that made sense. Kelly did seem

273

in safer territory when she was out of L.A.

"Maybe we should go back early," Doug murmured.

"Might not be a bad idea," Liam agreed. "Anyway, I'll know more after tomorrow."

"What's happening tomorrow?" Doug asked.

"I've got permission to interview Sumter."

"The husband?" Doug said.

Liam nodded, then shrugged. "I've got friends in the right places."

"Any possibility I could tag along?"

Liam looked at him, then shrugged again. "I'm going early. I'm out of here by seven."

"Look, like you said, I was a cop. I've still got some instincts, and I'm going to be around Kelly a lot now. I don't care what time it is, I'd like to tag along and meet the guy."

"All right, you're on," Liam said.

"Lord, he's really great!" Serena said, adding the mushrooms Jennifer had just sliced to the salad she was fixing.

"I like him," Abby, in charge of garnishes for the serving plates, informed Kelly sagely.

"Great body," Jennifer said.

274

"Great butt," Serena agreed.

"Girls!" Abby admonished, grinning. "It is a great butt," she told Kelly.

"There's more to a man than a body!" Kelly said.

"Well, of course there is!" Serena said impatiently. "Much more. And there should be much more. You're the baby in this group, but eventually we all age and our looks fade. What's important in life is companionship, dreams, ethics! But a great butt doesn't hurt."

"You know, guys, I haven't known him long at all," Kelly said.

Serena flashed a glance at Jennifer, who gave a knowing smile.

"What was that all about?" Kelly demanded.

"Nothing," Serena said.

Abby calmly placed a piece of parsley on a platter. "It means, dear, that they're both certain you've already slept with the man. And that it's not such a bad thing, because they believe they've acquired excellent instincts over the years and they think he's okay. Therefore, you're all right."

"Mother!" Jennifer protested.

Abby turned to give them all her sweet smile. "Am I wrong?" she demanded.

Jennifer and Serena were silent.

Abby looked at Kelly. "They're still a little wet behind the ears. I, on the other hand, have been around a long time. From what I've seen, I like the boy. I tend to be among the paranoid myself, since I've had to learn a few hard lessons during my journey through the years. But look at him out there, fitting right in with Conar and Liam, two fellows who have known each other for ages. And there's your boy, holding his own. Hang on to him, Kelly."

Kelly shook her head, smiling. "Abby, he's really not mine to hang on to. This is a working arrangement. And a short one at that. I think the video is slated to finish in five days. Budgets, you know. Then . . . well, hell, I don't know what I'm doing, but he'll go back to his world."

"And just what is his world?" Abby persisted.

"Well, he teaches. And dances on a professional circuit of some kind."

"I see," Abby said, studying Kelly. "Still, hang on to him, dear."

"He's just a nice guy."

Serena spun around, leaning against the sink, studying Kelly. "Hmm. But you have this glow about you now. Doesn't she, Jen?"

Jennifer whispered something to Serena

and Kelly was pretty sure that Jen said, *"Freshly fucked glow, huh?"*

"Jennifer!" Abby remonstrated. "There's never a need to use trucker language!"

"I didn't!" Jennifer said.

"Jennifer, my hearing is excellent."

"Excellent! Selective is more like it, Mom!"

Kelly groaned. "I'll take those platters out so the guys can start filling them up."

"Kelly," Abby said, "don't let those two gooses get to you. That one is a keeper."

"But not really mine to keep."

"Let's leave her alone, shall we?" Serena inquired. "Just so long as he's with her now, when all this is going on."

"Well, that's something we all agree on!" Abby said.

"Great. Good. Then maybe we could have dinner and talk about everything in the world *but* me and whether I'm having sex or not!" Kelly exclaimed.

"Sure," Serena said, smiling slightly.

"We'd never dream of asking for details," Jennifer said.

"Not in mixed company," Serena agreed.

"No. We'll do it later," Jennifer assured her.

"I think I hear a baby crying," Kelly said.

"Mine?" Serena asked.

"One of mine?" Jennifer demanded.

They looked at each other, then both started out of the kitchen. Kelly winked at Abby, who grinned and winked back.

They did talk about Kelly's situation, but even then, not until they were picking up the plates after dessert. Then Serena said, "Kelly, I don't like you at that house alone."

"I'm not alone," she protested, "I have Sam."

"Sam is a dog. You know that I adore him, but . . . I don't like you being alone."

"Serena, I've lived alone for a long time."

"I can stay out there," Doug said softly.

Kelly tried not to blush.

"I think you should both stay here tonight," Serena said.

"Serena, I have to go home! Besides, I can't very well move in for the rest of my life," Kelly said.

"Tonight, you should just stay here," Serena said.

"I can't leave Sam in the house alone, and Doug has said that he'll stay. You've got a crowded house right now, Serena."

"Hey, we're heading out," Jennifer said.

"Collecting the kids, the creatures, and heading on out."

"Am I a kid or a creature?" Abby asked.

"Sorry, Mom," Jennifer said.

"Serena, it just wouldn't make sense —"

"It would make perfect sense. Doug is heading out with Liam first thing in the morning," Serena said.

Startled, Kelly looked at O'Casey. "You are? Where are you two off to? Golf?" she asked.

He didn't exactly answer her, but she didn't realize that until later. "I'll go to your house and get Sam, if that's all right with you."

"Perfect!" Serena said.

"Serena, I don't have anything with me — "

"Oh, as if you can't wear my clothes!"

"Actually, it doesn't sound like such a bad idea," O'Casey said.

Kelly was more than a little surprised and certainly puzzled by his agreement. She had thought that he'd want to be alone — with just her. But in the frenzy to get Jennifer, the twins, her little boy, her dogs and her mom out, Doug also disappeared.

Alone in the entry with Liam and Serena, Kelly stared at them, frowning.

"Okay, where is O'Casey?"

"He went to get Sam."

"How?"

"I gave him the key I keep here," Serena said.

"But Serena —"

"But Kelly!" Liam said firmly. "You're better off here."

"Don't worry. You have connecting guest rooms," Serena said.

"That's not the point."

"I'll bet it is."

"I can't move in with you!"

"Just for tonight," Liam told her. "Your fellow and I are leaving early."

"And I should be afraid in the morning, in broad daylight?"

"We never know when we should be afraid, do we?" Liam asked. He kissed Serena lightly on the lips. "Mind if I go on up?"

She smiled, shaking her head. "Check on the baby, huh?"

"Absolutely," he said, and headed up the stairs.

Kelly stared at Serena. "I'm a big girl. And I won't be idiotically afraid if you people don't make me so!"

"We people love you. What? Is it a horror to stay at my house?"

Kelly shook her head. "Of course not. It's just that I'll have to go on living on my own. I don't want to get to the point where I'm afraid in my own home."

"Look, it's just for tonight, okay?"

"Sure you don't want to come to Florida with me?" Kelly asked.

"Oh, you'll be fine in Florida," Serena said with a wave of her hand.

"Oh?" Kelly inquired politely.

"Well, he'll watch after you. Doug, I mean. And since he was a cop —"

"What?"

"He was a cop. He never told you?"

"No, but I should have figured. All the signs were there."

"Well, it's a good thing. Why are you angry?" Serena asked.

"I'm not angry."

"Yes, you are. Anyway, it means he can protect you. And the fact that you're going to be protected shouldn't make you angry."

"It doesn't!"

"But you *are* angry."

"I'm not. And the fact that he was a cop doesn't really mean anything now."

Serena shrugged. "Well, yes and no. At least he can legally be armed."

"As an *ex*-cop?"

"Well, of course not. He's a licensed private investigator, just like Liam."

"What?"

"You didn't know that, either?"

"No, and how did you know it?"

"Well, Liam looked him up, of course!"

Kelly *really* should have figured. She didn't know why she was so angry herself. As Serena said, wasn't it a good thing?

Yes. And no. Because she had the odd feeling that he was only with her — that he had only taken the job — because her situation intrigued him! His instincts had kicked in. She was a possible case. No wonder he was seeing culprits wherever he looked! She should have known! He had such an edge.

There was a knock at the door. She heard Sam woofing. Serena stepped past her, opening the front door.

"Sam!"

He was ready to jump. He loved Serena. "Down, boy, I'll give you love on your own level, how's that?" Serena asked, hunkering down. She scratched and petted Sam, and he accepted her affection but then bounded past her to Kelly. Kelly lowered herself to the dog's level as well, staring over Sam at O'Casey.

He knew right away that something was

wrong, but he didn't say anything, listening instead as Serena said she'd show him his room.

"Come on, boy, we're heading to *our* room," Kelly said.

O'Casey gave her the slightest hike of a brow. Serena didn't even notice the expression. Kelly went up the stairs ahead of them. She had, at times, stayed with Serena before, when she had a flight and either Serena or Liam were giving her a ride to the airport. She went straight to her own space, entered the room with Sam and made a point of locking the door.

In the room, she paced. Fifteen minutes later, she heard the connecting door open. O'Casey entered, closed it and leaned against it, crossing his arms over his chest. "All right. What?"

"You're a cop!" she spat out.

He frowned. "*Was* a cop. What's wrong with that?"

"You never told me."

"You never asked."

"*And*," she informed him, "you have a private investigator's license!"

"Yeah."

"You never told me that, either."

"You never asked."

"Who the hell asks a dance teacher if

he's a P.I. on the side?" she demanded.

"What difference does it make?" he asked her.

She shook her head. "I'm not a person to you," she said at last. "I'm . . . I'm a curiosity, a possible piece of excitement!"

"Well, actually, you're very exciting," he murmured.

"That's not what I mean and you know it."

"Look, I never meant to keep anything from you. You never asked and the subject never came up." He hesitated. "Honestly, I didn't know that you didn't know. Your manager, Ally Bassett, knew. Shannon O'Casey, my brother's wife and the head of the studio, apparently told Ally that I'd been a cop. I just assumed you knew."

"Well, it makes me very uncomfortable."

"Are you aware that you're shouting?" he asked, his eyes narrowing.

"I am not."

"You'll wake the baby," he warned her.

"No, I won't. Sam and I are going to sleep now."

"Fine."

To her surprise, he didn't push the matter at all. He turned, exited the room and closed the door softly behind him.

Sam whined, thudding his stump of a

tail nervously on the floor.

"We don't need him," Kelly told the dog. But we do! she thought. No! Everything she had said tonight was true. Everything she had felt. Being in a music video had never really meant anything to him, she could tell. She had read that clearly about him. He had only taken on the job because he'd been told about the threats made against her.

"Sleep, Sam. We're going to sleep."

She shimmied out of her black knit dress and into one of the long old T-shirts Serena kept in the drawer for her, then crawled into bed. She lay wide awake, staring at the ceiling. Sam crawled up by her feet.

"You are the best protection in the world, you know," she told him softly. "And the best friend." And he was, of course. But . . . he wasn't a man. He wasn't O'Casey. He didn't have the amazing combination of muscles and grace, toughness and elegance, and . . .

Face it, she couldn't remember the last time she'd actually had what could be called a relationship. The right person just hadn't come along. She didn't go to bars and she didn't go bowling. And she hadn't had sex in . . . forever.

She winced, not ready to cast aside pride and forgive him. She had been taken. Subtly. And it hurt. And she didn't want to hurt more than she was already hurting.

She closed her eyes, wishing that the door would open again. That he would just burst in, ask no questions, scoop her up, hold her, touch her, excite her. But he wouldn't. He was O'Casey.

She could get up herself, but she'd rather die. And in a way, she felt like she *was* dying.

Then, to her amazement, the door opened. He was still in his dress pants, but shirtless. She could see the way the moonlight glowed on his chest and shoulders. He walked over to the bed, looked down at her. She could see his features, could read the taut form of his body.

Sam whined and wagged his tail. "It's all right, Sam," he said softly.

"It is?" Kelly inquired.

"Look, no commitment, no involvement. That's what you said you wanted, right?"

"I —"

"You pushed it today. Now it's my turn, my room. Sam can stay here."

"What?"

She was amazed when he did reach down and scoop her up, covers and all, dislodging Sam, who didn't seem to mind re-adjusting.

"All right, now. You've really got some nerve. I didn't pick you up!"

"You can't pick me up, that's the only difference."

"I beg to differ!"

"Shut up."

"What!"

"Sorry. Don't make so much noise. You'll wake the baby, remember?"

"You really do have a bloody nerve."

"So do you," he replied. "It was all right for you to strip to a robe in my hotel, so I guess I can be a bit on the aggressive side."

With that he turned and walked to the connecting door. " 'Night, Sam," he said, and closed the door with his foot. Inside he asked, "Any objections?"

"No. Not as long as the lines are drawn and we know each other for who we are."

"And do we?" he asked.

"I think so."

"I don't. I'm beginning to think that I don't really know you at all."

"But it doesn't matter, does it?"

"Not if that's the way you want it."

She bit her lip, ready to protest, but her heart was already thundering. She could feel his warmth, both the sensuality and security of his arms. And she didn't want to return to a room without him. She didn't want to let him go, didn't want to stop feeling everything that was racing through her. Without speaking, she reached up and threaded her fingers into his hair, drawing his lips to her. Her kiss was angry, almost violent.

"So, no objections?" he queried softly.

"What if I did?"

"They'd be rather hypocritical, but . . . no objections?"

Objections? Was he mad?

Somehow she managed a modicum of dignity in her reply. "I don't intend to say a word."

"Well, actually, I like my women to make a little noise," he murmured.

The next thing she knew was the feel of the mattress at her back and the man above her. And in the darkness, she didn't dwell on fact, fear or anger. Only on him.

Lance Morton sat in his own car that night, heedless of the fact that he had parked right in front of Kelly's house. He really didn't drink a lot. Nor, considering the fact that he was in the business he was — suddenly finding success and being offered all kinds of pills, booze and women

— was he a pill-popper or a womanizer.

Tonight, though, he just sat there in his rental car, staring at the house and finding that he was angry. He was the rock star, for God's sake! Didn't she have any idea how many groupies he could have with the snap of his fingers? No. There was so much she just didn't seem to realize.

He had waited before, thinking that she'd come home and he'd make his presence very well known. He'd apologize, assure her that he never meant to say a word about the night before. But she hadn't come home.

Then the dance teacher had shown up, the overgrown tackle. Lance had made sure the guy didn't see him. He'd slunk down almost to the floor.

Doug O'Casey had gone into her house — with a key! He'd come out with the dog and left again. It was then that Lance had driven his car even closer. Then he had broken out the beer.

Time passed. Eventually a cop car came around. He slunk deep down into his seat again, making it appear as if the car was empty. The cruiser went on by and Lance straightened. At last he looked at his watch and swore at the hour.

He twisted the key in the ignition,

bringing the car to life. The last thing he needed or wanted was to be arrested for having open booze in his car. But as he drove down the street, he thought about what he had seen.

The dog was gone. The house was really empty.

He jerked to a halt, turned the car around and drove back.

Chapter 16

Harvey Sumter looked like hell. His hair, what there was of it, was all but standing on end. He'd had a transplant at some time in his life, but it hadn't taken well. Now, as he entered, his fingers rose to his head. The man was, literally, all but tearing his hair out. He had a scruffy growth of beard, and the orange uniform he had been given to wear seemed to hang on his body.

His attorney was present, as was Detective Olsen, an old-timer who had been around the block a dozen times. He had seen the dregs of humanity, yet managed to come out of it all with something of a heart left and certainly a soul. He respected the work of technicians and scientists, but knew that it was a cop's perseverance and gut instinct that could bring in the suspect to make the forensics work. He had looked Doug over with an eagle eye and seemed to accept Liam's word that he was licensed and had a legitimate interest in the situation.

When Harvey Sumter was brought into the interview room with the single table and four chairs, the guard intended to leave the man's shackles on his wrists. Liam asked that they be taken off.

The guard took a look at the men in the room, then shrugged and did so.

Harvey took a seat, looking like a beaten man. At first, he didn't even seem curious about his visitors. He nodded listlessly at the introductions.

"Harvey, I'm here to tell you that you don't have to give any answers you don't want to give," the attorney warned.

Harvey waved a hand in the air. "My story isn't changing. I've told the truth from the beginning."

"What is your story, Mr. Sumter?" Liam asked.

Sumter looked around at last, noting Olsen with a nod, then Liam and Doug. He was obviously a fairly intelligent, educated man, his speech crisp and clear, as if he had been a professor or lecturer in an earlier life.

"Who are you people?" he asked. "Not you, Detective," he said to Olsen. "I know who you are, all right. But you two."

"They're private investigators," Olsen explained.

"I get two of you?" Sumter said dryly, amused. "I didn't hire you, did I?" He frowned, looking at his attorney.

"You didn't hire either one of us," Liam said. "We actually have other interests that include death threats to another party."

"The point is," Doug put in, "we're open to the fact that you might not be guilty, Mr. Sumter."

"Hallelujah!" Sumter said. "Funny thing about Dana — and there wasn't much that was fun about her, I can tell you. She meant to make me pay when she was alive, so she must be laughing in her grave right now. Sorry that sounds bitter, but I am bitter. Hell, yes, she was the queen of the bitches. God forgive me for speaking ill of the dead, but I've got kids. Grown up now, but my daughter's trying to believe me. My son . . . oh, God. I just wouldn't have done it, no matter how I hated her. Hell, I wouldn't kill anyone. I couldn't kill anyone. It just isn't in me."

"Well, now, Mr. Sumter," Detective Olsen said. "Most men — and women, for that matter — have a point they can come to where they can kill. For some, it's protecting their own lives, for others, the life of a loved one. But for some, it's just a point of anger and frustration so great, they can't abide it anymore."

"I hated my ex-wife, that's no secret," Sumter said flatly. "But I didn't kill her. And I will deny it until the day I die."

"Your prints were in the house."

"Of course. I still saw her, now and then. We kept up a decent front. It was her idea. Appearances were everything to Dana. And we had children."

"You have no alibi for the night she was killed."

He lifted his hands. "I'm not a young guy. It's not like I go to clubs and women fall all over me. I was home, watching television."

"But there is no one who can verify that fact," Olsen said.

Sumter looked at him, then slowly shook his head. "She's got me, hasn't she?" he asked softly. "I'm an innocent man, but I'll be convicted. I'll go to the chair. If I don't, I'll spend the rest of my life in prison."

"Look, Mr. Sumter, I don't think your wife got herself brutally murdered just to get even with you," Doug said. "Did you know of any threats made against her?"

Sumter laughed. "Hundreds of them.

Maybe thousands. Actually, she was gleeful about the amount of hate mail she received!"

"Can you tell us anything that could help find the real killer you believe is out there?" Liam asked.

Sumter moaned and brought his hands to his face. "God! Don't you think I'd have spoken by now? I've tried and tried to remember any little thing she might have said, anything . . . The thing is, I didn't do it. I just didn't do it. But I don't know how in hell to prove that I didn't." He shook his head, then looked up from his attorney to Olsen, Doug and then Liam. "I swear before God Almighty, I didn't kill her. I'm guilty of a hell of a lot, but not that. I didn't murder Dana."

Olsen pushed back his chair. He nodded to Sumter and then to his attorney. "Thank you for agreeing to see us."

"Can you help me?" Sumter asked hopefully. "I don't know what a P.I. costs. I don't know what I've got, but my kids — well, one of my kids would help."

"You don't need to hire anyone, Mr. Sumter," Liam said. "We have an interest in this case."

"You'll help me then?" A desperate hope remained in the man's eyes.

"If being determined that we find the truth is helping you, then yes," Doug told the man.

Sumter rose, as if he'd discovered a new-found dignity, or a reason for living at any rate. "Thank you," he said quietly. Then he walked over to the waiting guard and offered his hands up for the cuffs.

"Why didn't he get bail?" Doug asked as they left the holding cells.

"The judge thought it was one of the most heinous crimes she'd ever witnessed," Olsen explained.

Doug arched a brow. "I don't mean to discredit the violence of a strangling, but worse criminals have received bail."

"The fellow killed the dog with one kick to the head. The judge is an animal lover. I'll be in touch if I learn anything, Liam. Mr. O'Casey, a pleasure. If you learn anything, either of you, I'd definitely better hear about it!" He walked to his car, leaving them in the parking lot.

"Gruff fellow," Doug commented.

"He's all right."

"I imagine. What was your take?"

"He's either innocent or a damned good actor."

"Better than half the men on screen," Doug agreed.

"So you think he's innocent?" Liam asked.

"Yep."

"Too bad," Liam murmured.

"Why?"

"I agree with you."

"Well, it's good for Sumter. If he can be proven innocent, anyway."

"Yeah, good for Sumter. Bad for . . . well, others, since that means there is a killer on the loose out there."

They started for Liam's car. "Are you going to tell Kelly about this visit?"

"Haven't you already told her?" Doug asked dryly.

"She thinks we're golfing."

"Where does Serena think we are?"

"Here."

"Kelly will know," Doug told him.

"Yeah, guess you're right. So, what are you going to do?"

"Head back to Florida."

"It's probably a good idea. But what if the Ohio woman *was* killed by the same man?"

"You're sure it's a man, right?"

"Unless it's a woman who happens to be with the World Wrestling Entertainment," Liam said dryly. "It takes some strength to strangle someone the way Dana Sumter was snuffed out."

"Good point. But the thing is, Dana Sumter was definitely killed here in California. In Florida, at least Kelly is away from the soap. And it was on the soap that her accident occurred, so . . ."

"Florida. It's the smartest move," Liam agreed.

The tango. Body contact as close as one could get, not even the clothing in between seeming to help much. It was a strange feeling. She felt that she knew him incredibly well, intimately well. But she had been really angry that morning. She didn't know if Serena was supposed to keep the men's destination a secret, but she hadn't managed to do so.

To her credit, Serena was at a loss. She felt that Kelly should be thanking her lucky stars that her dance teacher had turned out to be the next best thing to a personal bodyguard. Better than a bodyguard, because, in her experience, bodyguards weren't always the most brilliant of men.

Kelly hadn't said a word when they had returned. Not a word. Serena had asked them about Harvey Sumter. Liam had replied that in his opinion, the man might well be telling the truth. O'Casey hadn't offered an opinion. After brunch, he had told her that if she was feeling up it, they should head to the studio. It was agreed that Sam would stay with Serena for the afternoon.

Once there, O'Casey became all business. Kelly missed a step, her concentration off.

"Sorry."

"It's all right," O'Casey said, breaking off to start the music over again. By the stereo system, he paused, his back to her. "You know, you can still have me taken off the project. It would make Lance happy, I'm sure."

"Do you want to be taken off the project?" she asked.

"You know I don't."

"I actually seem to be learning the tango," Kelly told him. "Why would I have you taken off?"

"I just want you to remember that it's your call."

"Actually, I'm not the producer, financier or casting director," she said sweetly.

He turned to look at her. "A word from your lips to Marc Logan's ear and it would be as if God had spoken."

"Perhaps."

"Ah, what power you have!"

"Can we get back to work?"

"Sure. Actually, you work well when you're mad."

"I'm not mad."

He ignored her and walked back. In a perfect stance, he waited for her to come into position. He counted as they moved. "Heel leads!"

She gritted her teeth, wondering how he could look directly in front of himself and see her feet. Mirrors, of course. "Nose forward, toes forward."

"They are!"

"The head doesn't turn until we snap around."

"Right."

"We should go to Florida tonight."

"What?" She tripped over her own feet. Drawing away, she frowned.

"We should get out of here. Tonight. I can make the arrangements."

"I can't leave tonight."

"Why not?"

"I have to be in the sound studio on Monday."

He frowned, and she realized that he had forgotten that fact.

"I'm going with you."

"I'm not so sure you should."

"Why not?"

"Well, if you'll recall, you tackled Lance Morton."

"If you'll recall, I also gave him a ride home that night."

"He could still get nasty about it," Kelly warned.

"I could get nasty right back. When you think someone is attacking someone else, you don't usually give them time to pull a gun, a knife or make a run for it," he said dryly.

"That's right. You were a cop, and now you're a P.I. It could be a series. Half drama, half sitcom. The *Dancing P.I.* has a ring to it."

"Would you please just get over it?" he demanded, annoyed.

"Right. I won't mention it again," Kelly said sweetly. "Tango. My nose and my toes facing the same direction. Contra body movement."

He broke away, going to start the music over one more time. "I am coming with you."

"Do what you want."

He walked back to her. She slipped into position.

"How long does it take?" he asked.

"How long does what take?"

"Recording."

"Maybe an hour, maybe several. We'll have to see exactly what the musical director wants."

"Isn't it what Lance Morton wants?"

"Theoretically, yes. But I would imagine he's taken a lot of other people's money, so . . ."

"Got it."

"It can be very boring," Kelly warned.

"I can be very patient."

She made a wrong turn, misreading his lead, and collided with him, crunching down hard on his toes. He barely winced.

"Sorry," she murmured.

"You're not feeling for the lead."

"Yes, I am."

"All right. I'm not supposed to be strong-arming you out here. You need to learn to understand what my movements mean."

"I'm trying. Believe me, I'm trying."

He broke away from her. "That's enough for today."

"Sorry, I guess I was horrible."

His back was to her. He'd gone to turn off the stereo. He turned and faced her reflectively. "Actually, you're still doing really well. Your turns are coming along nicely, getting very sharp. You're an excellent student. Which is good, since time is limited."

"Well, thanks," she murmured.

A little embarrassed, she headed out of the studio quickly. He locked the door, calling out to her. "Wait up!" She waited impatiently.

"It isn't dark yet!" she told him. "This is a public lot. On a busy street."

He walked straight up to her, obviously irritated, challenging and aggressive, in her space.

"Let's see, you fall down a cliff and are nearly run over. Two big-time near fatalities on one life. Then, let's see, there's a man sitting in prison who doesn't appear to be a killer. I'd say it doesn't matter much whether it's light or dark, day or night. You need to watch it."

She put her hands on her hips and stared back at him. "An asteroid could fall out of the sky!"

"It could, but none of the space agencies have reported such a danger," he said smoothly. "While it was just yesterday that you were nearly run over."

She was startled when he dropped her at Serena's house and didn't come in. "I've got some errands to run," he told her.

"You might want to remember, my car isn't here."

"I'll be back."

"I can get Liam or Serena to give me a ride."

"No. I'll be back."

She sighed, looking away.

"Does it really hurt to be safe?" he demanded angrily.

She stared at him again. "No." *It hurts to know what your real interest is!*

"I'll be back," he said more softly.

She nodded. "I'll be here."

"Thank you," he said.

She hesitated, then sighed. "No . . . I guess, thank you." She turned quickly and headed into the house.

Doug went up to his room to make the call. He didn't intend to use the hotel phone, he always made his calls on his cell. But his room was private and quiet.

Quinn answered after two rings.

"Did you find out anything?" Doug asked.

"Yes and no. I flew to Ohio myself last night," he said.

"Yeah?"

"Nothing like on-hands experience. I went over everything I could with the Sandusky boys."

"And?"

"If they come up with a suspect, they'll

be hard-pressed to make any kind of charge stick. The autopsy definitely found that death was caused by drowning. But there was no sign whatsoever that she was forced under. Nothing under the nails. No bruises. Just a mixture of booze and alcohol in her system. The coroner is convinced that she passed out and slipped under."

"Accident."

"Or suicide," Quinn said. "Or a killer that was damned clever."

"There's that, yes."

"Anything on your end?"

"Yeah. I got in to see Harvey Sumter."

"And?"

"He's convincing."

"A lot of killers — especially when they feel justified about a crime — can be convincing."

"I know."

"But . . ."

"He's still convincing."

"Anything else you need?" Quinn asked.

"You looked up everything you could about the cast and crew of *Valentine Valley*?"

"Yeah, and the truth even read like a soap. I can imagine they're very gun-shy on that set. Murder, mayhem — they've had it all in the past. And I don't mean just in the scripts."

"Yes, I've heard. But what about the people still involved?"

"The actors all check out. Some of the crew members come and go, so it's difficult to get a real feel for the entire situation. The heads have been a little slimy at times, but they were all cleared when it came to any violent crime or even any suggestion of violent crime. We're looking at drugs, sex and plain old bad behavior, but nothing that would indicate anyone there suddenly freaked out and decided Kelly was really her character."

"Thanks."

"All right. When you coming home?"

"I'm trying for Monday night." He hesitated. "Kelly was nearly run down yesterday."

"Run down?"

Doug described the incident to his brother and said, "So . . . someone's out to kill her? Or a lousy driver?"

"I think you're right. You should come home as soon as possible," Quinn said.

"Dana Sumter's husband said something that got me thinking about her."

"And that was?"

"About how important appearances were

to her. Which makes me think we ought to be delving more deeply into her past. Will you see what you can dig up on her for me? And I don't mean recent stuff. I think it might pay to go way back, high school days, even."

"I'll do more digging and get what I can," Quinn promised. "Keep in touch."

"Yeah . . . hey, wait. Do me another favor. Find out everything you can about the band, Kill Me Quick. I read a number of pages on them, but I want what's behind the stuff that's public knowledge."

"All right."

"Hey, one more!"

"Shoot."

"Her agent, Mel Alton."

"I thought the man was her best friend."

"He is, but it never hurts to know more about your friends, right?"

He rang off with Quinn and logged on to his own computer. His concentration grew as he went from Web page to Web page. Anything he could find on the band itself, specifically Lance Morton, was trite and packaged, so he moved on to Dana Sumter's sites — and there were plenty. Nothing caught his eye at first. Then he noticed that there seemed to be a year missing out of her life, right when she should have been going from high school to college. *Curious.*

He quickly went through a number of other sites. Anyone who had attempted a bio on her had come up with years for all of her academic pursuits and achievements. Except one. *What had she been doing that year? And did it mean anything?*

He went on to another site, one that actually listed her representation through the years. Staring at the computer screen, he froze. Why the hell hadn't he known this?

He was startled when the room phone rang. "Hello?"

"It's me, Kelly."

"Hey."

"Did you forget me?"

"Not likely," he murmured.

He heard her yawning. "It's nearly midnight."

"You're kidding."

"Not likely," she told him.

"Look, I'm really sorry. I can be there —"

"It's all right. Sam is my big concern, but he's here with me. Don't worry about getting me."

"I'll be right there."

"It's all right. Honestly. I'm just going to go to bed. I'm really tired. Good night."

The line went dead. He stared at it for several seconds, then rose. The information he had gathered from a ceaseless reading of Web pages raced like wildfire through his mind. But there was nothing he could do with it at the moment. And Kelly had called.

Liam was still up when he reached the house. And though Doug had been afraid he was going to feel like an idiot standing on the porch, Liam seemed to think it the most natural thing in the world that he had arrived.

"Sorry, I didn't realize how late it had gotten. I'm surprised you're still up," Doug said.

"One of the twins decided I needed to do a little walking," Liam told him with a shrug.

"I didn't wake any of the kids, did I?"

"No, but if one of them does wake up, I might let you do a little walking."

"Not a problem," Doug told him.

Liam yawned. "Make yourself at home. I'm going up."

"Actually, I've got a question for you."

"Shoot."

"Did you know that Mel Alton represented Dana Sumter twenty years ago, when she was just getting started?"

"No." Liam frowned. "How did you find that out?"

"It's on one of her Web pages."

Liam looked sheepish. "I went through a lot of those Web pages."

"There are dozens of them, and I found the info only on one. Also, she's missing a year from her life. Right after high school. She got her diploma, but her college entry is listed a year later. And there's no mention anywhere of what she was doing then. Waitressing? Seeing Europe? It's as if she dropped off the face of the earth for that year."

"I'll see what I can find out. And I'll tell them down at the station, see if they can find anything out."

"Thanks. Let's get some sleep, for now."

"Yeah."

Liam yawned again and started up the stairs. Doug followed. On the second-floor landing, Liam bid him good-night. Doug went into his own assigned room, hoping he'd see Kelly sleeping there. She wasn't. He walked to the dividing door, opened it and tiptoed in.

Sam, who was at the foot of Kelly's bed, wagged his tail. Doug patted the dog's head, warning him to silence. "She's sleeping, boy. I don't want to wake her."

And she was sleeping. Soundly, so it appeared. Even in sleep, she was a mass of contradictions. With her eyes closed, she looked young and very innocent. But the richness of the sweep of lashes over her cheeks seemed to hint at the seductress in her. Then there was all that hair — red, splayed out like a sheet of silk, deep and luxurious. She was wearing a simple T-shirt, but the soft cotton molded to her form. On Kelly, the garment was the most erotic lingerie ever conceived.

He hesitated where he stood, thinking that he should leave her be. He really didn't want to wake her. "What do you think, Sam?" he whispered.

The dog wagged his tail again.

"You're with me, huh? You think it's okay?"

The tail thumped, so Doug silently slipped out of his shoes, socks, shirt and pants. He carefully moved back the covers and climbed in next to her. Sam adjusted, allowing him room. Doug lay in the darkness, studying her face. A few moments later, she moved, gravitating toward him. When she turned her back on him, he slipped an arm around her. She moved into the curve of his body, still sound asleep, and yet more comfortable against him. Soft, warm. He stared up at the ceiling, holding her, hoping that the warmth didn't become too much. Then it didn't matter. He was glad just to sleep beside her.

Chapter 17

Mel Alton met them at the sound studios. If he was surprised to see Doug escorting Kelly, he didn't show it. Doug didn't know a great deal about recording, but he was pretty sure that the place was state-of-the-art. The entry lobby was grandiose, with music symbols designed into the rich carpeting, lots of hardwood and a huge open ceiling overhead at the entry that allowed a view of the lofty studios on the second floor.

"Kelly, Doug, good morning," Mel said cheerfully. He grinned at the receptionist. "I'll take them up from here, Sheila."

"Sure thing, Mr. Alton," Sheila told him.

An elevator took them up to the second floor, where they went to the green room. It was supplied with bagels, croissants, coffee, tea and a machine that made cappuccinos, espressos or lattes at the press of a button.

"What do you think?" Mel asked.

"Nice place," Doug said.

"I have to admit, very impressive," Kelly said.

"Marc Logan started it about three years ago, mainly to service his own label. I don't think he ever intended to make money on music, he was just one of those people who had always been an armchair musician. When the studios were completed, though, they came into high demand. It's strange, some people just have the knack. Logan got into this for his own amusement, but he's already making money. Go figure," Mel said. "Croissant, anyone? This whole spread is for you, Kelly."

She arched a brow. "Aren't the boys in the band due in?"

"They're not on call until twelve. Kelly, you don't need to sing with people, you know that. They're just laying your tracks this morning," Mel explained. He turned to Doug. "She's still a theater girl at heart. She was just a baby when she started on *Valentine Valley*, but before that, my girl was in a major production of *Annie*."

Doug looked at Kelly, arching a brow. "Live theater."

"It will always remain my favorite venue in the world," she informed him coolly.

"I didn't know you'd done live theater," he said.

"Well, we all have pasts, don't we?" she inquired politely. "What I'd really like right now is tea with lemon. Anyone see tea bags?"

"Right here," Mel told her. "And the hot water is . . . there."

As Kelly made tea, Doug helped himself to juice and coffee.

"Kelly, Ally called me about your return to Miami. The island is booked as of Thursday, so I thought a flight out tomorrow or Wednesday would give you a few days to get there and relax."

"I booked our flights," Doug said. "We're out of here tonight."

Mel stared at him with surprise. Despite the reserve and distance she had put between them since finding out about his past, Kelly hadn't seemed irritated that Doug had taken the matter in hand, nor annoyed that they were going so quickly. Maybe she thought that he would ease off once they were in Miami.

"You made the arrangements?" Mel said to Doug.

"I happened to be online and checked flights. Kelly is bringing Sam, you know. He had to be booked as well. It seemed to make sense to move down there. I want to bring Kelly into my studio, Moonlight Sonata, and let her work with Jane and Shannon. They can give her more of a feel for hand and arm positions and movements."

"Oh," Mel said. "Well, that makes sense, I guess." He cleared his throat. "Kelly only flies first class. It's in her contract."

"I know that," Doug told him.

"Well, naturally, turn in your receipts and you'll be reimbursed," Mel said.

"Right," Doug said.

"Wait a minute. I don't have a hotel booking until —"

"It's all right, Mel," Doug said. "Kelly wants to stay with friends of mine. My brother and sister-in-law, actually."

Kelly shot him a questioning glance.

"Oh?" Mel said worriedly. "Kelly, contractually you're entitled to the best accommodations, you know. I can make some calls —"

"Mel!" Kelly said. "I'll be fine. I want to get to know these dancers, to better understand how they can be so perfectly sharp in their movements, how their hands move . . . The more time I get to spend with the real thing, the better."

"But —" Mel began.

"Shannon holds a number of champion-ships for smooth dancing — that includes the tango," Doug said, stepping in quickly.

"I see." Mel looked at Kelly, then smiled. "So, you do think I steered you in the right direction, doing the video."

"Absolutely. But if I'm doing it, I'm doing it right, Mel," Kelly said.

"I'm sorry to say, but I can't be there that early. And I can't stay all the way through," Mel said.

"Hey, you're tops already," Kelly said, offering him her warmest smile, one filled with years of affection that Doug suddenly found himself envying. "You go above and beyond. I know you have other clients, but you hold my hand very well."

Mel smiled at her. " 'Cause you're the sweetest, kid."

The door to the little room opened and Marc Logan entered, grinning from ear to ear. "Miss Trent! Mel . . ." He frowned as he looked at Doug, as if he'd forgotten his name.

"O'Casey," Doug said.

"Right, right. Sorry, Mr. O'Casey. I hope you've all found everything you need."

"It's a lovely layout, thank you," Kelly told him. "These are fantastic studios. I had wondered why you weren't recording in Miami, since there are so many top-notch studios there. Now I know."

"Oh, we're going to be this big in Miami, too," Logan said cheerfully. "But, since you actually live out here in L.A., and I've got this . . . well, here we are."

"You brought all the musicians to me?" Kelly asked.

"They may be the next hottest thing on the chart," Logan said, "but right now you're the lead player."

"I don't mean to diminish my own importance, Mr. Logan —" Kelly began.

"Marc, please."

"Marc. But I'm sorry to say, the entire world does not watch soaps."

Logan came forward and took Kelly's hands. "You, my dear, are simply a dream come true. There's nothing I wouldn't do for you."

"Well, thank you," she murmured, drawing back. "I'm flattered. I hope I live up to your expectations."

"Oh, you will. You will!" Logan assured her. "Well, if you're ready, you're set up in nine. Gentlemen, you can watch from outside, of course."

"Outside" meant beyond large sheet-glass windows. Within the room, there were huge pieces of equipment and rooms within rooms. Logan brought Kelly in and introduced her to the people working the equipment. She was given several sheets and placed in one of the recording booths.

"This shouldn't take that long, it's just backup," Mel told Doug. "And Billy Oddhan, the fellow in there with the beard and really long hair, is one of the best. Logan may be the money, but Billy's the real producer, the guy who knows how to mix everything. Often you listen to CDs that are just great, but when you see the group live, they're horrible. That's because a good producer makes the sound." Mel snapped his finger. "The producer is the real talent."

He wasn't expecting an answer and Doug didn't give him one. Instead, he watched as Kelly was directed, as she listened through her earphones and was given visual cues.

"I'm not getting even a hint of what she's doing," Doug told Mel.

"They've got her doing backup, undertow and the chorus. She has a few lines and a few sung syllables," Mel explained. He pointed into the studio at the massive music machinery. "It's really something the way they can take the best bits from each recording and splice together the best version. She'll lay the chorus several times for them, do a line by line if they want and be done. Actually," Mel said ruefully, "I could have insisted we be in there. We could have been in the booth with headphones, too."

Mel sounded a little irritated. Time to strike, Doug determined. "How come you never mentioned that you were Dana Sumter's agent at one time?"

Mel seemed to turn to stone. Heartbeats of silence ticked by. Then he turned to Doug. "I represented her for all of about two minutes. And I haven't seen her since."

"Oh?"

"I wasn't high enough on an A-list ladder for her at the time," he said. "She hired me and fired me in the same week."

"But you might have mentioned it," Doug persisted.

Mel waved a hand in the air, obviously angry. "This is Lala Land, remember? Thousands come out here hoping to make it big, but for those who get a foot in the door, it's really not such a big place. I'm willing to bet half the people out here in the business wind up connected with one another in some way. Even if it's brief or by a few degrees of separation."

"I see," Doug murmured.

Mel frowned, looking at him. "Like hell! There's no one more worried about Kelly than me. And to prove it, I'm going to see that no one fires your ass for being a presumptuous upstart."

Doug inclined his head.

"Hell, and I had liked you!" Mel muttered.

Doug stared through the glass. "We're both looking out for Kelly's best interests, right?"

"Absolutely. And she knows that about me."

Doug stared at him again. "But *I* wasn't in California when Dana Sumter was killed. And I wasn't on the set when Kelly had the 'accident.' "

Mel stared at him with tremendous dignity. "I swear to you, I would never hurt Kelly. Ever!"

"Glad to hear that," Doug murmured.

"If you think my representing Dana Sumter all those years ago could possibly mean anything, I'll make sure myself that Kelly knows," he said.

Doug studied him. "It may seem minor, but we're all in the dark here, aren't we?"

Kelly came out as they were facing off with each other. She emerged with Logan, the man once again telling her how pleased he was to have her aboard. Logan looked at Mel, grinning. "She was an ace. I knew she would be. I don't actually watch television in the daytime, but Lance told me about your stint as a night club singer on the show, Kelly. I knew we had a winner."

"Well, thank you," Kelly murmured.

"She's my girl!" Mel said proudly. He flashed a glance at Doug.

"I think the boys in the band should be showing up any second, if you want to wait around a bit, have more coffee or something to eat," Logan said.

"Actually, I'm taking my dog on the plane tonight, so I'd like to get to the airport early and spend some time with him," Kelly told him. "I hope you understand."

"Of course, of course. Thank you, Kelly. Have a safe flight. Mel, take care. And you, too, Mr. . . ."

"O'Casey," Doug said.

"Mr. O'Casey. Hell, you'd think I could remember that!" Logan gave them all a wave and disappeared back behind the glass windows.

Kelly went on tiptoe and gave Mel a kiss on the cheek. "Thanks for being here."

"You'd be my one and only if I were a little richer," Mel told her, then said,

"Kelly, did you know that I once represented Dr. Dana Sumter?"

She cocked her head, an ironic smile on her lips. "You and half the agents in the state! Why?"

"I just wanted to make sure you knew. Doug seemed concerned."

Kelly looked at Doug. She seemed truly puzzled. "Some people stay with one agent forever. Some, like Dana Sumter, go through them like . . ."

"Like toilet paper!" Mel said softly. He turned to Doug, as if he'd proved his point, then smiled suddenly, glad of Doug's intrusion. "Doug, take care, and take care of my girl."

"I intend to," Doug assured him.

As they departed the studios, Doug asked, "Did you really know that about Mel?"

"That Mel represented Dana once? Not really, but I did know that she had been with dozens of agents. And I mean dozens." She changed the subject. "I'm staying at your sister-in-law's?" she inquired as they headed for his rental.

All right, Doug thought. So he'd table the discovery for now. Kelly truly seemed to think nothing of it. And now that Liam knew, the police would certainly be on it.

There was nothing else he could do now until he found out just what Mel had been doing the night Dana Sumter was killed.

"Doug. Hey, Doug! Are you with me?"

"Sure, sorry! Are you staying with Shannon, right? In a way. She has a place on the beach, but she and Quinn like to be on his boat, down at the marina. I've been living in her place. Nice house, near the beach, with a yard. I was thinking about Sam, as well."

"So I'm staying with you?"

"Is there a problem?"

"Well, there are always problems," she murmured. "But at this point . . . fine."

When they reached his car, he opened the passenger door for Kelly. As she sat, he noted a car tearing into the lot. A rental. A foreign car. A dark gray sedan. And as he watched, Lance Morton emerged from it.

Had the vehicle rushing down the street the other day been black or dark blue, dark green . . . or dark gray?

The roses were on the porch when they arrived at Kelly's house. It was a beautiful arrangement, but an odd one. Half of the roses were a stunning, brilliant red. But the other half were . . . black.

"An admirer?" O'Casey asked her, frowning.

She shrugged. "I don't know." She reached for the flowers.

"No, don't touch them," he said. He stooped down and picked up the vase, looking for the florist's card. There wasn't one. Just a note. It wasn't handwritten, but typed. "Bloodred roses for a bloodred beauty," he read to Kelly, looking at her.

She shrugged. "Well, there's no threat in that, is there?"

"No, but what are they doing here?"

"They're for me?" she suggested dryly.

"But from a fan?" he said.

"Probably."

O'Casey shook his head. "Shouldn't they have gone to the show, then? You don't just give your address out, do you."

"No, of course not," she said.

He looked around. "I'm calling Liam," he told her.

She fitted her key into the door, exasperated. "They're flowers!" she said. "Are you bringing them in?"

"No. I'm having them taken to the police."

"They're just flowers!"

"That shouldn't be here."

"You're making me insane!" she told him.

"Sorry. Just trying to keep you alive."

She nearly slammed the door on him. When he pushed it open and came in behind her, Sam made a beeline for him — ignoring Kelly. She found herself more irritated than ever and spun on O'Casey. "Okay, you saved my life at the crosswalk. I'm grateful. But my life is enough of a mess! Don't go throwing your own psychological dilemmas into the mix."

"I don't know what you're talking about," he said, his eyes hard.

"You! You're ridiculously suspicious. And of Mel, of all people! Quizzing him, giving him the third degree, I'm certain. And now the flowers. Apparently you liked being a cop, and now you've got yourself back into an investigation. I really don't think you care one way or another about dancing in this thing. You want to know who killed Dana Sumter. You want to *solve* this mystery. And you're making me insane!"

She didn't think that it could, but his jaw set to a harder line. "Are you learning the tango or aren't you?" he inquired.

"Could you bring my flowers in, please?"

"No."

"O'Casey!"

"There's no florist's card on it, just the

note, with no identification of where it actually came from."

"Someone might have delivered them by hand."

"What someone? Don't you understand? The someones out there shouldn't have your home address!"

"So you're going to have the flowers taken to the police station?"

"Yes, just like I'm sure Joe Penny had the really threatening fan mail sent to the police."

She threw up her hands. "Great, then. Go for it. The flowers would die, anyway. Take them in."

"I'm not leaving you."

"You're going to call Liam?"

"You bet."

She let out a sound of pure exasperation. "All right, fine. But I'm begging you, please stop looking for evil intent in every single thing that happens!"

He stared at her for a moment. "Sam, come on, I'll take you out," he told the dog. He glared at Kelly. "Lock me out."

"You bet!" she told him.

Fifteen minutes later, she was tempted to ignore the knocking at her door when he returned. He did, however, have her dog, so she opened the door, clearly still irritated. But they didn't exchange words. Liam was driving up at that very moment. She frowned, looked at O'Casey and realized he'd used his cell phone.

"Interesting arrangement," Liam told Kelly.

"It's pretty," she protested.

"Maybe for Halloween," he said.

She sighed. "I don't know what you're both so worried about. Whatever they mean, they're just flowers," Kelly said.

"Black roses. Black, like dead roses," Liam said softly.

"But they're not dead. They're just treated," Kelly said.

"I don't know. Like I said, it's an interesting arrangement. I think that we should bring them in to Olsen." He glanced at his watch. "I'll just hang around until you're ready. We'll take the flowers in to the station and then I'll drop you at the airport."

"Works for me. Kelly?" O'Casey asked.

"Does it matter if it works for me?" she murmured.

Both men stared at her. She shook her head and returned to her bedroom to make sure she'd packed everything she might need for the coming weeks. But then she burst back in on the two.

"What?" O'Casey asked.

"Sam."

"What about Sam?" Liam asked. "We can keep him again, if you think that will be better."

"No, no . . . I need to get to the veterinarian. I want to sedate Sam a little. It'll be a horrible flight for a dog."

O'Casey and Liam exchanged glances. "Okay, we go by the vet, then the police station, then on to the airport," Liam said cheerfully.

O'Casey nodded and Kelly went back to check on her packing a second time.

Chapter 18

When they arrived at the police station, Liam went in alone. Kelly was certain Detective Olsen would find their concern over the delivery of a bunch of flowers to be an infringement of valuable police time. But he must have accepted them, and the explanation, quickly enough. When Liam returned to the car, O'Casey asked, "He have any comments?"

"They'll check for toxins of any kind and see if they can locate the florist," Liam said. Then he turned around to Kelly in the back seat. "Olsen said it was a good thing we brought them in."

At the airport, Kelly found that she clung a little too tightly to Liam.

"Stick with that guy. He's all right," Liam told her.

"Well, I won't have anyone else, will I?" she murmured.

"We can pop on a plane ourselves, if the

330

going gets too rough," Liam said.

She laughed. "With three kids and a dozen pets. Sure, you can pop over anytime!"

"We can, you know."

"I'm fine," Kelly assured him. "It's the people around me who are having problems."

"Almost going over a cliff, then nearly being run over. I'd say you have to be careful, Kel."

She frowned. So much for O'Casey staying silent!

Horns were beeping everywhere. Liam had to move. He patted Sam on the head, shook O'Casey's hand and waved to Kelly one last time.

Inside the airport, crated and sedated, Sam seemed to be doing okay, but Kelly kept him with her as long as she could. It always made Kelly nervous to take Sam with her on a plane. She'd read such terrible things about what could happen to large dogs in the hold. But she didn't want to leave him behind. Not now. Besides, the vet had assured her that, with the tranquilizers, Sam would be just fine.

Whatever his thoughts on the subject, O'Casey managed not to voice them. Once on board, Kelly accepted a few glasses of champagne, intending to sleep during the flight. And she did. Later, she discovered to her horror that she'd made full use of Doug during the flight, stretching out, plumping her pillow onto his shoulder and leaving him in a fairly awkward position throughout the many hours. Though he didn't complain, he did work his shoulder once they had landed.

As they collected the dog and their suitcases and exited the airport, Kelly said, "We could have had a limo pick us up, you know?"

"We're being picked up," O'Casey assured her.

Despite the early hour, the airport was bustling, and Kelly felt a wave of heat wash over her. The covered pickup area was heavy with exhaust fumes. Arriving in Miami was always a little like getting hit by a semi of humidity.

"There," Doug said. "The Navigator." He waved and walked toward the car pulling in for them. She didn't need to be told that the man at the wheel was O'Casey's brother. Though he was dark where Doug was light, they had the same eyes. He was slightly taller than Doug, but they shared the same hard, tightly muscled build. And there was something very familiar about the man's quick smile.

"Hop in the front," O'Casey said. "Sam and I will be in the back."

"Hey, I'm Quinn," the man at the wheel said, assessing Kelly quickly with an open grin.

"Kelly," she murmured. "Nice to meet you, and thanks for coming. I'm sorry you had to brave the traffic."

"No problem. My pleasure."

Sam stuck his head through the seats, licking her cheek, then turned to greet the man. He gave Quinn a big slurp on the cheek as well.

"This is Sam," she said ruefully. "Sorry!"

"It's all right," he assured her. "He's a beauty." He glanced at Doug in the rear-view mirror. "Shannon stocked some stuff for you guys. I thought you might want to adjust to the house, maybe get a few hours of sleep. When you're ready, she'll be at the studio. I'm available whenever."

"Thanks," Doug told his brother.

"They work late at Moonlight Sonata," Quinn informed Kelly. "But if you don't mind, we'd like to have dinner with you two around ten."

"I don't mind," Kelly told him. "That would be lovely."

Quinn moved the car out into the traffic.

Sam made smudges all over the window with his nose, anxious to see everything they passed. Le Jeune Road took them to an expressway. Kelly was glad to realize she knew where she was.

"Do you like Miami?" Quinn asked her casually.

She grinned at him. "It's like L.A., minus the mountains."

"No mountains, but great water. Do you dive?"

She shook her head. "But I'm willing to get to know the water. I don't actually dance, either."

"She's lying. She's already gotten a really good tango down," Doug said.

Quinn smiled, looking ahead as he drove.

"Do you dance, Quinn?" Kelly asked.

"Have to. My wife makes me," he said. "But if you want to talk about two left feet . . ."

From the back, O'Casey added, "Shannon really is world class. And my old-timer of a brother here has learned to move damned well on the floor."

She smiled, realizing that she enjoyed seeing O'Casey with his brother. The relationship seemed to be a really good one. It softened something of the hard edge that could wrap around O'Casey, the dead-set determination and single-mindedness that could rule him at times.

As they drove, both the O'Caseys pointed out landmarks. She already recognized some of them. The view from the causeway as they crossed to the beach was stunning. The water rippled; the day was clear. It was a workday, but many people were out, on foot, on bicycles, moving along as if they didn't have a care in the world.

Shannon's house was in the South Beach area. When they arrived, Sam bounded out of the car, and though the yard wasn't fenced, he somehow recognized it as his own — for the time being. He raced from side to side.

"It's a lovely place. Please thank your wife," Kelly said.

Quinn laughed. "Doug pays rent, but we're happy to have you here."

There were pictures in the living room as they entered, and she recognized Doug and Jane in several. Jane could have been a contortionist. She'd been captured in various movements of incredible grace and agility Kelly was certain she could never mirror — certainly not in another week!

"It's all okay?" Doug asked her as he and Quinn brought in the luggage.

"It's great," she said.

"All right, I'm getting out of here. You two must be beat," Quinn said.

"I slept on the plane," Kelly said, but yawned. "It wasn't all that comfortable, though."

"Sorry," Doug said dryly.

"Oh, I didn't mean . . . um, you were a great pillow, really."

Quinn laughed and headed for the door. Kelly noticed a look pass between the brothers before Doug quickly said, "I'll walk you out. Kelly, go ahead and wander around, explore."

She nodded, thinking that she'd like coffee, but wondering if something without caffeine would be in order, especially if she hoped to get a nap in before practice. In the kitchen, she was touched to see a big bag of dog food waiting on the counter — Sam's brand. Their arrival had been carefully thought out. It was evident that Doug had talked to his brother and told him what to have in the house.

As she made tea, she decided that she was ravenous, having forgone dinner on the plane, and was digging around in the refrigerator when Doug reappeared. He seemed somewhat distracted. "What's wrong?"

"Nothing."

"Now, there's a crock. You walked your brother out because he had some little secret to tell you."

"Not a secret."

"Then what?"

He let the question slide, coming to join her at the refrigerator. "You must be starving. What are you in the mood for?"

"Food."

"An omelet?"

"Sure."

He didn't actually shove her aside, but he took charge, getting various ingredients out of the refrigerator. "Can you manage a toaster?" he asked her.

"I think so," she told him.

"Bread is over there."

They'd been left a choice of bread as well, everything from white to whole wheat and multigrain. She turned to O'Casey. "Do you want to choose the carbs?"

"You choose."

She opted for the multigrain.

He obviously could cook. The eggs were whisked, the ham and cheese chopped. Within minutes the pan was sending out an alluring aroma. He looked up, aware of her stare, and said, "Police academy."

"What?"

"We often wound up studying the books

at one another's houses fairly frequently, so we learned to cook."

"I see. You learned to be incredibly suspicious and how to cook. That's great."

"How do you like your omelet, a little runny or well done?"

"Cooked all the way through."

"Coming up."

"Juice?"

"Sure."

In another minute, they were seated at the counter. Kelly was so hungry, she completely forgot conversation until she had finished every bite on her plate.

"That was great," she told him honestly.

"I strive to please."

"Then could you please point me to a shower? I'm beginning to feel the itch of being on a plane all night."

The bath was charming, with a lot of deco features. She knew the house had to have been built in the twenties. There were a number that had been built in a similar style in the L.A. area, especially in Beverly Hills. This house was on a more modest scale, but what it lacked in size it made up for in charm. It was neat and clean, but lived-in — comfortable. Kelly didn't know whether to give the credit to O'Casey or his sister-in-law.

Doug called from the bedroom that he was taking the dog into the front yard area as she stepped beneath the water. She was thankful that the old place had a good water heater. Emerging a few minutes later, still warm from the hot water and sated with the meal, she knew that she could sleep. As she towel-dried her hair, she heard O'Casey and Sam come back in. Then she heard water running and assumed that Doug had taken the shower in her wake. Yawning, she stretched out on the bed in her towel, and a second later her eyes were closed.

She was groggy when she heard his voice. "Kelly, you'll be more comfortable under the covers." Blinking, she rose — and realized she'd already lost the towel. But it didn't matter. He knew what she thought, that he was a cop first and foremost in his heart, no matter what he said. The barrier had been established, just as the relationship had been.

He turned down the bed and she crawled back in. "You must be really exhausted," she murmured. "You didn't sleep on the plane at all." She felt his arms come around her.

"I don't think I could ever be so exhausted that . . ." He didn't finish the sen-

339

tence with words. Instead, she felt his lips against the nape of her neck, her shoulder blades . . . He moved against her. And he was right. For a man who should have been very tired, his behavior was incredibly vivid and electric.

She wasn't so exhausted herself, she realized. Either that or he had a true talent for awakening her. Yes, awakening her *and* arousing her.

His lips and fingers created the most exquisite heat, stroked with dampness, offered touches that were beyond intimate and far beyond eliciting. She turned into him, mesmerized, allowing the seduction, then flaring into excitement herself, bursting into an equal hunger, like a match tip newly struck. She began returning every touch, every stroke, every erotic caress. . . .

He deftly moved the length of her body about, finding the line of her back, the rise of her hip. The back of a knee. The flesh of her inner thigh. Higher. Lower. The deepest, most central zones. . . .

She was amazed, growing ever more comfortable in his arms, yet challenged, brought to new heights. She was stunned by the movement, the rhythm, the deep thrust and equally evocative slow withdrawal . . . and the feel of his muscles beneath her fingers, against her.

She closed her eyes, oblivious to everything but the longing and then the climax that came with such a volatile burst of ecstasy that it seemed to shatter her very essence.

Later, snuggled against him, she was surprised to realize that she finally felt safe. But what if he weren't with her? She closed her eyes, not wanting to think about that. There were times one should just be grateful for the moment.

She snuggled more tightly into his arms and discovered that he was awake. "O'Casey?"

"Hmm?"

"You should be sleeping."

"I will be."

She lifted up onto an elbow and stared at him. "Just what did your brother tell you?" she demanded.

"It really wasn't anything that important."

"Well then, what?"

He looked at her, those cobalt eyes shooting into hers. "He's been doing some research."

"So what did he find out? Anything earth-shattering?"

"Maybe yes, maybe no."

"What?" she demanded.

"Our friend Lance Morton happens to be from Sandusky, Ohio."

Her eyes narrowed. Inwardly, she admitted to a little spasm of unease. "Lots of people are from Sandusky, Ohio," she said.

He rolled to look at her more closely. "Yes, that's true. But Lance Morton just happened to be back in Ohio visiting his mother on the same night that Sally Bower drowned in her bathtub."

Chapter 19

Kelly refused to be disturbed by the information about Lance Morton. Doug had a damned good intuition that, although he might never be able to prove it, Lance had delivered the roses as well. Despite all this, however, sheer exhaustion enabled him to sleep. It was strange to realize that he could do so easily enough because Sam was out in the living room. If anyone came near the house, the dog would sound an alarm.

But the hours passed in quiet. He rose before Kelly, showered, dressed, put on coffee and took Sam for a run. Back in the house, he sipped coffee and logged on to the computer, going to work. There had been something about Lance's bio that disturbed him, and he now knew what it was. The information had mentioned an "Ohio" or "Midwestern upbringing," but didn't pin down an exact date or place of birth. He went through everything he could possibly find on the man, including city records. No one seemed to have his exact date of birth. He could find the man's school records, but those just told when he went into first grade. So he had to be about . . . about the age a child would be, if Dana Sumter had disappeared for a year to have a child.

He needed something far more than what he knew about Lance Morton, just as he needed to know more about Mel Alton.

He'd taken Kelly out of California, but it might not matter much. Too much of California would be coming to Florida. And soon.

He glanced at his watch. He figured they'd actually gotten to sleep about ten and it was four now. Kelly should be moving. But as he walked toward the bedroom, he heard the roar of the shower. She was up.

She emerged from the bathroom in black capris and a T-shirt, ready to work, but frowned at his expression. "Oh! I was thinking work in the dance studio, but we're going to dinner after, right? Should I be in better attire? Should I take something?"

"No, no, sorry, you're just fine for a casual late night around here," he told her. "I think we invented casual."

She walked into the kitchen and poured coffee. "What are they saying now about the situation in the Middle East?"

"What?"

"The paper. I was looking at the headlines," she said.

"Ah . . . nothing much has changed," he told her, folding the paper.

"I see. You're still fuming over the fact that Lance Morton was born in Ohio."

"Not only was he born there, but he was there when Sally Bower died."

She leaned on the counter. "Have I ever told you who else was originally from Ohio?"

"You?" he asked.

"No, but Serena was born there."

"Have I been trying to malign everyone born in Ohio?" he asked her.

She smiled. "No."

Sam had come up to her. She scratched his head, then apologized. "I'm sorry. You woke up and took him right out, didn't you? And you fed him?"

"I like Sam," he told her. "It's okay."

"But he's my responsibility. I wanted him here."

"Kelly, it's all right."

"I should take him out again . . . we'll be

kind of late tonight, right?"

"Home by midnight, I'd say."

"I'll take him for a run."

"No, just get your stuff together. I know the neighborhood."

When he returned, she'd drunk her coffee and was ready. The studio was just down the street, so it didn't take them long to get there. Kelly was pensive as he parked.

"Something wrong?" he asked her.

She glanced at him. "Um, actually . . ."

"What?"

"I'm feeling overwhelmed."

"Why?"

"I've seen your partner dance."

"And Jane just about worships the ground you walk on!" he assured her. "Come on, you'll like the place."

He realized that she was nervous, and liked her all the more for it. So much for his determination not to get involved. She'd been far too easy to want. So there was sex, an involvement in itself. But now . . .

All he could really come up with was the fact that he liked the way she laughed, the intelligence in her eyes, her quick smile, the dryness of her humor at times, the humility and a certain innocence that had somehow remained with her through the years. She was just Kelly — and that was pure seduction.

"Let's go up," he suggested, and took her hand.

As usual, there was a lot of activity going on in the studio. Shannon was there, apparently having just finished a practice with her professional partner, Ben. Jane was working with a kid named Bob Cramer. Sam Railly was working with a new couple, and Rhianna Markham was with one of their local high school football coaches.

When he entered with Kelly, Shannon's eyes widened just a bit and a smile curved her lips. She caught Ben's hand and walked over. "Hey!" she murmured, and kissed his cheek, then waited expectantly to be introduced.

"Shannon, Ben, Kelly Trent. Kelly, Ben Trudeau and my sister-in-law, Shannon."

"How do you do?" Kelly murmured.

"You really are even more stunning in person," Ben said admiringly.

Kelly flushed. "Thank you."

Shannon laughed. "You are, but don't let us make you feel self-conscious."

Doug realized that the music had stopped. The new couple, the football coach and Bob Cramer were all staring. So were Rhianna, Sam and Jane.

"Sorry, I guess everyone wants to meet you," Shannon said.

"It would be my pleasure," Kelly said quickly. She walked over to Jane first, greeting her with a kiss on the cheek.

Doug watched as Jane introduced her to the others. Kelly was charming and sweet. She apparently really did like people. He mused that he had probably been the one to create the hostility he'd felt when they first met. He had expected her to be a certain way. A diva, a star. High maintenance. But she was one of the most down-to-earth people he had ever met.

"Watch it," Shannon murmured to him.

"What?" Startled, he looked down into his sister-in-law's sparkling eyes.

"You're looking at her with wolf's eyes."

"What?" he repeated.

"Hungry eyes," she murmured. "With a little bit of alpha-dog possession thrown in. I hear you're getting close. Just be careful," she warned.

He stared back. "You should know me by now. I'm always careful."

"You're usually too careful. That's why you've got me a little scared. She seems very nice, though."

"Hmm."

"The studio will clear now. Jane and I are going to work with your girl alone."

"I don't leave her alone."

"Doug! She'll be with me. We'll lock the doors. We cleared the schedule, I told you. Besides, Quinn wants to see you. He'll be at the café across the street."

"Oh? Why isn't he here?"

"You know your brother. He'll only take so many lessons. Especially from me!"

Kelly was signing autographs. The new couple had wanted their progress books signed by her and the football coach had her sign his agenda, saying how grateful he was that he still carried a real paper book rather than an electronic gadget. Kelly signed for everyone, chatting with them and thanking them all for their interest. Then, as Shannon had promised, everyone but she and Jane departed.

"I'm really being thrown out?" Doug asked.

"Why don't you show us the routine first?" she suggested.

"All right. Kelly?" Doug said.

She stared at him, then at the two women. "You want me to dance . . . now?"

He smiled. "If they see our routine, they can give you little pointers."

"It's similar to what we were doing with

the dancers at the auditions, right?" Jane asked.

"I'd really love to see it," Shannon said.

Kelly winced. Doug walked over to her, and he couldn't help grinning. "Coward!" he teased.

"That would be about the gist of it, yes," she whispered back.

"Kelly, you can do it."

"Actually, I'm not as afraid of doing the video as I am of dancing here, now, with those two watching!"

"They're not the enemy, you know. They really want to help. Remember how it goes? You walk to me with the sweeps, into the hold, tango basic, medio corte, promenade, tango basic, doble corte, promenade left turn, basic, Argentine link, death drop, back for the count, chasse corte, flare promenade, basic, the lift, and spin and out."

"I —"

"Trust me," he told her.

"I have the rough track right here!" Jane called cheerfully. She walked over to the stereo, slipped in the CD. The music started.

"I'll catch you, no matter what you do."

"But they'll know!" Kelly said, a little panicky.

The music had begun. One thing about

Kelly — she was, beyond a doubt, a performer. He imagined that no matter what was going on in her life, when a curtain opened, or a director yelled action, or the music began to play, she was ready. And she was.

She felt that she didn't have the stance, assurance and speed of a dancer who had long been in training. And maybe she didn't. But she had stature and poise, and he was stunned himself at just how well she did that day, how well she remembered the steps and how well she executed them. Her body movement was exceptionally good, and she was in perfect position for the lift. She spun out of it when he brought her down as if she had done it a thousand times. She flushed, meeting his eyes as the music ended. Both Shannon and Jane burst into calls of encouragement and applause.

"Wow!" Jane congratulated her, hurrying forward. She looked at Doug, indicating that she was impressed. "You did all that in a few days in California! I'm impressed."

"I'm a good teacher. Thanks for being shocked!" Doug told her.

Jane elbowed him lightly. "Kelly, that was really unbelievable."

"We'll help you with your hands, head

positioning, arms . . . just a few little things," Shannon said.

"I'm telling you, though, you were fantastic!" Jane said.

Shannon turned on Doug, a small smile teasing her lips. "Your brother is waiting for you."

"All right, all right, I'll leave you guys. But don't go teaching her any bad habits!" he charged them.

"Hey! Who taught you?" Jane demanded.

"I'll be right across the street," Doug assured Kelly.

She smiled at him slowly. She was happy and proud, he realized. And something about the way that she looked at him . . . well, it was more than sex. It was involvement.

"What does Kelly think of it all?" Quinn asked him. They were seated at the café right across from the studio. The glass windows looked out to the street, and every once in a while they could see one of the women move by.

"She insists that everything happening is circumstantial."

"Well, you've got to admit that it might well be circumstantial," Quinn said. "Especially the fact that someone hails from Ohio. It's a fairly well-populated state."

"That's true. But I did some probing as well. Do you know where Lance Morton was when Dr. Dana Sumter was killed?"

"California," Quinn said. "They had a bunch of gigs in the L.A. area. But playing clubs in L.A. is not really a shocking thing for a band to do. Do you really suspect him?" Quinn asked.

"I want to," Doug admitted. "I want to find out that he's a freak for advice divas for some reason and that he killed the women. Then we can see that he's arrested, and Kelly will be safe."

"But you don't believe that he is guilty," Quinn said flatly.

"I can't figure the motive. He's never been married, so he hasn't been taken or cleaned out by a wife."

"Maybe the person who drove the murderer insane wasn't actually a wife. You don't need a marriage license to hurt, use or make someone crazy," Quinn said.

"That's true." He shook his head. "Mel once represented Dana Sumter. But I understand that everyone in the business in L.A. represented her at one time or another. Finding enemies against Dana Sumter . . . well, it's almost too easy."

"Right. But was the woman in Ohio actually murdered? If it *was* murder, someone very clever is running around the country with a vengeance — and an agenda."

"Something has to come together. Let's say both cases were murder. I need a suspect who could have been in Ohio and in California, able to get to both of the dead women and Kelly." He hesitated, looking at his brother. "I checked online and hacked into airline files this morning. I don't think Mel was in Sandusky anywhere near the time the diva died."

"Well, that would be something," Quinn said. "If . . ."

"If we knew for sure that she was murdered," Doug finished.

"Then there's the whole issue of Dana Sumter having disappeared for a year. I've been thinking along that track. What's usually behind a young woman's sudden disappearance for a year's time?"

"Pregnancy?" Quinn said.

"My thoughts exactly."

"If she had a child and gave it up for adoption, those records would be sealed. And if someone went nuts and killed her because she was a mother who'd abandoned him or her, why go after anyone else, including Kelly?"

"I don't know, but it's worth pursuing."

"I agree."

Doug hesitated. "In a way, I'm starting to wonder if I did the right thing, bringing Kelly here. I had thought the danger was surely in California. That's where the accident happened on the soap. That's where she received threatening mail. That's where she was nearly run over. But what if someone involved with this video is after her?"

"Give me names, whatever information you have," Quinn said. "Jake can use the station to do a thorough scan on them. We'll find criminal records, if there are any. At least she has her dog with her. He'll provide some protection."

Doug frowned suddenly. "You know, Dana Sumter had a dog."

"And the dog was killed," Quinn said quietly. "I don't think we need to let Kelly know that, do you?"

"She's in denial, anyway," Doug told him. "Do you know what she'd say? Dana Sumter had a little dog. She has a big weimaraner."

Quinn swallowed some of the coffee in the mug before him. "Doug, can you blame her? She's sure as hell not going to want to believe that she could be in any danger making the video. She's already smarting from the fact that she's been put on paid leave with the soap. She wants to do the video, needs to do the video. Should she be frightened out of every job she's offered? Think about it, from her point of view."

"Maybe she just shouldn't work for a while."

"That could kill her career."

"Better a dead career than a dead woman!" Doug insisted.

"Then there's only one answer. Get to the bottom of it." He hesitated. "And watch out for situations you can't control."

"What are you suggesting?"

"Leave this area now, quietly, without telling anyone who doesn't need to know. I know the place where you're filming in the Keys. The guy who owns it is anxious as hell for the business and the prestige that will come with the video, but he owes me a few favors. So we can slip you in, quietly and ahead of time. You and Kelly should head on down, get there before everyone else. For a few days, you'll have peace and quiet. And when the others arrive, you'll know the lay of the land."

Doug sat back, studying his brother.

After a minute, he nodded. "You can arrange it?"

"Yep."

"All right. Thanks."

"I'll get Shannon to reschedule her appointments for tomorrow. We'll drive down with you and I'll look the place over as well."

"All right. Good deal," Doug agreed. He looked up at the windows. He could see Kelly as she swept smoothly by the glass, apparently imitating an arm movement one of the women had suggested. She looked great. He felt a cold tremor of fear, just what he hadn't wanted. He was too involved. And being that involved meant he couldn't take any chances where she was concerned. She was just going to have to listen to him — whether she liked it or not. Whether she decided to have him fired or not. No matter what happened, he had to be with her.

Kelly was exuberant. No, she couldn't compare with Jane or Shannon, but they taught her a number of little tricks with arm, head and eye movements that, added on to what she had learned from O'Casey, at least gave the appearance of being a pro. She was still riding high on the comprehension and learning when Shannon finally said that they'd worked hard enough for the day and it was time to quit.

"And you know, videotape is good," Shannon reminded her.

"It can be edited," Jane agreed.

"Too bad they can't edit our competitions!" Jane said, grinning at Kelly. "I was out there with Doug one time when my heel caught in my skirt."

"What happened?" Kelly asked. "Did you fall?"

Jane shook her head. "It turned into the longest dip in history. We did a lot of stretching and preening until he read the problem, flicked off the hem, and we went on. There are all kinds of saves."

"We have one student who mixes up steps all the time. But she's great at pretending that they never happened," Shannon said.

"And if you do go down completely, which Shannon managed to do once, you just pretend that you're supposed to be on the floor and use those arm tricks to look as if you meant to do it."

"But you shouldn't worry. It's video!" Shannon said cheerfully. She glanced at her watch. "The guys should be back."

The O'Caseys arrived just a few minutes

later, along with a man introduced to Kelly as Mike, Jane's boyfriend. He was sandy-haired and good-looking, with a scar on his cheek. "The down side to being a hockey player," Jane told Kelly in a whisper. He seemed nice, and obviously adored Jane. Kelly wasn't sure why she found that to be such a relief.

Dinner was at a little out-of-the-way place on Washington. It was one of the nicest occasions Kelly could remember, completely relaxed. Mike told horror stories about his life on the ice, making them laugh as he explained some of the ridiculous fights that occurred in the rink. She heard more tales about competitions and dancers. And she found herself thinking that O'Casey was a lucky guy to have such good friends, relatives and associates. But she also noticed that every time a discussion about the video came up, Quinn or Doug steered the conversation in another direction.

When dinner had ended and the different duos split up, O'Casey told her, "We're going to go ahead and take off tomorrow for the Keys."

"We are?"

"Yeah. It will be nice," he said, slipping an arm around her shoulders as he walked her to the car. "Quinn and Shannon are going to take the day off and drive down with us. We'll stop in Key Largo — Quinn's business partner has a home there. Maybe we can even head out in his boat for a few hours. Then we'll move on down to the resort where we're filming."

"Can we go ahead of time?" she asked him, wondering why she was feeling so suspicious.

"Quinn knows the guy who owns the place. He owes him a favor."

She sighed. "The two of you want to check the place out, right?"

He stopped walking. "You really think it's such a bad idea?"

She shook her head and walked on by him.

"Kelly, damn it, what's the matter with knowing the lay of the land before other people arrive?"

She turned and stared at him. "Here's the problem. They say there's no such thing as bad publicity. Most of the time, that's probably true. But not always. I can't become a hot house flower. I can't let people believe that I'm a liability!"

"That's right. You've just got to get back on that soap!" he said disdainfully.

"It is my livelihood."

"It's a role you've grown attached to."

"It's good work."

"Is it worth dying for?"

"Everything going on could well be co-incidence!"

"Answer me. Is it worth dying for?"

"No role is worth dying for!" she snapped back. "But tell me this, would you live your life running around in fear every moment? No, you wouldn't."

"It's not a matter of running around in fear every moment. It's about finding out what is going on."

She turned again, heading for the car. "Fine. We'll go tomorrow and we'll scope out the place."

As they drove, she was startled when he said, "You were actually in a rut, do you know that?"

"What?"

"The show. It was easy for you, comfortable. And you were afraid to take chances doing something else. All right, go ahead and believe that I don't know you enough to peg any of your motives." Blue eyes shot her a steely glance. "But I am getting to know you. And I think you could do anything you wanted. As long as you get through it alive, this might be one of the best things to ever happen to you."

"Great. Now you're going to analyze my life! This from a man who isn't certain if he wants to be in law enforcement or entertainment!"

She struck a nerve, she was certain, because he fell silent. When they reached the house, he immediately went for the dog's leash. While he was out, she brushed her teeth and went straight into bed. She waited, heard the door open and close, heard his words as he talked to Sam. But he didn't come in. Eventually, she fell asleep.

Chapter 20

When she awoke, there was already commotion in the house. Hearing voices, she knew that Shannon and Quinn had arrived. She leaped up, grabbed clothing and made a beeline for the bathroom. When she emerged, coffee had been brewed, Shannon was moving around in the kitchen and Quinn and O'Casey were studying something on the computer. Naturally Sam had already been taken out. He was lying on the kitchen floor, happily slobbering over one of his rawhide chews.

"Good morning!" Shannon said cheerfully.

"Good morning," Kelly said, stooping down to pet her dog. Being a loving creature, he gave up a second on the chew to catch her chin with a big lick.

"He's a great dog."

"Thanks. I think so, too." Kelly rose, noting Shannon's energy as she moved about. "You're in a good mood," Kelly noted.

"I am. I never do anything like this, just take off for a day in the Keys. I rather like it."

"Well, I have an admission for you. I've never been there."

"You're going to love it! You've got a bathing suit, right?"

"Packed somewhere."

"Find it! We'll meet up with Dane and Kelsey and do a day of it."

"Aren't we going to the resort tonight?"

Shannon nodded. "Dane has a small private island just off Key Largo. The resort is another thirty or so minutes down. We'll take the car to Marathon, where Dane will pick us up and drop us off. We'll leave Doug's car at a lot in Marathon, and Dane will get Quinn and I back."

"Sounds awfully complicated."

"It's not." She smiled. "Life can be so uncomplicated in the Keys!"

Quinn and Doug made an appearance in the kitchen.

"Good morning," Quinn told Kelly.

"Good morning," she murmured.

"Everything all right?" Doug asked. "Do the plans for the day meet with your approval?"

He was still distant, almost hostile. She wasn't sure what he wanted her to do, crawl under a rock until they discovered just exactly what had happened to Dana Sumter? Some mysteries were never solved. Murderers often got away with their crimes. More than a hundred years later, theorists were still arguing over the identity of Jack the Ripper. She couldn't spend her life giving up everything and being afraid.

"The plans sounds great to me," she said. "I'll go make sure that my suit isn't at the very bottom of my luggage."

Despite Doug's mood, the drive was nice. And she had two eager tour guides telling her about the division of the little cities they passed, all Dade County and often considered part of Miami, but actually little municipalities with identities all their own. The streets took them to the highway and the highway down to the tip of the mainland — Homestead, Florida City. They stopped for gas — and a sniff and mark session for Sam — before heading down the long stretch of US1 that would take them to the Keys and back. The day was beautiful, and off to either side of the road the water sparkled brilliantly. Osprey nests sat high atop poles, and as they drove, Quinn made a point of showing her the different avian life that flourished in the area.

"Hurricane warnings down here are a real bitch," Quinn said. "Imagine evacuating with just one road in and one road out."

"I think I'd be afraid to live down here," Kelly told him.

"You're living out in a city where people warn that the 'big one' could strike at any time, and you'd be frightened by a storm?" Doug demanded, speaking to her at last.

"I didn't say I'd be frightened by a storm. I'm not sure I'd want to live in the Keys, that's all. One road . . . that's a little hairy."

"Aren't you forgetting how quickly, easily and without warning the earth seems to shift in L.A.?"

She realized that he was referring to the "accident" she'd had on the set. "I guess we're all willing to accept certain dangers," she said with a smile.

Quinn explained that the Keys were mapped by mile markers and that she could find any distance and any address along the entire stretch of the islands by referring to them. After about twenty minutes, they came into an area of civilization again, and Shannon announced that they had reached Key Largo.

They met up with Dane Whitelaw and his wife, Kelsey, at a little coffee shop with outdoor seating. Kelly noted right away that everyone there seemed to know one another. Dane was tall, dark and very striking, with impressive cheekbones. Kelly decided there was Native American blood in him somewhere. He had a laid-back, easy assurance about him, and she could well imagine he would do good work in the field of private investigation. His wife, Kelsey, was an artist. One of her pieces, a magical oil of a sailboat on the water, was hanging in the coffee shop. She and Shannon knew each other well, yet neither of them made Kelly feel like an outsider. As they ordered different coffees and late-morning doughnuts, the talk revolved around the weather, the season, the water, fishing, diving, tourists, traffic and general sundry affairs.

"Damn, but those are good doughnuts," Shannon murmured. "I think I'm going to order another one."

"I thought you were doing Atkins?" Kelsey teased her.

"Well, I was. But it doesn't work for a dance teacher," Shannon said.

"She's hungry all the time," Quinn explained, smiling affectionately and moving closer to his wife so that her hair brushed his chin.

"Ben said the lifts were getting hard!" Shannon said, shaking her head.

"It's looks to me as if you can afford another doughnut," Dane said politely.

"Except that we've packed lunch on the boat," Kelsey said.

"What if you and I split a doughnut?" Kelly suggested.

"There's a deal for you," Dane said.

They wound up ordering three more doughnuts and each of the women ate their own. When they were done, they transferred their belongings to Dane's Range Rover and headed back north over the main road. Back in Largo, they turned off it onto a series of streets, and finally into some barren land, then across a stretch of road that barely seemed to be above water level.

"It does sink at high tide," Shannon told her. "But the place is beautiful."

It was rustic, charming, surrounded with foliage, very solitary and lovely. Sam immediately went wild, running about, enjoying a rare taste of real freedom.

When they went into the house for

Kelsey to grab a few last-minute items, Kelly noted the crib in the living room and the pieces of baby paraphernalia about the place.

"We have a little boy. Justin," Kelsey told her. She grimaced. "He's with my mom — who had a baby just a year before he was born."

"Your folks must be young!" Kelly said.

Kelsey laughed. "Young enough, I guess. But it's really great. I watch my sibling and my own infant at the same time. And Mom is great, returning the favor. So we're entirely yours, free and clear, for the day."

Dane's boat was a huge yacht. Not new, Kelsey assured her, just well tended. Dane loved to sail, and with Quinn and Doug aboard, he had the right number of mates on hand. Though Kelly was a bit worried about Sam, he proved to be a perfect sailor, just sitting as if he were on guard as they cast off.

As they moved out into the Atlantic, Kelly found herself enjoying the day despite the fact that Doug remained cold and distant. His brother and the others were as kind and warm as could be. And as they sailed, she found it was fun to be a female on board this particular venture, because her sole duty seemed to be to lie in the sun and relax. The movement of the vessel surging across the water was lulling, and, she found herself not sleeping, but in such a state of contentment, it was almost like being semiconscious.

Suddenly she jerked up, startled to attention by cold water dripping on her sun-warmed stomach.

"Oh, sorry, did I wake you?" Doug, shirtless, shoeless and in cutoffs, was seated by her side, offering her a frosty plastic cup of something that had been dripping on her stomach.

"No, you didn't wake me."

"Ice-cold lemonade," he told her.

She took the drink, sitting up, and looked at him warily. He seemed more wired than he had last night, almost combustible.

"Thanks," she murmured. "So . . . what? There's something new bothering you, I can tell. Has there been some kind of threat against redheads in general?"

"No," he said, shaking his head. "I just got a call from a friend of yours, though. Someone else who is concerned."

She groaned. "Liam, right? Why does everyone I seem to know right now have to be in the field of private investigation?"

"You may wind up being a lucky girl,

that so many people in your life happen to be in the field."

She nodded. "Okay, what was he calling about?"

"Another woman has been killed."

She swallowed a sip of lemonade carefully. "And . . . ?"

"And she was a radio advice personality."

"Oh!" Kelly murmured. He was still staring at her. "How did she die?"

"Hit and run. She was killed crossing the street right near her place of business. Killed, Kelly. Witnesses described the car as a dark sedan. Some said black, some said dark blue. Some even suggested charcoal-gray. She was thrown thirty feet and declared dead at the site."

A huge splash jolted Kelly from the silent stare she had been giving O'Casey in return.

"Sam!" he said, jumping up.

Kelly jumped up as well, but there wasn't anything to worry about. Dane had dropped anchor not a hundred yards from an island with a white sand beach. Sam was following Shannon and Kelsey as they swam toward it.

"It's okay," she said quickly, and smiled though her heart was thudding. She wasn't sure just what Doug O'Casey's real feelings were for her, but he did care about Sam. "He swims well. He runs into the Pacific all the time. He must be in seventh heaven here, the water's so warm."

Doug was looking at her again, his eyes shielded by the sunglasses.

"Doug!" she said, her tone pleading. "Honest to God, I don't know what you want me to do. Should I run around shaking all the time? Hole up in a cabin in remote Montana? What?"

He shook his head. "I want you to take this seriously."

"I am taking it seriously. Please, I'm going along with every suggestion you make. What more can I do?" She bit her lower lip. "Where was this woman killed?"

"West Palm Beach."

Her heart took a little dive. Close. A couple of hours north of their present location. In Florida.

"When?"

"Early hours of the morning."

She exhaled. "The police will certainly be looking for the car."

"Yes, they will be."

"What more can I do?" she asked softly.

"Quit the soap."

"What?"

"Call a press conference. Get on all the news channels, the entertainment shows. Talk about things you want to do in the future. Make it evident that you're not an advice therapist of any kind."

"I don't see how that . . . I mean, if I'm really being targeted, how will that —"

She didn't have to finish speaking; he had already turned away. Slipping his sunglasses into his waistband, he dived off the boat and into the water.

Dane strode around to her location. "You coming?" he asked.

She nodded, trying to smile, and dived into the water.

Before diving in, Dane sent out an inner tube that carried a cooler and a dry pack with towels and utensils. While Kelly was still wringing the excess water from her hair, Dane passed her, dragging the tube. The others joined him to open the cooler and the pack. A couple of sheets were spread on the sand, drinks were popped open and a spread of sandwiches and salads was laid out.

Kelly found herself suddenly and deeply resentful; she might have really enjoyed the day. And she became determined to do just that, no matter Doug's words or his tense, quiet mood. While she accepted a sandwich from Shannon, he walked on the beach, throwing a stick for Sam to retrieve. His throws were long and hard, but Sam didn't mind.

Dane took a seat by Kelly. "If you look to the south, you can actually see the edge of the island where you'll be working."

"It's that close?"

"As the bird flies, very close. The islands loop beneath the state, so there's a bit more of a curve than appears. You'll see. We won't sail later. I'll motor the two of you over there in a few hours."

She studied the man. "I'm sure you heard about the hit-and-run in West Palm Beach," she said.

He nodded.

"Do you believe I'm in serious danger?"

"You could be."

"So what would you do?"

"Stay the hell away from the soap and any resemblance to your soap character."

"I'm already doing that."

He shrugged, looking out to the water. "No one can tell you what to do. We can only advise."

"Doug thinks I should make a big deal publicly about quitting the soap."

"That couldn't hurt."

"But then again," she persisted, "if there was — is — a real psychopath committing these murders, he's already convinced that the character is a real person. In his sick, warped mind, I'm already labeled."

"That's true."

"So . . ."

"Wouldn't you rather be safe than sorry?" he asked.

She thought about that a minute, then grimaced and rose.

Doug was standing by the surf. She walked in his direction. "Hey." He turned to her. "You took me by surprise," she told him. "Yes, my life is worth more to me than any role. And yes, I've been comfortable. But I've liked my work. Maybe I should be more daring, stretch my sights a bit. I don't know. I really don't know what I feel yet."

"Then you should think about it," he said, throwing the stick again. Sand blew around them with his effort.

"Hey, I'm doing everything you say. I'm spending every minute with a one-time cop!" she said teasingly.

He was silent.

"Now," she told him, "you're supposed to assure me that you've been trained, you made it through the academy head of your

375

class and, yes, you're sticking with me. I have you, don't you see? I'll be all right."

That brought him around to glare at her. "Kelly, hell. Am I supposed to say that yes, it's in my blood, I'd take a bullet for you? It doesn't work that way. *This* sure as hell doesn't work that way."

"Look," she said. "Think about the timing, Doug. Could the car that nearly hit me be in West Palm Beach now?"

He turned away from her, and she realized he'd already been wondering about that. She wanted to walk to him, slip her arms around his waist and rest her cheek against the sun-heated flesh of his bare back. But she forced herself to keep her distance.

"Kelly, I don't think it would hurt to make the kind of announcement I suggested."

"You may be right. Can you give me a little time to think it out? Please? Couldn't we just have today as . . . as a great day with friends?" she asked wistfully.

He remained stiff as a board for a minute, then he eased. And she did run to him, touch him, feel the heat and inhale the salt scent of his skin.

He lowered his head, nuzzling her forehead. "I'm just not sure how much time you dare take to think this all out," he warned.

"Today. A day on the water, in the sun. One perfect day to enjoy — and forget everything else."

Kelly stood at the helm with Doug, watching as they approached the island. The sun was just setting. The colors that touched the horizon were fantastic, brilliant shades that suddenly shot across the world, paled and appeared again. There were a few clouds in the sky and they took on the colors of the dipping orb in the western sky. The breeze was light, perfect. For a few minutes, Kelly forgot any hint of danger. She was completely mesmerized by the sky, the sensual touch of the salty air and the man who stood with his arms around her as they rode the waves. This was pure bliss. This was something she could do forever. She could die happy here.

Chapter 21

The little resort isle was absolutely beautiful. There was plenty of room for a sailboat such as Dane's to dock, and the owner, Harry Sullivan, was there to greet them.

Harry was a tall, slim man with sun-bleached hair, a ready smile and a slightly haggard look. Doug had never met Harry before, but both his brother and Dane knew the man fairly well. Harry greeted them both first as one of the dockhands helped Doug secure the vessel. By the time Doug jumped from the boat to the dock, hellos and greetings had gone around. He shook Harry's hand. The man was looking very pleased, but a little skeptical regarding Sam.

"We are pet friendly," he murmured, "but he's a big dog. Bigger than we usually get."

"He's not that big!" Kelly said. "And he's a very good dog."

"Yes, yes, of course. And he's yours, so I'm sure he'll be fine! Miss Trent, it was an honor knowing you were coming to begin with, and now — having you here for some private time — I am really thrilled. I haven't said a word to anyone. We've cleared the schedule and haven't taken any bookings, and with plenty of room to spare, the place is all yours."

"Wow!" Shannon murmured, elbowing Quinn. "Why didn't we stay?"

"Because you said the studio was too busy," he reminded her.

"Why do I do things like that to myself?" she murmured.

"Well, you can at least come up and see the main house, right?" Harry asked them.

"Of course you can. Right?" Kelly said to Shannon.

Harry talked about the construction of the place, and how a channel in Miami had been dredged, with the fill being bought and brought here. "The pool is around back. You can swim right up to the bar. Never understood myself how folks could need a pool when we have one of the prettiest little spits of beach you'd ever want to see! Aren't that many beaches down here, really. Our beach, like everywhere else, has been . . . enhanced!" he said cheerfully.

Kelly turned, grinned at Doug and continued following Harry. Sam, like a model
dog, stayed at her heels. Just inside the en-
trance was a huge fountain surrounded by
more foliage. The fall of the water was apparently calculated to a T. Along the concrete rim, there was ample seating.

"I think they're having you folks dance
there," Harry informed them.

"Good to know," Doug said.

Harry stopped, indicating areas. "To the
left, there's the check-in desk. To the right,
the main restaurant. Behind it, the spa
area. Normally we offer just anything your
heart could desire by way of mud baths,
massages, facials, you name it. Mr. Logan
didn't want a bunch of personnel on the island, though, so those folks are already on
leave. Upstairs there are shops, a little
coffee spot and a midday grill. Want to
keep exploring here or would you rather
see the rooms?"

"I wouldn't mind seeing the rooms,"
Kelly told him. "The sand is setting in!"

"Seeing the rooms sounds good to me,"
Doug agreed.

"We've got cooks on. I'll see that something is sent to Miss Trent's room. She has
the largest suite, of course," he murmured,
reddening slightly as he looked at Doug.

"Of course," he agreed complacently.

"The kitchen is fully stocked," Harry explained. "So once we're there, you can order off the menu."

"We should just take off," Shannon murmured.

"Please," Harry told her, glancing at Quinn. "Come on, Quinn, get her to stay for dinner, at least."

"Sure, we'll stay. All right?" He looked at Dane and Kelsey, who agreed.

The rooms were out by a trail in back. They could also be accessed from the dock by following the paths around the little hill to the summit. The guest rooms were charming, imitating a Hawaiian style. There were three wings — one to the right, one directly behind the main building and one to the left. Harry headed straight for the building to the right and to the door at the seaside edge. "You're gonna love it!" he assured Kelly.

"I know I will," she told him.

There was truly nothing not to love. Her "suite" was larger than his house, Doug thought, marveling at the size and decor. He looked at his brother. Quinn had never fully described the place. Quinn just shrugged.

"Bedroom is upstairs. It's like a little

town house," Harry informed them.

"The place can't be entered with a master key if the guest is inside?" Doug asked, cutting him short since he was going to go on again about the wonders of the place. He didn't need to; they were evident.

Harry frowned. "No," he said. "You have your sliding glass doors to the porch and the balcony off the bedroom, but there are old-fashioned rods that slip in to secure them at night. And the front door has a lock, a dead bolt and a chain."

"Are you happy?" Kelly murmured to him.

"Yeah, I think so," he returned.

They went up to see the bedroom. The bed was a huge, canopied affair — extremely inviting. And the bath offered a nice whirlpool, double sinks and gilded fixtures.

"I'll set you all up on the porch for dinner," Harry said happily, pleased that they were impressed with the room. "Grab a menu and dial room service. They'll be waiting!" Then he left them.

"Wow! I love this!" Shannon said, picking up the resort book with the room service menu. "This place definitely works for me. Quinn, why haven't we ever come out here?"

"Because you seldom want to spare any time, my love," he reminded her.

"I'll spare some," she promised. "Great menu!"

"Mind if we guys pick something out first?" Doug asked her. "Then we can go back and make sure we have all of our stuff off the boat."

"Absolutely," Shannon said, handing over the menu. "You hurry, then we can take our time."

Doug, Quinn and Dane picked out their entrées, left Kelly to order and headed back to collect the rest of the things from the sailboat. Sam ran back and forth, not sure whether to follow Doug or stay with Kelly. "No, you're fine here, boy," Doug told him. "Stay with Kelly. Watch Kelly." But as Sam obediently trotted back to his mistress's side, Doug noticed Kelly watching him oddly. He tried a smile. "Rare, please. Remember, I like my steak rare."

"You're in danger of mad cow, you know."

"Well, like you said, we have to live, right?" And with that, the three men headed for the boat.

Dinner was definitely enjoyable. They

ate out on the porch where they could savor the ocean breezes and the subtle hint of the surrounding flowers. And Kelly felt that she definitely needed to take more time for just such occasions in the future. Except that . . . what if there was no future? For a moment she suddenly felt a seizure of the fear that the others had been experiencing for her. And beyond that, what if she found herself alone in it?

The chill that seized her when she actually admitted she might be in real danger remained, despite the fact that she and Doug were leaning back together in the lounge and the others were all chatting about something. He was with her now. Wasn't that what mattered most?

Suddenly he eased her up. "Sure."

Sure what? She hadn't been paying attention.

"Quinn, Dane and I are going to walk around a bit. Then we'll see them off," Doug explained.

"Oh. Sure."

"Be back in a few minutes," he said, staring at her meaningfully.

Shannon sighed. "They want us to go in and lock the door," she explained.

"Even here?" she said.

Doug shrugged. "Never hurts," he told

her. And since she'd so recently felt such a chill regarding the possibility of her own demise, she decided not to argue the matter.

They went in. Kelly was startled when Kelsey Whitelaw handed her a piece of paper. It was one of the white, lace-edged place mats, and on it Kelsey had sketched a drawing of her and Doug on the lounge. As she stared at it, she suddenly found it hard to swallow. Kelsey was an excellent artist. She didn't just capture the substance and form of her subjects, she created real emotion in a simple sketch. The drawing was beautiful — to Kelly, at least. Her eyes were wistful as she looked out at the sea and leaned against Doug. His arm was around her, a protective quality in his hold. And there was something both tender and tormented in his eyes. The drawing was of people, separate and together, an element of a deep bond between them in the quick work of art done with a cheap hotel pen and a simple place mat.

Kelly looked from the drawing to the artist, suddenly afraid that anyone seeing the picture would know just how deeply she cared. And yet, she knew she'd never part with it.

"It's . . . lovely," she murmured. "Thank

you. You're damn good!"

"Well, thank you," Kelsey told her.

"She's wonderful!" Shannon said, and Kelly found herself smiling. Shannon was a wonderful friend, ready to fiercely applaud and promote those around her.

"I like what I do, thank you," Kelsey said. "And Shannon, thank you very much."

Shannon laughed. "You should see the painting she did for me, from one of the competitions. I've never looked better."

"You're a great subject," Kelsey said. "Hey, Sam's at the door. That must mean the guys are back."

After the goodbyes were said, Doug and Kelly found themselves alone. He went around immediately, securing the doors. Kelly watched, leaning against the kitchen counter. She had slipped the drawing into a drawer, afraid for him to see it.

When he finished with the locks, he stopped at last, looking at her. He was still in his cutoffs, and his shoulders were even more bronzed after the day in the sun. His chest rippled. He was a man who could wear a suit exceptionally well, but he could wear nothing at all with even greater appeal.

"So . . ." he said.

"So?"

"Have you thought —"

"Yes, I've thought a lot. And I don't want to think anymore tonight." She lifted a hand before he could speak. "Please, I promise we'll really talk in the morning. But tonight . . ." She allowed a wistful smile to curl her lips. "Let's just enjoy this paradise."

"Hmm?" he queried. "Just what did you have in mind?"

She sighed with exasperation, then smiled again. "Well, I was thinking about a whirlpool bath large enough to accommodate two quite comfortably. There's a great minibar, fully stocked with champagne. Bubbles in the whirlpool. Your body. Mine. That really terrific bed."

He moved toward her. "Lots of steam, bubbles . . . naked, writhing bodies?"

"Does the concept draw the least interest?"

He was silent a moment, then a light of amusement and something more came into his eyes.

"O'Casey?" she murmured.

He stepped past her, then paused, turning back to whisper in her ear, his breath a seductive touch of heat, his voice husky. "Beat you there," he said, and with a spurt, rushed toward the stairs.

She burst into a run, coming after him,

halfway knocking him down on the steps. Without a word, he swept her up and they continued up the stairs together, laughing . . . and then breathless.

In the morning, Kelly called Mel and they talked a long time. He agreed that, even if she didn't mean it, it might be a good thing to announce that she was doing the video and then leaving the vicious character of Marla Valentine behind.

"My only concern is that this will give them every excuse to sever the contract," Mel told her worriedly.

She winced, biting into her lower lip. She didn't think that she'd ever been so afraid in her entire life.

"I can look for something different, Mel," she told him. "You're a good agent, and I'm staying in the public eye with this video."

He sighed. "Let me think," he told her.

She discussed the conversation with O'Casey. "He's worried."

"You won't be working on *Valentine Valley* if you're dead," he said bluntly. "You won't have to worry about the character being killed off."

"Let him get back to me, please?" she asked.

He agreed, but she knew he'd been on the phone to Quinn and that Quinn had been into the police station with Jake Dilessio. As of yet, the police in Palm Beach hadn't been able to hunt down the car involved in the hit-and-run. She knew, as well, that Doug had talked to his brother for some time because he had paced back and forth out on the porch with his cell phone, claiming that the reception was better out there.

Once he hung up, though, he allowed the day to be everything that it might have been. They had a resort to themselves and they used it, going from the pool to the ocean, along the trails and back to the room.

By five, Mel had gotten back to her. "I talked to Joe Penny and he went nuts. But your tango teacher is right. You can't work if you become the victim of a wacko."

"Right. Thanks, Mel."

"If I put out some feelers, I know there will be some good stuff out there for you," he promised. She just wished he sounded a little more sincere and a little less forcefully cheerful.

Doug had told her that he had a friend at one of the local network stations. And if she gave them an "exclusive," the news would be picked up nationally. Mel thought it was a good idea, as long as their current location wasn't given away, nor mentioned as the site where the video would be filmed.

That afternoon Doug's friend arrived, compliments of Harry Sullivan, who went to Marathon to pick up the man himself. The man had the improbable name of Afton Clark, and he was a tall, striking African-American with one of the deepest, richest voices she had ever heard. He interviewed her against the backdrop of the water but far enough from the hotel so that the location couldn't be gleaned from the tape. Sam was seated by her feet for the interview, like a perfect gentleman.

Afton's questions were friendly, as if they were doing something for one of the entertainment channels. She was pleased when they finished, which she wasn't always after an interview. She had liked the man very much. When he had left, Doug told her dryly that Afton had been in the academy with him, but he'd left the force after being interviewed himself at the scene of a crime, then approached by the station.

"It's his voice," Doug told her.

"Great voice, yes. And he's very attractive. Well, the die is cast," she said.

"So it is," Doug said. "Scared?"

"Yes."

"I swear to you, it was the right thing to do."

She shrugged. "We'll see, won't we? But I don't want to think about it anymore. Now I want to go out on the Jet Skis."

Doug grinned slowly. "I'm sure Harry will allow us the pleasure," he told her. "But . . ."

"But what?" she demanded.

"The tango," he reminded her. "Tango practice."

"Oh! Right!"

They used the entryway for practice, and she was amazed to discover that it had actually become fun. Tremendous effort had turned to knowledge, and the comfort of knowing more about what she was doing gave her a certain freedom.

After two hours' rehearsing, they hit the water. They left Sam sleeping in the room. Then, as the sun began to set, they shot along the waves together. Kelly found it incredibly exhilarating. She couldn't remember when she had laughed so much.

They dined on room service out on the porch once again, with O'Casey swearing that they wouldn't talk about anything related to the danger she might be in. The night was magically romantic, the absolute stuff of dreams. Champagne and grapes in bed, the coolness of the sheets, the heat of his body.

There was only one flaw. Late that night she awoke and realized that he wasn't with her. Then she heard the undertone of his voice and knew that he was out on the balcony — on the phone again. He never really forgot that he had designated himself her bodyguard.

Chapter 22

Doug had never imagined that the crew would be so large. Besides Jerry Tritan, there were two assistant directors, Herb Essen, Jane and the other three dancers, an assistant to Herb, three production assistants, makeup personnel, costumers and gofers, cameramen, soundmen and lighting technicians. Then there were the boys in the band — Lance Morton, Hal Winter, Aaron Kiley and Ron Peterson. Mel arrived with Marc Logan and Ally Bassett.

The day began with a meeting that included the full cast and crew. Though Jerry Tritan did the speaking, explaining his vision for the shoot, Marc Logan was there looking on the whole while. Ally Bassett watched everything with a sharp eye, and though she was quiet, Doug knew that if she thought anything wasn't working right for Kelly, she'd be speaking up.

They hadn't had a chance to talk, but he

could see that Ally remained concerned, and Mel and Kelly had conferred with her briefly before Kelly had done her interview.

Despite the fact that she had hired him, Doug found himself making a mental note regarding Ally's age. Where had she been when all of these things had occurred? He planned to find out, just to be thorough.

Doug had to admit that he was impressed by Jerry Tritan, who believed that the video should be a story, capturing the viewer's eye just as the song captured the listener's ear. He talked about the sheer romance of the tango and how Kill Me Quick had managed to capture the absolute sensuality of the dance. And how, as well, love could be as frightening as it was beautiful, since passion was a fiery emotion, evoking the deepest and darkest of human sensations.

Schedules were handed out with exact locations and cast member requirements. Jerry Tritan was hopping right in; he meant the shoot to be hard and fast. Looking at the schedule, Doug saw that he and Kelly were required to be in every scene being rehearsed and then filmed. They were due in costume and makeup by twelve.

He wondered if Kelly would still be nervous; she wasn't. She was happy that Jane had arrived with the barrage of people. Doug was happy, too, because Jane could go where he could not — places such as the rooms reserved for women's makeup and changing.

It was a long day that went well into the night, and Doug found himself incredibly proud of Kelly. She would meet his eyes with humor and challenge frequently when they were working. She had an advantage over him; she was accustomed to this type of work and far more patient. Several times he wanted to shout to one of the men holding a light reflector to please get it right; they were doing the exact same thing over and over again.

Not only that, they filmed the same thing from many different angles. They wanted the exact same footage while it was daytime and while it was night. They wanted footage with the backup dancers and without them. They wanted it *with* Lance Morton lip-synching his own lyrics and without. They wanted it with just Lance, then with the entire band, with their instruments, then without their instruments.

Herb Essen stepped in now and then. He

had choreographed the tango the way he had wanted it with Doug before they'd had the auditions. For the most part, it had seemed, the man wanted to leave it at that and work with the others. But apparently, from the director's point of view, there were things to change. This angle, that angle. The position of the backup dancers around them. Herb was kept very busy.

It was a long, grinding day. Once, Doug turned away, ready to scream, only to discover that both Kelly and Jane were staring at him, very amused. And only one thing kept him from exploding and telling them all just to go to hell. Kelly. There was no way in hell he'd leave her alone anywhere near Lance Morton — or any of the others, for that matter. He was there for the long run, sticking like glue.

He wasn't sure why Lance Morton got on his nerves. Except, of course, he was on Doug's suspect list. But why would the guy have murdered Dana Sumter? If there was a motive, he had to find it.

Doug was almost certain that Lance had delivered the very strange arrangement of flowers to Kelly. And he was from Ohio. In addition, he had returned to Florida right after his own session at the recording studio, which meant that he could have driven to West Palm and run that woman over. That meant Lance had been in California at the right time, in Ohio at the right time and in Florida at the right time. Doug had checked out Lance's flights and his hotel. The singer had come into Miami International and spent his first night on Miami Beach. Still, it was only an hour's drive up to Palm Beach.

And to make matters worse, every time there was a break, Lance sidled up to Kelly, reminding her that they'd be dancing together in several of the scenes.

He knew he wasn't being fair to Lance. Besides, if he was looking for a possible psycho among the video crowd, there were plenty of people to choose from. Marc Logan was a total sleaze. Mel had represented Dana Sumter. Jerry Tritan twitched. And Herb Essen was . . . a decent guy, Doug had to admit. Had always been. Hard-working, exacting, yet able to be kind to dancers even when turning them down. Maybe Kelly was right; maybe he *was* too damn suspicious.

He knew that he was driving her crazy, but he was driving himself even crazier. He had been certain he would feel that Kelly was safer here, but instead he felt more aware of a noose tightening.

Around nine o'clock Jerry Tritan announced that the dinner break he'd delayed now signaled the end of the workday. He applauded them all. "Thanks, folks. It was a long day, but a good day."

Doug noticed Ally Bassett talking to Kelly; then she came to him. "I have to leave soon . . . but Mel will be here a bit longer. I just wanted you to know how much I appreciate you having taken the job. And now more than ever. Is it working out for you?" The question seemed intense.

"Yes, fine, thank you."

"I hope we did the right thing, making her do that interview."

"I believe we did."

"Well, then . . ." She looked around, then stared at him again. "You stick close to Kelly, don't you?"

"Yes."

She let out a little sigh. "Yes, that's important."

"You trust me that much?" he asked her.

"You weren't in California when she had her accident," Ally said flatly. "Anyway, I'll keep in touch." She conferred with Mel and Marc Logan, and then she was gone.

"Hey!" Lance called suddenly, interrupting the director.

"What is it, Lance?" Jerry asked, a note of weary patience in his voice.

"My cell is gone."

"What?" Jerry said, frowning.

"My cell phone. It was on that light base thing over there. Now it's gone."

"Did anybody take Lance's cell phone?" Jerry asked. There was no reply.

"Lance, you must have put it down somewhere else," Jerry said.

"I didn't. I put it right there," Lance said stubbornly.

"Okay, everybody, let's stop everything and look for Lance's cell phone," Jerry said, his patience at its final limit. But apparently he meant it. Everyone wandered around, looking for the cell phone, but it wasn't to be found.

"Someone took it!" Lance accused.

"Call it in lost and get a damned new one!" Marc Logan said, obviously irritated. "These people have worked long and hard. It's dinner, folks. Dinner. You're through for the day."

The company split, the cast talking, heading in all directions, the light and camera crews breaking down. Jerry wandered over to talk to Marc.

"Can you believe that? Someone here is a thief!" Lance said to Kelly.

Doug joined them. "Do what Logan said. Call it in lost. Here, you can use mine to do it."

"I don't know who the hell to call. We're not with the same company," Lance said, obviously sulking.

"Get a P.A. to help you, then," Doug said. "Kelly, Sam probably needs to go out, huh?"

"Sam! Yes," Kelly said, apparently eager to leave the situation herself. "I need out of this dress, too. I'm going back to costumes to change."

"I'm coming with you."

They left Lance on the beach, his mood obviously dour. In the main section of the hotel, they split to go to their different changing rooms. Doug was impatient as he shrugged out of the elegant tux he'd been given. He hurried, making his way back to wait at the door for Kelly. Then Jane appeared, along with another girl who had been chosen from the auditions and Ally Bassett.

"Kelly still in there?" he asked.

"I never saw anyone change so fast in my life," Jane told him, grinning. "She was worried about Sam."

"Thanks," he said, starting to head for the trail to the back — and to Kelly's suite.

"Hey, you coming to dinner?" Jane asked.

"Yeah. I just want to get Kelly."

He hurried to her suite. When she didn't answer his bang on the door, he used his copy of her key to get in. She wasn't there; the back sliding door was open. He hurried through, feeling panic surge through him. Then he spotted her. She was standing on the beach, Sam running up and down on the sand by her.

"Kelly!" he snapped.

She turned, startled, and he rushed to her, taking her shoulders far too roughly.

"Dammit, what's the matter with you?" she demanded, shaking free.

"Why did you run off?"

"I didn't run off. I came to let Sam out."

"Kelly, dammit, don't be alone here."

She backed farther away, staring at him. "I'm not alone. I'm with Sam. You know what? I definitely want to live, but this is getting ridiculous. There are dozens of people here. I'm with my dog. I left California, did an interview denying my character on the show and got far away from the people involved with the soap."

"I don't think we should be staying here," he murmured.

"O'Casey! Stop it. Please!"

He took a deep breath, aware that he was pushing too hard, aware that it was his own fear of inadequacy that was prompting him.

"Kelly, that dancer I was involved with was killed in front of a crowd of hundreds. She was tricked into too much alcohol that had been laced with drugs. It looked like an accident, but it was anything but."

"O'Casey, you're driving me crazy," she said, almost at her breaking point.

"Look, I'm sorry. I know that I pressured you out of California and out of the show. Away from the past. But there's a lot now to indicate that maybe . . ."

"Maybe what? That the killer planned for me to be hired for this video?" she asked impatiently.

"All right, maybe that does sound a little preposterous."

"That he was able to rig a set in California, then manage to be on the crew of a video?" she asked.

He set his jaw stubbornly. "Kelly, listen to me. Dana Sumter was killed in California. Your accident was in California and you were nearly run over in California. Now you're here, and a woman was killed in West Palm Beach."

"Yes, but Sally Bower died in Ohio and I sure wasn't there."

"But Lance Morton was."

"Why don't we just go ask him if he was in Florida, then?" she demanded.

"He was."

"How do you know?"

"I tracked his flight."

"Right, that's what you do on the cell phone all the time, right? Have your brother check out every little incident and movement."

"Yes, Kelly, that's what I do."

"Kelly?" They both spun around, hearing her name called. It was Mel. Apparently, he'd tried her door, then come around the building to the beach side.

"Hey, Mel, over here!" she called back, then said softly to Doug, "It's Mel. May he join us?"

"Sure." Doug grated his teeth. "But you should know this. Mel came in early, too."

"What do you mean, he came in early?"

"His flight to Miami came in the day after ours."

"Oh! Now you're suggesting that Mel wants to kill me?" Kelly demanded incredulously.

"I'm just telling you certain people have been in the same area when things have happened, Kelly. That's all."

She walked up to him angrily, her voice a

hissed whisper. "Guess what? Mel sure as hell wasn't in Ohio!" She turned away from him, hurrying to her agent, giving him a hug. "Hey! It was pretty good, wasn't it, Mel?" she asked anxiously.

Mel beamed at her, then at Doug. "It was great! Kelly, I was behind Logan, watching the camera. You looked stunning." He glanced at Doug, shrugging ruefully. "You looked pretty good, too, O'Casey."

"Aw, shucks. Thanks."

"Are you two coming to dinner?"

"You bet. I'm starving," Kelly said. "Let me just get Sam back in."

They walked back to the open rear of Kelly's suite, and Doug damned himself. He'd come running out, leaving that back door open in his anxiety to reach Kelly. Leaving the door open for anyone to slip in.

Chapter 23

O'Casey was definitely her shadow, Kelly thought wryly. And it should have been fine. She knew she was growing more and more dependent on him, or on his being with her at least. And she loved the moments when they weren't discussing her situation, loved it when they were in the heat and tumult of passion, when they laughed, when she just lay beside him and studied his face, feeling his breath, his warmth, the beat of his heart. . . .

If they were an actual couple, she realized, he'd be driving her insane. But then again, she was fairly certain he wouldn't be acting so crazy if the world were just . . . normal. O'Casey had confidence. He wasn't the type to need assurance every other second or to be irrationally jealous. If he were really in her life . . . not that she knew exactly what her real life was anymore.

At dinner that night, he was particularly intense. When she rose to grab a napkin off another table, his eyes followed her the whole way. Anytime anyone talked to her, his eyes narrowed as he listened to every word. And his brow furrowed tightly anytime Lance Morton talked to her. She could almost see hackles rise on the back of his neck.

Kelly was very grateful for Jane Ulrich, who kept the conversation going at their table. She was light and cheerful, talking about the area to Mel, informing him that he really needed to swim with the dolphins while he was here. Jane managed to make it all seem so . . . normal.

When they returned to her suite, O'Casey reminded her of a caged cat. He was distracted, absentminded, and couldn't stop pacing around the room. It was late and she was exhausted. She just wanted to lie down with him and actually voice her pleasure in the work that day. She was proud of herself. It had been real challenging remembering to keep all her body parts in the right position at the right time. But she fell asleep before he ever came to bed.

She woke up in the middle of the night. He wasn't beside her. She assumed that he must be out on the balcony, on his cell, but he wasn't. She rose, slipped into one of the resort robes and tiptoed to the landing, then down the stairs. She found him in the rear area, behind the kitchenette and in front of the beach-side porch doors, where there was an Internet station. Sam was lying by his feet.

"Before you ask, it's a chart I've been keeping," he told her.

"A chart?"

She looked over his shoulder and was startled to see the extensive detail of the report. He had names, dates and places. A little flutter of anger seized her when she noticed Mel's name. O'Casey had been following his movements all the way from the date Dana Sumter had been killed.

"You know," she told him, "suppose the person doing this is none of the above? It's not usually that easy, is it? In most cases of serial murder, there's a profile."

He spun the chair around, looking at her. "Did you ever see clips of Ted Bundy? He wasn't just normal in appearance, he was a good-looking man, intelligent and articulate."

"But he targeted a type of woman, not an occupation!"

"Still, a type of woman. He was after

young women with long brown hair. This fellow is out for those who give advice."

Kelly shook her head again. "Those involved with this video have been living rather normal lives for years. Wouldn't something have to cause a mental snap to suddenly plunge a man — or woman, for that matter — into murder?"

O'Casey was silent, and she knew that he agreed with her question.

"That's it, isn't it?" he murmured.

"What?"

"It's not just a matter of tracking who was where, it's a matter of finding out what might have happened in someone's life to cause a . . . breakdown of some kind." He switched off the computer suddenly. "Early call tomorrow," he said.

She smiled. "I have an early call tomorrow. The scene with Lance. You don't have to be there, you know."

"Yes, I do."

"Do you really think he could be a psychotic killer?" she asked.

"Doesn't matter. I don't intend to leave him alone with you."

"We're hardly going to be alone. There will be a whole crew there."

"I told you, I saw someone killed once —"

She lowered to her knees, touching his face. "I know. Someone was killed in full view of others. And I'm so sorry. But O'Casey . . ."

His features were so intense. He responded to her touch, catching her hand, kissing her fingers and then her palm. She had never known that the brush of lips against her hand could be so erotic. Or that someone could make her feel so very cherished with such a light touch, then set her on fire as his fingers moved beneath the robe, stroking her collarbone, sliding around her breast. He drew her up onto his lap and into his arms. His kiss fell upon her lips with tenderness, then an eager hunger. He rose, holding her tight, his lips still welded to hers. And when they broke, his voice was husky, the tenor and depth of it setting fire to her just as his touch had.

"I'll be there with you," he said.

She smiled, leaning back, and curled her arms around his neck as they moved toward the stairs, knowing where his kiss would fall when they reached the top.

Hours later, he was back at the computer. There was one person missing from the picture — in Florida, at least.

The bio for Matt Avery under Household Heaven was typical PR schmaltz, but there were some interesting facts to be gleaned from it. He'd been raised by an adoptive father, a high school teacher, but he'd gone to the best schools, expensive schools. On a teacher's salary?

His parents had been killed in an automobile accident several years ago. They'd gone right off the Pacific Coast Highway, and died in a fiery heap just inches from the ocean. Somehow, with the death of his parents, he'd inherited something of an estate. Again, Doug thought, an estate? On a teacher's salary? Money had come into that house from somewhere, but from where?

Again, he couldn't help thinking about Dana Sumter's missing year, and the fact that she might well have had a child. He pulled out his chart. Lance Morton. Matt Avery.

He dug back into the computer, checking the Web sites of each man. He looked for the basic information on their lives. Both of them were the same age, Matt just a few months older than Lance. And both could well have been born that missing year in Dana Sumter's life.

He put through a call to the West Coast. Getting through to the jail wasn't easy; it was late out there now. Luckily, he knew people with the right pull. And soon enough, he was talking to Dana Sumter's ex-husband, Harvey. The fellow had been sleeping and seemed very confused.

"Do you know if your wife had an illegitimate child before you were married?"

"What?"

"Did your wife have an illegitimate child before you were married?" Doug repeated.

At first, only silence came over the lines. Then, "What makes you ask that?" Harvey said, sounding confused. "She never said anything before we were married, but somewhere along the line, in the middle of an argument, she implied that she might have given up a child. She was trying to make me see just how important a career was to her. I don't know it for a fact, but, yes, I believe she might have had a child out there. I didn't ever bring up the subject again. After all," he said with bitterness, "it had been in her past."

"There's a year missing from her life when she was quite young," Doug said. "Do you know where she might have had this child?"

"Hell, no."

"Was it in California, do you know?"

"Look, I don't even know for sure if

there is a child. Does it mean something?"

"I don't know, but I'm going to find out."

Doug woke early and anxiously slipped from bed, careful not to wake Kelly. She was the one with the early call, but there was still time for her to sleep. Downstairs he put a call through to Liam Murphy. It was the middle of the night in L.A., but he couldn't be sorry. Serena, sounding entirely confused and disoriented, was the one to answer. When she heard his voice, she was alarmed. He apologized quickly, assuring her that everything was all right, and asked to speak to Liam. Again, he apologized. Liam, sounding half dead, tried to be polite.

"Phone records? You need a subpoena —"

"Not when you know the right people."

Liam groaned. "Not even Detective Olsen can just —"

"You've got to know someone."

"I'll try. What are you trying to prove?"

"I don't know, exactly," Doug said. "I've checked out a lot of past histories, and it seems that everyone professionally involved with Kelly has an ex-wife. I can't imagine that a marriage gone bad years ago would suddenly set someone off now, unless it's some kind of a repeat thing. That's why I want to hunt down any recent associations. A bad breakup. Something. Anything that would indicate a recent relationship that went bad."

"You talked to the husband last night?"

"Yes, and I was right. He said that she'd had a child before their marriage."

"Where?" Liam demanded.

"He had no idea and she wouldn't tell him."

"We wouldn't even know where to start looking for those records."

"We start with the people we know — Lance Morton, Matt Avery."

"I'll do what I can," Liam murmured.

"I've got friends I'm going to ask at this end, too," Doug told him.

"Good. It's actually morning for them," Liam told him dryly.

"Look, I'm really sorry about the time."

"Wait until you have twins," Liam said.

"Sorry, really."

"Since it's for Kelly's sake, it's all right," he said gruffly.

"One more favor," Doug said.

"Yeah?"

"Matt Avery."

"Yeah, yeah, you gave me his name."

"I have one more question about him."

"The guy is an ass. You want more than that?"

"He got his money from somewhere. I want to know where. Also, I'd like to find out about his whereabouts over the last several months."

"I'll do my best," Liam told him, and hung up.

Doug quickly put a call through to his brother. He woke Quinn as well, but knew that his brother would deal with it. After he rang off, he started coffee in the little kitchenette and went to wake Kelly.

Kelly absolutely couldn't believe that Lance Morton could be a killer, especially not the apparently very organized man who had killed Dana Sumter. Lance simply wasn't bright enough. He knew music, and he had one hell of a voice. But other than that . . .

The song spoke of a man's love for a tango dancer, and how he would rather see her dead than in the arms of the partner she preferred. Therefore, there were "dream" moments in which he held her in his arms. Lance didn't have to dance, he just had to pretend to sing while holding her.

Jerry Tritan, apparently, didn't find Lance the brightest penny in the mint, either. He'd wanted a fair amount of rehearsal, and he was filming it, just so he could see where Lance was going and what needed to be said to him to improve the scene.

There wasn't anything particularly repulsive about Lance, but something about the way he held her made Kelly long to recoil. His fingers moved a little too suggestively on her skin. When Jerry called, "Cut!" Lance held on a little too long, pulling her a shade closer before releasing her.

Told to wait while some tape was being rerun, he slipped an arm around her shoulders. "You know, I really believe I'm going to be the hottest thing out there once this hits."

She smiled. "There was a lead singer of a hot band who once said he was better than any of the Beatles. No one's seen anything from him in years. Modesty can be a good thing, you know."

"I am modest. I'm just saying that I'm going places and you, Kelly, could be with me."

"Wow," she couldn't help but murmur dryly.

"Really, I think you're the most beautiful thing in the world."

"That's very sweet."

"Ready on set!" one of the P.A.s called.

"Think about it!" Lance told her, pulling her into his arms with a lascivious smile. "You can ditch that dance teacher and come with me to Marathon today — I'm going to pick out a new phone. You can help me. I'd cherish your advice."

She stared at him, incredulous.

"Yes, I'd let you choose for me," he said, his voice silky.

"Gee, Lance. Sorry, but I'm going to have to pass on that one."

"If you wait too long, I may be snapped up. I mean, you are the ticket, Kelly, but a man has needs, you know."

"I'm sure."

"Quiet on set!" Jerry snapped.

They fell silent, listening to his new direction. "Lance, no, no, no!" Jerry said. He started to come toward them, apparently forgetting that he was on the edge of the concrete fountain. Jerry fell like a ton of bricks. As he crashed down, he howled in pain. The place broke into chaos.

Kelly heard Marc Logan cursing above it all. "Dammit, Tritan!" So much for empathy.

She backed away, knowing that Jerry was hurt but not wanting to add to the rush going on around him. She saw that O'Casey had stepped forward, and she was certain he'd probably had some medical training in the police academy.

Kelly hung back, concerned and feeling helpless. Jane came to stand by her side. "I think he's really hurt!" she said worriedly.

"I'm afraid so," Kelly murmured.

In the next moments, a straight gurney was rigged. Harry, O'Casey and a number of the others carefully lifted a still-moaning Jerry, hurrying to get him to the dock, where an emergency medical assistance boat would get him to the mainland. From there, he would be rushed to the nearest hospital, in Homestead.

Eventually Marc Logan returned to the throng. "All right, folks, everyone has the day off. But if you go sightseeing, it's on your own! We're going to be seriously over budget already!"

"A day off!" Lance said cheerfully, reaching Kelly and Jane. "We could really make an afternoon of it," he told Kelly.

"Thanks, but . . . no thanks, Lance."

He turned to Jane. "How about you, hot stuff?"

Jane looked at him as if he were crazy.

Kelly slipped an arm around her, pulling her close. "Jane is dating a professional hockey player. A really big fellow, you know? The guy's been in so many major fights on the ice, he doesn't even have any of his own teeth left."

"Gotta go," Lance said. "Ladies, your loss."

They both nodded. When he had walked off, Jane burst into laughter. "Kelly! Mike has all his own teeth."

"Sorry. Couldn't help myself."

"You got rid of him, that's what counts. But, Kelly, what will happen now? Do you think that Jerry is seriously hurt? And what about the video?"

"He may have a broken bone . . . or maybe several," Kelly said sadly. "But don't worry. A lot of film has already been shot. Marc Logan isn't going to let it go to waste, I'm certain."

"I hope you're right."

People were milling around in groups, worrying on the one hand, determining how to spend their day of freedom on the other.

"People, people!" Harry Sullivan announced, raising his hands as he entered the center of the group. "I'll have the launch ready for a trip to the main islands in thirty minutes. Jump on board, anyone who wants to explore the Keys today. You can rent a car if you want, there are a few places. And you can get a decent meal at Vinnie's — that's where I pick up and drop off. I'll come in and out a couple of times during the day. Last trip back here will be at ten. After that, you'll need private transportation or a room somewhere else."

One of the girls on the light crew called out to them. "We're heading down to Key West. Want to come?"

"Wait, wait, wait!" one of the lighting guys interrupted. "My group is going diving. Anyone want to join us?"

"Thanks," Kelly returned. "To both of you. I'm not sure yet what I'm going to do with the day. But thanks for the invitations."

"Yep, thanks!" Jane said as well, then turned to Kelly. "What are you going to do?"

Kelly shrugged, then told her dryly, "Nothing until I hear from the almighty commander, your partner."

Jane giggled. "He sure can get a bone in his craw, huh?"

As she spoke, they could see O'Casey returning from the dock area. "How does Jerry look?" Kelly asked him.

"He smashed up his face, but I don't think he broke his nose or his jaw. Luckily he didn't break his neck. Nothing on him appeared to be too swollen, so he may just be sore. The launch will take him straight up to Key Largo, and he'll be in a hospital soon. We saw to it that he wasn't moved, though he will be jostled a bit in the boat." He offered them both a smile, then looked around. "So, the mice have scattered already."

"In a flash," Jane said.

"Do you know where people are off to?" he queried.

"Diving, driving to Key West, and I'm not sure where else," Jane said.

"I'm going to go let Sam out," Kelly announced.

"Can I tag along with you?" Jane asked. "Oh, sorry! Unless you want to be alone."

"Please, do come along. You can see my little retreat," Kelly told her.

O'Casey was looking around. "Hey? Are you coming?" Kelly asked him.

"Wow, I love it!" Jane said, marveling at the size and scope of the suite. "And I do mean wow!"

O'Casey walked on through, heading to the back to let Sam out. He stood on the back porch, letting the dog run around crazily out on the sand. He watched Sam for a minute, then made a turnaround so sharp it had military precision.

"I think we should go into Marathon, just take in some tourist stuff for the day." He glanced at his watch. "It's nearly three, but we can take in a late lunch. What do you think?"

"Tourist stuff?" Kelly echoed. "I'd want to take Sam."

"No!" Jane said. "I mean . . ." She flushed. "Why don't you two go in and I'll baby-sit. Dog-sit, that is. I'd love to stay here with him. I've never seen a suite like this in my whole life."

"It's fine with me," Kelly said, "if that's what you really want."

"Oh, I would love to live this fantasy! Watch a movie, do my nails, soak . . . pretend I'm incredibly wealthy," Jane said.

"Keep the doors locked," O'Casey said.

"Why?"

"Jane, I'm serious. If you plan to stay, you need to keep the doors locked."

"But Sam may need —"

"Let Sam water something in here, Jane. Keep the doors locked. Promise."

She looked at Kelly, warning her that O'Casey definitely had his oddities.

Kelly already knew that.

Doug's cell phone rang as he awaited Jane's assurance. He answered it, then snapped it shut and called Sam back in.

"We're out of here, Jane. Keep those doors locked!" And with that he put his arm around Kelly and led her out the front door.

Chapter 24

A number of the cast and crew, including Lance Morton, were headed to Vinnie's for lunch. To Kelly's surprise, O'Casey was eager to join them.

"All right, what's going on?" she asked, leaning toward him as they slid into one of the wooden benches at a picnic-style, rustic table. "Wait! I know. You're going to tell me that Jerry's fall was all part of the conspiracy."

"No, I have to admit, he looked as if he just fell," O'Casey replied.

"Then . . . ?"

"Quinn is driving down."

She didn't have a chance to ask him why because Mel came over and slid next to Kelly. "Well, if this doesn't just kind of beat all," he said.

"Any word yet?"

"Broken arm, and that's it. Jerry will be back to work the day after tomorrow."

"So, we're off for two days then?" Kelly asked.

"No. Herb Essen is going to take over working with the dancers tomorrow."

"But Jerry is the director," Kelly said.

"Doesn't matter. Logan says his budget is too high already. He wants people working, not running around enjoying the Keys." He pulled out the menu. "So, Doug. This is your neck of the woods. What's good down here?"

"Fish. It will be fresh," Doug told him.

Across the room, Kelly could see Lance flirting with the waitress and one of the camera girls.

Mel turned to Kelly. "You're doing well, here, right? You're okay?"

"I'm fine," she assured him.

"I'm going to head on back. To L.A."

"That's fine, Mel. You've been around way more than I could expect," Kelly told him.

He studied her, a rueful smile on his lips. "Well, you've had me worried." He looked at Doug. "Your newscast showed, you know."

O'Casey shook his head. "Actually, we didn't watch."

"It was good. You were charming," he told Kelly. "And Sam at your feet was a nice little extra, too." He looked across the table at O'Casey. "It's being picked up by all the entertainment shows, just as you suggested. So . . ."

"Go home and make money on your other clients. I'm fine," Kelly assured him.

Their waitress came by and they all ordered the fish. She swore it would be fresh, just as Doug had suggested. The girl looked a little harried, but then again, they had more or less bombarded the place. Most of the cast and crew were here, along with Marc Logan, who sat with a few of the production assistants scribbling notes as he spoke. The place was busy; lots of confusion.

O'Casey's phone rang. "Excuse me," he said, rising. "Can't hear in here."

"Interesting fellow. Very intense," Mel said as they watched Doug weave his way through the tables.

"So are you driving back up to Miami to head out?" she asked.

"I've got all my things with me. I thought I'd hang around until night then drive up and see what they have in the way of a red-eye. But as it is, I can take an afternoon flight that will get me in by the evening. Kelly, listen, if you feel unsafe in any way, unhappy in any way, call. I can hop right back on a flight out here."

She set her hand over his, squeezing. "It's all right. I'm fine. I'm sorry about Jerry, yet I'm relieved that it doesn't appear to be any kind of a conspiracy." Kelly heard her own phone go off. And when she answered it, she realized that, for once, O'Casey wasn't being secretive — it really was impossible to hear.

"Excuse me," she told Mel, and slipped out to the dockside area of the restaurant. She could see their launch listing in the waves, and Harry Sullivan reading his newspaper as he sat at the helm, an arm draped over the wheel.

"Hello? Hello?" she said. There was silence for a second and she felt a chill seeping into her. "Hello?"

"Kelly!"

"Yes?"

"It's Jane."

"Oh!" Relief filled her.

"Kelly, you need to come back."

"What's the matter?"

Jane hesitated on the other end, then said, "I'm really worried about Sam."

"Sam?"

"Kelly, he must have gotten hold of something bad. He's frothing at the mouth, and he growls at me when I try to get near him. He's sick, Kelly, really sick, and I don't know what to do."

"I'm coming. Now. Right now." She hung up and rushed back into the restaurant, looking for O'Casey, but he hadn't returned. And to her amazement, Mel had left the table as well. She hurried over to where Lance was sitting with his crew. "Have you seen Mel or Doug O'Casey?" she asked him.

"No, but I'm here!" he told her.

"Listen, if you see either one of them, tell them that I headed back to the island — there's something wrong with Sam."

"I'll come with you —" Lance said, rising.

"No! No, thanks!"

Kelly ran out, hoping that someone would pay her tab. She hesitated briefly, looking back for Doug, but she didn't see him and knew she couldn't wait.

She rushed down the dock, yelling, "Harry! You've got to get me back to the island!"

He dropped his paper, taken by surprise. "What? Now? But the other folks are all . . ."

"Harry!" She actually hit him on the shoulder. "My dog is sick. Get me back to that island!"

"All right, all right!" he muttered, and hurried to release the tie ropes.

"What have you got?" Doug asked his brother. "Are you headed down?"

"Yeah, yeah, I'm driving down. And you may be fired."

"From the video?"

"No, from your day job, remember? Moonlight Sonata studios, my wife's place."

"Why?"

"I had to bring roses to a woman I know at the phone company. Shannon definitely arched a brow at that, but I did come up with a lot of paperwork."

"I won't be fired."

"Don't kid yourself. Shannon likes to get those roses herself."

"What did you get?"

"Interesting information. First, the threatening call you received for Kelly came from a phone booth on the beach, just as we suspected."

"That's no surprise."

Quinn continued. "My friend talks to a lot of her cohorts at other companies. You know, the concept of getting 'phone records' isn't what it used to be. Hell, everyone is with a different company. And everyone has a cell phone."

"But have you got anything?"

"A lot I could probably get arrested for."

"Quinn, what have you got?"

Doug paced the restaurant parking lot as he waited for the information. As he wandered over to a shady area secluded by a bunch of sea grapes, he saw a number of people beginning to wander out of Vinnie's. He wasn't in the mood for any of the really cordial invitations others in the group were handing out.

"To start, all I can get on Lance Morton, as far as Ohio goes, is that he calls two numbers in Sandusky. One is his mother's house. The other number belongs to an old girlfriend. Apparently they've stayed in touch."

"How do you know that?"

"I called her."

"You called her?"

"I told her I was a reporter doing research on his background."

"Go on."

"They were a hot item once, but he cheated on her and she gave him his walking papers. The guy tried to make it up to her, but she was obstinate. Now she's not so sure she did the right thing — she believes he's going to be big-time."

"Okay, so he had a bad breakup with his girlfriend."

"Well, this may or may not mean anything, but she contributed to her school paper at the time. She wrote an advice column. And, listen to this. She said that once, when they had a big fight, he got violent."

"How violent?"

"Shoved her around. She told everyone and he was nearly arrested, but she didn't press charges."

"But they're friends now?"

"So she says."

"The guy is a dick," Doug muttered.

"Careful. You may have decided you just don't like him, but that doesn't make him a killer."

"I know that."

He was vaguely aware of the sounds of car motors and boat motors revving around him. Staring out at the parking lot, he saw Mel Alton deep in conversation with Marc Logan.

"What else have you got?" Doug asked.

"A fair amount. I'll give you a couple of quick pieces of information Liam Murphy dug up in California."

"Talk to me."

"Mel Alton."

"He was in Ohio, too?"

"No. Again, this may or may not mean anything, but his ex-wife intends to take him back to court."

"Child support?"

"And more alimony. She believes she deserves more, having supported him through college. She's claiming that her support of him curtailed her own possible future and income. I have more papers, too. Pages and pages of them. Lots of phone records on anyone I could think of and have a hope of obtaining. I didn't think you wanted to get faxes at the resort, so I got Liam to send the stuff from his end to me. I have it all for you. Actually, I have more than you asked for, but sure as hell nothing that's a bull's-eye."

"What else can you tell me quickly?" As he watched the scene in the parking lot, Mel broke away from Logan and headed to his rental car — a dark green Buick sedan. Behind him, Logan was walking toward a Lincoln Continental. Black.

"Liam must have some really good friends at the phone companies out there," Quinn continued. "He pulled the records for Dana Sumter's house, cell and place of business. He figures her killer must have called in when she was giving out her advice."

Lance Morton appeared in the parking lot, his arm around a pretty camera girl. She was laughing, flushed with the excitement of being with him. He headed toward a dark blue, muddied Oldsmobile.

"Anyway, I have scores of numbers and addresses."

"Good."

"Remember your questions about Matt Avery?"

"Yes?"

"Apparently his mother had been socking money away for years. Where it came from can't be traced. And get this. He's out of town a lot, 'working' vacations. And guess where he takes those vacations?"

"Where?"

"An old family mansion in Palm Beach."

"Has he been there recently?"

"According to his secretary, he's out of town now. But she won't say where he is."

"Thanks."

"All right. I'll see —"

The phone suddenly went dead in Doug's hand. He swore softly but knew that Quinn had probably driven into an area where there was no satellite reception. He tried to call his brother's number back but was immediately switched over to the answering machine. He swore again, clicked his phone shut and started back into the restaurant.

The table he had been sharing with Mel and Kelly was empty. Most of the other tables had cleared out as well. He recognized two members of the crew and asked them if they'd seen Kelly. They hadn't. One of them had seen her on the phone a while back, but they hadn't seen her since. He swore again. Where the hell had she gone? Sweat broke out on his brow.

"Hey!" the production assistant he had talked to earlier called. "She might have gone back to the island. The launch left kind of suddenly."

"Thanks!"

He walked out to the dock. The launch was indeed gone. Trying to suppress a surge of panic, he dialed her cell number. To his amazement, he heard a phone ringing by his feet. He looked down and saw that Kelly's cell had fallen on the planks. Either she had dropped it in her haste to get somewhere, or . . . someone had forced her onto the launch.

He dialed the hotel number, gritting his teeth as he went through the automatic response system that would let him key in her room number. His feeling of unease nearly exploded. The room number rang and rang and rang.

There was only one boat at the dock, a small, beaten-to-pieces little motorboat. He hurried back into the restaurant. "Hey, anybody know who owns the boat out here?" A fellow with gray hair down his back and a Grateful Dead T-shirt answered.

"It's mine. You want to make something out of it?"

"No. I want to pay you to use it."

The fellow perked up. "How much? How long do you want it for?"

"I don't know — the day, I guess."

The man named an exorbitant price. "Hell, you take credit cards?" Doug asked.

"What you got?"

Doug opened his wallet, sifting through the bills. He offered a wad to the man. "Take it or leave it."

"I'll leave it, 'cause you're desperate."

He didn't mean to, but he caught the fellow by the collar of his shirt. "I can steal it or pay you."

"Shit! Pay me. I ain't goin' nowheres today, anyhow!" he said, handing Doug a key. "She's worth a small fortune, you know!"

"Like hell!" Doug called back as he left the restaurant.

He raced back to the dock, slipped the ties and turned the key in the ignition. Halfway across the water, he was swearing again. The motor was pathetic. He could have swum more quickly. He could see the little islet in front of him, but he couldn't reach it fast enough.

Kelly couldn't believe how sick Sam had gotten so quickly, but it was true. He looked liked hell. She'd tried to call O'Casey when she got on the launch, but realized that she'd dropped her cell. And she had meant to call when she reached the room, but after one look at Sam, she didn't remember anything.

"I gotta get him to a vet, fast," she told Jane. Sam didn't growl at her; he whimpered pathetically. His eyes were glazed and he continued to foam at the mouth.

"Yeah, I think you're right," Jane agreed.

He was a big, heavy dog. Kelly went to scoop him up in her arms.

"I can try to help you," Jane said nervously.

"No . . . no, just go ahead of me, will you? Get Harry and tell him we're heading back to the island."

"Of course!"

Kelly moved as quickly as she could with

Sam in her arms. When she reached the dock area, Harry was just coming in.

"You've got to get me to the closest vet," Kelly told him.

"What? He probably just ate some grass or something. If you —"

"Get her to a vet!" Jane shouted.

Surprised, Kelly glanced at Jane, who shrugged. "I'll come with you."

"No, you wait here. Tell O'Casey where I am. Hey, where will I be?" she asked Harry. "Hurry!"

He gave them a mile-marker number and Kelly hurried to the launch, carefully balancing as Harry tried to help her while keeping his hands and digits far from Sam's head.

"Hey! My car's the little silver BMW in the rear of the lot," Jane said, tossing the keys at Kelly. Harry caught them just in time.

"Go! Go! Go!" Kelly yelled.

Doing the best he could to get power out of the beat-up boat, O'Casey was startled when he saw the launch from the island whipping by him. The wake tossed him heavily. It looked as if Harry Sullivan was the only one aboard. With one hand on the helm, he pulled out his cell. He dialed the hotel, swore again as he waited for the re-corded message and keyed in the room number. Still no answer.

He was closer to the island than the docks at Vinnie's. By coaxing the engine, he could be there in a matter of minutes.

The dock was empty. The entire island seemed to be empty. He raced through the main house of the hotel, out the back, to Kelly's room. The door was ajar. He flew toward it, pushed it open. And heard a scream.

Chapter 25

The folks at Vinnie's were great. One of the waiters rushed to the dock, ready to help her, but she warned him that Sam wasn't himself.

"Is there anything I can do?" the fellow asked.

"Yes, thank you! Harry, toss him the keys, please." With Sam in her arms, she used her head as an indicator. "Can you run ahead and open a silver BMW for me?" she asked, and the fellow obliged.

"Harry, let Doug O'Casey know where I am!" she called over her shoulder. She didn't know if Harry answered her or not.

The waiter opened both the back and front doors for her, and she carefully laid Sam in the back. As she got into the driver's seat, thanking the waiter again and taking the keys back, she noted that O'Casey's car was still in the parking lot. She could write him a note. Except that . . . she didn't have time. Sam was barely panting anymore, barely breathing.

And O'Casey! Damn him. Where the hell had he been when she needed him? He'd taken one of his secretive phone calls and simply disappeared. But she couldn't worry about him. Not now. Not when tears were nearly blinding her and she had to get help for Sam.

She gunned the motor, jerked the car into gear and headed for the exit. For a moment she was disoriented, trying to decide which way was north, which was south.

Right! she screamed at herself mentally. There's only one road. And she was stuck behind a Sunday driver. She honked the horn, but the car drew more to a crawl, probably assuming she was just being an ass.

The opposing traffic was heavy, so she prayed for a passing lane.

Finally one came up and she gunned the engine, sweeping around the slow mover. Clutching the wheel in a death grip, she leaned over, desperately looking for the mile-marker signs and any sign that would indicate the vet's office.

She nearly drove past it, then came to a dead stop in the middle of the road. She heard brakes screeching behind her, and as she pulled into the lot, someone cussed at her from an open car window. She ignored the words, desperately throwing open the back door and reaching in for Sam. And with him in her arms, she burst into the office.

It was a small but friendly-looking place, with light blue walls that were hand-painted with creatures — puppies, kittens and fish. She rushed to the counter, where a young woman with a blue streak in her dark hair was sitting, talking on the phone.

"One moment, please. You can take a seat," she told Kelly.

Stunned, Kelly stared at her. Then, somehow balancing Sam, she managed to reach over the counter, grip the receiver, jerk it from the girl's hand and return it the cradle. "Sorry. I'm really sorry. But I need help. Please . . . my dog is dying!"

"Oh, my God! You scared me to death!" Jane cried.

Doug stared at her. He didn't bother telling her that her scream had surely scared him just as badly. He didn't think it was possible to feel a greater sense of unease.

"Where's Kelly?" he asked, his heart thundering.

"She took Sam to the vet. She's all right," Jane said quickly. "But something was terribly wrong with Sam. He was foaming, Doug. And I couldn't do anything because he wouldn't let me near him."

"Foaming?"

"He must have gotten into something on the island. I don't know, a plant . . . a dead fish. Something. He was violently ill. But Kelly has him and Harry was taking them back to the mainland so she can take Sam to a vet."

"Where?" Doug demanded.

She gave him the mile marker. He turned to leave, then spun back.

"Why was this door open?" he demanded.

"Damn it, Doug, I had just walked back in!" Jane said.

"Get in and lock it. Do you understand?"

"Yes, sir!" she said resentfully.

He didn't have time to apologize or explain his misgivings. Sure, Sam might have gotten into something. But in his present state of mind, Doug didn't believe it. Sam had been poisoned.

He gave Jane a last look. "Lock yourself in!" Then he raced back to the dock, where the pathetic piece-of-shit motorboat awaited him. Since Harry wasn't back with the launch, he had no choice. Swearing, he hopped back in.

Halfway back to the main island, the motor sputtered, coughed and died. He cranked it again and again, but to no avail. And there was no other vessel on the water to be seen! He looked to the sky. Pretty soon the sun was going to begin to set. Then he kicked off his shoes, stripped off his shirt and dived in.

The receptionist, realizing Sam's shape, jumped up and called for the vet. He appeared, running out from his inner offices at the commotion. One look at Sam and he knew there was serious trouble.

"Excuse me, folks," he apologized to his waiting clients and patients. He strode straight to Kelly and reached for Sam.

"I've . . . I've got him. I can carry him!" she said. She was afraid that, in Sam's present condition, he would try to bite the hand that was trying to help him.

"Miss, let me take him," the vet said firmly.

"He could . . . he wouldn't usually . . . he could bite."

"I think I'm all right."

Sam didn't make any attempt to bite, for he had gotten far too weak. His head lolled as the vet carried him straight back into one of his patient rooms.

A big fellow tried to stop her from following, blocking her way, speaking in gentle tones. "The vet can handle him from here. It might not be pretty. He's in a bad way."

"I have to come in!" Kelly cried.

"If she wants to come in, let her," the vet called back.

The following minutes were a nightmare for Kelly, yet she knew she would never be able to express her gratitude to the man who worked on Sam. Tests might determine what had brought him to his state near death; for the moment, it was important only to get it out of his system.

Sam struggled only slightly as he was hit with a needle. Silent tears slipped down Kelly's cheeks as the vet, a burly assistant at his side, worked to pump Sam's stomach. It was horrible. But when the vet had done what he could, he said the words that Kelly longed to hear. "He's still breathing and his pulse is steady, but he's weak and exhausted. I'm going to have to keep him overnight."

"I can't leave him!" Kelly said.

"Please, he won't really be alone. I'll watch him through the night, I swear. I live in back. And if I need anything for him, the office is right here."

Kelly burst into tears and would have sunk to the ground if the vet hadn't grabbed her.

"I'll do everything I can for him. He looks like a fighter. Come on out now and let us get a little information from you. Jimmy will make him comfortable." Jimmy was apparently the huge bear of a man who had tried to stop her, but who was as gentle and tender with Sam as an angel.

The vet continued. "Sam will sleep now. We've taken some samples from him and we'll run some tests, find out what caused this."

She managed to nod, and for the first time, she really saw the fellow. He was about fifty, with kind brown eyes and dark, graying hair. He was tanned and lined, as if he lived in the sun and didn't give a damn about the effects. There was something very solid and reassuring about him. His name was Dr. Emil Garcia.

"I really think it's going to be all right," he assured her again. "Sorry, but I really do need some paperwork. Are you up to it?"

"Yes, of course. Thank you. Thank you so very much."

So she filled out papers. And it wasn't until she had answered all his questions about Sam — about where they had been, what he might have eaten — that he nodded slowly, staring at her again.

"You're the soap star. Working on the big video deal, right?"

When she nodded, he told her quietly, "This was possibly a case of willful poisoning."

"But . . . he's going to be all right?"

"I will do everything in my power to see to it."

"I should just stay here, stay with him," she said numbly.

"Miss Trent, I promise you, if there's any change, I'll call you immediately."

She managed a wry smile. "You can't. I lost my cell phone somewhere."

"I know the number to the resort. Really, there's nothing you can do. And you look like hell yourself. You need to get some rest. For the moment, Sam is out of the woods. He needs rest." He frowned suddenly. "If you're not feeling up to driving, I can have someone take you back to Vinnie's."

She shook her head. She meant to get

Jane's car back. And she was very anxious now to find O'Casey.

"I can drive. If Sam is going to pull through, I can do anything."

"I can't give you any guarantees, but I think we got to him in time," Dr. Garcia said. He smiled. "I'm serious. He's a strong, healthy dog."

He escorted her out to the waiting room, where the number of people and pets had grown.

"I think we've pulled him through, folks!" he said.

There was a round of applause, and a woman with a fluffy mutt rose, coming to Kelly. "Oh, there, darling, it's going to be all right! Thank God. We're all so happy for you."

She smiled her thanks. And when she finally left, she was almost feeling good.

The sun was setting, the sky streaked with stunning colors. Even as she clicked open the car door, the colors were changing before her eyes. She had noticed that about the Keys. The sky would be touched by brilliant, glorious colors, and then they would deepen to richer hues of mauve, crimson and magenta. Then, with little warning, those colors would blend to darkness — true darkness.

She had never seen it this dark in L.A., or Miami, or any major city for that matter. The lights of man's existence were simply too strong. But here, the darkness was complete. And she was glad that there was only one road, because she was pretty certain she knew just how far she had to get and where she was going.

Exhausted, she revved the engine, fought the temptation to go back in and look at Sam one more time, and moved the car out of the drive, ready to enter the road.

There were a number of people either seated at little shanty tables or milling around dockside at Vinnie's when Doug crawled out of the water. He was soaked and shoeless. They all stared at him, but he walked past them and headed for his car. He crawled into the front seat, then pulled his keys out of his soaking pocket. It was already dark.

As she drove, Kelly's mind was on Sam. Had someone actually poisoned her dog? And if so, her claiming that she wasn't Marla Valentine hadn't meant anything. And not only that, there were surely a number of advice therapists out there — qualified and self-proclaimed — who re-

447

mained in danger, as well. No one should have to live like that — ever.

She was deep in thought, the only illumination the pool of light created by her car's high beams. She had on her brights, but not even that power could illuminate the deep pitch darkness of the world around her.

Suddenly she winced, narrowing her eyes. There was someone behind her, someone with their high beams on. Since there were no cars coming in the opposite direction, she flicked her lights, indicating that the driver should pass. But the driver didn't.

The blinding light came more fully upon her and she realized that the driver at her rear was tailgating terribly. Again, she flicked her lights, but the car came closer. She sped up and it did the same.

For the first time, fear gripped her. She was on a lonely stretch of highway, in pitch darkness and the person behind her was not just an irate and careless driver in a hurry. Whoever it was meant to drive her off the road.

She wondered just how fast Jane's car would go. She needed to speed up, drive like a maniac until she could reach a gas station or any little piece of civilization where she could turn off.

The car behind her came closer, then revved up on her side. She was terrified of a crash. Instinctively and foolishly, she jerked her own wheel. Her scream pierced the night as her vehicle went shooting off the pavement and into the utter and absolute darkness.

Doug pulled into the vet's parking lot. The office lights were still on, and as he reached for the door, he noted that the vet was open until seven several nights a week, probably to accommodate the clients who worked nine to five.

He realized he must have been a sight when he burst through the door, barefoot and in soggy cutoffs. The few people remaining in the waiting room chairs stared at him as if he were a madman. And he probably looked like one.

He strode to the reception window. "Kelly Trent? Is she still here? She came in with a sick dog named Sam."

"Yes, just a bit back."

"Is she still here?"

The girl didn't seem alarmed by his appearance. They were in the Keys after all. Shirtless, shoeless guys in soaked cutoffs actually weren't that rare. It wasn't his mode of dress that had alarmed the others; it was his manner of pure panic and tension.

"I'm sorry, she left just a few minutes ago. But the dog is doing very well."

"She left?"

"Yes."

"In a car?"

"I am assuming so," the girl said politely.

He should have checked on Sam, but he was still feeling too uneasy about Kelly. Of course she had driven. She'd had Jane's car. It must have been one of the cars he had driven past to get here. He thanked the girl, nodded to the people who looked as if they wanted to inch away from him and headed back out.

Getting into his car, all he could think about was the information his brother had given him. Quinn! Quinn would be at Vinnie's now, wondering where the hell he was. If he'd passed Kelly, she should be at Vinnie's by now.

He reached into his pocket for his cell phone, then cursed himself as water drained from it. He tried pressing the digits. Nothing.

The car seemed to plunge through a mire of grass, brush and slush forever.

When it came to a halt, the jerk sent her flying forward, then backward. She tensed, waiting for a terrible bang, but there was none. The car had simply come to a halt. And by the grace of God, it hadn't gone into the ocean.

She listened and could still hear a wheel spinning. The blaze of her lights revealed nothing but brush and grass ahead, trees all around her. She sat there stunned for several seconds, not hurt, just sore from the tension that had seized her and the jerking around. Her heart was thundering in her chest.

Then, after a moment, she jumped to life, exiting the car as if she had suddenly been set on fire. There might be a gas leak, she thought. The vehicle might be ready to explode.

She had traveled deep into the embankment, and though it had appeared to be solid ground from the road, she was ankle deep in water. She was on the Atlantic side of the island, and the road, she was certain, had been built up. Therefore, here, on the embankment and in the shrubs and growth, she was caught in a mire of seeping ocean water and fill.

The road seemed a long way away. There were lights, she realized. Not just cars that were passing by, but lights that belonged to a car that had parked. Despite her absolute physical misery and her fear of things that might be beneath her feet, she felt the urge to move back. Then a rustling, sloshing sound caught her attention. Someone had indeed parked up on the road and was now walking toward the car. Someone . . . who had forced her off the road?

She turned away from the car, looking into the darkness of the overgrowth around her, wincing as she wondered about snakes. Terror drove her onward. She tried very hard to move silently through the darkness, but her heart was too loud. It, alone, could surely be heard.

Move, move, move! Trying not to slosh, she headed toward a mangrove. Someone was coming, that was for certain. She could hear the sound. But could the someone hear her as well?

Doug shot down the highway at the safest speed he dared, his feeling of anxiety growing all the while. He saw the skid marks on the road first, then the trail that stretched into the foliage. His heart seemed to leap to his chest. It wasn't nec-essarily Kelly. People in a hurry wound up in accidents all the time. No, it wasn't necessarily Kelly . . . but instinct forced him to slow down.

He jerked his car to a halt and leaped out, eyeing the car down the embankment, alive with lights, mired in the muck. He stood there, every muscle screaming as he recognized that it was, indeed, Jane Ulrich's car deep in the foliage, as if it had shot right off the highway to land hundreds of yards away.

Kelly.

The front door of the car was open and lights blazed, clearly showing that the car was empty. He nearly cried out her name, but then he shut his mouth. There was another car besides his own, pulled off the road. Someone who had stopped to help? Or maybe someone who had driven her off the road? He didn't know.

He did know that it was a dark green Buick sedan, the same car he had seen Mel Alton enter just hours ago. Alton, whose ex-wife was suing him for more money.

He couldn't take a chance. No matter what his fear that she might be lying dead or dying in a pool of marsh and water, hurt, dazed or worse, he had to stay quiet.

He couldn't see her anywhere in the area illuminated by the still-blazing car lights. She had to have moved on her own. Or . . .

she had been moved. But the other car re-mained on the embankment. So he started to move carefully into the wet, mucky ground.

Kelly strained to see the trees ahead of her. The beams from the car were so bright they made everything not in their path twice as dark. But the sloshing had come from a different direction. She had to get into the trees.

There was an eerie glow coming from the limbs of the gnarly tree. The thing was fantastic, with roots crawling above the wa-terlogged earth as well as below it. She winced as her footsteps caused her to splash through a puddle, and reached out for the trunk of the tree, slipping around it.

A scream nearly tore from her throat as a hand came out from behind the trunk, catching her around the face and neck . . . clamping over her mouth.

Chapter 26

Quinn looked at his watch with growing impatience. Doug wasn't picking up his phone and Kelly wasn't picking up hers. He'd ordered tea at first, then when more time had gone by he'd decided he was starving and ordered something to eat. He'd even studied the papers in front of him until his eyes were swimming, hoping to make some connection between numbers.

The launch from the islet wasn't at the dock and there wasn't a single soul around that he knew. Finally he let out a sigh of impatience. As his waiter strode by, he reached out and caught the fellow by the wrist.

"Hey."

"Hey," the fellow returned, stopping short and eyeing him uneasily.

"Sorry, I didn't mean to grab you like that." Quinn released the fellow's arm. "Do you happen to know who Kelly Trent is? Would you recognize her if you saw her?"

The man's eyes widened. "Oh, sure! Yeah."

"Well? Have you seen her?"

"Oh, yeah! I saw her. I helped her!" he said proudly.

Quinn shook his head. "Helped her with what?"

"Her dog. She got off the launch with her dog, who was in a really bad way. Looked as if he might have gotten hold of one of those toads, you know? Really lethal creatures. Anyway, he was foaming, lolling in her arms. I saw her get off the launch and I opened up her car for her. She was real nice, even though she was in pretty bad shape, too."

Quinn rose. "Where was she going?"

"To the vet?"

"Where?"

The waiter told him. And Quinn threw way too much money on the table, gathered his papers and headed for his car.

"Kelly!" She heard her name shouted almost the second the hand came over her mouth. "Shh!" she heard then, and in a split second she realized it was Doug who had stopped her because she knew his touch and scent.

She opened her mouth to speak, but he eased back, drawing his fingers to his lips. He mouthed words to her anxiously. "Are you all right?"

"Kelly!" They heard her name again, called with anxiety.

She started to ease from his hold, a sigh of relief leaving her. "It's just Mel!"

"Stay!" he told her.

"But it's just Mel! I know his voice."

"Stay here!" Doug commanded, shoving her back toward the tree. He moved out, in silence. In the stygian darkness, he disappeared almost instantly.

She silently cursed him. At first, she was just alone in the darkness. Then there were the sounds. Grass-moving footsteps.

Her breathing, loud as a windstorm. More shuffling in the foliage, closer and closer to her. Then . . . a howl. And then . . .

"O'Casey! It's me! Mel Alton. What the hell is the matter with you?"

Kelly couldn't stand it any longer. She could suddenly see both men emerging into the dim light cast from the car headlights. They'd been down on the ground; O'Casey had tackled Mel. Then he had helped him up and was frisking him, as if he were still a cop and Mel a tried-and-true offender.

"Hey!" Mel protested again. "Would you stop it! Jesus, what's the matter with you! Kelly was in that car. We have to find her."

"I'm here, Mel! I'm right here and I'm fine!" Kelly cried out, sloshing her way back from the mangrove tree.

O'Casey was glaring at her, obviously irate, but Mel looked at her with such relief that she wanted to go hug him.

"Kelly!" he cried, sounding just like a father.

Screw O'Casey. She ran to Mel and stared at the other man, defying him to suspect her agent of any foul play.

"Kelly, what happened?" Mel asked anxiously. "Some guy at the restaurant said that you'd taken Sam to the vet in Jane's car. I was trying to get to you when I saw the car in the marsh."

"Some guy told you about the vet?" O'Casey said skeptically.

Mel brought Kelly closer to him, frowning. "Yes, and if you don't believe me, we can go back and find the guy!"

"How long have you had that car, Mel?" O'Casey demanded.

Mel never answered. There was another shout from the road, loud and menacing. "Doug! Kelly!"

"Quinn," O'Casey muttered. "Over here!" he shouted.

A moment later, Quinn had reached them. He looked over the situation. "What the hell is going on?"

Kelly realized that she wasn't sure anymore. Had it just been a bad driver? Or had she purposely been forced off the road? She winced, afraid that it was the latter and that someone really had tried to poison her dog. But if she acted afraid, God knew what these two would think she should do next.

"Quite frankly, I'm not certain. I was forced off the road."

"Interesting," Doug said. "Mel, did you force Kelly off the road?"

"You son of a bitch!" Mel began. "How —"

"Hey, hey, hey," Quinn said. "We'll get to the bottom of the situation. First off, everyone all right?"

"I'm fine," Kelly said quickly, but she wasn't. Every muscle and joint in her body now seemed to be screaming.

"Look," Mel said, "I parked — get that, I parked! — up on the road when I thought it looked like Jane's car down here. You know you've got some nerve!" he told Doug angrily. "Who the hell do you think you are? I've worked with Kelly for years. Years! You're an upstart. I don't care who you were . . . are. Right now you're just the hired help, the dance instructor! I would never hurt Kelly. Never!"

They could hear the sirens then.

"I called the cops," Quinn said.

"Well, for your information, I called the cops, too — 911!" Mel said.

A second later, a Monroe County sheriff's car pulled onto the embankment. A flashlight bore down on them. "Anyone hurt?" an officer called out.

"No!" Quinn called back. "But there has been an accident. This lady was sideswiped."

"Well, then, let's get everyone up here and start finding out just what we can, all right?" the deputy shouted down to them. Obviously he wasn't alone. His partner was walking through the marsh to the scene.

"Let me see your phone," O'Casey asked Mel.

"What?"

"Your phone. You said you called 911. I want to see your call history."

"Fine. Go ahead!"

Mel handed O'Casey his phone. O'Casey opened it, hit a number, looked at it, then snapped the phone shut and returned it.

"How about an apology?" Mel demanded.

"Hey, folks!" the deputy called. A young man in his early thirties, he had a pleasant but solid attitude about him. "Let's talk. Who was in the car?"

"I was," Kelly said.

"Anyone else?"

"No."

"And no one's hurt?" the officer asked.

"No."

He turned his flashlight beam on the car, then looked at them all. "Let's go up and sort this out."

And so they did. Kelly explained what had happened, where she had been. Doug explained that he had followed her. And Mel explained that he had been due to leave but had decided to stay another night. At the restaurant he had heard about Kelly rushing to the vet with Sam. As her *friend*, he emphasized, and not just as her agent, he, too, had followed. Then Quinn explained that he had been waiting for his brother so long that he, too, had asked questions and heard about Kelly's trip to the vet.

Both the officers looked at them, somewhat confused. "Okay, where's the dog?" one of them asked.

"Still at the vet," Kelly said. She almost added, He might have been poisoned! But she refrained. She wanted to get through the current situation and out of it. She needed time in peace and quiet to determine her own next action. She wasn't a fool and she didn't want to die. But she had been scared to death. And she was very angry.

"All right, Miss Trent, what happened?" the older officer demanded.

And she told him. She told him exactly what had happened. As she spoke, she saw that Doug glared at Mel all the while. She ignored him and hoped that Mel was doing the same.

The officer wrote a report and called for a tow truck. Then he apologized to them all. "I'm sorry, but I don't think we're going to be able to do anything. You didn't see the car at all, right, Miss Trent?"

She shook her head. "The lights . . . they were just blinding."

"And you really don't know if it was just a road-hog jerk in the kind of hurry that could have killed someone or if . . . well, if it was someone playing lethal road games?"

Kelly shook her head, praying that it was coming to an end, that they were going to let her go.

"Someone is trying to kill her," Doug stated.

She looked at him with horror.

"There have been several murders across the country of advice-therapist types," Doug continued, his eyes like steel as they rested on her, his jaw set hard as concrete. "Kelly played an advice therapist on her soap."

"I know," the younger officer said, and flushed. His partner stared at him. "Yes, yes! I watch the soaps on my days off, all right?"

His partner shrugged after a moment. "Sure."

"I think that someone was purposely trying to run her off the road," Doug said, still staring at Mel.

Mel, usually calm, dignified and collected, had had it. "You ass! Your car is up there, too!"

"All right, all right," the older officer said. "Miss Trent, if you think —"

"I think that we've all been through a bit of stress," she said sweetly, calmly. She glared at Doug, then looked to Quinn for help. "I can't tell you anything about the

463

car that sideswiped me. Nothing. And I am so sorry. You've got my name, license, insurance card . . . and the tow truck is coming. My friends here are worried about me, but honestly, there's nothing to do except for everyone to cool down some."

"We can go into the station —"

"There's no reason," Quinn said, producing his wallet and showing his own license. "My brother is licensed, too. There really is nothing that can be done. If Kelly didn't see anything, and if her report is properly filled out, we'll just wait for the tow truck, then go get some rest."

The older officer peered at Kelly. "You're sure you don't want some medical help?"

"I would be horrified to take the time of an emergency medic to look at a few mosquito bites," Kelly said.

As she spoke, the tow truck arrived. The driver was a cheerful old fellow who took a look at the car and then the people. He shook his head. "And no one was hurt?" he said.

"No," Kelly assured him.

"The air bags didn't deploy?" he asked.

Again, Kelly shook her head.

"Need a ride yourself?" he asked hopefully.

She smiled. "No, I'm fine, thanks." She took a step toward Mel, glaring at Doug. "We've got three cars here. Thanks, anyway," she repeated. "Mel, I'll drive with you. The O'Caseys can follow in their cars and we'll all meet up back at Vinnie's."

Not about to allow an argument, even though she knew that Doug was furious, she slipped her arm through Mel's and thanked the officers again. Determined to leave behind the site of the accident, she hurried into the passenger's seat of Mel's car.

He crawled into the driver's seat — and looked at her before starting the engine. "Kelly, I would never hurt you. I can't even believe that anyone could suggest such a thing."

"It's all right, Mel. I know. And please don't hold it against Doug. He's really determined to look after me."

She was surprised when Mel laughed. "Actually, I'm indignant, but I do forgive him. I forgive him because it's all for you. But I'm not going anywhere now. I'm staying right by your side."

She touched his shoulder, squeezing it. "Can I use your cell phone?" she asked him.

"Sure." He dug it from his pocket. She slipped the vet's card from her own and dialed the number. Dr. Garcia answered. "Sam still okay?" she asked anxiously.

"Sleeping restfully," he assured her. "And you?"

She arched a brow. Could even the vet know about the accident already? "I'm fine."

"You left here in such a state, frankly I was more worried about you than the dog for a while. Don't worry about Sam. I'm doing paperwork right next to him now."

"Thank you so much," Kelly said.

"My pleasure."

She hung up and turned to Mel. "You know, someone might have tried to poison him."

"Yeah, this whole thing is looking just great," Mel muttered. "You left the soap because you might have been in danger. And God forgive me, I pushed this video on you." He glanced over at her quickly as he drove. "I pray it wasn't . . ."

"It wasn't a mistake."

"I'm just praying now it wasn't a lethal mistake," he muttered.

They pulled into Vinnie's parking lot, the O'Caseys right behind them. Once there, she noticed at last that Doug was in nothing but cutoffs. She frowned, looking at him.

"Long story," he said with a wave of his hands.

"I suggest a beer," Quinn said.

"Why not?" Mel agreed.

That Doug was really angry was more than apparent to Kelly. He was stiff as could be as he sat across a table from her.

The waiter who had helped her was still working, and though the place was hopping, he made a point of stopping by. "You all found one another. Good."

The man shrank back slightly when Mel grabbed him by the arm. "This is the young man who told me where Kelly had gone. Right?"

"Oh, yes, I've been telling people what happened all day," the waiter said cheerfully. He cleared his throat. "Um, my arm." Mel released him.

Doug grabbed him. "You've been telling people . . . all day?"

The poor man frowned, staring at his arm again. Doug wasn't going to release him until he answered, that much was obvious.

"Yeah, all kinds of people. Sir . . . ?"

Doug let go, still staring at him.

"People around here were concerned. The group from the island has been coming and going, and they all asked. For a while, even all the folks sitting around at the tables were talking about it." He paused, smiling. "Sure, folks are interested in you, Miss Trent. But it's a nice group around here. People really care. How did you make out? How's your dog?"

Kelly smiled. "Doing well. Thank you so much. The vet is great."

"He sure is. Left some fancy practice in New York City to come down here. The Keys have a way with folks, you know? Can't compete with the big cities for big business and high-powered jobs most of the time, but, hey . . . it can compete with the sunsets. What can I get you folks?"

They all opted for beer. The waiter gave Doug a look that suggested he sure as hell needed one, maybe a lot of them.

As the waiter walked off, a man came forward. "Where the hell's my boat?" he asked Doug.

"You might have told me the motor was about to die," Doug said.

"You didn't ask!" the old fellow said. "So where's my boat?"

"On the water. We'll get it towed in to-morrow."

The old man grinned. He had a one-toothed smile. "Fix the motor for me, too?"

Doug glared at him.

"Hey, it was worth a try! You can pay me for it. Actually, though, I'd prefer if you fixed the darn-tootin' thing."

"You got any money on you?" Doug asked his brother.

"Some. And an ATM card," Quinn replied.

"Ah, come on. You're a couple of healthy young fellows. Looks like you've been around boats," the man said.

"How about this? We'll see," Doug said. "We'll get her towed tomorrow and see what we can do."

The fellow smiled, nodded and walked off.

"What was that all about?" Kelly asked.

"I've been chasing you since I got off the phone and found out you'd left Vinnie's."

"I'm sorry, I couldn't find you!" she told him.

"I was right out in the parking lot."

"Look, Sam was sick. I had to go," she said angrily.

"Clams, anyone?" Quinn said, looking up from the menu. "They're really good here."

"Lay off her," Mel said.

"All right, I'll do the ordering and the three of you will all take a breath," Quinn said firmly.

The tension at the table could have been cut with a knife. No one spoke. Then Kelly turned to Quinn. "Clams sound good to me."

By the time they reached the resort that night, Kelly was really exhausted. And no one was prepared for a furious Jane.

"A phone call! One of you could have given me a simple phone call!" Jane stared at the group of them, shaking her head. "You're all filthy, do you know that? I'd better get some explanations. And why am I not asking about the dog, you wonder? Because I called the vet, of course, a man who actually answers his phone!"

"Jane, I'm sorry. Really sorry!" Doug told her. He reached into his pocket and produced his cell phone, showing her that it was dead. "I took it swimming."

"Oh, great. You went swimming." She pointed at Kelly. "You lost yours, right?"

"Yeah . . . it didn't seem to matter much at the time," Kelly said.

"Actually . . ." Doug murmured, reaching into his other pocket. "It's not lost. I found it on the dock." Kelly arched a brow in his direction. Her phone was as dead as his. "At least I have it," he told her.

"Well, that's true. It's not lost anymore."

Jane spun on Quinn. "You have a phone." She frowned. "And what are you doing here?"

"I was just in the neighborhood?" Quinn suggested.

"But you have a phone, right?"

"I'm sorry, too, Jane," Quinn said diplomatically.

Then Jane turned on Mel. "You have a phone, right? Or did you go swimming, too?"

"No, I have a phone," Mel said. "I just didn't know we were supposed to call."

"I didn't know what the hell had happened or what was going on!" Jane accused them.

It was time to tell her, Doug decided. "Jane, actually . . . there was an accident."

"An accident!" she said. "All right, I know Sam is okay and you all look fine. Was anyone hurt?"

"Your car," Kelly told her.

"Oh?"

"I was sideswiped, run off the road," Kelly said.

"But . . . you're all right?"

Kelly nodded. "I'm really sorry, Jane. I'll see to it that it's fixed."

"The car is the least of it. I have insurance," Jane said. "You were sideswiped? Run off the road?"

Kelly nodded.

"Did they get the guy? No, of course not," Jane said, answering her own question. "It would have been some idiot in a real hurry, then too much of a coward to make sure that you were all right. Some ass who would leave a driver stranded in the middle of nowhere!"

She was angry, disgusted. They all knew that kind of driver. It didn't occur to Jane that there might be any more to it, so Doug decided not to push the point. Hell, maybe Jane was right. But he didn't believe that — not for a minute.

"All right, I'm going to go shower," Mel said.

"We're locking up for the night," Doug told him. He still mistrusted the man. The only reason he was willing to give Mel the benefit of the doubt was the fact that he really had dialed 911 into his phone. And even though a voice at the back of his head warned him that it might have been a cover-up, he was going to force himself to be decent to the man — for Kelly. But that didn't mean he wouldn't be watching him.

"So I don't have a car?" Jane murmured

after they had said good-night to Mel.

"I don't think it's in bad shape, but it was towed to the nearest station. We can check on it in the morning," Doug told her.

"You might have been killed!" Jane told her, truly horrified by the thought.

"I always buckle up," Kelly said. "And now I'm really glad it's a habit."

"Anybody want a drink? I want a drink!" Jane said. She delved into the minibar, pulling out a miniature whiskey. They all stared at her as she twisted the top and swallowed it down, making a face. "No one else?" she said.

"I want a bath more than anything in the world," Kelly said.

"Then I'm getting out of here. Except I'm taking another drink. My room didn't come with an open minibar!" She took out another miniature, then looked them all over again and shook her head. "Good night."

"Wait, I'll walk you to your room," Quinn told her.

She frowned. "It's only a few doors down."

"I'll walk you."

"Oh, Lord!" she said, looking from Quinn to Doug. "The two of you make me nervous as hell! All that stuff about locking the doors and now I can't walk a few steps on my own."

"I need to get to Doug's, shower, then on the phone with Shannon," Quinn said. "Let her know I'm staying the night." He turned to Doug. "Key?"

"Yeah, hang on." Doug went to the kitchen counter and found the pack of keys he'd been given for his room, keys he'd never used. He gave them to Quinn, who motioned his head toward a manila envelope he'd left on the sofa. Doug nodded.

"In the morning," he told them. "Good night."

As Quinn walked Jane out, Doug heard her muttering. "An accident! Someone might have been killed and you all didn't even think to call me and tell me you were all right!" Naturally Quinn began to apologize again.

Kelly was already starting up the stairs as Doug closed and locked the door. "I'm taking a bath," she said.

"Yeah," he murmured.

She stopped suddenly, turned around and looked at him. "You're angry, aren't you? Because I went with Mel."

"I wish you hadn't, yes."

"Mel would never hurt me."

"You shouldn't trust anyone, Kelly. Anyone."

"You are angry."

"He has an ex-wife who is about to take him to court."

"If you're going to condemn a man for that, you could look at almost every male I've met in all my years in the L.A. area."

"He was there, Kelly. In California."

"Never in Ohio."

"Maybe that death wasn't related."

"Maybe none of this is related!" she reminded him.

"Kelly, I know you're not a fool. In one day, Sam wound up in the vet's office and you were nearly killed. Don't trust anyone — including Mel Alton."

"What about you?" she asked softly.

He stared back at her. "Maybe you shouldn't trust me. But I'm all you've really got right now."

She didn't smile and didn't reply. She just turned and continued up the stairs.

He watched her, feeling the ache of tension creeping into his shoulders. He stared after her a long while, then turned to the manila envelope of records Quinn had given him. Picking it up, he walked over to the computer desk and sat down.

An hour later, he was still staring at

numbers. Phones, addresses, connections. There were calls between Marc Logan, Joe Penny, Mel Alton and Lance Morton. Naturally. They were all business associates. And there were also calls to Matt Avery. Doug found those interesting. The ones between him, Joe Penny and even Mel Alton were explainable. But why had he been in contact with Lance Morton and Marc Logan? There had to be something to that.

With names and numbers swimming before his eyes, he set the file down and walked around. He missed Sam and understood better just how crazed Kelly must have been.

He walked up the stairs, noting that although he'd been losing more and more of the dried sand on his feet and ankles since they'd left the scene of the accident, he was still dry and dusty with the stuff. His shoulders were red, burned from the heat today. He felt like a salt log.

Upstairs, he found the room dark and silent. Not wanting to disturb Kelly, he slipped into the bathroom and into the shower. When he walked out, Kelly was in the doorway, sleek, naked, arms crossed over her chest, staring at him.

He towel dried, staring back, stunned by

his own libido. This was surely serious. His focus kept slipping. And though he'd come out of the hot shower limp as a rag, he was now rising like a banner.

"I thought you were sleeping," he said, the words sounding inane to his ears.

"Obviously I'm not."

"What the hell are you mad at?" he demanded.

"You."

"Me! You're the one who went off with your agent."

"You have to quit acting like the strong arm of God!" she said, pointing at him.

He dropped the towel and walked over to her, pointing back. His forefinger poked her breastbone. "I swim half the distance from a stinking boat I halfway commandeered to get to a dock to chase you up and down the mainland only to find you in a ditch! And you're telling me to quit?"

She stiffened, staring at him, eyes burning. "Yes!"

"You little diva!"

"Oh!" She tried to think of something. "Would-be cop!"

"I *was* a cop."

"I am not a diva."

"You need to learn sense!"

"And you . . . you can't bully everyone."

"No?"

"No!"

He moved closer; she moved closer. They were both breathing heavily.

"Oh, hell!" Doug pulled her into his arms, felt the crush of her body, the unbelievable heat of her lips. He pressed his hands against the wall, pinning her there, staring into her eyes. "Still angry?"

"You bet."

"So am I!"

This time she leaned forward, finding his mouth. His hands slipped behind her back, caught her against him, lifted her. The steam from the shower was still swirling around them. He had been damp; in seconds he was soaked. The roar of their hearts, breath, movement, seemed to crash around them. Her legs were locked around his. They were slamming against the wall of the bathroom, the tile smooth against his hands, her back . . .

The volatile surge of excitement that had seized them burned hard and fast. In a few minutes, she lay panting against him. He eased her weight down. "Still angry?" he whispered.

"Well, actually," she murmured, "it's a little better now. And you?"

"Well, not so angry."

"Then what?"

He kissed her with all the tenderness their lovemaking had just lacked.

"What?" she whispered.

He drew her to him, bringing her back to the softness of the bed. He didn't reply until he had laid her down and come by her side, studying the beauty of her face in the dim moonlight that filtered in.

"Scared," he said softly. "I couldn't bear to lose you."

Chapter 27

In the morning Kelly's first thought was to call the vet. It was early, but Dr. Garcia answered his own phone and didn't mind in the least that she had called. "He's looking good," he told Kelly. "You can pick him up tonight, anytime."

"What do you think caused it?"

"I don't know yet. I'll have to wait for the lab results." He was silent a minute. "If you're worried, he's more than welcome to stay with me for a few days."

"Thanks," Kelly told him. "Can I get back to you on that?"

"Sure thing."

She thanked him again and rang off. Doug was out of bed already and she had a feeling he'd been up with the sunrise. He didn't seem to need much sleep.

She hopped into the shower, feeling good. Sam was going to be all right. An idiot had tried to run her off the road and succeeded, but all she'd suffered were some sore muscles and a few scratches. And she was living with a man who . . . drove her crazy. Made her insane. And also made her feel as if she were the most important being in the universe, the most sensual, sexy female living. But she didn't want to dwell on the feelings and she didn't want to think about what they meant.

Doug hadn't been in her life that long, but suddenly it seemed as if he *was* her life. And she liked it that way, didn't want to think what might happen when . . . when it was all over. Where did she go once this video was filmed? Her life wasn't in South Florida. His wasn't in California. Her life, she realized then, was never going to be the same again. In many ways.

Hearing the phone ring, she shut off the water. When she stepped out of the shower stall, the ringing had stopped. She dressed quickly and hurried down the stairs. A cup of coffee awaited her. Doug was at the computer.

"Our call is at nine," he told her. He turned around and grinned. "Fifteen minutes to spare. Quinn just stopped by. He said to tell you goodbye and that he'll hopefully see you back in Miami."

"Of course," she murmured, picking up the coffee cup. "I see he brought a bunch of papers. It almost looks as if you're studying race forms."

He shrugged. "Did you know that your old friend from Household Heaven kept in contact with Marc Logan?"

"No, I certainly didn't know that. I'm surprised Logan still hired me if those two are buddies!"

"I can't find anything indicating that they're buddies."

"Still, maybe Marc Logan did call Matt Avery about me. Who knows?"

Doug studied her for a moment. "I called Logan and asked him why."

"What?"

"Asking questions can sometimes help find the truth."

"Yes, but didn't Logan wonder why his tango dancer was asking questions about his phone calls?"

"Sure. He asked me what the hell business it was of mine. I explained to him that I'd once been a cop, and that even if he wanted to fire me, I'd still be here — at your insistence. I was going to be your bodyguard."

"And what did he say?"

"He laughed and told me to be a good

bodyguard. Then he admitted that Matt Avery had called him several times to try to talk him out of using you."

"See? I told you. I could sue Matt for that, couldn't I?"

"I don't know, but it wouldn't have mattered, anyway. Logan had his heart set on you."

He was still staring at her. "What?" she demanded.

"That was his explanation, but there were a few calls from Avery's office to Marc Logan's *before* this whole thing about the video started."

"So? They're both businessmen. They travel in the same circles. They've probably known each other for years. Marc Logan owns that recording studio we went to, you know."

"Apparently Logan owns a lot of other media outlets as well, under corporate names."

"And what does that mean?"

"I'm not sure. I'm still working on it. I'm trying to trace down what they all are and where they all are."

"You think it could be Marc Logan?" she said incredulously.

He hesitated. "Dana Sumter had a child."

"She had a couple, according to the papers. Grown now."

"No, no . . . an illegitimate child. He or she would now just be the age of Lance Morton or Matt Avery."

Kelly gasped. "How do you know?"

"It was a hunch, but her ex-husband verified it."

"So you think that one of them might have been that child, and that they grew up, found out she was their mother and killed her?"

"Possibly."

"Then the woman in Ohio, her death was accidental?"

"Again, possibly. But the woman who was killed by the hit-and-run driver in Palm Beach . . . I think she was definitely murdered."

"Okay, I can see feeling bitter and furious with a mother who easily gave up a child. A sick mind might not seek circumstances. But then why kill the woman in Palm Beach? And why attack me?"

"Association," he said softly.

"What does that mean, exactly?"

"I'm not sure. But I could swear, I'm almost there."

"Well, Marc Logan could hardly be the child of Dana Sumter."

"No, but Matt Avery could be."

"Matt Avery isn't in Florida."

"He could be. He isn't in California. And he owns that place in Palm Beach."

"Aha. Okay. Keep me in on it, huh? I am involved." She smiled at him then. "Sam is fine, by the way."

"I know."

"You called the vet, too?"

"You bet."

"He's a cool dog, huh?"

"The best."

"He may even like you best," she said lightly.

"No, that dog is yours all the way." He rose, stretching, and stared down at the papers again. "Addresses, phone numbers . . . dates, times. Something should be gelling. It's just out of reach," he murmured, "and I need it to gel *now*."

"You know," she told him, "there may be nothing to gel."

"There is. And I'm going to find it, and find it fast."

"How?"

"I'm going to delve and ask every rude question I can," he murmured. "I'm going to push the envelope until something snaps. But now we've got to go. Jane is going to meet us outside the women's changing room and stick with you all through makeup."

"Did Jane used to be a black belt or was she a cop, too?" Kelly asked.

"Neither. She's company, there to make sure that no one entices you away again without me."

It turned out that Jane and the other backup dancers weren't needed that day. Herb Essen wanted to get the interaction between Doug, Kelly and Lance Morton.

Lance looked bad that morning, as if he'd gone overboard with his vices the night before. He was in a surly mood, as well. Kelly's feeling of things moving in the right direction began to fade quickly after they began work. And she couldn't really blame Doug. Lance was goading him.

The scene required that she be dancing with Doug when Lance, in his dream vision, swept her away. She would then move in his arms, just swaying to the music. It was easy enough. And the tango was close, but . . . twice when Herb yelled "Cut!" Lance kept her in a vise. And several times when the tape was running, Herb would call out an order to let her spin, but Lance would refuse to do so.

Herb called a break for lunch, swearing.

"You picked a loser, babe!" Lance told her, indicating Doug, who was coming to meet her. "You could have me, *can* have me, just say the word."

"Lance. A word. No," she told him.

He shrugged, walking away before Doug could reach them.

Things went downhill after the lunch break. There was a problem with one of the cameras, so everyone was put on hold. The day was slightly overcast, so Herb wanted more light for the scene. And getting the rigging to his liking took more time. Finally the sun began to wane and Herb Essen decided he liked the colors in the sky, so everything was reset.

Then, in one of the scenes, Lance pretended that his hand slipped and moved over her breast.

"Dammit, Lance!" she swore.

She should have kept silent. The next thing she knew, Doug was coming toward him. "Touch her again and I'll deck you," he said quietly.

"I didn't do anything. And if I did . . . well, what the hell. Are you two suddenly married or something?"

"Touch her again and I'll deck you," Doug repeated very softly.

"Gotcha!" Lance said, making a motion

like a shooting gun out of his hand.

They went back to work, but once again Lance made the slip. Doug came striding over.

"All right, all right!" Herb cried ineffectually, but this time Lance approached Doug, shoving him on the chest.

"Hey, can the testosterone!" Herb cried.

Lance pushed again. And again. The third time, he took a hard swing. Doug avoided it and instinctively swung back. A right to the jaw sent Lance spiraling to his knees, screaming in pain and fury. He jumped up, staring at Doug. "You're off, asshole. You're off!"

"Like hell," Doug told him.

They had a silent, stunned audience at first. Then Herb swore. "Lance, damn you, your face —"

"Me! This animal came at me like a gorilla!"

"Now, Lance —" Herb began.

But to no avail. Lance Morton was walking off the set. "You'll hear from my attorneys!" he said.

Jane ran up to Doug. "Hey, don't worry! There were witnesses. He started it."

Kelly looked at Doug worriedly. "He started it, but . . ."

"Kelly, what the hell did you want me to

do?" Doug demanded.

"I'll have the dancers, all of them, out here tomorrow, nine sharp, in costume and makeup!" Herb snapped, angry and disgusted.

"There's going to be trouble. Real trouble," Jane murmured.

Doug just shrugged. "Let's go eat in the room," he suggested softly to Kelly.

She nodded. "I'll give the vet a call again. Jane, are you joining us?"

Jane shook her head. "I'm going to eat with the crew, suck up, find out what people saw or think they saw, and what they think of the whole deal," she said.

Doug smiled at her. "Jane on the defensive," he teased.

"Hey! I want to be in this video. I want us both to be in this video."

"Jane, his behavior was totally out of line, and you know it."

"Yes, I do know it. Come on, Kel, let me go to the changing room and be your company. Then I'm going to suck up around the crew."

Half an hour later, Kelly and Doug were back in her room. "Dammit, I shouldn't have let him push me," Doug said, pacing.

Kelly was surprised. She knew he had felt he'd had good reason at the time.

"Look, he did push you," she said.

"That's the thing, he's usually a cowardly little creep."

"Well, he's always kind of creepy," Kelly said.

Doug shook his head. "Creepy but cowardly. He knew I could deck him. *Knew it.* But he kept at it, anyway. Almost as if . . . he had to."

It was then that they heard the firm knock on the door. Frowning, Doug stared at Kelly, then walked to it. He looked out. "The cops!" he said, shaking his head. "I wonder if they found out something about the accident. Or if they're here because . . ."

He opened the door to two men in sheriff's uniforms. "Douglas O'Casey?" the bigger, heavier one asked.

"Yes."

"You're under arrest for assault and battery, and attempted murder."

"What?" Kelly cried incredulously. "Attempted murder! That's ridiculous."

"May I see some ID, please?" Doug asked.

"Yessir," the larger man said. He took out a badge, flapping it in front of Doug, then closed it. "Deputy Smith," he murmured aloud. He looked at the other man.

"And your ID, please?" The second man looked at the first, then produced a badge. "And Officer Jones. Thank you."

Kelly kept shaking her head, frowning. "This is the most ridiculous thing I've ever heard!" she protested. "Lance Morton attacked Doug."

"Kelly, it's all right. You're arresting me? Not taking me in for questioning?"

"Sorry, sir. It's an arrest."

"Not your fault," Doug told the man.

"What are you saying?" Kelly demanded.

"I've got to go with them," he told her.

One had cuffs out. The other began reading Doug his rights. Doug turned, allowing the man to cuff him. He looked at her, mouthing words. "Lock yourself in. Don't open to anyone. Call the sheriff's office."

"But —"

He narrowed his eyes fiercely, warning her to be silent. She shook her head, still disbelieving the situation.

"Wait!" she cried in protest. "This is wrong, all wrong!"

"Sorry, ma'am, we've got the charges, and there were witnesses. Apparently, sir, you nearly broke a guy's face. We've questioned some folks and the witnesses agree that you went after Lance Morton with deadly intent," Deputy Smith said apologetically.

"That's a lie!" Kelly said.

"Well, hopefully it can be straightened out at the station," Smith said. He seemed to be the talker between the two.

"Right. We'll straighten it out at the station," Doug said.

Kelly was at a loss. Doug seemed far too willing to go.

"May I just say goodbye?" he asked.

"Sure."

He moved close to her, pretending to nuzzle her cheek. "Call the sheriff's office and then Quinn. Right away."

"But these are the cops."

He shook his head with a barely perceptible movement.

"All right, let's go now. With any luck, it will be straightened out and you'll be back here in an hour," Smith said, setting a hand on Doug's shoulder.

Smith and Jones. Surely whoever had dreamed this up could have been more original with the names! Doug thought. He hated the thought of Kelly being left, even for two seconds. What an ass he'd been! He'd opened the door.

At that point he couldn't have protested.

Not then. He cursed himself a thousand times over. Why the hell had he opened the door just because he had seen the uniforms? These fellows were armed. His licensed Smith & Wesson was upstairs, in his suitcase. He hadn't dared take a chance that they would pull out the guns and shoot him and Kelly then and there.

He had to admit, he hadn't been in the least prepared for such a ploy as this. He had thought the killer was working independently. The best way to get away with a crime was to have no accomplices, no one to give you away. How would this be explained? There was obviously a plan underway to get to Kelly now — while he was out. But how? If she really kept the door locked, if she called Quinn . . .

How much were these fellows being paid to impersonate deputies? The uniforms were good. The guns were regulation. The badges — except for the ridiculous names of Joe Smith and John Jones — were good, too. He was certain they'd been hired to kill him. But by whom? Lance Morton? No, he just couldn't believe the guy had the intelligence to plan anything like this.

So was Matt Avery in Florida, far closer to them than they had imagined? Was that it?

A cold sweat broke out over him as he suddenly saw what it was he had missed — until now. Now it was crystal clear. And he had to get back to Kelly. Fast.

The place seemed quiet as they walked him around to the docks. Cast and crew were probably in the main building, having dinner, or else they'd returned to their rooms. The launch was at the docks, but there was no sign of Harry Sullivan. And there was a small motorboat waiting.

What was the plan, then? Were they going to shoot him and toss him overboard? Or just toss him overboard in the cuffs, assuming he wouldn't be able to swim while shackled? He had to admit, the planning had been detailed.

And Lance Morton had been in on it, goading him into the fight. The two men, had they been questioned, had a sure reason for being here, for taking him. The fight had been witnessed. The attempted-murder bit was a little preposterous, but hell, a guy like Lance Morton might have tried to press such a charge.

Behind his back, keeping the movement small, he began working the cuffs. They weren't regulation, he was grateful to realize. If he worked them hard enough, without causing his hands to swell, he could manage to slip them off. It was something he had done often enough in class with tighter cuffs, sometimes amazing his academy mates. He just prayed he could do it fast enough.

Smith reached for his elbow to help him down into the motorboat and Doug allowed himself to be led. Seated in the front, he was aware that knowing what was going on might not be enough to save his life. It was important, though, to keep them thinking he believed every bit of their charade. "You guys know that this charge is bullshit, right?"

"Hey?" Smith lifted his hands, going for the motor. "We just work here, you know."

His right hand was out. That was enough. But there were two of them and they were big guys with guns. When would be the right moment to make his move?

The motor came to life and they moved out on the water. Doug had a feeling they didn't dare ditch him too close to Marathon, so that meant they'd need to get rid of him soon. Really soon. He was going to have to take his chance. If he could go for one of them, go for a gun, that would be best. But he could also wind up with a hole in his gut. Best just to make the plunge, dive in far and deep. In the darkness, they might just start shooting. And they might make a lucky hit. He just didn't have many choices.

He coiled where he sat, knowing that he was going to have to move like wildfire. He counted the seconds, getting ready. Then, his chance came, but in a way that set his heart sinking, his mind so numb with fear that he was barely able to take the opportunity.

A sudden darkness pitched over the water as the resort went into a blackout. Smith and Jones were both looking toward the little isle. It was his chance. And he was desperate.

He jerked to his feet, kicked Smith a hard blow in the back, sending him over. Before Jones could turn, he'd made a dive himself. He went deep, heard the pinging sound of bullets wildly flying by him in the water. He swam hard, deeper. The water was dark and cool. He tried to gauge the direction to the isle. His shoulders burned and then his lungs, but he stayed deep, not emerging until he had gone a good distance and was unable to keep himself from gasping for breath. He could hear the men back on the boat.

"Shit! Think we got him?"

"Do you see a body, asshole?"

"Can you see anything? It's too damned dark."

"We've got to find him."

"We just go back to the isle and get him."

"Hell, no! Someone might have called the real cops by now."

"How, idiot? We cut the phone lines."

"Cell phones, idiot."

"We've got to get him or we're dead ourselves."

"Do what you want, idiot."

"All right."

Doug heard a gunshot, then a plop in the water. He didn't know if Jones had killed Smith or if Smith had killed Jones. And frankly, he didn't care. The motor revved again. Doug watched and waited, then thanked God for the one small favor. The boat was moving away from the island, so he began to swim again, as hard as he could.

Chapter 28

The second the door closed, Kelly headed for the phone on the kitchen wall. She still didn't understand why he wanted her to call the cops when the cops had taken him away. Calling Quinn, though, that made some sense.

She hesitated at the phone. Doug had been a cop. Were the men who had come for him . . . not real? Could anyone have planned such an elaborate setup? Lance Morton, to get even? Surely even Lance knew that his performance that afternoon was on tape. He'd definitely provoked the attack.

She lifted the receiver. The phone was dead. Ice filled her veins. She rushed into the living room, to the table where Doug had tossed their wet and useless cell phones. She tried her own, praying it would work, then picked up his. Nothing. Both dead.

A sense of hysteria seized her. Dead. Dead as a doornail. Dead as she was intended to be. And Doug . . .

Her heart was in her throat, her limbs frozen. She had been terrified in the car last night, but this knowing that she was being stalked was worse. And Doug . . . He had let them take him without protest to buy time for her?

She jumped, screaming, as she heard a thud against the back plate-glass doors.

"Kelly!" She heard her name, recognized the voice. Mel. She walked toward the rear, knowing that she couldn't open the door, disturbed by his tone.

"Kelly, for the love of God!"

There he was. Light from the room played out on the porch. He was in slacks and a T-shirt, amazingly casual attire for Mel. He raised his hands, banging them against the glass. "Kelly!" His whole body was nearly flush against the glass. She was ridiculously reminded for a moment of Jim Davis's hapless Garfield, crushed against a window.

"Kelly!"

She shook her head, then gasped as something emerged from the dark behind him. Blood splattered against the glass. Mel's mouth formed into an O. There was an earsplitting explosion of sound and the glass shattered. Mel fell into the room with a crystal rain of glass shards. And then the lights went out.

The dock was empty when Doug reached it. Exhausted, lungs and limbs burning with his effort, he pulled himself onto the deck. He rose, thinking that the generator lights should have kicked on. But they hadn't. Someone had found out everything they needed to know about the island, all about the electricity, the phones and the emergency generators.

The darkness was complete. He made his way through it, desperate to reach the room. And Kelly.

"Kelly, Kelly, Kelly!" She heard her name in a heinous, bitter, almost whining whisper. It was a sound that crept right into her body. He was there, right before her, standing in the pool of shattered glass. But she couldn't see who.

Her mind was working desperately. He had a gun, but he hadn't shot Mel. He had struck him, causing blood to spatter. Then he had used his gun to shatter the glass. He wanted to terrify her and would use the gun if he had to.

She had to use the darkness to her advantage. As she inched back silently, she heard a footstep over the shattered glass.

"Sometimes I watched you, Kelly, and thought what a wonderful actress you are. Just an actress. But then I watched you and *knew*. You are her, Marla Valentine. You loved telling women what they should do with their men. You loved it because that's the way you are — cruel, rejecting, thinking that the fools who fall all over you should then have to pay. You believe it, Kelly. Every word of it."

She kept walking backward. Silently. She didn't think he could hear her movement because he remained dead still. He was relishing his words, believing he could smell her fear. He was convinced that he had time, all the time in the world.

And why not? The others were surely gathered at the main house. They'd probably been in the dining room when the lights had gone out. Someone there was keeping them together, finding flashlights. Someone there certainly had a phone that worked. But even then, it would take time for help to get to the island. So the killer knew he had some time to play. Like a cat with a mouse, he had time to torment his victim.

"Oh, Kelly, you and I both know that the woman who walks around pretending to be nice isn't the real one. It's Marla who's real."

At last she could feel the door behind her. Biting her lip, she turned, feeling for the chain, clenching her teeth as she slipped it free, desperately trying to keep the movement silent. She barely dared breathe. She finally got it, but sliding the bolt would make noise. She had to be ready.

"Poor Kelly. Nowhere to run. Well, hell, you've made me show my hand. But they'll never know. Do you know why? Because I'm careful. I know what I'm doing. I plan it out."

She drew the bolt, jerking the door at the same time, and ran out. A bullet whizzed past her head and thunked into a palm tree. She ran, not toward the water, but toward the trees and the brush.

Doug came around the back, stealthy and silent. He trod upon the darkened beach and headed through the darkness for the rear sliding doors. As he did, it suddenly clicked in his mind. What he had seen in the numbers. What the calls had meant. Why addresses of connections to pay phones had actually made tremendous sense, though they had appeared random.

He inched toward the rear and stepped on the glass. As he backed away, he heard a moan. Inching forward, he saw the body on the floor. For a moment, his heart leaped. He hunkered down. It was Mel, with blood on his forehead and all around him. But he was breathing, still breathing.

He couldn't stop to help him or even attempt to ascertain the injury. He paused, dead still, listening, and knew after a moment that the room was empty. He was growing accustomed to the dark and could see that the door in the front was open. Wide open.

Kelly burst into a thicket of palms and tall brush. There, she went dead still. There was help, at the main house, if she could get to it. But he would follow her. He would start shooting, probably. Did he dare? Everyone would see him. What would it matter? She had seen him. She knew. He had to kill her now.

She listened. At first, there was nothing. Then footsteps. Light footsteps, but with enough weight to cause the ground to rustle. He was coming closer.

Doug moved through the house, going upstairs and to his suitcase. His Smith & Wesson tucked in his waistband, he moved back down the stairs. Someone was moving in the house. At the foot of the stairs, he listened, waited. Then he made his move. With a sudden leap, he brought the night prowler down.

"Don't! Don't hurt me. It's not me, I swear. I wouldn't . . . I wouldn't hurt her!"

It was Lance Morton.

Crack. Rustle. Crack. Rustle.

"Kelly, Kelly, Kelly . . . come out and play! You know, your pretty boy was so clever, but there were just things he didn't know." There was suddenly a sound of laughter. "I can see you, Kelly. Stand up and face the music!"

The gun was pointing at her. She stood. He came closer, smiling. "See, Kelly, there's a lot people don't know, because money is power. Money can buy anything. Money buys people and it buys silence."

"It just never bought you anyone who actually cared about you, right?" she asked, keeping the conversation going. How long did she have?

"Ah, Kelly, we could have such a conversation. I never wanted it to end like this. We should have had time. You should have understood. But this is rather dramatic, don't you think? The police will be here soon. And I'll be long gone, of course!"

"Someone will pick up your pseudo cops, you know," she told him.

"I don't intend to let them live that long," he said. "Ah, Kelly! You really are such a pretty thing. I did dream of running my fingers thought that hair of yours before . . . well, you know. But I'm afraid —"

She had no idea if it would work or not. None. She just knew she was about to be shot. She bent over and snapped out one of her best, toughest yoga moves.

Her foot slammed into his wrist. The gun flew into the foliage.

"Bitch! I am going to strangle you slowly!" he swore.

Kelly ran.

"Get up, you idiot! I know it's not you!" Doug snapped, dragging Lance Morton to his feet. "Get out of here. Run out of the room, making as much of a commotion as you can. Shout, call out names, make a racket."

"Me! There's a maniac with a gun out there —"

"Damn it, do it! Run fast."

Lance stared at him.

"You know who it is because he told you to pick a fight with me today so that he could get rid of me. If you didn't do what he asked, he was going to shut down your video, right?"

"Bull! You came after me —"

"Get out. We haven't got time for this! Now! Or I'll shoot you!" Doug threatened.

Lance stood where he was.

"If he gets to her . . ." Doug warned, taking a step toward Lance.

"I'm going. I'm going!" Lance burst out the door, screaming. "Kelly, Kelly Trent. Hey, Kelly, anyone!"

He must have really expected a bullet, because he ran as if his pants were on fire, wildly waving his arms in the air. Behind him, Doug slipped out and headed into the brush. Just beneath the sound of Lance's wild gyrations, he could hear the brush moving.

She ran hard, then came to a dead standstill when she heard the commotion. Lance Morton! The idiot! Creating so much noise! And . . . stopping her pursuer, she realized dryly.

But Lance wasn't bright enough to do

that on his own. Her heart took flight. O'Casey. Somehow he had made it back.

She quickly weighed her position. She'd been forced around to the beach side and she couldn't make it to the house unless she went around the entire wing of the building — or slipped out into the water.

She shivered. The ocean at night. The ocean when she couldn't see. The darkness. Yes, the ocean, she thought, and started to run.

She had nearly reached the water when she heard the thunder of feet directly behind her. She turned and there he was, ready to leap upon her. She screamed. His face was twisted with fury, and she realized that he had expected to bring her down far more quickly and with far less effort. He was about frothing at the mouth, his weight slamming her down in the damp sand. The surf washed over them both.

"I poisoned your damned dog, Kelly. How'd you like that? The little yapper old Dana had went out like a light with one kick. That was part of it with you, Kelly, did you know that? You're still young. While she . . . she was old. She'd been at it a long time. The bitch! She was a bitch when she had my kid and gave him up, and didn't even tell me for years. Not until she could get something out of it. You do understand, don't you? She'd gone after me because she was young then, young enough to see me in jail. That was what she threatened. Then she came back into my life. And the funny thing was, I still wanted her. Even though she was older. Even though she'd been screwed by that idiot she married. Because she had steel in her. She could manipulate in a way that was exciting. She was something different, sexy. But you know what I found out? This time I wasn't going to let her get me. She'd been playing the trump card for far too many years. I had to shut her up — with my bare hands. Damn that felt good. Every time I heard someone sound like her . . . well, it became a challenge. But you, Kelly . . . you had me pulled in long before I knew that Marla Valentine was real, long before Matt told me about the real you."

"Matt!" Terrified, feeling his weight, feeling his spittle against her, she was not just playing for time, but truly amazed. "What does Matt have to do with this?"

"Well, he's my son, of course."

"Your son!"

"Dana was already blackmailing me, you see. Years later, knowing that it could never be traced or changed, she told me about him and I started seeing the boy. I'd already been watching you for so long at that point. And I knew that you were another of them, the worst of them. And when he told me what you did to him, I knew that you really were Marla Valentine. And I knew that, whatever it cost, whatever I had to do, you *had* to go." His face went taut and grim suddenly. "And now it's time."

His fingers curled around her throat, tightened. She tried to scream but could only choke out a sound. Then the grip eased. She realized that someone had Logan by the hair and was trying to rip him off of her. There were feet near her head, right when she heard the words, "Get the fuck off her. Now!"

A sudden shove of heavy weight crushed over Kelly, nearly causing her to black out. Then the weight was gone and the men were rolling into the water. They staggered up and Marc Logan was staring at Doug in amazement. He hadn't expected him to survive.

"You all right, Kelly?" he asked, his gun trained on Logan.

"Yes." It was a croak at first. "Yes!" she repeated firmly.

Logan shifted, his body movement bringing him closer to Kelly again.

"Stay away from her. I mean it. I could do a whole *Dirty Harry* thing here, you know. Frankly, I'd like to shoot you, but I was a cop once, and cops are supposed to make arrests, not be judge and jury. I do have something of a temper, though, especially where Kelly is concerned. And hell, I'm not a cop now, so keep your distance."

Logan continued to stare. "You're not going to shoot me."

"No?"

Logan grinned. "Don't you realize by now that I've been in that apartment? How do you think that animal got the poison in his food. Check out your weapon, muscle boy. No bullets."

"You know what, Logan? You have really lost it. Patting yourself on the back all this time for your incredible cleverness. But you're not so clever. There's no way in hell you'll get away with any of it this time."

"Yes, there is. Money can buy anything."

"You're wrong," O'Casey assured him.

"Anyone can be bought. I'll bet even you have a price."

"Again, you're wrong. 'Cause guess what, Logan, money isn't everything."

Logan laughed. "You talk a lot of shit for someone without a gun. So how are you going to stop me?"

"You don't have a gun, either. Face it, Logan, I can knock you flat."

Logan started to laugh, hunkering down, almost as if he were just going to sit in the sand. "Thing is, muscle boy, I *do* have a weapon!" He reached for his calf and came back to his feet suddenly, brandishing a knife. "Always prepared."

He made an instant feint for Doug.

"O'Casey. Watch out!" Kelly cried inanely. Doug had hopped back, agile, quick, but Logan was gearing up to lunge again.

Kelly rolled quickly, going for his legs. Logan eluded her, but Doug was ready. He spun around, left foot slamming out. He caught Logan hard in the gut. Logan staggered. Another lightning-quick blow disarmed him. He faltered back and made a lunge for his knife, but Doug stepped on it. The man began to run.

"Ah, hell!" Doug said, and went after him.

Down the beach, he tackled Logan. He did have one hell of a right jab. Logan went still, and Doug rose slowly, coming toward Kelly. He reached down, helping her up. She was trembling.

"He hurt you?"

She shook her head. He looked back toward the shattered glass of her back door. "I think we need a new room, huh?" he said.

"I . . . Mel! Mel is hurt, Doug."

"I know. Let's go to him. Help is coming, though. Can't you hear the boats?" Suddenly she could hear sirens on the water. He put his arm around her. "Kelly, I should have known! The calls between Logan and Avery. Avery's mysterious past. There had to have been something. Logan had been paying Matt's adoptive mother and paying in cash. And then there were the other calls, made to Dana Sumter's station and her house — from a pay phone on the same street as Marc Logan's glorious new sound studios. I should have known. I could have . . . I could have lost you."

She still didn't understand. She was shaking in the balmy night, her knees suddenly weak. She wanted to just let him hold her, tell her that this was really over now and that she would be safe from now on. With him. But then she remembered.

She swallowed hard. "Mel . . ." she murmured.

"Right."

They turned and hurried for the man, who was prone and bleeding, half in, half out of the shattered glass entry. Kelly came quickly to her knees. Doug was already at Mel's side. "Looks like the blood is from his temple, not a bullet wound. Logan must have given him a really hard hit with the butt of the gun. His pulse is weak but steady."

"Oh, Mel!" Kelly murmured.

To her amazement, Mel's eyes fluttered up. "Kel . . ."

"I'm all right. It was Logan. He's out in the sand."

Something of a smile touched Mel's lips. "I take it all back, Kelly."

"What's that, Mel?"

"You're . . . high maintenance. I definitely deserve fifteen percent." And with that, his eyes closed again.

There were men running around on the beach — deputies, med techs. "Over here!" O'Casey cried.

A moment later, she was leaning against him, and they both watched as Mel was tended to, then lifted, ready to be taken to a hospital. Only then did Kelly turn at last and collapse into O'Casey's arms.

*Light
and
Revelation*

Epilogue

There was conjecture, there was truth, there was admission — all to be put together. And when it broke, it was sure to be the scandal of the decade.

It wasn't that night, with the madness and confusion, that anything began to come clear. That night, there was worrying about Mel, med techs crawling all over, the emergency launches, the deputies and the questions.

It wasn't until several days later, when dozens of papers and programs broke with the story, that Kelly really began to comprehend it all herself.

But the basis of the matter was this; nothing had been coincidence — except for the death of the poor woman in Ohio. She had died on her own, and it was doubtful that anyone would ever know if it had been an accident or suicide.

Thirty years before her death, Dana

Sumter had indulged in an affair with an up-and-coming businessman named Marc Logan. She had known that theirs was not the forever-after kind of affair, and she had used her age to milk him for a tremendous sum of money. Rather than using an unexpected pregnancy as a means to receive more at the time, she had given the child up for adoption, not telling Logan the truth for years.

Logan had taken the adoption out on the parents, seeing that they met a fiery end upon the California beach. He had befriended his biological son, without betraying the truth. But by associating with his past lover, he had become embroiled again — until the sharpness of her tongue once again turned him away. And worse. It sparked a calculated fury within him that set him on a course of determined murder, starting with the woman who had created such irrational hate in him.

The publicity, Mel told her ecstatically from his hospital bed, had made her one of the most sought-after personalities in the country. Joe Penny had called, saying that, of course, she could be written back into the script.

Kelly was with Doug, secluded in the house on Miami Beach, when Mel called

518

her, eager to give her another offer. It was evening. They had taken Sam for a walk along the beach, arm in arm, just watching the sunset. The odd thing, of course, was that they had done rather little talking since it had all broken. They just spent the time together.

On the phone, she first chided Mel for working from his hospital bed. He sighed. "It's what I do, Kelly. Hey, I love to wheel and deal. But this is it, my last call for the night. I . . . I have a visitor. My ex-wife is coming."

"Oh, no, Mel! She doesn't want to give you paperwork or talk about legal action while you're in the hospital!" Kelly protested.

He was silent for a minute. "No . . . she's just coming to see me. She was upset when she saw the news, when she knew that I'd been hurt."

Kelly smiled slowly. "Mel! You think you might get back together?"

Doug, lying on the sofa reading the paper, looked at her, arching a brow. She smiled with a shrug as Mel said, "Who knows. But she is coming to see me. Anyway, as to another offer —"

"I've taken an offer," she said.

"What?" Mel demanded.

Doug jerked around and stared at her.

She smiled again. "A very handsome and articulate fellow named Afton Clark was approached by a cable station . . . You'll get the paperwork and the contracts, Mel. We're going to host a show together. Tentatively it will be called *Miami Magic*. What do you think?"

"I think you should let me handle the business."

"I'm staying here, Mel."

"California is still the place to be."

"Not for me."

"Hey! Does Ally know about this?" he demanded.

"Do you care, Mel? You've never really liked her."

She could hear his soft sigh. "She was the one smart enough to find a dance coach who was an ex-cop," he admitted.

"I'm glad you're getting along. Since you're working from your bed, anyway, you can call Ally for me and the two of you can whine about me together. It will be great. But get some rest, dammit! And see your ex-wife. We'll talk later. I love you."

She hung up, smiling at Doug, who was still staring at her in astonishment.

"Why don't I know anything about this?"

he demanded. "And Afton didn't mention anything to me!"

"You were out with Sam when he called," she said. "I haven't actually agreed yet, but . . ."

He rose, walked to the chair where she was sitting and hunkered down before her. "You want to stay here?"

"For now."

"Why?"

"Because your life is here," she said softly.

"But that's not fair."

She stretched, reflective. "Well, I was thinking maybe you'd like to make this bodyguard arrangement more . . . permanent."

He lowered his eyes, then looked up and smiled. "Kelly, I'm a dance teacher about to start doing investigations on the side. Am I what you really want? Am I enough? You could probably have anything in the world that you want right now. Every talk show in the nation is eager to get you on. You could have anything."

"Including you?" she asked.

"I would have curled up and died if I lost you," he said.

"You don't have to lose me, ever. You know that, O'Casey, right?"

He stared at her. "Does that mean you know full well just how much I love you?" he asked after a moment.

"It means that I hoped!" she whispered.

"Does that mean a Hollywood wedding?" he said.

"Are you asking me to marry you?" she asked.

"I am basically down on my knees . . ." He shifted, going fully down, taking her hands. "Yes, I'm asking."

"O'Casey," she murmured. "Kelly O'Casey. I like it. Has a nice ring."

He leaned forward and kissed her. The lock of their lips deepened. Breathless, she broke away.

"You're sure?" he whispered.

She nodded. "You are everything I want," she told him.

He smiled, rose and lifted her up into his arms.

"In the mood for everything?" he asked.

"Oh, yes!"

He walked into the bedroom with her. And it was only later that she fully realized she had just gotten everything. And for a lifetime.